Kathy,

Mary Quigley's Da

Me da used to say: "Were it not for bad luck, the Irish would have no luck at all!"

Mary Jaffe

Mary Jaffe

(née Scott.)

KITSAP
PUBLISHING

MARY QUIGLEY'S DA
A TRAGEDY OF AN IRISH IMMIGRANT COUPLE AND
THEIR CHILDREN CAUGHT ON THE KANSAS-MISSOURI
BORDER DURING THE CIVIL WAR

Publisher's Cataloging-In-Publication Data
(Prepared by The Donohue Group, Inc.)

Names: Jaffe, Mary, author.
Title: Mary Quigley's da : a tragedy of an Irish immigrant couple and
     their children caught on the Kansas-Missouri border during the
     Civil War / Mary (née Scott) Jaffe.
Description: [Poulsbo, Washington] : Kitsap Publishing, [2021]
Identifiers: ISBN 9781952685859 (softcover) |
     ISBN 9781952685866 (ebook)
Subjects: LCSH: Irish Americans—Middle West—History—19th century—
     Fiction. | United States—History—Civil War, 1861-1865—Fiction. |
     Frontier and pioneer life—Middle West—History—19th century—Fiction. |
     Family secrets—Fiction. | LCGFT: Historical fiction.
Classification: LCC PS3610.A3663 M37 2021 (print) |
     LCC PS3610.A3662 (ebook) | DDC 813/.6—dc23

Illustration by Trent Shad, trentshadburne.my portfolio.com

Library of Congress Number 2019921222

Kitsap Publishing, 1451 NW Finn Hill Road, P.O. Box 1269, Poulsbo, WA 98370
Rev. date: 08/09/2021

To my grandmother and namesake, Mary Quigley, and her sisters Ellen and Annie, I dedicate this work. (Annie was believed to have been "lost" in her family tragedy of 1877. Remarkably, I found her resting place 135 years later in Independence, Missouri.)

To my loving, intelligent, and patient husband who encouraged and tolerated me throughout his physical vulnerabilities and suffering of seventeen years. He passed a year before I finished my book, but he was my rock who made this possible.

To my mother, who passed on the history gene, and my father, who passed on passion and my uncanny feeling of familiarity with a grandma I never met in life.

To our immigrant and slave ancestors, who prevailed through hunger, sickness, and natural or man-made catastrophes and inequities. They embraced opportunities and sacrificed much to rise above it all. From the 1600s to today, they built a country and kept their families as whole as they could under their circumstances. All were part of the complexity of our nation, including my Scots-Irish family who were fervent and active abolitionists while being officers in the Indian Wars. Such unresolved events and unreconciled antitheses remain America's open wounds. Fortunately, my Celtic family has embraced the addition of many other DNA cultures, as have most "American" families who might not be aware of their own histories. Each culture has given a boost to the strength, health, and intelligence of the family and sent it into hundreds of amazing story lines.

Like Mary Quigley's da, we are your legacy: good or bad.

CONTENTS

PROLOGUE

Little Mary Quigley could not know, but the moment of her parents' deaths would long outlive her. Mary could not know how her parents' names would be intoned or shrouded in mystery and shame for decades. To some degree, those moments damaged or changed everyone she loved.

Those moments would be relived all the days of her life and would become her family's legacy after her passing. Those moments would become her darkest secret, her greatest burden, and the focus of endless conversations and searches for truth by her children and grandchildren whose existence she had not yet contemplated. None would ever hear or think of Mary Quigley without pondering Mary Quigley's da.

CHAPTER 1

FARM OF MARY AND JOSEPH QUIGLEY, PLEASANT HILL, CASS COUNTY, MISSOURI, SEPTEMBER 13, 1877

Alone and silent, her back pressed against the dark-stained south side of her family's small farmhouse, Little Mary peered carefully around its southwest corner. She saw Uncle Mike Quigley, brother of her da, Joseph Quigley, sitting under the dying walnut tree in her da's broken three-legged chair. The hired hand, Melvin Knight, sat on the back steps around the northwest corner of their house.

Less than an hour before, in a tragedy of her da's making, Mary and her five siblings had fled for help and safety. Mike and Melvin believed all six Quigley children were now in refuge at the Collins's farm or at Michael's. They were unaware of the curious nine-year- old Mary's presence at the back of the house where she silently watched Uncle Mike shivering in distress. Mary also trembled from the horror of what her da had done in their home.

Mary glanced south and noticed that her ma's Jersey milk cow was headed from the far end of the pasture to the shed. It was unusual for Polly to come up so early. Mary returned her gaze toward Mike to determine whether he thought Polly was revealing Little Mary's presence, or if she was merely curious about the crumbled Mary McManus lying on the shaded ground.

On the sunny side of the house, Michael was sorting out this event the best he could and had begun his unbearable vigil for the sheriff to arrive with questions. It was approaching time to milk, but he would wait until after the sheriff had come and gone. With his bloody, wounded hand, Melvin could not help, and the children were gone and could not help. Mary thought that maybe Mr. Hill would send his boys over to do Quigley chores after they had finished their own.

Hoping Mike and Melvin would stay out of the house Mary prayed, "God, please be with me; make them stay where they are."

Mary watched in the fading sun as Mike quietly questioned and comforted Melvin, who was audibly sobbing. Mary wondered if Mike had looked into the lifeless hazel eyes of his sister-in-law, Mary McManus, lying in the brown September shadow of late afternoon on the other side of the house. Except for Mass, which Joe had quit attending, neither Mary McManus nor her children had seen nor spoken with Uncle Mike since Joseph's drunken attempt to retrieve a sow the year before. Joe had threatened to shoot and kill Mike in the midst of a two-year struggle over hogs.

Mary wondered if Mike had leaned over Ma's pale, lifeless body to tell her how very sorry he was that his brother had finally done this to her. Mary had already spoken to her. She had told her dead ma that she was sorry that she and Ellen could do nothing to stop Da. She asked God to wake her mother up. "I need you, Ma. Please, God." But she knew it wouldn't happen.

Not many months ago, Little Mary's drunken father had driven her ma and siblings from their home into the cold. As usual, Melvin had intervened because Mike had given up interfering out of fear and disgust. Surrender from the problem had brought Mike's family some peace. Mary knew it also brought guilt for letting Mary McManus Quigley and her children down. Mike's absence from their lives had been painful. Mary saw it in his face the day she stood on his porch as he told her he could no longer come to her home to save her family.

For several years, Mary McManus Quigley and her children had been forced to handle Joseph on their own or with the minimal interventions of the Hills, Collinses, or other neighbors who attended from the road when the children's screaming reached a devilish pitch.

Only an hour earlier on this September afternoon, Mike's dread-filled vision had been delivered in shocking reality. It arrived with Ellen galloping bareback up the lane with Little Thomas. Without benefit of halter or saddle and holding fast to the dark mane of Joseph's sorrel mare, for Mike to see Ellen galloping up to his house with a small brother hanging onto her was terribly out of the ordinary. *How those children can ride!* he thought. *But why is she here ... like this?* Mike called toward the barn for his oldest son, John.

"I'm afraid it's Uncle Joe," John said, and he was right. This was going to be the event they had feared the most: the inevitable and irreversible tragedy caused by an enraged, drunken Joe Quigley with a revolver in his hand. He had threatened over and over. This time, he had done it.

The tortured looks on the children's faces did little to prepare Michael and John for Ellen's precise and appalling revelations: "Ma's lyin' dead in the yard. Me da shot her! I think Da's dead too. Melvin's hurt."

Mike asked, "Are you sure, Ellen?" Upon hearing the account, Mike immediately sent John into Pleasant Hill for the sheriff and doctor. Uncle Mike ushered Ellen and Thomas into the house to be with his wife, their aunt Mary Murphy. Not knowing what to expect about the other children, he then headed the mile down the road in his little cart to his brother's farm. He hadn't grabbed his rifle; if his brother was dead, he wouldn't need it.

From the back corner of the weathered farmhouse, Little Mary continued watching Mike balance Joseph's three-legged chair on a stump. She could not read or hear his thoughts, but she would listen to him and Melvin. The air was dead and quiet. Because Melvin was talking out across the backyard, and Mike was sitting out where she could hear, she could almost comprehend every word they said.

Mary wanted to run, throw her arms around the kind uncle she had missed, and wail, "I'm sorry, Uncle Mike. We tried, but Da wouldn't stop." She practiced the words, but her legs wouldn't let her move.

Mike briefly looked toward the shed and glanced at Joe's wagon. He said to Melvin, "I don't know where I can take Joseph in that wagon. The church is done with Joseph's soul. Maybe the Reeds will take him. He can't be buried in Holden or Independence. He committed a mortal sin; he broke God's sixth commandment. Mary can be sent home to Garnett or Westphalia with her family in Kansas. The church will welcome her there. If not, the McManus or Agnew family will produce one of their own priests, but they can't be buried together."

Polly stood listening to Mike and chewing her cud. Mary saw that the need for her to soon be milked had not registered in Mike's rattled mind.

Contemplating what she was about to do, Little Mary knew that Mike and Melvin had left her da's frail body on the bed, slumped over against the wall. There, Melvin had seen pieces of Joe's brain still dripping. She had heard him say so to her uncle. This confirmed her understanding and fears of the third gunshot. She saw Melvin's hand from the first gunshot as he ran after Ma.

Joseph's beloved wife, Mary, lay still warm, faceup in the brown weeds of autumn. Little Mary had just seen the bullet hole through Ma's left breast, and she saw her blood soaking her dress as she was still alive and running around the corner of the house to find her children.

After Mary fell, the children were dispersed, and before Uncle Mike arrived, the nineteen-year-old hired hand, Melvin, had collapsed in silence and utter shock on the back steps. After Lawrence Collins scooped up Little Michael and took him to the Collins's home, Melvin had sat alone, blood flowing from a ruined hand, until Uncle Mike arrived. Now, Mary was hearing him continue to sob as he waited for his father, Elder Jokob Knight, to come with a doctor who Mike assured him would be coming. These were the same steps where her ma had stumbled out onto the yard to bleed out her life before her stunned daughter Ellen and screaming sons: Michael, seven years; Joseph, five years; and Thomas Edward, only three.

Mary heard Melvin answering Mike's questions, repeating the details, and sharing opinions: "I don't understand, Michael. He loved her. He didn't have to kill her. The family would have been fine in Kansas after he died. He should have known that. I think he was dying. He was in pain and thought crazy things.

"The yelling between Joseph and Mary was desperate, and the girls were both in the house. Mary stayed in, but Ellen came running outside yelling, 'Da's goin' to shoot Ma. Do something, Melvin!' Then she stayed outside with the boys, like she usually did. That's when I rushed into the house and tried to help Mary." Now standing behind the south end of the house, Little Mary could hear the echo of the catastrophe that brought audible wails of grief from Melvin as he recalled the event.

Mike asked, "How ye doin', Melvin?"

Melvin answered, "My hand's on fire and throbbing, and I can still see Little Mary rushing past me with Annie before it happened. She almost knocked me over. Before she took Annie and ran, that little girl, in front of a raging father with a gun, yelled out, 'Ye can't do it, Da. Ye can't take away our ma or our Annie! Yer soul will burn in hell, and ye know it.'

"Before she ran, she said, 'Christ before ye, Da; Christ beside ye; stop it, Da, or we'll be hatin' ye forever then!'"

Melvin went on about the unfolding events of the afternoon: "Little Mary looked straight at him, took Annie from her mother and wailed, 'Christ shields us, Annie!' Then she fled out the front door and across the porch, allowing the door to slam when Joe shot me. He shot me when I lunged for the gun. I could not take it from him, and when it went off, I wasn't sure if it was the door or the pistol I heard."

After a pause to wipe his nose on his sleeve, he continued, "Outdoors, Ellen heard the first shot, screamed, and ran around to the front. She probably heard Little Mary bursting through the front door because I heard her yell to the boys, 'Out front! It must be Mary and Ma!' So Ellen and the boys ran out front where they met Little Mary fleeing toward them with baby Annie tight in her arms. Mary stopped, looking toward Ellen and the boys, but Ma wasn't with her.

"Right away, there was the second shot that hit their ma. I was just standing, shocked, outside the bedroom door behind her. The children usually hung tight together outside the kitchen door. That's where most fights ended, so Mrs. Quigley and I ran toward the kitchen door and down the steps. This time, everything was different. The kids were all out front." Again, Melvin stopped talking, and Mike gave him a moment to overcome his emotions.

As Mary waited for Melvin to regain his composure, she felt as though she would shatter. She again felt tears streaming down her face, and she found herself shaking with a kind of rage she'd never before felt. In her nine-year-old soul, Mary realized that the responsibility to terminate life and destroy their family had been passed to a sick, withdrawal-crazed drunk with a gun in his hand. He had neither right nor need to kill Ma, but Da no longer possessed rational or spiritual gumption to rise above his misery. His soul was gone. All he had left was his gun and his sickness.

Knowing what Melvin would say next, Mary recalled holding tight to Annie and running, knowing her ma would soon be dead. The realization had frozen her legs when she reached the bottom of the porch steps. In her head, she relived the moment she hesitated in the yard enough to hear all three shots: one shot for Melvin, one for Ma, and one for Da at his own hands. Again, in her tear-blurred eyes, she recalled standing immobile with Annie, staring into the terrified eyes and bleeding mouth and breast of her dying ma. Mary closed her eyes and saw her screaming siblings turn to Ma, and Ma stumble. It was Melvin's demand for her to keep going that propelled her body to run past her family. She remembered how horrible it was to run past her mother. Oh, how she hated that moment, as much as all of them.

Melvin continued, "As the bullet ripped through my hand, Mrs. Quigley stepped forward and commanded Joe to hand over the pistol. He did not. Instead, he stood up on the bed, trained the barrel on his wife's heart, and pulled the trigger. I was standing right there behind her. She was less than an arm's length in front of him."

Melvin told Michael that Ma stumbled as she reached the bottom of the back steps. Melvin reached down to lift her up. Little Mary saw that he was still stumbling upright with her as they cleared the northeast corner of the house. Ma took several more steps, following behind the screaming voices of her children.

As Little Mary stood watching her mother and her siblings, Melvin shouted, "Keep running to Elizabeth's, Mary! Don't stop!"

Melvin explained that Ellen and the boys, aware that their mother and he were behind them, swung around to face their mother as she struggled toward them. "Reaching out toward her children, Mary's left knee landed on the ground. Her other foot tangled in her petticoat. Her body failed at that moment and pulled her over to her left side and then to her back where the children heard and saw her take her last red, frothy breath. She was dead when she fell to the ground."

With her ma lying dead, Little Mary ran past them while still in her panic to get to the Collins's farm for help.

"Little Joseph, screaming out of control, also panicked and ran after his sister Mary," continued Melvin. "I called for him to come back, but he ran across the field, off in the direction of his sisters. Mary had not stopped to take their sure-footed pony. She just ran the distance with her sturdy little legs and thick braids flying.

"I told Ellen to snatch up Thomas Edward and run to the barn to fetch her da's bridle and her heavy saddle blanket. Just yesterday, she had braided a few thick strands of the mare's mane for Thomas. Forgoing the bridle, she grabbed the sorrel's black mane, led her to the fence, and climbed up two railings to hop on. Thomas did likewise, and Ellen pulled him up to her. In a flash, they were off to your place, without benefit of saddle or bridle. The children used the cavalry and Indian tricks Joe taught them without even thinking about it. They had learned to move fast, as though someone was after them. When there was chaos, they were always one step ahead of their da."

Melvin told Michael that, alone with the stoic little Michael who was no longer screaming, he returned to the kitchen to grab a dishcloth to wrap around his mangled hand. It was when he looked down that he realized his little finger was missing.

The sweet little Michael who had his da's charming looks and his ma's kindness said, "I'm sorry ye lost yer finger, Melvin."

Planting Joe's trembling son on the back steps, Melvin gingerly walked back into the bedroom to examine the result of the third gunshot.

In a darkening puddle on the floor, Melvin saw his finger. He left it where it lay. Stepping over it, Melvin picked up Mary's prized hand-stitched bedspread folded over the end of the bed, pulled it carefully from under Joseph's bare feet, and took it to Mary. With it, he wiped the blood off her mouth. Protecting his bleeding hand, he gently laid it over Mary's torso and her chest wound. There he left her. He could not bear to pull it over her face. He was a Mennonite, but he loved the Catholic prayer that started with "Hail Mary, full of grace." Melvin told Michael that the kids and their ma sometimes prayed together while doing their chores in the barn.

"Honestly, Michael, when I saw Mary lying there, that's how she looked, full of grace. I wanted her to see the face of God and the angels who were coming for her, so I left her face looking up to heaven. I guess that sounds silly," Melvin continued.

"When Lawrence Collins arrived, he said he and the Hinshaws had heard the shots. He said he heard Mary and Joe shouting and the children screaming the day before and the day before that. Heading over to check on the family, he passed Mary and Annie, and then Joseph who were running toward his house. Lawrence told me that Mary yelled out, 'Ma's dead. Ma's dead 'cause me da shot her! I think Da's dead too.' Not stopping, Lawrence sent them ahead to his wife, Elizabeth.

"After checking Mary and Joe to see if either was still alive, and talking with me, Lawrence lifted Little Michael up on his shoulders and carried him back to his place to be with Mary, Annie, and Joseph."

Hearing Melvin tell his story, Mary recalled that after leaving Annie with Elizabeth, she had immediately turned around and ran back toward her farm. She'd seen Lawrence on the road, returning to his farm along the path beside the harvested field with the frightened Little Michael on his shoulders. Lawrence had not seen her lying still beside a corn furrow.

Mary saw in her mind how Mr. Collins had looked straight down at the ground so as not to stumble with Michael. However, from his viewpoint, her little brother saw her out in the field as Mr. Collins passed. Michael helped his sister, as he usually did. She recalled how

8

she'd looked at him, placed her finger over her mouth, and shook her head vigorously. She'd then mouthed the word "no," and Michael had obediently turned his head toward the Collins's farm and rested his chin on Lawrence's head. Michael had then begun to whimper in great wails, like an abandoned puppy. It was so loud that it echoed across the cornfield and seared Mary's heart.

Φ

Little Mary believed that in the confusion and preoccupation of the afternoon, she might have time to go unnoticed and unmissed in the Collins household. This was her only opportunity to return to her farm to retrieve her book. Also, she hadn't said goodbye to her mother and hadn't told her how well she would watch over Annie. She had also yearned to hear Uncle Michael and Melvin's conversation because she was so confused about what was going to happen to her parents and siblings. From the corner of the house where she was now standing, she had heard all she could stand, but no questions about where the children would go had been brought up.

Also, her heart was still pounding in her ears from running in her panic to the Collins's farm and back to her own, and reliving, in Michael and Melvin's words, all the horror. Mary tried to hear the crickets, the chickens grubbing, the lowing of Polly, or other calm sounds in the silence of ensuing dusk. Now at her farm, she again relived her own screams and those of her little brothers and Ellen. It became a sound avalanche in her head. She shut her eyes, but when she recalled her bleeding mother stumbling to her death, she opened them and looked toward the creek across the field. It was a beautiful scene in the late afternoon sun, but the screaming from this occasion and others resounded in her head.

She didn't want Uncle Mike and Melvin to hear the sounds inside her head. To keep the noise or the scream she felt building in her now from leaking out, she pursed her lips tightly, stuffed her muscular fingers in her ears, stopped breathing, and closed her eyes again. With closed eyes, she recalled her beautiful mother lying behind her in the front yard, the bloodstained coverlet hiding the little hole that had taken her life.

She had turned and run away from Ma with Annie. Melvin made her do it, and in the moment, she hated him for it. She had handed over the little sister who needed her. Annie would get hungry. Things needed to be done, and here she stood frozen, waiting to go back into the house. She would find Mrs. Collins and retrieve Annie after she secured her book.

Mary opened her eyes to again peer around at Uncle Mike. The still, cooling air now held Michael and Melvin's low conversation to the chilled ground. The residue of quiet speech served to focus Mary. Like the whispered prayers off the lips of the visiting nuns in morning offerings, Uncle Michael's tenor voice compelled her to listen until the deafening sounds in her head disappeared—and a full awareness of where she was finally caught up to her. She heard her parents' names, "Mary" and "Joe," over and over from the men's conversation, but the other words were lost, and she could no longer put the sentences together.

As Mary silently braced her spine up against the backside of the second bedroom wall outside, she became aware that time had not stopped. She moved herself forward, around to the front of the house, and up the steps of the front porch. The sheriff and other men from town would arrive up the driveway into the yard outside the kitchen door to take her breathless parents away. If she remained hidden, she could watch. She wished Ellen were with her.

Mary found herself standing alone in the darkening shadows of a partially cloudy autumn afternoon, peering out the front door of her silent house at her still mother lying faceup among spent thistles. She turned and walked toward the bedroom where Annie had been born only four months earlier. To move forward and retrieve her little prayer book, Mary needed to release her grip on her parents' bedroom doorjamb—and accidentally placed her hand in the sticky blood of her mother. The realization brought an urge to scream. Instead, it turned into a moment of silent internal sickness.

When Mary had walked past that tiny pile in the grass that was her mother, a similar sickness brought forth a whimper and moan in her throat that she swallowed. In the doorway of the bedroom, her breath rushed from her contracting ribs, and the tears that had escaped her momentarily began pouring from her eyes again. She collapsed to the floor on her knees, and her bottom landed on the heels of her feet. She heard herself grieve again as her mother's blood appeared—a charcoal shadow on the curved fingers of her cupped palm now settled in the filthy petticoat that covered her lap. The hot tears dropped down, rinsing her mother's blood into her palm.

Whispering into her heart, Mary sought courage. She recalled Sister Bernard telling the story of Mary, the mother of Christ, washing her son's body at the foot of the cross. Mary thought of her own tears that tried to wash her mother's blood from her hands in a final tender gesture of love. It gave her comfort. Her mother's blood would shield her. Then she recalled that her beloved mother was still lying on the cool earth drawing away her warmth. She wanted to run outside, place her arms around her mother, lay her mother's lifeless head in her lap, as the Blessed Mother had done with her son, but Michael and Melvin were sitting outside the house waiting, and her time was running out. She whispered, "God's shield to protect me" and stood up.

Little Mary had returned for the precious Irish prayer book Great-Uncle Terence Magrath had given to her mother. Mary hardly knew her mother's uncle, but her mother cherished it not only for what was in it and how it was made but what it symbolized. Her mother had told her about the history of the Irish people. The cerulean-blue leather book, the same color as the Virgin Mary's gown, with gold leaf lettering represented the tenacity of the Irish monks. They dared to beautifully preserve the forbidden Irish language from a condemned religion. This book was a fanciful, hand-transcribed work of Saint Patrick's Lúireach Phádraig and other common Catholic prayers.

Terence Fitzgerald, who had traveled the world among the last Irish aristocratic linen merchants, had secreted that book among his vast library. Fitzgerald, the defiant Catholic Irish academic merchant, had miraculously packed his library on a ship. Without family to escort it, the private library, one of the largest in America, sailed from England. The little blue leather book had hidden among the treasures, and it had been passed on to Mary McManus when she married. Originally, that book had been removed and gifted from a dusty shelf in Rome. Little Mary had imagined it being passed on by the hand of God for her to inherit. She knew it in her soul. It would bind her to her mother, and she would keep it hidden, as her mother had.

She had taken up the little book's purpose by learning the Pater Noster as well as the Lorica in her parents' native tongue. On this day and others, those Irish words had given Mary and her siblings the strength of the legendary McManus warriors. Her mother had promised it to her, and now she would walk into that room and reach into that top drawer where it compelled her forward past the sorrow. As she stepped forward, the falling yellow sun burst through the wispy clouds and pierced through the window, landing on the dresser at the end of the bedroom. It was God's invitation.

Mary reached through the glow, and in it, she heard the prayer book's whispers. As she touched it, the voice of Sister Bernard at vespers fell on her. It urged her to be strong, to turn her head, and to look behind the light. There she could look straight on the face of her father in the dark shadow. Mary turned and calmly whispered, "Why, Da?" She had done it. She had spoken to the unrecognizable form slumped in the darkness beyond the light where she discerned no face or head. Was that truly her father?

She heard nothing back. She waited briefly. In the silence that followed, she realized that her da would not be speaking. There would be nothing she could explain to Ellen. That she had been here at all should now rest among her secrets. Her da was as dead as he had made her ma, but God no longer spoke for him. He was not there for her, and Mary would never gaze upon his handsome face and would never dance with him around a parlor as her mother played the piano. He would never sing his beautiful Irish tunes again. Mary would never laugh with her da again. He would never mistreat their family again. He would no longer drink up their mortgage or household money, destroy their precious things, or strike her ma. His destroyed soul had gone away with his ruined body—the beautiful place Christ prepared just for him that he had destroyed.

Mary loved her da. He had secretly told her that her confident voice and large, sure hands had made her gifted to work with the animals. He told her that her boldness made her a true chieftain's daughter, born to rise above the rest. Her singing da had held her dirty, freckled hand and walked with her amid the rolling fields of golden grain. He had taught her how not to go after the horse and how to make the horse come to her. He was teaching her how to speak to the mule at the fair—and how to lure him to their barn. Mary allowed herself to giggle because she knew Da didn't mean for Mary to steal a mule. *Or did he?* There was so much love and devilishness left to be shared between them. *Why this?* This would remind her of all the ugliness of heart and soul that led to this.

Da had kissed her ma and told her she was the only girl for him. *Why had he treated Ma so badly?* Like Da, Ma was so special and different from the other mothers. Mary's questions would never be answered. She would hide them in her soul. She would pray and forget about answers that could not be uttered by the dead.

Mary slipped the little blue book in her petticoat, ran out the front door, and in Irish whispered from her soul: *Chríost in aice liom / Christ beside you.*

Seeing the sheriff's entourage in the far-off distance, she crawled on her hands and knees through the broken weeds to her mother. Young Mary Quigley looked over her mother's lightly freckled porcelain face and promised to care for Annie. Like the dew, her tears dropped down and wept for her mother, whose soul had already left the earth. She glanced up to look for the angels. They had come and gone. In their place, she saw the harvest moon rising boldly above the horizon. Mary promised on the moon to her mother that she would keep the book as close to her as she kept Annie and that she and Ellen would keep their family together forever—just as Ma had done when they all went to live in the wagon after Da threw them out of their home.

Mary knew her mother and her McManus family would be ashamed of Da, so she promised to tell not a soul what had happened on this day. "I love ye, Ma; I love me da as well. I will pray for ye both, but this will be our secret. Ellen is as good as the angels, Ma. She will

13

keep the secret as well as I. I have to go, Ma." She kissed her mother's cold, blue lips and saw that blood had been wiped from them. Had the angels washed her ma for meetin' with God? She thought so.

Mary crawled around to the south end of the house, leaving a second trail of broken weeds in the yard. She waited for the sheriff to greet Michael and Melvin. When the little group of men had swung around east to be with Mary McManus at the front, Little Mary ran out west behind the hog shed. Polly greeted her with a calm lowing and began to follow her to the coop. The chickens had returned to roost.

Quietly, she slipped back through the rails and into the kitchen to get the clean milk pail off Ma's pantry counter. She ran back into the shed, grabbed a handful of mash, tossed it into the pan in the coop, and locked the door behind the hens. Then she made a dash around behind the trees. Polly's rough, pink tongue caught up to the side of Mary's face. It wiped away a patch of salty dust and tears. Mary looked into Polly's sorrowful eyes and dropped on her knees to milk their faithful, dripping Jersey. "I know, Polly. I'm missing me family too. It's all right to weep; you're a good mother, Polly. I want to take ye with me, especially for Annie, but I'm not sure I can. Maybe I'll come get ye tomorrow. I'll try, Polly."

Φ

It was supper when she arrived, exhausted, at the back door of the Collins's farm, standing in the moonlight with her pail of milk. Mary saw that Lawrence had lit his lantern and placed it before her brothers Joseph and Michael, who were in the little kitchen eating biscuits and eggs he had cooked. Elizabeth Collins was not there. "Mr. Collins, Annie needs her supper. Where's our baby sister?

It's been a long time, and she can't wait. She's a very tiny thing, and Polly has sent her milk to Annie. Here. Look!" Mary proudly held up her full pail and bribed Lawrence with a woeful smile.

"You're right, Mary. Annie needs milk, but Elizabeth took Annie up to your aunt Mary's place. There's a lady there who has milk for Annie."

Mary's heart sunk. She wavered a sigh and began to sob.

Lawrence held up another lantern. Where Mary's tears had captured layers of dust on this ghastly day and Polly had tried to clean her, Lawrence could almost count the episodes of crying on her freckled face. Her dark, thick braids had snagged thistles, corn stubble, and a chicken feather, and one of her white ribbons was missing. He saw smudges of blood on her apron and her sleeve, but he wasn't sure if he wanted to hear from Mary where she had been or what she had seen and done.

"Darlin' Mary, let me take yer milk pail. Wash yer hands first, then come into the kitchen, precious girl, and sit with yer little brothers to eat. They have missed ye. Where have ye been, sweet one?"

Mary did not answer, but she stepped forward just in time to see Joseph reach over and take a piece of Michael's biscuit. Michael, though he was older, started bawling, jumped up, and threw his arms around Mary. "I want to go home, Mary. Is Ma better now?"

Lawrence had momentarily stepped out of the room to get another chair. He could not have answered Michael's question.

Mary answered, "Yes, Michael. Ma's better, but she has to go home to Kansas to be with Ma and Pa McManus. Maybe we'll get to Kansas to see her, but not tonight, Michael. You'll be with me. We'll go back home later to sleep, but don't tell Lawrence I said so. We'll camp in fresh hay in the wagon. Polly will be there with us." Upon hearing of his ma's "trip" to Kansas, Joseph said, "Yer a liar, Mary, Mary Stinkweeds! Ma's dead, and ye know it! She can't get better, and she won't be makin' no trip to Kansas. Yer a liar, Mary, Mary Stinkweeds! Tell Michael the truth."

Mary burst forward, slapped Joseph firmly across his face and exclaimed, "Don't you ever talk like that again to me or anyone else, Joseph Franklyn Quigley. From this moment on, things are exactly what Ellen and I say they are—and don't ye ever, ever forget it! We're yer boss now!" She looked at Joseph's plate, took his biscuit in her sizable and dirty hands, broke it in half top to bottom, scooped a fried egg into the center, replaced the top half and jammed most of it into her mouth. Mangled biscuit sandwich still in one large mitt, she took Joseph's empty milk tin, cradled Polly's milk pail with its warm, creamy milk, and commanded, "Come on then, Michael.

Stay away from us, Joseph. Yer evil. If ye don't behave, ye'll go to hell like our da! Be good—or I'll drag ye back and lay ye down next to Da so they can take ye away with him."

Carrying the biscuit, the ever-obedient Michael followed Mary briskly out into the moonlit dusk. They scurried to the Collins's barn and sat with the barn cats on the steps out in front of the manure pile. The Collins's kittens looked much older in the approaching darkness. They weren't frisky, showing interest in the buttered biscuit, or looking for fun from the children. They ambled out along the fence to creep, sit, and pounce on the newest litter of juvenile field mice.

Sharing her last piece of sandwich with her little brother, Mary noticed that the mother cat was not so concerned about the kittens anymore. Now her kittens were on their own. Eventually, they disappeared into the field, and Mary held Michael as the two orphaned children wept in loneliness under the moonlight. She wanted to always keep little Michael close and protect him. She hated the way Joseph was acting. When things were terrible, he had a way of making them worse. She would stay close to Michael and keep him from going bad with Joseph.

CHAPTER 2

JOSEPH IN THE CAVALRY,
KANSAS-MISSOURI BORDER, MAY 1862

On a drizzling May morning, Joseph Quigley and three other cavalry scouts received their intelligence assignment after breakfast. Their scouting mission was to travel covertly and somewhat independently along the rivers below Harrisonville, their headquarters, in Cass County. They would travel as far south as Bates and Saint Clair Counties, then meet up in a small town north of the Grand River in Henry County. They would then circle back north and east of Harrisonville, as far as Rose Hill in Johnson County and into Pleasant Hill, back into Cass County, before they returned. The diameter of their search area was more than fifty miles, and they would have a week to complete their job. They were to check bridges and look for signs of a growing Confederate regular or guerilla encampment north of the confluence of the rivers flowing into the Osage west of Osceola.

Osceola had been sacked by James Lane and his Kansas Jayhawkers in September, eight months before. He had plundered from the inhabitants, freed slaves who had nowhere to go, and murdered nine local residents. Lane's sacking set up greater hostility toward the Union among nearby settlers. The Confederacy had literally taken up residence along the Missouri side of the border. Having so few men was extremely dangerous, but it was less likely to draw attention than a patrol. Hopefully they could gather information without meeting their demise, which had happened here and there over the past year. Scouts from the cavalry were going out and not coming back.

Noting the presence of enemy but not engaging unless absolutely necessary was critical. If there was an engagement, they were to return to Harrisonville immediately. In April, Joseph's first cavalry action had been a skirmish at Little Manqua, a day's ride south and east of Clinton. The Second Battalion was spread throughout the border region on larger patrols with other militia and Federal Regulars. Joseph's tiny patrol was to hunker down when necessary. Certainly, they would engage only when they were at a very clear advantage. A good secesh was a dead one, as long as killing him didn't invite in the family.

Through raids and skirmishes, six towns in the area had been burned to the ground in 1861. Shortly after arriving at their home in Big Creek, Joseph and Michael's families became victims of a raid. It destroyed them, and it prompted Mary's return to the relative safety of her McManus family in Anderson County, Kansas. Since then, there had been a dozen serious encounters in which civilians and soldiers had been killed, livestock destroyed or stolen, homes emptied or burned, and farms abandoned in and around Cass County.

Joseph felt compelled to serve. More than three-fourths of the Missouri Home Guard volunteers came from Cass County. He decided he would not retreat to Kansas. He couldn't leave his future in the hands of the secessionists. His Irish history had been the colonization and theft of his ancestors' land, faith, and livelihood by the English. The Irish were forced to subdivide land until their families could no longer survive. The potato had provided enough protein to exist on their one-acre plots—until the potato blight arrived in 1845. Joseph's family had tried to ride it out, but they emigrated in 1849, on one of the greatest waves of starving immigrants to that time. The Irish had believed that in America, the farmers' food would not be sent to another nation as they watched their own families die. Through seven famines, his ancestors had seen their great harvests shipped to the European Continent as they starved. As a consequence, the Irish formed fierce attachments to their land.

Now, he wasn't certain that conditions wouldn't starve them out again. Joseph could not walk away because various factions of this battle were stripping farmers clean of food and personal property. Farmers were literally being left with empty houses, no livestock, and empty larders. He had to save a place for his brother's family, himself, and Mary and hold on to it. He was young, and he would prevail.

Φ

Always, something unpleasant prompted cavalry reconnaissance missions such as the one Joseph and his peers were beginning. In the days before, the mail coach into Pleasant Hill had been held up by a small band of Confederate guerillas. A couple of MSM (Missouri State Militia) uniforms had been stolen. The locals were caught off guard, and they reported to the militia in Harrisonville that there was good evidence that many more than those three secesh scoundrels were in the region.

The Home Guard to which Joseph and many of his friends belonged in 1861 was transitioned into the cavalry in the spring of 1862, but they would never be in great enough numbers to overcome the bushwhackers and secesh guerillas. Rumors had been coming in about the various locations of Confederate gatherings. It was believed there could be a large attack on the way, gathering from the west along the Kansas-Missouri border west of Butler, or more likely, from the southwest, out of Arkansas. In spite of the large number of Union soldiers camped in Butler, the vast majority were artillery. There was limited cavalry, so intelligence was lacking as to where and when Cass and Johnson Counties might be targeted. Due to rumors and people's efforts to excite the cavalry into action without hard evidence, intelligence could be sketchy. However, it seemed in 1861 that the area could reel completely out of control, thus the new cavalry had been formed and formally trained by the brigadier general of volunteers, John Schofield, who had been sent in by Lincoln to organize Joseph's battalion and other volunteer units.

Since the 1861 Confederate victories at Wilson's Creek and Carthage, in Greene, Christian, and Jasper Counties, no place could be safe without increased and constant vigilance. General Schofield's assignment, in response to Union losses, had been to recruit and train the local cavalry specifically for increased bridge surveillance, guerilla scouting, and continued harassment of the enemy. For a full year before enlisting in the new MSM, Joseph and his neighbors in the Home Guard had been protecting bridges, looking for Confederate camps, and skirmishing with the enemy. Joseph was an incredibly good shot and was recognized for his effectiveness at hitting his targets.

Cavalry sharpshooters were the spine of the regular army, and Schofield's volunteers in the militia brought their guns or were issued them to employ the same sharpshooting talent as the "regulars," though they were not officially called sharpshooters, as was the First US Sharpshooters regiment in the regular Union Army. Joseph brought to the guard and the MSM his own Navy Colt Revolver and a Sharps Rifle he had acquired as a young adult in Westport. Both Merrill's Horse Second Missouri Volunteer Cavalry and Joseph's Second Battalion, Company C, were employing the same skills as the First US out of Harrisonville and Sedalia.

In smaller units, scouting on exceptional horses and selectively firing on their targets at near or distant range were guerilla skills and concepts that Schofield believed in. He convinced his friend Abraham Lincoln that his volunteers needed to be taught guerilla tactics along with traditional battlefield sword skills. It was fully approved. Also approved was the unfortunate but practical decision to not take prisoners since there was no prison to house them, and with the small numbers in the scouting units, traveling with prisoners would endanger the men.

In 1861, Joseph's company had participated in skirmishes in Parkersville, Harrisonville, Jonesborough, Old Randolph, Bush Bridge Road, Butler, on the Grand River, north of the Mississippi, Dayton, and Wadesburg. Joseph's faithful and powerful steed, Fitzgerald, had proved himself a remarkable warrior horse and best companion in all situations. Therefore, both had survived in fairly good shape. Joseph did have an ever-cramping stomach, caused by poor food and too much whiskey, and Fitzgerald had sustained a superficial bullet wound on his right rear fetlock that quickly healed.

In his first months, Joseph fretted at night over the killing. Earlier, he had harbored a secret regarding a personal action he had been forced to take. After time in skirmishes, Joseph no longer wasted his emotion over the recipients of his bullets. He was praised for his accuracy. All he cared of dead men was whether they wore gray coats or carried a secesh flag or didn't. Killing men was not as bad a consequence as injuring a horse in his encounters. He liked an opportunity to recover them, along with mules or wagons and the food to feed them. Nearly all the men felt the same way. Their resources were limited, and replacing lost resources was critical to their survival. Like the enemy, they got their hands on as many livestock as they could.

In camp, they sat and relived their successes, but Joseph never revealed that his first hits were not in a cavalry skirmish. In his mind, it was self-defense, but his story would remain untold due to the unique circumstances: he had bribed a thieving secessionist to get Fitzgerald.

He had not bragged to the men from the Home Guard he later met, though they often shared tales of bravery when confronted by the enemy. Joseph knew this was a different situation than standing in your barnyard to save the farm.

Joseph had learned from his sister Ellen and the men in St. Louis from his steamship ride to keep his mouth closed about everything. He felt justified, but he knew in his gut that revenge from the Neumann family could catch him. Like the loss of a mother, such things never went away.

Joining the Militia Cavalry was the logical next step from Home Guard: Joseph and many of the other men of the guard had been personally victimized to the point of losing their homes, families, property, and livestock. In the cavalry, Joseph had his beloved horse and weapons, and he was looking forward to the eleven dollars a month he would be paid.

Because the Union was short on trained, healthy horses, the men brought in their own. Each had to be proficient in certain commands and free from any diseases or defects. Fitzgerald was a one of a kind at a hair less than seventeen hands high. The military wanted horses that were fifteen to sixteen hands tall. Though he was beyond the limit, he was exceptionally strong, healthy, and remarkably well trained. It was the kind of horse used by the German cavalry, bred through the centuries. The cavalry knew they could benefit and hoped the striking, healthy gelding would survive the first major battle in which Joseph remained on his horse. At induction, Fitzgerald was immediately valued at only $90, including Joseph's equipment. His actual value was far greater, but the government did not pay more.

Φ

The four soldiers on this mission traveled quickly on the main road west out of Harrisonville, toward Kansas. Two companions, Alexander and Matthew, had already served with Joseph in the Home Guard. Their enlistment in the Second Battalion of the MSM was a continuation of a commitment to their fellow settlers who needed protection from Confederate guerillas and the Union's Kansas Brigade under the command of the Kansas senator, James H. Lane, and his partner, Charles Jennison. Jennison was an ardent vigilante abolitionist with little regard for determining who the enemy was before looting, plundering, and even shooting civilians who had not been given due process. In their zeal to drive out secessionists, the brigade scoured and burned indiscriminately across Cass and other counties in Missouri. In one campaign, the brigade began in the northwest corner and moved south along the entire distance of the Kansas-Missouri border to "clean up" Missouri of Confederate sympathizers.

In the voluntary guard, Joseph and his companions, Alexander and Matthew, had fought side by side in skirmishes that stretched north above Kansas City, east beyond Sedalia, and south, nearly to the Arkansas border. They had been over most of the territory of twelve border counties and were continually doing more. As cavalry scouts, their Missouri experience gave them the advantage of knowing hidden vantage points, bluffs, ravines, and streams that Confederate scouts from Louisiana or Tennessee just couldn't know. Traveling in very small units, they could get from one place to the other more quickly and more efficiently. They could advise their officers as it was deemed appropriate. As advance soldiers, scouts, and marksmen, they could support regiments from the regular Union Army who hailed from Iowa, Illinois, or Ohio.

Unfortunately for Joseph's companions, the local Confederate guerillas around the Harrisonville cavalry, sometimes being former neighbors, knew as much about the local geography as the Union volunteers. That evened the score and kept them nervous. Some of the Confederate boys had farmed in the same township or attended the same church as the Yanks, but that didn't bother Joseph during battle. If Joseph didn't shoot his neighbor first, his neighbor would shoot him—and with equal enthusiasm. He'd been shooting at some of them from his teamster days in Westport. He had recognized faces.

His third companion in this mission, Frederick Schmidt, was a problem for Joseph. He did not trust him, and he did not like him. He felt Frederick was completely out of place, and Joseph had convinced himself that Frederick was, perhaps, someone he had met from his past but could not place. He refrained from asking Frederick straight out because Joseph, as did the others, always looked over his shoulder. Danger was sure to be there. He didn't want to welcome it.

Frederick was sociable but not likeable. He didn't share personal information, but he would share information about hunting, fishing, and other trivial tidbits of information of no interest to anyone but himself. Missourians were hunting and fishing to stay alive. They were not associated with hunting clubs. Frederick's styles and interests were detached from the suffering of Missourians. He was a know-it-all who didn't seem to know reality. Unlike the others, he seldom expressed information about his disdain for the secesh. Had the Confederate guerrillas done nothing to him or his family?

There was also never talk about his family. He didn't appear to have an opinion on politics or war. He was detached from the purpose. He preferred target practice. He practiced shooting often and was an excellent shot, but he did not discuss his past service in St. Louis. Why had he traveled all the way to Harrisonville to reenlist? There were plenty of Confederates to the east. There were too many questions that normally would have been answered by now. He didn't belong.

The road Joseph's small troop took out of town, if continued, would have led Joseph to his wife, Mary. She was living about sixty miles down the road in a tiny cabin next to her older brother, Daniel McManus, and his wife, Mary. Nearly due east of his farm was the location of the 1858 prewar massacres on the Marais des Cygnes River. On the Kansas border, just east of that place, was where Joseph was headed. The attack on the Cygnes by John Brown helped start the war. The area was dangerous and required extreme vigilance.

Mary McManus's family were farming just west of Garnett in Anderson County. Some lived less than a hundred acres south in Westphalia Township—and many more to the north, on the border of Franklin County. Mary's highly regarded maternal Grant family and her paternal aunt Margaret's erudite husband, Terence Magrath, had helped found the community of Emerald—about twelve miles north of Daniel's farm. They and other families who had been close in Ireland had made their investments together, settled within miles, and like an ancient clan, positioned themselves for success and dominance in the area.

As Joseph rode along in the disappearing rain, he bitterly thought of the day at the end of last summer. Now it was raining; then, it was a drought. The crops had not survived, and families were barely eating. His brother, Michael, and his wife, Mary Murphy, had done well the year before, in 1860, and could have ridden out the drought. Joseph and Mary had no fat in their larder and had been living on Michael's largesse when they were forced to flee Big Creek in 1861.

By then, Joseph and Mary had only been married about a year and a half. Riding along, he thought about their bickering and Mary's incessant criticisms of him as husband and farmer. Joseph loved and admired Mary for her strength and intelligence, but he resented being bossed and blamed. He did not understand her intolerance of his desire to enjoy the saloon with his companions when he went into town to buy supplies or get mail. He wanted to talk with other men about attacks and hear the rumors about anticipated troubles. He wanted to drink as much as he needed. What was so terrible about going home intoxicated? Other men did what he did, and he never heard that their wives complained as his did.

Mary would have supper ready long before he got home. Why did she then complain? Couldn't she wait? Couldn't she eat by herself? She constantly reminded him that they could not afford the whiskey or wasting of food. What if they had children? Would he be drinking up their money needed for seed crops? What if they lost their milk cow? Where would the money be to secure another? She had threatened to stop cooking his dinner. What kind of woman would do that? Besides, what made her such a great farmer?

Though his father was a tailor and brother a stonemason, they lived and worked on a farm. She hadn't come to America until she arrived in Philadelphia in 1852, at the age of fifteen. He met Mary when she was sixteen. Her father had been a linen merchant and world traveler. He wasn't a farmer. They were from the town of Newry, County Down, and they had once lived in a large and well-appointed home.

Joseph's last vision of their Big Creek home was that of a juvenile Murphy cousin, John, who had come to live with them and provide help others thought Joseph needed. Using Michael's youngest oxen, Joseph recalled John driving Joseph's empty Hiram Young wagon down a path at the back of a field toward the ravine—the one where he had killed his pursuers not that long ago. Fitzgerald was loosely tied to the back of the wagon. The Murphy boy was to park the wagon on the downhill side of the ridge, chop down a tree or two, and pull them behind the wagon wheels to secure it. He would then ride Fitzgerald back to his home in Independence, using the same trail that Michael and Mary were using, back in the direction from which the raiders had come. The young ox was let free. Joseph recalled that he was going to use Michael's saddle horse to round him up if he could be found after Lane's raid was over, but they decided the Union raiders had taken him in the attack.

Mary was preparing her little cart being pulled by their limping workhorse as the Jayhawkers burned their way closer to their farm. The Jayhawkers surely wouldn't want a limping workhorse to feed. Joseph's brother Michael and his wife, Mary Murphy, had, with advance warning from John Murphy, grabbed what they could and escaped in their wagon heading west—hiding in the trees of a western ravine with a marginal road and hoping to buy time and distance off the main roads.

In his mind, Joseph remembered looking into the distance and seeing the rising smoke from the houses and barns ablaze. How many men are there comin' our way? he had wondered. They had to flee.

Before climbing in her cart, Joseph's wife Mary had whispered a surprise to Joseph that she might be expecting a child. On this day, the baby would have been several weeks old, but it had not arrived. Mary, terrified and tearful, only spoke about it in the chaos of that day but never mentioned it to Joseph or anyone else again. Her sister-in-law Mary Murphy had already lost a child and had been very stoic, and young Mary McManus didn't want to show weakness.

Standing defenseless, Joseph recalled his highly distraught wife in the midst of the raid, crying hysterically over the loss of their little brown milk cow. Standing under the protective roof off the kitchen, she had screamed, "Joseph, they're taking our Sunshine!" Mary grabbed an iron fry pan from her cart, held her belly, and followed off after two men screaming, "Drop that rope now!" In tow, they had the cow her sister Margaret had given her. It was quietly brought into the country by a cousin in Philadelphia, and nobody else had such a wonderful cow. "Our family needs Sunshine! That's my cow!" One of the men looked back and laughed at Mary, though they had shared the revelation that they had never seen such a cow before.

Following after Mary to take her back to the cart, Joseph vowed to not forget that man's face. Pitifully outnumbered by Jayhawk vigilantes, Joseph had no chance to shoot the man without being shot in return. He barely held his temper in check. Also, he needed to keep his guns hidden. These Yanks knew that the recent Irish were generally not involved with secesh issues. For now, they were not worried about Joseph and Mary as spies or leaders. They just wanted their animals, wagons, crops, bedding, or whatever else they needed.

The lives of Mary and Joseph, his brother Michael Quigley, Mary Murphy, and their four small children had been caught in the upheaval of pre-Civil War conflict that nearly every Missourian experienced on either side. In the wrong place at the wrong time in history, they had been lucky to escape with their lives and some household items. It seemed they were ruined before they hardly had started.

Φ

Traveling out of town in the rain, Joseph was cold, wet as usual, and he had envisioned more from life. Their Big Creek house was gone—burned to ashes along with their dreams. Joseph was to find that, all day, his mind would not cleanse itself of the latent idea of that baby with himself and Mary together in that sweet little house where they had begun their married life. Stressful though it was, he smelled freshly baked biscuits in his mind, Sunshine's rich butter, and revisited the mocking face of the Kansan vigilante. He wished he had shot him.

About eight miles out of town, Joseph's small detachment had left the westbound road and dropped due south. They knew that wearing civilian clothing did not guarantee safety, and they traveled cautiously and briskly in the lessening rain. Joseph and Alexander were at the head, and Alexander was the levelheaded and responsible corporal. Joseph looked plaintively toward Kansas, and without realizing it, he slumped down in his saddle, his hands surrendering the reins to his horse.

In response to Joseph's indifferent body, the shiny, muscular horse immediately took off on a working trot. It was the beautiful gait the horse used when showing off his magnificent bay body in parades. His neck he held erect, his head was tilted slightly down, tail flowing, and there was no rocking motion as he sped out in front. Joseph sat perfectly straight, his legs working the stirrups to keep a perfectly level profile, as they sped down the recently repaired road. Joseph did not immediately correct his athletic horse, but he understood the reason for his spontaneous antics. Fitzgerald was assuming the head position because Joseph had handed himself over to ambivalence. Fitzgerald did not like a tentative rider. He had sensed resignation and taken control over his rider.

Joseph knew, however, that not even the sure-footed Fitzgerald could keep this up once they hit the rougher terrain ahead. If he did not contain his spirited horse, he would be disciplined. The cavalry soldiers were spread thin throughout the county and beyond in the collection of intelligence. A cavalry at war could not risk behavioral problems in either their men or their horses. Because Joseph was expected to be somewhat invisible and to maintain his regulatory position in a "column of two," he reined in his beast with a commanding du go mall / slow down.

To the other riders, it was immediate magic. Without a sound or a flinch, Fitzgerald had broken his gate and dropped back, following Alexander's horse—Bucephalus III—step for step. Joseph was conforming and sat significantly higher and tighter in the saddle to control Fitzgerald.

From behind Joseph, came the question in a German accent, "Joe, your horse Fitzgerald learn Irish, ya? How he do that?"

Joe met the inquiry with a ridiculous question of his own: "Frederick, how did ye learn German?"

After some time in contemplation, Frederick answered, "My mother."

"So did Fitzgerald. He learned to speak from his ma, but Frederick, did you know that Fitzgerald is not Irish?"

"Ya?" asked Frederick, who already knew the horse was German.

"Ya," replied Joseph. "He is a large, handsome Hanoverian. His da had a German accent like yers. Does that make it even more remarkable that he understands Irish?"

"Ya?" asked Frederick. Then he continued, laughing, "Ya, Fitzgerald is big like German and not tiny and hungry like Irish. You Irish. How do you feed him so gut?" He looked intently at Joseph and raised one eyebrow. "All other Irish horses—what they say, skinny?" With two pinched fingers he made a gesture of thinness.

"Frederick, not all the other horses ridden by Irish are Irish horses. You eejit, no horses were brought over on our boats. We would have damned well eaten them, so they never could have gotten here. Yer Lucky is not skinny. Frederick, how long have ye had yer nice, fat, and healthy horse? Where did ye buy such a fat horse? I heard that all the fat Missouri horses of St. Louis ended up in the Confederate Army anyway. Is dat true?"

Ignoring the question, Frederick continued, "Joe, how does Hanoverian horse mother sound speaking Irish?"

Joseph leaned over into the ear of Fitzgerald and audibly asked, "Fitzgerald, could ye speak in Irish for Frederick? He wants to hear how yer ma sounded when ye learned to ... speak."

Without an apparent cue, Fitzgerald let out a high-pitched neigh, a snort, and kicked up his heels.

All four men were amused by Fitzgerald's response, adding to the fascination about Joe's talents as well as the intelligence of Fitzgerald.

Joseph turned and quietly commented, "Frederick, Fitzgerald is insulted by yer questions, and he wants me to stop talking to ye. He is vorried about consortin' mit the enemy."

"Ya?"

With a perfectly delayed timing, Joseph turned about in his saddle, stared in an intimidating way into Frederick's familiar slate eyes, and replied, "Ya!" He continued looking in Frederick's eyes, scratching his own brain for answers and trying to intimidate Frederick. It seemed that this man was stupidly flirting with revealing himself. He thought, *Why does he ask so much about my horse? What does he already know about me and Fitzgerald? Why does he keep talking about it? Does he want to reveal his secrets so I can turn around and shoot him, the damned spy?*

During the pause in talk, gnawing in Joseph's brain was not only Frederick's question about how he fed Fitzgerald so well, but there were pieces of a conversation only days earlier that annoyed him. It involved Frederick and a group of men sitting around their fire, finishing their morning coffee, and waiting for the dreaded order for a drill. As usual, there was talk of food, bragging about what someone had done here and there in a skirmish, amusing stories about exceptionally bad or good officers, and conjecture about the enemy. Most men in the group who had not served in the Home Guard were new to the military. Joseph had thought that about Frederick, but his preconceived notions didn't fit after limited observation.

Frederick had clearly been a soldier, but he didn't seem to love his horse. After riding, he didn't remove his bridle right away. He tethered Lucky loosely or not at all, and in the mornings on outings, they were always waiting on Frederick to retrieve Lucky. Which did Frederick prefer: getting shot or getting away? His carelessness jeopardized patrols. Frederick was competent in the drills, and he didn't mind mindless hours sitting around camp. The rest was seriously lacking.

Frederick always seemed to be looking at Joseph. He would be studying Joseph as he sat quietly listening to others. If Joseph got up, Frederick's eyes followed. Joseph had begun to avoid Frederick's line of vision or would get up and move out of his sight when he felt it was necessary. After several days of this, Joseph decided he had seen those big slate eyes somewhere before. His precious little brother Charley had large gray eyes, but they were kind. Frederick's moon face and pie eyes were unsettling, even when the men were at ease around the fire.

When the subject of food came up, one of the greenhorns suggested that the Confederates ate better than their Northern counterparts. "I reckon they knows what to do with one of them big Missouri hams they steal. I hear them secesh boys always got lots of tender meat."

"Don't believe dat!" Frederick said. "Soldiers at Sugar Creek was, for a week, with three days of crackers in their pockets. Officers eat dat ham—no private eat dat ham!"

It was spoken with such conviction that Joseph believed Frederick might have been there. Joseph thought, *And being in St. Louis, how do you know that, Frederick? A Confederate who served for Sterling Price would know about that.* Neither Joseph nor anyone else around the fire had heard about three days' worth of crackers handed out to last for five days. Where would that come from? All the men turned to Frederick and examined him with furrows in their brows.

Joseph's company persistently entertained the subject of Sterling Price as leader: Where was he? What was his plan now, after Pea Ridge? Would he show up in Cass County next?

Joseph listened and waited. He decided to pull Frederick off guard, and he asked, "You ever been in Ireland, Frederick?"

Frederick laughed. "In Ireland?" "How 'bout Arkansas?"

No answer came. It was such a surprise that Frederick immediately seemed not to hear Joseph. Everyone understood the accusatory tone in Joe's voice and looked at Frederick.

Frederick looked down at his pants and pretended to flick a bug off his knee, emotionally exclaiming, "What is kind of bug?" Joseph glanced over to Matthew to check his expression and, hopefully, rattle Frederick. He asked, "Where were you in February and March, Matt?"

"Right here in Cass County. Where were you, Joe?"

"After enlisting in the militia in February, I went to visit my wife and fatten my horse in Kansas. You know I've been here since April." Looking at the man seated next to him, he asked, "How about you, John?"

As John explained about his mother dying and packing up his little sisters to go live with an uncle, Joe looked for signs of emotional squirming in Frederick's face. There was only one man, Padraig, between John and Frederick. Frederick was calmly, and with a sympathetic face, poking the dwindling fire back to life. Joseph realized that Frederick had a well-rehearsed answer and was ready to supply it even if Padraig didn't tell his story. Joseph resisted asking Frederick if he'd ever been in "one of them Shakespeare plays." He wanted to accuse Frederick of acting. He wanted to question how long he could keep it up before they all knew the truth.

Joe would watch and wait. He suspected that Alexander and Matthew might have begun to question how this "transfer" of Frederick to this regiment might have happened. Most of the men were unfamiliar with regular or volunteer operations or didn't care about such things. Most of them enlisted where they lived. Times were irregular everywhere, but Joe had decided that the friendly Frederick was a plant—and not a transfer.

He told both the corporal and his commanding officer. It intrigued Joseph that neither acted surprised. They told Joseph it was a serious accusation and that he had no proof. Both told Joseph he needed to refrain from expressing his opinion again, and they told him it was inappropriate material for general conversation among the men. It was "dangerous and unfounded" and could result in a murder among the men.

CHAPTER 3

SCOUTING THE KANSAS-MISSOURI BORDER, 1862

The four scouts traveled on together, in twos, following Alexander's lead until afternoon was approaching and they reached the road headed straight east to Garden City.

Alexander called out, "Halt, gentlemen." When the men had all stopped, he continued, "It's been a good day. I don't think we'll find anything until we move on a bit closer to the border or somewhere past Austin or below Dayton, but this is our place to split up."

Alexander reviewed the details. "Joseph and I will cover Miami and Cygnes. We'll continue tonight until we get below south branch. We'll camp as close to the border road as we can and will start out tomorrow, planning to meet up at Papinsville day after tomorrow. Matthew, ye and Frederick find yer own ideal camping site, but drop south off the Grand below Dayton." Handing his map to Matthew, Alexander pointed and continued, "Go southeast as far as Johnstown or Montrose, then turn north, cross at Clinton, and head back northwest into Creighton along the north bank of the river. Take note of every bridge and crossing—but avoid the Ford. It's easy to get lost, and it's likely flooded; there are a lot of dangerous dead ends. It's unlikely any large force of men will be camping in there because of the recent flooding, and ye don't want to get cut off or boxed in, even though the weather looks to be improving. We'll meet Friday night in Creighton, on the west side of town near the post office."

Frederick piped in, "Joseph, you sure you want to skirt secesh border by yourself? I hear it is fearful place."

Joseph answered, "But it is less fearful without ye, Frederick." Alexander laughed.

Frederick ambled off behind Matthew and cheerfully called out, "Look at Matt, Joseph. You must learn to trust. We will get along fine. You? Good luck in middle of gray coats by self!"

Joseph ignored Frederick, who made ridiculous comments in an effort to be humorous.

As Frederick was rambling on in his heavy accent, Joseph glanced toward Matthew and mouthed, "Christ beside you, Matt."

Matthew recognized the prayer given by Saint Patrick himself for the monks in Northern Ireland being hunted by the English soldiers. Matt knew the prayer that Joe's wife had learned to recite in Irish. Mary was raised not far from the very spot in Ireland where the miracle of the prayer had happened. The prayer to ask for Christ's protection had made the monks appear as deer in a fog to the English soldiers. For two centuries, it had sustained and given courage. For Matt, Joseph, and Alexander it brought comfort but never took away concern. Christ was probably not going to be above, beside, before, or behind Matthew, but Joseph hoped it would remind Matthew to keep looking in all those directions while in the immediate presence of his enemy, Frederick.

Φ

On Lucky, Frederick ambled east down the road behind Matthew, appointed point man by Alexander. They traveled directly either east or south for five miles before reaching the banks of the main stream, barely talking the entire distance. Because Frederick usually rambled on but was quiet, it seemed to Matthew that he was annoyed, bored, or distracted. Matthew did not believe that Frederick's heart was in his job. It wasn't until they stopped for a brief break that Frederick began to talk to Matt about their camping site. The thought cheered him, and hunting and fishing seemed to be at the top of his concerns. It had become an absolutely beautiful day, and they were entering a wildlife-abundant area along the river.

Matthew knew that Frederick thought of himself as a great hunter. Who knew any different? Seeming to be indifferent to his task, he began telling Matt about his many trips hunting as a small child with his grandfather in Germany. He was proud of his marksmanship and expressed excitement at the prospect of bagging a duck or goose for dinner. Matt was up for good eating, but he didn't feel indiscriminate shooting was a "covert" activity when conducted in the middle of enemy territory.

Matthew reminded Frederick that if there were guerillas hiding beside them out along the river, a gunshot might bring an unwanted investigation by a unit. Also, he suggested saving his bullets for the enemy. "Besides," added Matthew, "bullets are gettin' hard to acquire."

It was unusual that Matthew would have to remind a fellow soldier about noise or bullets. Matthew had no confidence that Frederick had done quiet, independent scouting. Perhaps he was accustomed to "camping" with a regiment of five hundred where hunting and loud storytelling might be a more appropriate activity, but probably not. He discouraged Frederick from hunting in favor of fishing. He also suggested that he talk less robustly.

Always with a hook and some line in his haversack, Frederick said he was just as anxious to find a good spot to drop in his line as he was to shoot something—anything—but he cheerfully put aside his idea about hunting. "Ya, maybe you become the hunted when you hunt around here."

They quickly crossed a main intersection between the larger road that went across the river and north, back into Harrisonville and one that led to the former town of Dayton. The small settlement of Dayton had been burned to the ground in a raid only five months earlier, and few inhabitants were left on the rich farms between the town and Grand River. Anything left would be an ideal spot for guerillas to hide. Matthew suggested that they sneak across the river and check for secesh south of Dayton if they could get across. Otherwise, they would have to approach it from the Creighton side once they met up with the others. Frederick disinterestedly replied, "Oh, ya," as though he could not have cared less.

Eventually, both agreed on a spot to bed down around a north-turning bend far out of sight of the busy road to Harrisonville. It was upstream from a confluence with one of the larger tributaries and appeared to be an animal crossing above deeper water just downstream that ran flat and meandered into the large swampy area. From their map, it appeared they were approaching the ford. Early in the morning, they could continue a mile or two east and then depart southeast from the river to circumvent the large, nearly impenetrable area in their way.

At their chosen site, the egress from either side of the river was not too wide. On their side of the river, the bank was wider, quite sandy to one side, and it had nice river rock. Downstream, on their side of the bank, it was somewhat muddy. Willows grew in the high water, and numerous logs jumbled here and there indicated that this spot gathered up flood materials where the bank had been eaten into and there was a place for things to shove up against the bend. It left deeper water on the north side, as the stream moved over to erode the side with less resistance.

At their campsite, it was obvious that animals and even locals had crossed often before the river altered. Because nearby Dayton residents on the opposite bank had nearly all fled, it probably wasn't used too much now.

Leading down the bank from the level area above was a white oak. It sat in front of a cluster of sweet-smelling cottonwoods and birch. Beyond the thorny bushes to the east was great shelter for secluding their horses with some new grass that grew out in an opening beyond the crest of the bank. It might have been a lightning strike and small burn. Matthew saw blackened trees along the perimeter and pointed out deer hoofprints leading down to the water.

Matthew was always nervous, so he looked for escape routes, lookout places, and usable advantages in the topography. During his inspection of the area, Matthew noted significant camp smoke coming from the horizon far east of their site. He told Frederick that they best assume it was secesh, as they were the only Union they knew of scouting in the area. Most Union had gone north due to the problems in Independence. The large Union force in Butler was artillery. He pointed the volume of smoke out to Frederick, but his "Ya, ya, ya" response indicated greater interest in fishing.

After dismounting, Frederick and Matthew dropped the reins of their horses and gave them a long drink. Matthew relieved Brother from his bridle and led him by the halter out to get a drink while he was free from his bit. Lucky and Brother waded out a little bit from the muddy bank and found clean water under the surface where it was a little deeper.

Matthew briefly discussed with Frederick how close they would travel to the distant campfire tomorrow so they could make an accurate accounting of what they saw, and he demanded they keep their own fire small and not leave it burning into dark. Matthew told Frederick they needed to stay off the open bank, crawl back into the shrubs, and keep their horses tethered deep into the trees and shrubs along the bank. That way, they would not be visible in the moonlight if secesh headed their way on night patrols.

Returning to flat ground above the bank, Matthew pulled long grasses, piled them, and laid out Brother's grain on top so it would not fall in dirt or sand among the weeds. Brother hated his feed bag, but Matthew didn't like wasting grain in the dirt. After Brother had eaten his oats, he tethered him hidden among shaded birches and not too far from where he had chosen to bed down.

Φ

After caring for Lucky, Frederick searched out a good fishing hole. He walked to the ridge of the bank and continued east around the bend seeking a trail to the large jam down river. He whacked his way down and found the perfect spot with lodged logs and limbs with new leaves—a good place for him to drop his hook. He fashioned a pole from a willow. It was going to be a beautiful evening, the first in a very long time, and the moon would be nearly full. The last sun of dusk was perfect for river fishing.

Frederick noticed a few bugs flitting around above the water. However, it was a little early in the year for the salmon fly and saddlebags that brought good fishing. Because of the rain and cold, it had been a late spring for bugs. Frederick thought he saw a mantid and was hopeful. Unfortunately, there were no more of either to be caught. Because he had no bait, he dangled himself out on the jam and flitted about with the bare hook trying to tempt somebody out of the "depths" of the log shadows. It failed.

Returning to the willows, he scrounged around the new green leaves for caterpillars and was finally successful. However, nobody was biting either his bitter caterpillars or grubs this late in the day. If he wanted fish in the morning, he would have to add worms to the bait menu.

When he returned empty-handed to the small campfire where Matthew had a little bite of bacon and hot coffee ready, he apologized and promised more in the morning. Matthew had already whittled the willow skewers for cooking fish and was noticeably disappoint-ed, though he was ready with a piece of bacon for Frederick. The meal was sparse, but it would not be the first time a soldier would be depending on accumulated fat to carry himself over a scouting trip. Soldiers were used to constant states of feast and famine. He and Matthew had eaten well for a week at Harrisonville, so they were prepared for meager fare for a few days. Perhaps they could eat a real meal in Clinton. Often, soldiers were so accustomed to going hungry that they couldn't hold down a full meal when they finally found one.

As the moon rose and the sun set, Frederick watched as Matthew went to his haversack, returned items, and retrieved his blanket. Frederick sat by the fire, face toward to the river and his back turned to Matthew.

Moving Brother away from the tough grass, Matthew stood con-cealed from Frederick behind Brother. He laid the blanket back across Brother's back and quietly loaded his rifle. He then stepped to Brother's hind flanks, turned ninety degrees, and from behind Brother's rump, pointed the barrel at the back of Frederick's head. His trigger finger was one blink away from firing. Matthew's in-stincts and the warnings of Joseph told him that he was in a kill-or-be-killed situation, but his angels and good fairies got the better of him. He backed around behind Brother, who had stood perfectly still and quiet, and led him back into the trees. Matt sensed that Frederick might have turned around and just missed seeing Mat-thew stalking him.

Was Joseph wrong? Not usually. Being a devout Catholic, Matt asked Christ's forgiveness and retired, rifle and blanket in hand, to the edge of the brush. He laid down some small, new branches and settled in near the ridge of the bank. He was tucked far enough in, back up against an oak, that no deer or bushwhackers would find it necessary to lope over him in the night. There were so many shrubs and trees that Frederick could not easily sneak up behind him as he lay sleeping. With the moonlight in front of him, Matthew would have had a clear view.

He trusted that Frederick would take care of the campfire and would retire to the other side of the trail to the river. He was right. Frederick settled in farther down the bank, in a place that would not afford him a good opportunity to get at Matthew. Matthew relaxed and decided that he might get some sleep. However, he had begun perceiving a coldness expanding behind Frederick's practiced smile. Frederick did not fit; he was not one of them.

Φ

The sun had already risen when Matthew awoke. He had heard Lucky and decided that Frederick was returning or retrieving items and preparing his fishing expedition around the bend. Before rising, he heard steps in the water and thought Frederick was leaving the camp area by wading downstream to the logjam rather than coming up the bank and disturbing Matthew. It occurred to Matt that Frederick was being thoughtful, though he was usually most thoughtful when indulging himself and not others.

Matthew stood up, grabbed his rifle and blanket, and began his move out of the brush, a move designed to savor more time lying in the rising sun. When he stood up, he didn't see Frederick. Glancing west, upriver, Matthew saw a low mist rising. Smelling cooked fish in his mind, Matthew lay back down, closer to the sandy beach, which was warming and drying in the early moments of morning. After a few minutes with his eyes facing east, he turned his back to the bright sun, eyes closed, facing somewhat southwest, up toward the bending ridge. His back was turned directly away from the shady direction in which Frederick was fishing.

Suddenly, Matthew felt the shock of something hard being smashed across his temple. On instinct, Matthew stumbled up on his hands and knees and called, "Fredrick, help, quick!" He grappled for the loaded rifle under his blanket. Almost to his feet, hands on the ground, he turned toward the river and saw Frederick over him, smiling and saying, "Ah! Good morning, Matthew." With the butt of Frederick's rifle already positioned to come down, Matthew felt another massive thump to the nape of his neck. He pitched forward, planted himself facedown in the sand, and slumped into blackness.

Φ

Frederick dropped his rifle, grabbed Matthew's feet, and dragged him to the edge of the river. As he was going to roll him over on his back to check for breathing and dump him in the water where he planned to shoot him, he heard men in conversation. They were approaching west from across the river! One stopped at the top of the bank, riding from the direction of Clinton and faced away from Frederick, and was talking to the man approaching from the east, behind him.

Frederick scrambled for his rifle, tossed it into the bushes, snatched Matthew's blanket, and threw it over him. Matt's feet stuck out at the bottom, his arms above his shoulders, but Frederick, eyes on the rider, tucked Matt's sprawled-out arms underneath the blanket and set his own hat over Matt's head to hide the bleeding. Frederick calmly sat down and waited.

The first man came down to the water and dismounted, to give his horse a drink.

Frederick pretended that he could not hear or that he was drunk. He clumsily wobbled up on his feet, pointed to his ears, and shook his head in a negative gesture, hands out as if to indicate he understood nothing. He motioned toward Matthew, tipped an imaginary bottle in the air to indicate that Matthew was a drunk who had apparently passed out where he fell. In a heavy accent, he muddled things about being too drunk to cross the river; he would be making coffee; and they were heading into Clinton to buy a horse.

The man who had not come down to the water dismounted briefly from his horse and relieved himself in the bushes.

When the horse finished his drink, his rider led him up the bank, and both men saddled up. They momentarily turned east, seemed to signal another rider who might be coming, and then rode away from the river in a northerly direction. Frederick hoped whoever else was coming along would ride diagonally toward the others rather than stop at the crossing.

Believing the first men would not return, but not knowing if the others might approach, Frederick uncovered Matthew and rolled his limp body parallel to the river with his head pointing east. As Frederick began to check for signs of breathing, he suddenly heard more voices. He hadn't expected more than one man. He shoved Matthew's body out into the river. Frederick was sure Mathew would float to center stream and drift out of sight of the men behind the trees on the other side of the river. Even if they came down to the water, Matthew would be out of sight around the north-bending river. They wouldn't be looking east toward the sun for a body floating around the bend away from them.

The water was very shallow, and Frederick lost control of Matt's limp body, which didn't want to float far or fast. He was dragging on the bottom. In a panic, Frederick kicked Matthew's feet out to catch deeper and swifter-moving water. He didn't want to be caught out in the shallow water with a dead body casually drifting along. In pushing Matt's feet first, the water caught his legs and began to swing them out in slow, clockwise motion with Matt's head and shoulders pivoting on the sandy mud and protruding stones under the water. Through his broken skin, Matthew was bleeding out into the water, but it was impossible for Frederick to identify pulsing because of the movement of the water and the reflection of the bright morning light. To his horror, he had not pushed Matthew out far enough. As he heard and looked for the men approaching, the water began to forcefully direct Matthew back toward the bank and behind an old black log that had lodged, butt up, in the mud. The stream was somewhat gravelly and shallow in front of the log, and willows were protruding out of the pea-sized gravel. The water behind the log was

41

deeper, and Matthew's body was neatly parked there, feetfirst, where the men coming down the bank could not see him.

Frederick grabbed Matthew's blanket and was washing his hat off in the river when the men noticed him across the bank. Frederick thought they were too far away to notice blood or be interested in details across the water. Dragged body marks in the sand, one man, but two horses, a rifle tossed partly hidden in the bushes, a hat lying on the ground by the second horse, blood in the sand, and a man washing his hat should have been indicators to Frederick that he was no professional. There was no campfire, but there was a random haversack on the ground near the second horse. And, of course, there was the body floating, faceup, behind a rotten log along the shore.

The men rode their horses into the water so they could drink and called across to ask Frederick if he was all right. Again, he acted deaf and told them his buddy was off looking for caterpillars and grubs in the willows so they could catch a fish for breakfast. He told them he was on his way to buy a horse in Clinton.

The man pointed and called back that there were large catfish downstream toward the swampland if they were going that way.

Frederick thanked them, forgetting that he couldn't hear. The man looked at him and stood there for a moment.

Frederick then added, "Thanks for telling me where is Clinton, ya?"

The men looked skeptical, but they turned and rode back up the bank, one at a time. The second man turned and looked toward Frederick, and then they both rode away quickly, looking as though they were anxious to catch up to the other two men up ahead of them.

Frederick flew into action. He had to get away quickly! How many others would come along, forcing him to modify his story and making this more difficult than it needed to be? Normally, this kind of thing didn't rattle him, but this was too much. He thought of putting a bullet in Matthew before he left, but if the men decided to come back, they might hear the shot or see him in action. Matthew hadn't stirred, and the water was cold. Frederick decided not to be concerned. He didn't check Matthew. He simply put Matthew out of his mind, got on his horse, and rode back west toward the Kansas border.

CHAPTER 4

JOSEPH ON THE MARAIS DES CYGNES RIVER

Joseph had, by far, the superior and best-fed horse so he was assigned the most dangerous territory. His horse skills were legendary. Although Joseph could be intense and somewhat unpredictable, he was remarkably creative when he was not drinking. He was willing to risk doing things that kept himself and his companions out of tricky or hopeless situations. Like a weasel, he was able to snatch a hen from the chicken coop before the rooster knew what happened.

Alexander and Joseph camped safely among the trees and woke early to an unusually beautiful day. They agreed that they would meet, possibly tomorrow or the next day, where Miami Creek crossed the main road to Butler and Harrisonville. Upon reaching the final bend, north of a fairly sizable slaveholding secesh plantation, Joseph would cut northeast and travel to the main road.

Upon reaching Miami Creek, Joseph shook Alexander's hand and said, "Christ be with ye, friend."

"And with ye, Joseph." Alexander immediately turned east and started his scouting alone on the north bank.

Joseph crossed the small tributary and continued due south. He could connect with the Marais des Cygnes River in a few miles where it ran out of the ravines of Kansas and southeasterly, somewhat parallel to Miami Creek to his north. Even with persistent thoughts of Mary sitting at her spinning wheel by her fire in Kansas, Joseph knew he would not be riding close enough to visit. As soon as he reached the Cygnes, he would be riding away from her and eventually to where both tributaries met at the main road to Harrisonville, a departure from their original plan.

His trail continued easily until it led into the creek. As Joe scrambled up out of the full-flowing Miami creek bed into an open field, his main concern was being forced to cross a flooded Marais des

Cygnes downstream. He might get himself and Fitzgerald in trouble by attempting to cross back to the north side to rejoin his troop, especially if a critical bridge was gone.

Bridges were on close banks, where the water tended to be deeper and swifter. The river was already flooded, and washed- out, burned-out, or blown-out bridges were almost never the best place to cross. He didn't want to be chased, guns blazing, as he plunged his beloved Fitzgerald into a raging river full of broken timbers, lodged tree branches, or large pieces of twisted metal. Joseph thought, *God doesn't watch too well over me. Does he show me the same love that he shows some scoundrel like Frederick? It would be just like an unlucky Irishman like me to drown or have Frederick catch up and finish me off.*

As Joseph continued due south beneath golden, clearing skies, the frequency of blue-eyed grass indicated fields growing back to the natural open prairie. Again, it reminded him of the loss of the little farm on Big Creek and the necessity of sending his hungry wife without him across the mean Kansas border. He reached down and pulled on the tallest plants to form a little bouquet of blue blossoms that he slipped under Fitzgerald's bridle. He sped up.

Alone and perpetually fearful, the great sadness that lay in all the grief that had been heaped upon him in his twenty-four years swept over Joseph. Looking at the little blossoms of the prairie plant lifted his heart. They reminded him of the bright blue flowers that proliferated along the gray, stone walls of the Irish childhood he barely remembered. It moved him to his most pleasant and one of his last images of his ma.

He remembered crying as a five-year-old and picking the dainty blue flowers along the wee road with her and his little brother, Charley. His mother was a beautiful woman. She had handed him a bouquet and kissed the tears off his cheek. He had been holding Charley's hand, but he had been too young to remember the circumstances of his unhappiness. He thought it might have been about helping his ma carry her butter. He loved little Charley. Maybe Charley wanted to carry the butter. Joseph never could sort it out, and there was nobody left to ask.

During his adolescence, Joseph had lost contact with Charley and his sister Ellen. Joseph felt nostalgic comfort when he thought about his little brother holding his hand and his ma's beautiful, freckled face. He could see Ma when he saw his own reflection. He and Charley had her singing voice, some of the same facial features, and the thick, black curly hair, and light eyes—something that amazed blond-haired, blue-eyed Americans. They did not understand the "black Irish" Celtic genes. Many had never seen blue eyes with black hair.

Joseph's significant other lasting image of his ma was her sudden departure from the ship when they arrived in New York Harbor. He remembered his father barely helping a man in a uniform lift his ma's failed body up the dark stairs to the sunny top deck. Michael's mother, also named Margaret, had died when Michael was about seven years old. Their da had married Joseph's mother shortly thereafter. Michael loved Joseph's mother. He had known her longer than his own mother. Michael's half sister, Margaret, and Joseph's other siblings came along nearly every other year after that. Neither he nor Michael had quit thinking about their love of their mothers since stepping ashore in America. Michael loved both Margarets and thought both would be proud of him. Of course, Joseph had never met Michael's mother.

Like crumbs on the steerage floor, five members of his family were swept away by illness. It made Joseph cry when he thought about it. If his beautiful ma could have kissed him or touched his hand as she departed, he would have felt better about losing her. Maybe he could have gotten over it. Now, as he traveled along dangerous open lands, riverbanks, and through woodlands looking for the enemy who wanted to kill him, his childhood and arrival to America seemed an eternity away.

He suddenly realized he was distracting himself from the enemy. *Where is Frederick? Is Matthew staying behind Frederick?* Joseph's level of trust in Frederick had steadily eroded from little to none. He was still convinced that he had seen those eyes somewhere in the past, which was not good. He heard the persistent "ya" in his brain, and it irritated him. He decided to let it inform him. He focused on every evil person he had met. He was not the man at Big Creek who stole Sunshine, but he had probably met him without realizing it.

Joseph didn't think that a lot of Confederates looked like Frederick. Some Confederates were Irish—something he didn't understand—but most Germans sympathized with Lincoln and the North. He had run into exceptional German soldiers on the side of the Union from Iowa and Missouri in the past year. Like the Irish, some of them were dark, and some were light. Joseph didn't remember seeing any German redheads. Germans liked beer, but they tended to stay sober more than the Irish. Joseph knew that not all Germans were bad, but this one was. The only other "bad" Germans he had encountered were the Neumann family in Strother. He tried to connect his familiarity there.

Joseph's morning had been easy enough to allow his mind to drift and to become too easily distracted from his mission. Throughout the early afternoon, Joseph had quickly traveled parallel to the dangerous Kansas border. Now he was only a few miles east of a primary staging area of the Confederate guerillas. Here, each step required extreme caution and thoughtful calculation. He was enjoying the brilliantly blue sky and good visibility, but all his senses were fully alert to signs of the enemy. The spring grasses were lush and provided decent cover.

After traveling about four miles unimpeded across the stunning Missouri prairie, Joseph noticed in the distance a small, spread-out herd of about seven horses and a mule in a field that had been fenced. They were grazing freely outside some railings that were still standing. The farm had apparently fallen into complete disrepair, though the cabin was still intact. It seemed occupied today. The sun was still high. Its blazing golden light cast dark shadows along the tree line to the west of the house where a bend in the river flowed northeast. What few windows the structure had were likely on the west side where the sun had reached its tipping point and would begin to descend.

If he passed on the bright side, he thought he could be more easily seen as he moved toward the shadows. Because Joseph needed to be to the east, he chose that direction instead, even though it meant he'd be out in the open for longer. He moved directly east until he perceived a slight dip in the land. Then he began to turn gradually toward the river. The tall stands of grass moving in the breeze would help hide a full profile of Fitzgerald. Perhaps the shadows were long enough to obscure or confuse someone's view of what was moving behind the newly greened clumps. Going left would also keep him farther from the horses grazing behind the cabin.

"Ciúin síos / Quiet down," Joseph whispered as he dismounted. Holding his reins tight below Fitzgerald's neck and muzzle, Joseph walked very slowly beside Fitzgerald. He crouched low, peering out across the tops of the grass from under the horse's neck. Joseph continued to look for light emanating from within or other signs. The sun was just dipping toward the horizon so he could not be sure that light inside was a fire and not a reflection coming through a window from the west. He wasn't close enough to discern the difference. There appeared to be a wisp of smoke from the chimney.

The small herd was the only sign of livestock—no chickens, no pigs of settlers—but Joseph was particularly concerned about who might be in the house, which was about sixty yards away. There were no stallions among the herd, and the mares or geldings, quite a distance off, did not appear interested in guests. They seemed to be separately staked and focused on the grass, which had been cultivated a few years ago by settlers and not the prairie. They didn't act anxious to cut loose. They weren't rogue horses that had broken free and were roaming east of Confederate territory; everything had a temporary look and feel to Joseph. They were likely secesh.

Joseph had told Fitzgerald that his fairies could make him invisible. Pulling tight and down on his reins made him lower his head. Joseph had taught him to simultaneously tuck his tail down between his legs and to hush to a barely audible nickering. Fitzgerald had learned the signals that there was great danger. It brought confidence to Joseph, and he childishly imagined himself as a great Celtic chieftain with a spiritually endowed warhorse. When Fitzgerald nickered in the midst of danger, Joseph whispered, "Capall maith / Good horse."

Most of the small homesteads not destroyed by fire along the border had been emptied of their owners by Jayhawkers, guerillas, or other close calls with certain death or destruction. Log cabins or otherwise, they were falling into serious disrepair. People had given up. Food supplies were gone from their cellars. Livestock being led through their parlors by strange men had replaced baptism celebrations, wakes, and Christmas dinners. With the year's persistent rain and nobody left to plant, the prospects for finding anything other than scatterings of grains that had seeded themselves outside the grasp of a combine was very unlikely on these farms.

Other than in the midst of battle, this careful travel and tense moments were when Joseph most appreciated Fitzgerald, his trusted friend. He was relieved that the burden of Frederick as companion was not with him. Had Joseph been the one chosen to ride along the Grand, he surely would have alleviated Frederick from the inconvenience of living and, by now, would have dragged and released his rotten soul downstream into the swamp. His other two companions would have been grateful for his actions, and the three soldiers could have continued on with relief.

Fitzgerald, who kept his ears perked up and nostrils working, was how Joseph got through these adventures unscathed. Joseph's alert, low profile in the saddle signaled to Fitzgerald not to be spooked by sudden movements or sounds. Fitzgerald stayed alert but steady.

Even though Fitzgerald could puff up like a stallion from time to time, in the fields and along the streams, he was prepared to drop and play dead when asked. Joseph's reassuring, quiet utterances of Celtic words for warrior horses produced pride and confidence in man and horse. In the theater of war, they became equals; they were that perfect pairing of warriors born to battle.

Once out of sight from the little house, Joseph remounted and continued to the river and its protective tree line, which was less than a hundred yards ahead.

Joseph's plan was to travel along the north bank until a flatter and more ample crossing presented itself far to the east of the cabin. Ahead, he saw a break in the silhouette of trees. They crossed to the south bank and traveled east, downstream, to make anyone from the cabin who was tracking believe he had continued away from the cabin along the south bank. Joseph and Fitzgerald traveled far enough that most trackers would quit looking for the familiar signs of doubling back.

In due course, after meandering north and south along the bank, sometimes walking in the water and then continuing on, Joseph drove Fitzgerald into fairly deep water in an unlikely spot. He then turned him back west, pushing upstream so that any trail underwater was unseen in the daylight or would be washed away in minutes. Eventually, they came to a crossing behind the cabin.

On the far side of the crossing, they scrambled up the steep grassy bank and continued west. After about forty yards, they dropped back into the water, moving back down toward the cabin to a stand of tall trees on the far bank not easily accessible walking upstream from the crossing. The large oaks were on elevated land directly behind the cabin. They grew closer to the water than they normally would because the stream had shifted, and the bank had been eroded by water. New leaves and cottonwoods provided complete coverage from the sides and behind. However, Joseph found a wide-open view. He could now see the light in the cabin and more smoke coming from the chimney, and he could smell meat cooking.

If Joseph climbed into a tree, he would have a perfect vantage point across the bank and along the back and eastern side of the cabin. It was one of those beautiful evenings when the full moon rose before the sun set. There was a hint of apricot creeping on the western horizon, and the moon was anxious. Venus had begun glowing over Joseph's shoulder. Even as night approached, he could pick a single target and probably a second from his vantage point. Hopefully they would be looking down and could not place a flash if he missed his mark.

He led Fitzgerald to the right position. Joseph then sat in the dark shadows on Fitzgerald's back and securely tied one end of a rope around the trunk and above a limb of a sturdy tree. The rope could not slide down. He coiled up the loose rope and directed Fitzgerald across the short but cold, deep distance to the other side. Once on the north bank, Joseph jumped off his horse and walked partway up the bank. Throwing the rope up over a limb about six feet above the ground and tying as he had across the river, Joseph looped the end around his small saddle horn and had Fitzgerald back up until it could get no tighter. The rope was now strung between two trees about five feet above the deepest water of the stream. Nobody would look for him to cross here. He could come or go from one side to the other without his horse, and if he fell off, he wouldn't necessarily make a big splash. It was a short distance to drift to the shallow crossing.

Man and horse quietly returned to the south bank. Behind the tree line, along the field above the river, he removed Fitzgerald's bridle, tethered him, and placed a feed bag of oats over his muzzle. Joseph gave him a hug and pat around his head, uttered "Capall maith / Good horse," and brushed the cold water off his shiny coat. When he could, Joseph took care of Fitzgerald before he tended to his own needs. While brushing, he planned and kept one eye on the cabin.

Joseph, aware of the smoke and the smell of bacon, shivered from his wet feet and legs and thought of a warming fire in a cozy house. The smells of comfort brought on his desire for a strong drink that could heat his bones and put the stress of the Confederacy and stalking assassins out of his mind. For now, however, he would wrap himself in his blanket, eat his meager hardtack, and wait for some inevitable event he could not fully predict.

CHAPTER 5

WAITING FOR THE ENEMY

Joseph dozed for a short time until he heard activity from the cabin. Within two hours, sunset would arrive. The moon was now in view in the blue sky when men came out and headed to their horses.

After enjoying his bag, Fitzgerald had been freed to forage among the mixed grasses along the once-tilled field behind. Conveniently, he was nearly standing over Joseph.

The moment Joseph heard men speaking and saw movement, Joseph called for Fitzgerald to drop. "Fanntais / Fall!" he whispered. Joseph crept up and cuddled behind the warm Fitzgerald with his rifle propped on the horse's shoulder. Fitzgerald lay flat. Field glasses pressed to the bridge of his nose, Joseph peered out from behind his animal, through the leaves and shadows, at the figures in the field across the river.

One by one, the men had begun to gather up their horses in preparation for departure. They had returned bridles and haversacks, and they were tightening up cinch straps on the horses. As the men busied themselves, another man came riding up from the north, leading a second horse behind him. The rider loosely tied both horses to one of the posts out front and walked briskly out to greet the man closest to him who had been intently watching.

Joseph assumed they were all seceshes, though he noticed carefully and studied body movement insecurities among the men. All three men behind the leader momentarily stopped their activity and turned toward the stranger as their hands hovered above their holsters.

They were facing the wrong way, and the breeze muffled their voices. However, it was probably a case where they were all secesh but not connected to the new rider. Now at ease, it appeared to Joseph that the first four men were in the process of sorting out who would lead each of the seven horses. It seemed they were changing things up. Perhaps things had not gone well on their way here. Maybe that's why they stopped at an unusual time of day: to calm down their animals and grab a bite before continuing on to Trading Post, Kansas, about two hours across the border.

They seemed to single out the most aggressive horse to be on a single lead with one rider. That required fixing a third snap on a longer line for the horse that would be distanced from the aggressor. Such a move might add to an already difficult challenge. Joseph knew it was a tricky job to lead more than one unknown horse. Maybe the rider had figured the horses out by now, but adding the third horse was iffy at best. He smiled. *And what will they do with the mule?* he thought. *Have they forgotten their mule? Surely not.*

The arrangement problem amused and interested Joseph as much as anything else. As a professional mule drover, he entertained himself with the crazy idea of allowing the mule to lead the entire entourage. The head rider, hooked to the mule, would follow the mule while leading the aggressive horse. Joseph had known mules that could lead the entire string back home if they were hooked together properly. He joked to himself that it would work only if the mule and the lead rider were like-minded and had agreed exactly—down to the blade of grass—on their destination.

How will ye behave in the moonlight, sweet girl? Will ye want to stop, sit down, light a cigar, and count the stars—like me Elizabeth?

When Joseph was seventeen, he took up smoking cigars at the local pub. When he was sleeping in the shed with his mules, he would take a cigar back home for his mule, Elizabeth. She enjoyed a cigar now and then, but Joseph couldn't trust her to smoke alone in the barn.

Maybe this mule should be placed just behind the rider and in front of the aggressive horse to give her a kick in the face when she gets out of line. He liked that arrangement, and the image brought him a good laugh. There was nothing like a smart Missouri mule in the mix to add interest to your life.

Joseph thought, *What if Fitzgerald were forced to go along with strangers without me? How might he ruin their day if he were there? He absolutely could ruin their day!* Joseph gave him a little pat, whispered, "Capall maith / Good horse," and assumed that Fitzgerald would have made Joseph proud if he were placed with a mule. *He and Elizabeth could have showed them all!*

Joseph continued to watch the theater in the dusk across the river. As the newcomer moved closer in acknowledgement of the men who were tacking up their horses, he didn't appear to have already known them. However, he thought himself important enough to interrupt their activity by insisting on shaking all their hands and becoming familiar. The lead man with the newcomer shared information Joseph could not hear, but when the stranger turned south, lifted his left arm, and pointed downstream, his voice carried directly across the river in Joseph's direction.

Joseph became suddenly and intensely aware that he recognized his voice. There was no mistaking that he spoke with a German accent. Joseph was stunned when the voice said, "Ya?" His rigid start alerted Fitzgerald who twitched with his reaction. Joseph's spine turned to frozen steel. Before him was the devil, Frederick, and Joseph knew whose horse Frederick had. *It's Brother!* Joseph's heart thumped wildly in his chest. He couldn't see the painted blanket on Brother's rump, but he didn't need to. It was Matt's horse, and Matt wasn't on him. "That secesh bastard!" he whispered to Fitzgerald, who obligingly pinned back his ears.

Joseph looked intently through the glasses toward Brother to see if Matthew's limp body had been draped over Brother's rump or saddle. Nothing! *Where is Matthew?*

Fear, grief, and rage lived within Joseph. They were daily visitors that motivated him, especially in the midst of battle. In this moment, Joseph knew where to direct all the intensity of these emotions. His focus narrowed, and his brain rushed. He lay stone still, took deep breaths, and prepared to murder Frederick.

After talking briefly, all the men reengaged in preparing the horses to move. Eventually, and to Joseph's delight, all but Frederick got on their faithful steeds and traveled directly west—toward Kansas.

Godspeed, thought Joseph cynically. *In spite of yer woes, don't turn around and come back until I'm finished with Frederick.*

The main road to Trading Post was only a few miles northwest of this spot—practically in the backyard of the post, which was not more than a handful of miles away once they got to the road. Surely there would be Union soldiers there. Joseph hoped so, but his greater hope was that they would be long gone and would not hear Joseph's potential gunshots.

Joseph also hoped he wouldn't run into any Union soldiers from Kansas. He would feel compelled to shoot them as much as he would the secesh. They couldn't stop their harassment of Missouri settlers, believing they were all enemy and using it as an excuse to rob them of everything. His scouting party had to be reminded that General Schofield had sent down a special order that the cavalry was not to shoot Kansas Army assumed to be errant. They were to be reported—not shot!

After removing bridles from Lucky and Brother, and relieving his horse of its saddle, Frederick led them out to the edge of the field and tethered them fairly close to the riverbank, directly across from Joseph. Joseph could have shot him right then and there, but they needed to talk about Matthew. Frederick had his pistol in his belt, and Joseph didn't want a gunfight with a marksman, so he allowed Frederick to move inside the cabin. He would likely rebuild the fire, eat, and nap before he moved on. Fitzgerald stood as Joseph placed him at ease by saying, "Ar a suaimhneas / At ease."

Frederick, no doubt, thought that running into the cabin was his fortune. Joseph wanted to prove it otherwise. He fastened his rifle to his shoulder strap, loaded his pistol, returned it to its holster, placed his field glasses in his haversack, stuffed two handfuls of oats into his ample pockets, and led Fitzgerald back to the tree. He looped a short rope knotted on either end around his tight line, stood on another limb of the tree next to the rope, and said, "Fan / Stay!"

Joseph pushed himself off the tree and quickly glided down the rope to the cabin side of the stream. He looped the rope section around his neck and then crept up the bank. He was only feet away from the horses. Taking out a handful of oats, he casually and quickly walked toward the two horses. He first turned Brother's rear to the cabin, faced him, and whispered, "Capall maith / Good horse."

Brother knew a little Irish, looked up, and neighed a familiar greeting. He quietly acknowledged Joseph with a nodding head, and Joseph offered him oats.

Lucky jealously stretched out his neck and reached his nose over for his share. Joseph made Lucky beg a little, but eventually Lucky was also eating out of his hand. Crouching low and watching the cabin, Joseph swiftly pulled out their tethers, wound up the leads, and led both geldings lickety-split down the bank and across the river. Up the bank the horses went, and they appeared content when reunited with Fitzgerald, who had already been directed to get up and greet his friends.

Once the two were tethered down an incline on the field side of the bank—well behind the trees and out of Frederick's sight from the cabin—Joseph moved Fitzgerald a good fifty yards upstream and tethered him by himself, "Fan / Stay," Joe ordered. Fitzgerald would not like this arrangement, but he was trained to handle inconvenience and discomfort like a soldier.

Taking his blanket, his rifle still on his shoulder and pistol under his coat, he climbed up into the large tree, using the length of rope, and relaxed against the main trunk in the crotch of a giant limb. He was now considerably higher in the tree than his line, and the great limb reached out across the river, making it unlikely anyone would think him there from the other side. *This is where raccoons spend their nights.* The leaves above and in front of him glistened and rattled in the moonlight breeze.

With the short utility rope, he untied the two knots in the ends, let out its doubled length, and tied himself in the wide crotch of the tree, legs spread out and up on the limb so as not to be visible from below. The rope would tug at him, not hang him, if he fell asleep and started slipping off the tree. He positioned the blanket around his shoulders, checked his weapons, and pulled out a cracker. Easily, he was within ten yards of his target if it ended up on the line above the river where he wanted it. He shut his eyes to the beautiful night sky and stilled his heart and breathing. He would wait for the target to show up.

Φ

As daylight was breaking, Frederick walked outside to realize that he had lost his horses. It wasn't unusual. He could shoot the whiskers off a squirrel, but he couldn't drive a stick into the ground. He whistled. Lucky answered him anxiously, tugged on his line, and looked toward Frederick, but he couldn't see Frederick and couldn't go anywhere. Frederick called and whistled again. When Lucky answered the second time, Frederick looked across through the trees. He continued to walk directly, but cautiously, toward the sound of the horses. He couldn't be sure that the horses didn't have company. The river was too deep for crossing. He then saw the rope in the tree. How convenient. From here, he could not see if the horses were tethered or who else might be on the downside of the bank below the horses.

He thought that the men from last night might have put it there for some reason—maybe to move something across the river or to cross over if they didn't want to get wet for their trip west. Maybe passing children had placed it there to jump in the river. The rope looked old and well used.

There were many large limbs up the giant tree, but there were too many leaves, and he didn't think anyone would go up there. He had heard nothing. He didn't recall any of his fellow troopers who carried enough rope for this. Certainly not Alexander or Joseph.

Frederick turned his face north, jumped up to reach the rope, and walked his legs up the trunk of the tree to wrap them around the rope. He used his legs and arms to climb horizontally, hand over hand backward, up the gentle incline of the rope. Like a child, he was enjoying the speed at which he was moving across the river.

Frederick moved a little more than halfway up the rope before he heard, "Halt! *Willkommen*, but don't move, Frederick."

Frederick stretched his head slowly back to face the barrel of Joseph's rifle pointing down at him from the large tree branch above. He could see the top half of Joseph's face above the site of his Sharps.

57

Frederick thought for a moment that he could reach up and grab the rifle, but he knew Joseph would keep the rifle slightly more than an arm's length away. If he reached, Joseph might pull the trigger. He would have to think of how to talk Joseph out of killing him.

"So, Frederick, you've come to tell me where Matthew is. Ya?"

Now shaking, Frederick answered, "Ya. Sure. Trust me. It was all an accident."

"An accident, Frederick? If ye *want* to live, there are things I need to know. When ye lie to me about accidents, it makes me want to see daylight through yer mouth or forehead. Don't talk until ye can imagine how it will be to have sunshine where yer brains used to be. We've seen men without their brains before. Use the tiny brain ye have now and think seriously. Make a good decision, Frederick, because yer floating downstream without a brain is a beautiful thought."

"Frederick, is Lucky worth ninety dollars?"

"Oh, ya, Joseph."

"Well, I don't think so, but that's what I'm going to ask for him when I take him back home to Strother. And what's the price on me head, Frederick? What am I worth?"

"What?"

Frederick was shocked to hear Joseph talk about Strother. When he rode along on one of the deliveries to Stone, he was wearing a mask.

Mocking his surprise, Joseph continued, "What is what, you ask? Do you not understand there are things I need to know? Don't try to be an actor, Frederick. This is not the time. I know who ye are. I remembered where I first heard 'ya' and saw those dull gray eyes peering out over the mask. Do ye now understand? Ye are the assassin, and I am yer target. Ya?"

"Ya, I understand."

"That is good. Let's play a guessing game. Where do ye think I first heard ye say ya?" Choose one: Westport, Harrisonville, or on the way to the farm in Strother?"

"Was Strother, I tink."

"There was a man in charge of the removal of unknown goods off me wagon, and his name is what?"

"His name is Stone. Stone Neumann."

"Yer doing well now, Frederick. Do ye still want to see the daylight with your eyes, or do you want to drift downriver in blackness to be reunited with your friends in hell?"

"I want to live, Joseph. I can help you find Matthew's body. I tell you, it was accident."

"Is that what ye want me to say to the captain when they threaten to sentence me for yer death, Frederick? 'I'm so sorry, Captain, but me trigger finger slipped as I stood in a tree after waitin' all night for Frederick to come climbing up me rope? I am so sorry I killed me assassin, Captain, but trust me, it was an accident!' How much did Stone offer ye to kill me? Was it Stone? Count to three, Freddie, and may Christ be with ye, pathetic devil!" "No, Joseph. Vait! Vait! On your head, five hundred dollars. Stone will give me five hundred dollars, but I think it vas money from Howard or the captain of David Tatum. They both wealthy, both put money in pot."

"Only five hundred dollars? Vat? Fitzpatrick is now worth more than half that, and ye know it."

Quickly Joseph slid down the tree. "Come along, fool, and find Matthew's body."

Φ

Joseph carried two weapons. One was a Colt Navy pistol that he kept secluded beneath his coat when in civilian dress. He had used his Colt to coax his beautiful new Sharps rifle from a nervous John Miller in a meeting before leaving his warehouse.

As Frederick stood on a fence rail, hands loosely tied together in front of him, Joseph coached him, with that same revolver, how to sit backward on Lucky's saddle. As Frederick had a McClelland's saddle—not a western-style saddle like Joseph's—Joseph told him it wouldn't be too bad. Joseph sat beside him on Fitzgerald, tied Frederick's hands behind his back, and fastened them on the ring at the front of the saddle. Frederick's feet didn't fit in the stirrup, but Joseph stuck them there anyway, and then he tied them together under Lucky's belly. It was a perfectly miserable position, and Frederick strained to imagine how he could survive the trip.

Joseph returned his rifle to the holster behind his right leg, and off they went, three horses and two men, one of whom was backward on his horse, strung together, to ride across the dangerous, warrior-infested prairie of western Missouri.

Frederick was so well strung up that he would not get away if he fell or jumped off the horse. He would be dragged. Frederick would be miserably uncomfortable, and Joseph was glad. Joseph didn't plan for him to get off his horse for any reason until they met up with Alexander or they found Matthew.

It was very early when they had left the cabin, and Joseph made excellent time. Unfortunately, they had a long distance to travel. Joseph straightened out the bends of the river, crossed the river in a couple of places, and got to the broad bank at the plantation around eight o'clock. As he was preparing to travel for another hour, Alexander came riding straight to the river bend in their direction. Joseph was greatly relieved to see the person he was expecting to see. It didn't always happen so smoothly.

After wading Frederick around in the cold river to clean out his pants, the two cavalrymen moved north with their wet companion into a secluded area above the river. They untied his legs and pulled the suffering Frederick out of the saddle, now sitting face forward thanks to Andrew. After building a campfire close enough to Frederick that he could dry out and putting on the coffee, they tied Frederick by the wrist to one tree and by the foot to another. Alexander and Joseph interrogated their prisoner in his exhausted state until he was nearly repentant.

Though the details of the "accident" changed more than once in Frederick's "final" accounts, it was obvious to Joseph that Frederick continued to lie. He was almost too tired to lie, but he had apparently rehearsed his lie so well that Joseph thought that Frederick might have begun to believe himself.

Joseph wondered why Frederick had made no accusations regarding Joseph's dealings with the stolen guns and the extortion with Stone Neumann and Mr. Miller. Perhaps he had been told that regardless of the outcome in his new profession of spying assassin, Neumann's name was never to surface. In the end, this was not about supposed justifications for Frederick's behavior. Murder was murder.

Joseph decided not to reveal to Alexander the origin of his acquaintance with Frederick, no matter what might come out of Frederick's mouth. He was no traitor against the Union. Nobody had told him what was in the boxes he hauled. However, he would have killed Frederick over that secret had he felt no loyalty to Matthew. Since they needed Frederick to explain Matthew's disappearance, Joseph let him live—at least until it no longer worked in Joe's favor. Then, he'd have to figure it out.

Alexander and Joseph ate dried meat dipped in hot coffee, and then they drank meat-flavored hot coffee. Joseph had been awake all night and had drunk nothing hot for two days, so his body could hardly resist sleep once he warmed up and relaxed. Frederick had stopped talking until Joe threw a blanket over him.

Frederick smirked. "Joe, what is traitor? You should tell Alexander why I ask that question, ya?"

Joseph answered, "Well, Frederick, that's your problem, ya? Yer the Confederate spy and hired assassin who has probably murdered a Union Militia soldier. Yer not even a good German. Alexander and I didn't kill Matthew. I'm a Union soldier and a good businessman, Frederick. Don't ask me to do yer thinkin'. Ye need to pray for God's forgiveness. Yer the one who will be answering to the US federal government—not I. Yer not as brilliant as the three Irish boys ye've come to murder, and Alexander and I will not listen to yer stupid lies any more than the captain will. We don't want to put ye to sleep, so be goot boy and go to sleep on yer own, ya? Maybe ye can find Matthew in the mornin'."

Φ

In the morning, Alexander again asked Frederick to come clean about Matthew.

Frederick responded, "I tell you, it was accident. When we found a good place on river, we were watering horses. Lucky in front, Brother over right side behind. Matthew, he lean over to wash face, but too close to Lucky. Lucky spooked and kicked Matthew in head." Frederick patted his right temple to show. "Maybe he kick him someplace else ... back of head? I don't know." Joe asked, "Did you see that happen? If you didn't see him kicked in the temple, why would ye suggest he was kicked in the back of the head as well?"

"I tell you, I standing in water drinking from hands cupped. I did not know until I turn Lucky around, so leading him to riverbank. Matthew just gone."

"If ye didn't see, man, how would ye know Matthew leaned over to wash his face? How would ye know he wasn't peein' in the river? Ye never mentioned that ye ever saw Matt dismount Brother."

"Ya, ya, ya, he dismount. I told you, Joe," responded Frederick, again growing agitated.

"The river is not that swift or loud," pressed Alexander. "How could he be just gone, Frederick?"

"I don't know. I think maybe secesh scout from distant campfire shoot him, and he drift downstream."

"And ye didn't hear shots? It would have been a rifle shot. Ye would have ducked, dived in the water, or crossed to the other bank to get away. If ye had thought a group of secesh were on yer side of the bank, ye would not have led Lucky and Brother toward them to go looking for Matthew! Then ye spent the night there, hopin' Matthew returns? From the dead? How dumb do ye think we are?"

There was a thirty-mile trip ahead of them before they even started a search for Matthew. Joseph dreaded it.

Φ

It was beginning to drizzle lightly in the late afternoon as the party traveled down the riverbank to the spot where the "accident" had happened. Exhausted, Frederick quickly admitted to the spot where he had last "seen" Matthew. With his hands no longer tied behind his back but his legs hobbled under Lucky, he directed Alexander, still tethered to Lucky, and Joseph to the edge of the water and pointed out where Matthew had been "bucked" into the water. Alexander reminded Frederick that it was where Matthew had been "kicked" in the head. "You said he was standing too close to the horse's hooves. Now you say he was bucked?"

Frederick said, "Ya, I remember now. He bucked off then kicked."

Joe interjected, "So Matthew made no sound as he was bucked off his horse, and he landed on his feet? What spooked Brother to buck Matthew off?"

Frederick felt a panic set in when Alexander, on his horse and closest to the log where Matthew's body drifted, glanced toward the back of the log.

Alexander said, "Of course, you didn't see any of this, so you could not have remembered it, right, Frederick? And now I see boot prints and blood?"

Frederick pushed up higher in his saddle to take a better, if not discrete look behind the log. He was so genuinely amazed and shocked to find that Matthew was not there that he audibly gasped. The water had receded, so Matt would not have been floating or covered, but should be lying on the ground there. Someone would have moved him—or he might have walked out himself had he not been dead. Frederick also saw blood and footprints in the mud and got nauseated.

Joseph saw the blood drain from Frederick's face and thought he might pass out.

With a wrenching stomach and shaking voice, Frederick looked away and quickly suggested that Matthew had probably drifted downstream.

There were at least three different sets of prints from men's footwear around the log and up the bank on the opposite shore. It was obvious that Matthew had once been behind the log, and Joseph and Alexander figured it out quickly. The prints had begun to flatten and fade from the drizzling sky, but there was no question about their existence.

Frederick sat quietly and wondered, *Did Matthew come to his senses, crawl up onto the log, and then get rescued?*

They saw drag marks in the mud next to the log and decided it was more than possible. It appeared to have been likely. Until today's heavy mist, it had not rained, and only two days of sunshine had passed.

They crossed the river to the north bank and saw more horse and boot tracks on the small outcropping at the crossing. One set of hoofprints was probably from a very large workhorse. Many men and horses had been here who hadn't just passed from one shore to the other, but they had lingered and not behaved in a usual manner. The large horse had not crossed the river to the south bank. He had walked down to the stream and then turned back up the northern bank.

If riders came upon Matthew's body that presented with no bullet hole, they might have believed he was a local man who had had an accident or died of illness. However, the circumstances indicated to Joseph and Alexander that this was likely the site of a crime.

Missouri was becoming strewn with dead bodies. Some had been rolled or dumped into mass graves after battles. Some had been returned to their families or buried by their families on the farms where they were shot. Infants and small children or grandparents who died were buried in a nice place under a suitable tree in the woods.

It made no sense that Frederick took Matthew's horse and rode away, leaving him to bleed out in the sand or die alone. In spite of the belief that men came back to get Matthew, Alexander and Joseph pointed out that the weaknesses in Frederick's contentions and numerous accounts pointed to murder or attempted murder. Knowing his goose was cooked and frantic, Frederick blurted out, "The men mit Amish hat come back and Matthew with them?

Matthew not dead! Oh mein Gott! Matthew alive!" He smiled as he said, "Wunderbar! Now you untie me. You know? Matthew alive."

Joseph turned to Frederick, slugged him to the ground, whipped out his pistol, and repeated, "Oh mein Gott, nothin'! We should kill ye right now ye secesh swine!"

Frederick completely lost control, whimpered like a pig being pulled by the tail to his slaughter, and began to thrash about on the ground like a spoiled toddler. "Please. I do not tink Matthew dead!" He got up to run, but with his hands tied behind his back and his feet hobbled, he couldn't.

Joseph grabbed Frederick by the arm and pressed his pistol against his temple.

In his corporal voice, Alexander asked Joseph, "Ye heard that he said the men had Amish hats? That large horse fits and would be easy to track, for sure, but not tonight." He pulled Joseph aside and quietly added, "Mr. Quigley, as yer corporal, I must ask you to refrain from shootin' the prisoner, even if he is deservin'. I know 'tis not frowned on when there is great risk, but he has not been properly charged with a crime nor has he had his hearin'. Ye cannot risk yer own court-martial. We will assure that he returns safely. Do ye understand, Mr. Quigley?"

Joseph replied, "Ye have me word, sir." "Thank you, Mr. Quigley."

They decided that they had a few more hours left of daylight, and they crossed to the north bank, and until they could no longer see in the dim light, they followed, westward, the footprints of the large horse.

They spent the night along the north bank of the South Grand. When they started out the next morning, along came a group of three Amish riders, one on a large horse. Matthew was not among them.

They confirmed that Matthew was not dead when they found him, but he was not in good shape. He was barely able to tell them that he had been attacked by the butt of the rifle of the man they had seen sitting on the bank—the same one now captive with Joseph and Alexander. The Amish men had all seen Frederick and were able to identify him as the attacker.

When they backtracked to help Matthew, Frederick had ridden off with Brother. They carried him on the back of the large horse to the Amish farm where they had stayed the night before. At the farm, a man and his son carted Matthew into Butler. They were aware he was from Harrisonville, but they knew there were soldiers in Butler who could help Matthew get medical help and eventually return him to Harrisonville.

Joseph and Alexander expressed their gratefulness and shook their hands. As they left, Joseph called out, "Christ be with ye."

The men tipped their hats and rode toward Kansas where they had started their journey a week before.

Frederick sat on Lucky, speechless. It seemed he felt no remorse as he expressed only about his discomfort and hunger. Once again, he stated, "It vas accident. You vait, Joseph. Your turn next."

Φ

Before beginning their fifteen-mile journey back to Harrisonville with their prisoner, Alexander asked Joseph to sit with him on a rocky spot overlooking the river. It was still morning, and Alexander and Frederick could arrive at their destination, Harrisonville, in about five hours. They would arrive in the afternoon. Before doing so, Frederick was tied securely to a tree on the bank of the river in sight—but not within hearing distance—of the two friends. Alexander and Joseph sat forty yards behind Frederick with their rifles and the horses and the rippling sounds of shallow water over a rocky riverbed.

Alexander said, "Joseph, I have decided that there are a lot of things going on between ye and Frederick that I do not understand. Ye are me friend as well as fellow soldier. I always agreed with ye that he is a spy, but it seems there is more goin' on between the two of ye? I don't want to step into a situation that makes it difficult to remain yer friend. I can't return with this man as a prisoner without hearing what yer connection is. What would the motive have been for Frederick to kill Matthew?"

Joseph answered, "Matthew may have been in the way. I can't explain what Frederick had in his head when killing Matt, but I know that he was hired to kill me."

Alexander continued, "Why would Frederick risk so much and face so much danger to chase ye down?"

Joseph answered, "He wanted five hundred dollars. A group of Cass County secesh were goin' to pay him. They thought they could use him in the future. Frederick was building a career.

"When I was a child, I ended up in Westport without me family. I worked me way up with the outfitters and became a drover. Eventually, I had me own wagon and teams I shared with a great older gentleman and eventually, two other friends me age. We did honest and good jobs for people, but I was young and taken advantage of by secesh. Without knowin' it, they put me in a bad position. I think they had me haulin' stolen goods from the Union Army, but I never asked, and they never told. I dealt with it on me own to get away. They weren't payin' me proper, so I asked for more compensation because of the danger. One of the participants in the theft bred prized horses. Ye might know him, but don't ask. You don't really need to know. It would not serve either of us.

"'Tis how I got Fitzgerald. They thought I was goin' to turn them in, so Frederick was sent after me. I can't tell ye any more than that. Ye have to believe me, Alexander, I never did anything against the Union, nor would I. Ye know that, don't ye? The secesh nearly ruined me, but I barely broke free with me life, so they came after me to get Fitzgerald back and get me out of their hair.

"Frederick has killed Matthew. He is the criminal, not I. I'm the one who brought Frederick back to face the music. Please don't implicate me in crimes I never committed. I didn't steal any goods. Frederick's gang and his family of thieves did. If they get him on that, it doesn't matter that he is an assassin out for me. They'll kill him because of Matt. Let Frederick do the explainin' about how his family committed treason. He might think it will save his neck.

"I think ye should return him to Butler. It's closer, and that's where Matthew was taken. When ye hand him off in Butler, ye whisper to him: 'Frederick, are ye goin' to tell them what ye know about a man named Stone?' Frederick will think that I told about their gang and that you know about everything and everybody. He'll lie so much they won't be able to trust him. You know he'll talk to save his own arse, and ye'll not be involved. You can drop Frederick off, grab Matthew's horse, and return to Harrisonville alone. Tell the commander that I took Fitzgerald and Lucky. Tell him Lucky was in poor health and limpin' and Fitzgerald needs a bigger shoe than they have in camp. I'll take him in to Strother to get his shoe fixed, and I'll be back to camp as soon as I'm done.

"I'm requestin' permission, sir, to go on ahead north with Lucky and Fitzgerald to get their shoes fixed. Strother is Frederick's town. If he asks, I'll tell Herman the blacksmith that I last saw Frederick in Butler, explaining things to the commanding officer of the cavalry about the man he killed."

Alexander replied, "I can do that, Joseph. I've told ye how I got to America, but can ye tell me where yer family is and how you ended up in Westport, a young boy by yerself? You seem to be very hurt by the loss of yer mother? Did she die in Ireland or here?"

CHAPTER 6

STATEN ISLAND, NEW YORK, MAY 1849

As the ship roiled and creaked its way to America, the open door to the steerage deck allowed a shaft of light to filter down from mid-morning to midafternoon. Two ventilation shafts from the top deck leading into other partially separated steerage compartments, one for single men, another for single women, barely fed enough air to maintain life in the darkness below. Several false walls roughly formed rooms that separated eighteen families with infants from single travelers. On an abysmal day in March, the Quigley family had stepped aboard fueled only by determination; their energy ignited by adrenaline. They loved God. Their da told them that God would see them through.

The sickly father, James Quigley, his fully pregnant wife Margaret, and their seven hungry children had been living directly behind the shaft of light. Only through luck, they had been given the breezy compartment at the bottom of the steps leading to the main deck of a three-mastered barque called the *Wave*.

With the other passengers aboard, the Quigley family of nine was quartered on three six-feet-by-eighteen-inch bunks made of slats. Situated at the foot of the main stairs leading to the deck, there was little privacy. People loitered in the Quigley space during storms that prevented them from sitting on the open deck above. Often, they came to breathe the fresh ocean breezes that wafted down, lifted their spirits, and helped relieve them from the fetid air of human waste. They also retched in the Quigley space as the waves tossed up any fluids left in their stomachs.

The *Wave* was built to accommodate a small crew, to sail well into the headwinds, and haul commerce. It normally carried staples—oil, bone, grain, and wool—between the UK and Australia. It conveyed less than ten passengers when engaged in commerce. On this journey, it carried 212 passengers more than the usual ten, including Margaret's infant daughter born several days before reaching Staten Island. The *Wave* had been "customized" to carry the potato famine diaspora to their destinations.

There was limited water—only cold saltwater for washing— and sometimes no food other than what either the starving people had brought themselves for the month or that provided by benevolent landlords. There were no bathroom or other hygiene facilities available on a commercial ship for more than the crew. People excreted in buckets, over the edge of the ship, or if they were too weak to rise from bed, their body fluids dripped through slats down onto the person lying below or simply to the floor. Unlike some famine ships, the Wave had no disciplined regimen for emptying waste buckets or cleaning the wooden surfaces.

For the Quigley family, there were three ship-provided mattresses of white canvas stuffed with seaweed. There were three pillows of the same material. The family took turns using their pillows, and they all had light blankets that were passed out to all passengers. People were usually so cold, however, that they slept in multiple layers of their heaviest clothing. By the time Margaret was no longer able to walk and she had bled, vomited, and given birth on her mattress, it was almost not usable. The family folded it over, and the male members of the family used the "cleanest" section to sit on for sleeping the last few days. James gave his wife, Margaret, his blanket and his beautifully tailored and clean Sunday jacket to lie on.

Some families paid their last farthing for these accommodations. Landlords, especially the absentee landlords living in countries other than Ireland, who had paid for the ship and food for their renters, often did so because it was cheaper than keeping them alive in Ireland or paying taxes on nonproducing land. Paying for tenant emigration was in regard to their own dwindling finances.

Michael, the nineteen-year-old son of James and his deceased wife, had been a blessing to his dying parents. Once they arrived at Staten Island, his herculean job was to focus on keeping Joseph out of trouble and otherwise fit into his parents' shoes as head of family in their new country.

After painting a picture of the reality of his circumstances on the ship, Joseph told Alexander about his arrival. "After half a dozen weeks on the Wave, on the forenoon of Thursday, May 3, 1849, Michael, who had gone topside to empty our family pot, noticed the fog had just lifted, and he saw land. He called excitedly through the door to me. I was standin' over Ma, 'Joseph, come, come!' I stuck me head out the door and out across the railing. I saw the shoreline in the distance. Then I realized that this would be where I parted with me ma and probably me da forever, so I turned and looked straight up through the sails to the blue sky of America.

"The riggin' had fascinated me from the first day, and I wanted to be sure it was memorized for life. That way, I would be leavin' the ship, but I would never forget how to tie the knots the captain had shown me as I wandered about where I didn't belong. I hated all the sufferin' and misery, but I loved the ship. I knew that, in his heart, Captain Lockhart would be glad to see me go because I'd sneak in and drink with the single men. To punish me, he taught me everythin' about the riggin' and the knots we had not used on the farm. The crew would come along and name a knot—and have me do it ten times until I did it as fast as I could. I still will never forget me first square knot! Captain would sit me down and have me tying until I got sober enough to go back down to me family. I don't know why he did that for me. He was very smart, that one.

"On the deck, the day we arrived, Michael saw how I was lookin' in the wrong direction. I was supposed to be lookin' at America, but before she died, Ma had explained to him that misbehavin', drinkin', or not focusin' where I was supposed to was how I acted when I was afraid, angry, or heartbroken. She told Michael I only seemed like a bad boy. She said that down inside I was a 'tender' boy. I was so embarrassed at the time, but I believed then that me ma was the only person who understood me. Now I know she was wrong. I was just different. Even when I was eleven years old, I always found somethin' to drink when I felt like it. Do ye know what I mean, Alexander? Once Ma said that about me to Michael, he started lookin' for signs. I guess, lookin' at and talkin' about the riggin' instead of thinkin' about leavin' the boat without me ma was what Michael was seein' in me. I remember bein' so angry and hurt about our situation I could barely stand it. Just like you and Matthew, there was nothin' any of us could do about any of it. Sometimes I think that's why so many Irishmen took to drinkin'. They couldn't get away from the English cruelty, famines, or not going to their own church. Nothin' was fair. Then we came to America, and so many of our parents and siblings died. Now we're fightin' a war."

Up on the deck, the passengers were allowed to flow freely for the arrival, even to the bow, where Joseph had been alone with the captain, tying knots. America's promising spring sunlight greeted them and their exuberance, and the sense of hope even crept into the frightened corners of Michael's heart. He later told Joseph tha-the was tellin' himself that Christ stood beside him, and he would be fine alone with all those children. At the time, he thought that maybe every sibling but Doroty would be with him.

Joseph recalled that, until the third of May, the last time they had been allowed on deck was to stand out in the rain in a harsh storm to wash excrement and vomit off their bodies. After cleanin' up, they had been sent back out in the darkness of night to collect drinking water in all the containers possible. On their arrival day, on deck, people around him were seeing their first sight of America. They believed it would provide them exceptional opportunity. Joseph and Michael could hear them celebrate that belief, in spite of their feeble condition. They said that God had finally answered their prayers. They had arrived! Joseph didn't feel that way. He wanted to lie down and die. God had not answered his prayers. He wanted to go with his ma, but he knew he was going with poor Michael and a handful of frightened orphaned half siblings, ages thirteen to three.

Joseph called down to his brothers and sisters to come up to the deck. As they came up, the light was so stunning to their eyes that they could hardly open them to see the green on the hillsides, the large mouth of an estuary, the dunes and wispy grasses along the sandy shores, and the white sails on the boats coming and going from the vast harbor.

After they went up, Joseph went down to see if Ma had woken up. He imagined that maybe, in all the excitement, she would. Getting to New York was her dream. However, still lying prone, Margaret Quigley, arms positioned around their deceased infant sister, Doroty, could not rise to join him. Joseph saw that her motionless and expressionless face did not appear to be faintly aware of the circumstances. It had not changed since Doroty's death. Ma really had grown tearless and lay perfectly still in a body that could resist no more insults and no longer moved with breathing. Her death was sinking into him.

Joseph recounted how he turned to his da who crawled up a few steps on hands and knees with Joseph's encouragement. He told Joseph that his heart was beating so erratically and his weakness was so profound that he could not go up on deck with him. Da was unable to stand up or look out beyond the ship's railing. Joseph tried, but he could not lift his da. Michael had told Joseph earlier that Da was riddled through with the fever and could not survive, so he needed to not push him to do things he could not do. It hadn't registered in Joseph's mind that he was losing both his parents at this moment in his life. Da's clothing was soaked in feces from his diarrhea, and his heart was giving out, but he slid down on his seat to the bottom step, held tight to the newel post, and asked Joseph to quickly get Michael. People rushed past or over him in their excitement, so Michael made a place for him to stagger over, next to Margaret and Doroty near the foot of the short bed.

Many years later, on their journey down the Ohio River, Michael had told Joseph that above deck, he had looked around at his fellow travelers in daylight and thought, *What a sight. So many malnourished bodies, sticks standing, children barefoot and in rags!* In various stages of typhus, dysentery, yellow fever, relapsing fever, and dehydration, there was no end to the list of ailments present. As a child who had lived through more than one period of hunger and disease, Michael had fallen victim to relapsing fever so many times that he had apparently grown immune. He was not infirm a day on the *Wave*. Joseph, too, had had his share of fevers and hunger, but his stomach had bothered him only when he ate certain things on his trip to New York. It was the hard oats, the stale white bread, and his occasional drinking early on, but not a contagion that got to him.

Staying below, Michael noticed that the littlest Quigley children, Mary and James, had more serious rashes on their torsos, and Mary's throat was nearly swollen shut with diseased tonsils. They had worsened. Both little children had every sign that was not good. James had started out premature and malnourished as an infant, and he had never quite caught up before this assault on his fragile three-year-old body. Michael knew James and Mary were soon to die. They were lying, dressed up like dolls by Margaret and Ellen, on their soiled blankets with their eyes closed. Tiny Mary even had on her Sunday bonnet, planned for her arrival by her sisters.

On Tuesday evening, while they were still able to do so, Da, Mary, and Ellen had set Doroty in Charley's arms and dressed Ma in her blue silk wedding dress, a surprise gift Da had made more than a decade earlier. It complemented her blue eyes, and she wanted to wear it to leave the ship.

As Michael lovingly tended to his little half siblings, Da tearfully told his son Michael that he had regretted coming to America. Forgetting his own misery, James grieved that this beautiful mother of their children would not be stepping out on fine, clean grass in the bright fresh air. Da cried as he said how beautiful Ma would have appeared, wearing her blue silk dress while "herding" her precocious darlings to greatness. His first thought upon their arrival was something that had struck him more than a week ago: that he should have stayed home with his family and met death there. They could have all lain down in the spring grass with their neighbors and died among the dear spring lambs—a pastoral image that gave him sweet comfort.

Joseph had overhead his grieving da say that, and he imagined himself dying in the grass while April lambs frisked about. It was very full of sadness. It gave him no comfort.

Michael later recalled with Joseph, going down the Ohio, how he thought through Ma's progression to death while the celebration went on above. By Tuesday, Ma's fever was long gone. On Tuesday morning, Margaret had stopped drinking. She had stopped vomiting and defecating by Tuesday evening. On Tuesday evening, they put the blue dress over her greatly diminished body. On Wednesday evening, she had turned an even whiter color, and by morning she was comatose. She was deceased by the time they arrived in New York Harbor.

Before their arrival, Joseph had been standing over her, crying, because she had not said goodbye or told him that she loved him. Doroty died only hours before that, but it had been met with no response by Ma. Ma had no tears to drop for her dead or living children. She may have known that she was taking Doroty with her and thought the rest would soon follow. When her Doroty died, she had already passed into her completely oblivious state. Joseph recalled how Margaret and Ellen, especially, fretted over Ma's need for water and her inability to drink it. They were inventing ways to get water down as they had not completely accepted or understood her resignation to death. They still hoped and expressed anger and frustration that she had "given up" too soon.

Putting such thoughts and reflections behind him, Michael, in the interest of knowing what should be done next, returned to the deck. He joined Ellen and Charley, but Margaret returned to be with Da and check on her little sister and brother. She wanted to hold them so they wouldn't be afraid to die. Joseph moved to be beside the little ones and got angrier about how unfair it all was.

Michael learned that Captain Lockhart dropped anchor off Staten Island to "organize" for disembarking. He needed to make a "final assessment" of his passengers and sort out the luggage. Michael also heard him say that the dead and those in their last throes would be lifted off first, but for the docking, all the passengers needed to be sent back down to wait for their inspection by a doctor and to be kept from the small mob of reporters and locals about the dock. A team of men, including a tall doctor and two marine-dressed employees had already arrived on the Wave by boat.

Once the Quigley family gathered, they stood beside Ma and Doroty and Da, who was still seated on the bed. Da asked his family to pray an Act of Contrition and the Lorica in Irish. They blessed themselves, and as they began praying, other families quietly joined in while the captain, doctor, and crewmen attended to the family next to them.

Michael, holding the limp and dying James's head on his shoulder, stood with tears in his eyes as his da said, "I'm sorry, Michael, that I have brought ye, such a wonderful son, into a world where ye have lost two loving mothers and many siblings. Stay good and faithful—and take Joseph to work with ye—he needs to be watched carefully. Take the children to Mass every Sunday. Ask cousin Margaret to help ye resettle the little ones, maybe in Pennsylvania, then quickly find a wife to help ye bring the family back together. The family needs to stay together. Pray for Doroty's soul to go quickly to heaven. She was not baptized, so she may be in limbo."

As the children all stood together in a tight little brood like chicks to hear the exchange, Michael promised, "I'll do me best, Da! We could not have had a better da! We'll all make ye proud, and ye'll surely see us all in heaven. I'll look for me full sister, Margaret, in Missouri when I get there."

Φ

As Joseph and Alexander sat by the river, Joseph said, "I was only eleven, so I didn't know what to think about going to work with Michael. I also remember thinkin' I might not go to heaven with Michael to see Da, and thinkin' how disappointed Ma would be if everyone but me showed up there. Da would not have been that surprised, I guess!

"Me da breathlessly rehearsed one more time where we were going on Mott Street in New York City. He handed Michael papers with cousin Margaret's address, and the names and addresses of cousins in Pennsylvania. Then he handed over his small linen pouch holding the last of his money. I didn't know at the time that we had any."

Joseph continued to describe how the captain, doctor, and the other men stepped next to the Quigley family of ten bodies at the bottom of the stairs. An assistant said, "Quigley, ten persons." Then the doctor examined each person beginning with Da. With the end of each person's notation, the doctor quietly called out "D," "T," "S," or "H" as the assistant repeated the designation and charted it.

When done, the captain called out, "Total please," and the assistant called out, "Deceased two, terminal three, sick zero, and healthy five." The captain said, "Total of ten, correct; thank you, sir," and they moved to the next family.

"In all, it didn't take more than a few minutes, and those men decided how half our family would disappear. I was so angry and hurt—I would have shot them if I'd had a gun."

Joseph continued to describe how Ellen took James from Michael's arms as a tarp was handed down the stairs by a crewman. Both Doroty and Ma, still holding her, were lifted by Michael and two other men up through the door and up to the deck where they disappeared from the family's sight. The children started to follow, but the family was ordered to stay below until all families were "sorted out."

People and activities were swirling all around them, but they were so absorbed in their own grief, shock, and loss that they didn't observe how the other families were being torn apart in the same manner as was their own.

Without further ceremony, the men carried Da off and scooped the two limp children—Mary, who was five, and James, only three—out of Ellen and Margaret's arms. When James was handed over, Ellen reached over and kissed Mary's little bare toes. Mary's eyes briefly opened, and Michael saw her smile at Ellen and then go limp again. All but Michael hadn't considered that the littlest two would be taken with their da, who could not care for them. Joseph, Margaret, Ellen, and Charley were absolutely shocked by the abruptness of losing their family, and they began to sob uncontrollably. They looked to Michael who reached out to embrace them all.

The families who had lost their deceased, terminal, and sick members to burial and quarantine were herded onto the deck first.

On the deck, the five Quigley children stood silent as half their family disintegrated. Margaret, who had been holding James or Mary for a month, threw her arms around Michael's waist and cried, "Michael, help me. The little ones are me angels. How can I live without me precious lambs? James's little hand on me arm and me lookin' down on his sweet face? For all his years, he could look to me. Can I not go with him? Please, Michael. I can help Mary and Da too. Let me go with them."

Michael answered, "We can only pray, Margaret. God and the angels will take care of their pure souls. Ye will be with them all again, in heaven. We'll be good, and we can be with them again. We must keep our faith, Margaret."

Margaret held Michael and said, "Please stay with me, Michael. I don't want to be 'settled' with aunts or cousins."

Above deck, Michael and his siblings were astounded by the sight of the Staten Island people who greeted the immigrants at the dock. Journalists, handkerchiefs pressed to their mouths, ferried over the five miles from Manhattan to meet immigrant ships that first stopped for their quarantine on the island. Reporters were recording their outrage at the numbers and deplorable conditions. "When will something be done," they said, "to protect the people of these beautiful and prosperous New York islands from the human refuse of Ireland?"

Some local people yelled out, "You're like the rotten potatoes in your baskets back home. You need to be inspected and 'tossed' somewhere else so as not to contaminate our island."

"Go home, papist Celtic heathens! This is not a dumping ground! Bury your rotten bodies somewhere else."

As the deceased and dying members of the Quigley family were being carted away, Michael, Margaret, Ellen, and Joseph were especially horrified.

Joseph yelled, "Shut it!"

Brazen little Ellen followed immediately with, "Ye eejit!"

Then they were distracted by a crowd of men along a roped-off section of dock, calling for the captain to let them aboard to help ferry passengers to their destinations. The crowd was moved back by dock employees who shouted, "Stay back! These people are contagious. Stay back! They're going into quarantine!" Water that was meant for the thirsty passengers was dumped on the curious who had ferried over to exploit the people who had nothing left to give. A young Protestant minister who wanted to "proselytize and save the souls of the papists" was abruptly turned away.

It was then that Joseph spotted Da with both the little ones in his lap, propped up in a very large wagon with many other "T" persons. The wagon was drawn by a team, Joseph noted, of very different and mismatched horses. He looked at their harnesses and straps, hanging this way and that. As the others watched Da head down the road and up a long hill, Joseph commented, again, on the mismatched horses. Behind his useless words, he hurt so profoundly that he couldn't look at the people riding in the wagon.

He couldn't acknowledge the reality. Joseph watched the horses so he would not die of sadness.

The horses were large, small, light, and dark, and he asked if anyone had noticed the two smaller horses with the painted rumps. A man on the dock told him they might be the "painted" ponies that came from the Indians. His siblings weren't listening to Joseph or the man, and they didn't respond, except for Margaret, who swiftly kicked him in the shins and told him to "Shut it, Joseph!"

Joseph commented, "Me sisters Margaret and Ellen didn't seem to crumble under their grief. They just yelled at me or hit me and carried on with their lives. Inside, I always wanted to die or me stomach would start hurtin' or me heart would be thumpin' till I had enough to drink and passed out. It's like some boys I know in the cavalry. Ye know what I mean, Alexander?"

Eventually, more wagons would arrive to get the rest of those bound for New York. Standing at the head of the passengers, the captain told them that after the ship was tended to with supplies, those left behind on the ship would be traveling the next morning on to Canada for an inspection and quarantine of their own. The *Wave* would not be sailing on to Manhattan with the healthy passengers. They would probably be taken to the quarantine processing center for baths, a meal, and maybe clean clothing, and then they would be released to find accommodations in the town of Saint George.

Michael was confused about how he would get to New York or pay money for "accommodations." He decided to stay calm, reassure the children, protect them, and wait. He asked his little family to wipe away their tears and show grace and courage during their processing. Joseph said, "We will show them what a strong and intelligent people we are."

Φ

The children were able to ride together in one wagon, barely hanging on to their bench fastened to one side, their luggage in the large box behind them. After clearing the flat streets of Saint George, up a steep hill, they quietly bumped along until they arrived at a long and tall wooden building. Michael, Joseph, and Charley were sent in one direction, and Margaret and Ellen were directed to go with the other females in another. As the families were again separated, Charley looked toward Ellen and bawled, "Ellen, don't leave me!"

She called across cheerfully to him, "Don't worry, Charley. I'll get ye on the other side, darlin'. Ye are me precious bu'ercup, and I would never leave ye!" Then she added with a wink and sarcastic smile, "Take care of Joseph for me, Charley. He'll require a lot of yer attention. Kickin' and pinchin' or name-callin' work on him good, darlin' boy."

Joseph said, "I turned around and yelled, loud enough for all to hear, 'Shut it, Ellen, ye leprechaun child of the devil!' It got me a few laughs from both lines.

"Infuriated and completely exhausted, Michael grabbed me by the ear, pulled me back into line and whispered, 'Of all the times to dishonor yer faithfully departed parents, 'tis not now, Joseph. You must grow up now and be good for yer family. Do not speak until you are told, and do not make eejits of the Quigley family! We are an aristocratic, faithful, and comely family and don't ye forget it!' "Without anyone but me noticing, Ellen hid her face beneath the collar of her coat, looked around it at me, stuck out her tongue, and mouthed, "Gobshite!"

Margaret explained to the boys what happened to the girls that had caused a ruckus. When she realized what was happening at the showers, she began to shake with fear. She had hardly been naked in front of even her mother at the age of thirteen, so she was shocked and felt threatened. Suddenly she was struck by the thought that these were Protestants preparing to kill her— and maybe eat her.

She hated them, and she feared them. She whispered, "Ellen, I think these are Protestants, not Catholics. Maybe they are going to kill us."

As the women attempted to take the girls' clothing, Margaret yelled, "Do not touch me or me sister! Back off now, Protestant!" They screamed, kicked, bit, cried, and held onto their clothing for their lives.

Margaret couldn't feel enough gratitude for two younger women and a mother who overheard what the girls had said and stepped in to shelter and reassure Margaret and Ellen so that they would not be hurt. They stepped around the modesty wall that led to the shelter and compelled the head matron to let go of the Quigley girls' clothing. They then used the clothing, instead, to hide their bodies from the Protestant women.

Being outnumbered, the nurses from the hospital typically backed off and saw no harm. The Irish women were polite, explained that Irish females did not, at any age, disrobe in front of others. They were helpful, and full of darlin', angel, and sweet thing. With that, they were getting the job done for the nurses, so they all got through the experience in relative peace.

The girls surrendered their dirty clothing in exchange for ill-fitting, but clean clothes of strangers. They had no idea where their clothes were headed, but a lady pinned a little paper on which she had written: "Quigley, May 3, 1849."

"On the men's side, Michael, Charley, and I were able to go through the showers together. Charley began to cry when he heard Margaret and Ellen, but I was well satisfied that the girls were gettin' what they probably deserved. If they'd been nicer to me, it never would have happened—whatever it was because I didn't know at the time. After their bathing ordeal, outside the building, Margaret ran to Michael. One of the young women who had helped and was traveling alone, explained to Michael what had happened to Margaret and Ellen and assured him that they would be fine. She also assured him that when they got separated downtown later, she would try to look out for them, but she'd been told there were a lot of abandoned and lost immigrants in the streets."

Soon, along came wagons that hauled the people back into the town. At the police station, everyone lined up and was fed a small bowl of salty, thick chicken soup. They learned that this was not usual, but occasionally someone came from Manhattan to help feed the latest boat of immigrants. Before they could eat, a lady from a church announced who had provided the soup, and everyone clapped. Best of all, the soup was hot, and they were cold. They had been scared and in shock throughout the day, and the evening was coming quickly. The hot soup tasted good and calmed their shivers, but after eating, they huddled together like lost lambs under scratchy but warm blankets that each received after their meal.

On the boat, the children had been eating nearly raw oats the family had taken onboard. After more than a month of a terrible, rough diet, food was hard to digest. From the hot, salty soup, they savored the delicious chunks of potato, cabbage, and turnips and sipped the broth with little bits of shredded chicken. They had also been given tea and milk. The tea was especially helpful for their writhing stomachs, and it made them relax enough to be able to sleep.

People were finding different places to sleep in a small group of buildings—one was a jail where the men ended up. The Quigley girls slept the first night on the cold floor of a school. They held onto one another as though they thought they would be snatched in the night. Margaret whispered in Ellen's ear, "Do na' worry, sister. I have ye safe," and they both began to cry from extreme exhaustion and sadness. They cried themselves to sleep in each other's arms and could hardly wake up in the morning.

For several days, they were pushed aside, directed, corrected, and advised. Also, they cried for their ma, their da, their deceased siblings, and each other. They whispered to each other, wondering what Doroty would have been like as a sister, and they sat on the cold, sometimes wet street and dreamed of their austere little cottage in beautiful Ireland where they had been hungry, but all had been alone together before a toasty fire.

In the darkness of the next evening, sleeping in a cold basement, Margaret asked Ellen, "Do ye remember when Ma cooked biscuits in the morning in her little pan? Do you miss the babies as much as I do?"

Ellen's tears gave the answer. They missed caring for their sickly little brother and sister, and they mourned their loss.

Margaret missed the creaking ship rolling endlessly and rocking her to sleep. She said, "Ellen, pretend that Mary is an angel, and she's lyin' here between us with her tiny wings curled up. Ma is lyin' behind us with her angel wings spread over us all. 'Tis a most lovely feelin', am I correct in thinkin'?"

"And Doroty?" questioned Ellen. They had not played with, cuddled with, or dressed Doroty. Doroty had never seen her siblings or smiled at them. For a moment, Margaret realized that in just a few days, Doroty was not as much on her mind, and she was like a stranger they didn't get to know.

"And Doroty's lying in Mary's wings, the tiniest angel of all. James and Da are with the boys right now. They're all watching over us, darlin', so no harm will come."

With that sad, sweet thought, the sisters could sleep.

CHAPTER 7

STREETS OF SAINT GEORGE

In the early morning hours of May 5, Michael hurried to the police station with Charley in tow. He, Joseph, and Charley had taken to sleeping on the damp ground of the city park as an alternative to the jail. When Michael woke up, Joseph was gone. After searching and calling, they found him nowhere in the streets. Charley had been sworn to secrecy, but after the police said they would do what they could, but did nothing, Charley finally could no longer hold his secret. Michael and the girls were too worried, and it wasn't fair.

The night before, while Michael was talking with another man who had also left the police station for the park, Joseph told Charley that he needed to find where their Ma and Doroty had gone. He told Charley not to worry and not to come looking for him if he was gone the next day, but he had to find where Ma was. Also, he wanted to find Ma's blue silk dress. He promised Charley he'd be back, but he was not to tell Michael anything other than not to worry.

Charley told Michael that he thought Joseph had gone up to the women's immigrant hospital to find out where Ma and Da had finally gone. Charley told Michael that Joseph would be back and not to worry, but Michael didn't wait.

Everyone in town could see where the hospitals were, so Joseph would be relatively easy to find. According to Charley, Joseph was going to find Ma first. He wanted to get up high enough to see out, to know where the dead women and their children went when they were taken from the hospital.

When Charley said Joseph wanted to get up high, Michael thought of the tall building where they had taken their showers. Michael also recalled the interest Joseph showed in the workman who came out of the closet by the chimney. They were walking out of the building at about the same time as he. The man took a drink then lifted the heavy handles of the handcart to move the dirty clothes to the little building behind the shrubs. Joseph frequently commented on what others thought were insignificant details.

Charley told Michael that they didn't leave dead people in the hospital. Joseph had told him that dead people had to be taken away and buried somewhere, and Joseph wanted to know where his ma and Doroty had been taken.

In Ireland, Joseph had seen families carrying carts stacked with stiff family members and neighbors who had died in the night. There wasn't enough material left in Ireland to cover the dead, so they were stripped before they were dumped in their graves, and the clothing was reused. Joseph couldn't stand the sight of it.

He knew that his "healthy" family's clothing had been removed to be washed, and he wondered if the replacements they were wearing had been taken from the dead. Would they have taken Ma's blue dress as well? He had looked in the streets of Saint George for Ma's dress being worn by an immigrant woman. The day before, Joseph had suggested that Margaret and Ellen should look for the dress among the women. Joseph had told Charley that if they found her, they would get it back from her—even if they had to tear it from her.

Joseph walked up the long hill to the place where Ma and Da had been taken and back to where he and his family had taken their showers.

The women's immigrant hospital was just up the hill in the distance from the bathhouse. From the bathhouse roof, he believed he would be able to see diagonally across to the back side of the women's hospital.

He had seen the workman exit a closet behind the chimney with a little flask to cart away the pile of clothes from the bathhouse. He stumbled down a trail shrouded with landscaping to what appeared to be the washhouse. He nearly dumped his load. There was smoke coming from the chimney, and hot, gray water was pouring into an outside drain and into a ditch than ran under a little bridge and then down the hill. The man had the classic red nose and rosy cheeks of a man who appeared to drink often. He would be a good one for Joseph to ask for help.

Joseph had learned how to intimidate others in order to get a drink or get favors for himself. He knew exactly the person to wait for when he arrived at the washhouse, hiding behind buildings and ducking behind shrubs. It was always a working formula for Joseph: "I won't tell on you if you will do this for me. If you don't, you might live to regret your decision."

So it was that Joseph was finally found drinking from a little jar the man had given him. Joseph had been looking over the treetops and searching for any sign of Ma. What he saw here was what he saw in Ireland. People had moved away to America to get away from death, but he saw that it followed them wherever they went.

He saw dead women and their children carried out of the hospital early in the morning and laid or tossed onto a cart. He saw no blue dress. Unclothed people were piled high. Then a horse came and hauled the cart out of sight down the side of the hill. One cart was hauled up the hill and out of sight. As he drank the man's poteen, he was able to watch and cry through his anger.

He felt the pain of a child whose parents had brought him to hell and then abandoned him to all these strangers he didn't love. His ma had told him she loved him best, but she hadn't needed to tell him in Ireland. He knew it the day his beautiful self was born. Yet, how had she let this happen to them here? She didn't tell him she loved him before she died.

Even worse, with her illness and the birth of Doroty, she had stopped talking privately with Joseph. As she lay sleeping, her arm fixed around Doroty, gray with death, he had lain his cheek down on Ma's face, and she said nothin' to him. There was no loving smile. She just kept sleeping. Maybe she didn't acknowledge Joseph because Doroty was here. She hadn't done this to him when the other children were born, but he was getting older. Maybe he was too much for her. He should have been a good boy more often. He should have been like Michael or Charley, but he wasn't.

A sudden thought occurred to him: In all those days she was sick on the boat, he never told Ma not to die, that he still needed her to stay alive. He had himself to blame for that, and it lay heavy in his heart as he sat there and hoped to die himself: a cold, drunken child, dulling his senses and clinging to a chimney on a roof, with no ability to reason.

Michael had talked the worker into finding someone to help bring Joseph down off the roof. Michael climbed up the ladder behind him because he did not want Joseph to get hurt. He assumed Joseph would fight him, but not a stranger. When Joseph was dragged down the tight closet ladder from the roof, he bit the man whose arm was around his neck. The man who had given him the poteen paid Joseph back with a hard knuckle rap on his head. Now, he was acting shocked that a boy like Joseph would be drinking, and where would he get poteen so early in the morning?

The sizable knot made his head as tender as Joseph's soul and was administered as a not-so-subtle reminder for Joseph to keep his mouth shut that he had discovered the man drinking on the job. Joseph could not be more miserable with his feelings of abandonment and a throbbing head.

Before he took his rooftop nap, he hoped they would find him dead and lay him down in the ground with his ma and da—if they were together. He hoped that all six of them would lie on the hill of Staten Island together.

Joseph told his family that he had also looked for Da in the men's house up the hill. What he saw instead were workers and a cart that carried dead bodies. They covered them with a sheet and sent them out into a field where gravediggers were working nonstop.

He told Michael that what they had seen in Ireland was happening here on Staten Island. Michael, Joseph, and Charley were taken off the hill and sent back to town in a wagon that was headed to the dock to pick up more quarantined passengers from Ireland.

Φ

On Tuesday, May 8—as Michael, Margaret, Joseph, Ellen, and Charley were free of lice and growing accustomed to not vomiting up occasional soup—someone decided the Quigley children should vacate the island before somebody died. The normal quarantine was for thirty days, but so many patients died after a week in quarantine that it was now the practice that the immigrants with no signs of impending death should leave before they caught a new disease and succumbed.

Notices were posted to go to the police station after seven days had passed to request any luggage that had been sent to the immigrant center. If they had a place to go and had obtained their property, they could get off the island. The streets of Saint George were bulging with frustrated and disgruntled immigrants, and more were arriving daily. Upon his arrival at the station, the director suggested to Michael that the Quigley children were too tough, smart, or mean to die—so "waiting for their deaths" was no longer required.

Upon hearing the news, Michael immediately turned to Joseph and thanked him for their early departure.

Their departure via ferry to Manhattan Island had been arranged by persons unknown. Nobody asked them for money, but they managed to reacquire their good clothing—except for Ma's blue dress. They reacquired Da's precious trunk, which contained Michael's masonry tools, put on their own clean clothes, and stepped aboard a little steamboat ferry.

Most passengers were looking over the bow of the boat toward Manhattan, but Michael's brood stood somberly under the trailing wood smoke, along the simple fenced barrier on the passenger deck, looking out over the stern. Michael watched as the boat gradually separated them only five miles away in distance but forever in time from Da, Ma, Doroty, Mary, and James. Michael saw the grief that was reflected in the faces of his half siblings. He could not believe what had taken place in six days. It was more like a dream than a reality. He wondered how the other children felt. He felt as though he had been cut adrift in a sea.

Joseph suddenly cut the silence and said, "I wonder if they could put paddles on horses' feet like a duck or seal? They could suspend them in canvas jackets and slip their legs through holes in the bottom of a boat. Do ye suppose it would work, Michael?" He added, "I hate me shoes, Michael. They're too small now. Can I take them off?"

Michael, arm around a whimpering Charley who said he missed his parents, looked down at Joseph, and he didn't appreciate his brilliant imaginings. He chose to ignore Joseph.

Joseph continued, "When ye get to land, the boat could have wheels, and the team could just keep walkin' straight away and out of the water, Michael."

Michael calmly answered, "Joseph, take off those shoes, and I'll tie a rope around yer neck. We'll just throw ye in, and we'll see if ye can paddle us to Manhattan Island! All that swimmin' in the freezin' water should quiet ye down some!"

Margaret and Ellen giggled through their tears at Michael's suggestion. Then they turned and gave Joseph contemptuous looks.

Michael said, "The word we use in America is no, Joseph. Everything from here on is no, so don't ask. And don't talk to yer brother and sisters now. We have things other than horses on our minds. We're worried about gettin' to Margaret's, so please shut it." Still irritated with Joseph, Margaret, sable hair shiny in the sun, new freckles splashed generously across her broad face from the sunny days on Staten Island, held tight to Ellen's hand. With malice in her heart, her green eyes turned to intense slits across her face, she turned toward Joseph and barely resisted the urge to kick him into the paddle wheel, the ocean, or back to Staten Island. Instead, she silently stuck out her tongue, kicked his bottom, turned around, and walked to the other end of the ferry to face Manhattan, tears washing over her beautiful rosy cheeks. As Ellen passed, she also gave a swift boot to poor Joseph's bum.

Margaret had decided that Joseph was what people called a "pain in the arse." Nobody but Ma and Michael recognized Joseph's inability to handle his emotions. Margaret and Ellen expected Joseph to take their somewhat tempered abuse in stride. Today, however, Margaret thought she saw tears in Joseph's eyes before he started his horse talk, and she thought there might be hope. She thought he just didn't care enough to remember to cry.

Joseph knew that he cared so much that he couldn't stand it. Margaret kicked him anyway. He was accustomed to it, and she thought it let him know what others were thinking. However, in that hour of leaving Staten Island, Joseph was thinking how he wanted to drink whiskey and fall asleep instead of riding the ferry to another unknown. He wanted everything to go away, but it wouldn't.

His other choice was to turn on his charm. To Joseph, it meant talking. It was something Ma told him would work because his face was so beautiful. She told him charm would win the war against anger or heartache. He would listen to Ma who told him that's what she did. She was pretty, so she talked to everyone and hid behind her smile. She would say, "Smile at yer enemy, Joseph. It keeps 'em guessin'."

It was nearly time to dock when the boys walked up and joined the girls who had found two empty seats on a bench where people waited to egress. Joseph helped Michael by taking Charley's hand when they jumped onto the landing dock.

Michael learned that the English minister Joseph called a murderer had arranged with their cousin Margaret Quigley for the family to be picked up at the docks in a wagon. There was an assistant who yelled out the name "Quigley" and directed them to their wagon. He had a cup for donations, but Michael had his hands full and was advised not to give any money that was not owed. Saint Patrick's Church, where cousin Margaret Quigley regularly attended Mass, would help out their parishioners who were expecting impoverished family immigrants. Having lost both parents, the Quigley children were especially vulnerable to the thieves who hung out at the ferry dock on the southern tip of Manhattan. Margaret knew that being picked up right away helped avoid theft.

The wagon sent to carry them to Margaret's apartment building was unique. It had outward slanting sides and two attached, parallel benches that were lids to bins underneath. A square iron frame was attached to four corner posts. Over the top, an oiled canvas draped itself over three bent hickory spines. There was a fancy, red fabric trimming fastened to the edge of the canvas top along three sides, excluding the driver's end. Two steps at the rear provided entrance into the large bed of the wagon. Compared to the other vehicles they saw, it was puzzling, but they were grateful for the ride. As they turned around a treed area and headed up Broadway, Joseph told Tim, the cheerful Irish driver, that he liked his horse. Then he asked, "Is he an Irish horse?"

Margaret said, "Joseph!" shook her head, and mouthed their new word of the day: no. She sighed in disbelief. "Perhaps Tim wants to point things out to us on our way, Joseph."

Surprised at the question, Tim laughed, "No, I think he's an American bay—probably from a farm out east of Margaret's, or maybe west in New Jersey. He's not my horse; he belongs to a friend."

Joseph answered, "Well, I really like him. I like a big strong horse. Can I ride him sometime, then?"

Ellen, who was sitting next to Joseph, bumped his knee, compelling him to stop talking, but Joseph ignored her. Michael glared at Joseph to stop him. Joseph returned a defiant look that said, "I'm in America now; I'm ignoring ye because I'm free." To keep the peace, Michael ignored Joseph.

Tim said, "Well, lad, this is a cart horse who works for a livin' by haulin' people. My friend and I have a couple of horses, and we take people places for money. We have two carts and two wagons. When he's not workin', he's in a stable not too far from here—a block up Mulberry Street. Maybe ye'll see us again. Ye can't ride him, but maybe we'll let ye take the reins for a bit. I can teach ye."

Joseph replied, "That I'd like to do, but ye would not have to teach me. I know it all now about horses. What's his name?"

"We just call him the bay."

Joseph blurted, "He might work for ye better if he was yer friend. Ye could at least give him a name, Tim. I can name him for ye. What's the big street we just crossed?"

"That's Lafayette, son."

"My name is Joseph. I don't have a father now, so I'm nobody's son, but we'll call yer horse Lafayette. Do ye like Lafayette, then?

"I'm sorry, Joseph. I heard that you children lost your parents, and I am sorry, but I like that name. Lafayette it is! It sounds good on him. He's a real big, good horse. He deserves a proper and grand name like Lafayette."

"See? I told you that ye'd like him as a friend more if he had a name. He'll like ye better too. I bet he learns his name in a day or two if ye talk to him and say his name every time. He'll work a little harder for ye. Me ma told me a name is how people know who comes into the world and who goes out of it. That's how we know where they are. Even animals love it when ye know them."

Tim laughed and agreed.

"If I didn't have a name, people would have to call me the brilliant, handsome Quigley lad without a mother. Problem is, in Ireland, there are too many of us motherless Quigley lads to know which one I am." Joseph yelled, "Yer a damned good horse, Lafayette! Ye are now known, loved, and will always be remembered!"

Margaret instantly gave him a good pinch on his leg and whispered, "Joseph, if ye say one more stupid thing, I'll stuff yer socks in yer mouth!"

They traveled silently for a couple of blocks down Canal Street. After crossing Lafayette, the ground had become smelly and the street muddy. There was considerable construction to the southeast. Michael was pleased to know that the area was within very easy walking distance of Margaret's Mott Street address. Being a stonemason with considerable experience, he thought he would be able to get a job right away. He'd get over there as soon as he could—maybe tomorrow morning if it worked out with the kids. Suddenly, his heart sunk, and he realized that in all the activity, Joseph's blabbing, and the grief, he had neglected his continuous attention on his most precious possessions—his tools. His heart sank. The trunk had sat alone on the ferry as they stood on the deck, and he hadn't checked it since.

Michael grabbed for the trunk at his feet, lifted the lid, and fumbled around for his sturdy, leather bag. Relieved at finding it, he untied the linen straps, unwound them, and revealed his mason's hammer, several jointers, a blocking chisel, his header, offset and tracing chisels, a stiff brush, and a tool for repointing lime mortar. These tools might keep what was left of the Quigley family alive, and he could not afford to lose sight of them for a moment. Thankfully, they would be headed straight for their cousin Margaret's apartment, and he would not see them moving about among strangers.

While tidying up his belongings, Michael's mind drifted back to Ireland. As he rode along, he looked at the buildings of varied quality amid the shacks and shambles in the alleyways. In Ireland, Michael's da was respected for his artistry in weaving and tailoring. Michael was glad he was a stonemason. The local stonemasons had not hesitated in accepting a very young Michael Quigley into his apprenticeship. He was a sturdy teenager at fifteen, and they thought he might be a natural, given his father's talent with his hands, as well as the reputations of other Quigley masons.

In a few short years, Michael began building his own reputation around his village, especially having been apprenticed to Mr. Jackson. Michael believed it was Mr. Jackson's training more than it was his own talent that made him skilled. Mr. Jackson was called upon to fix ancient structures falling into disrepair. On those occasions, he took his youthful Quigley apprentice with him. Repairs often taught Michael the most. He had repaired many bridges damaged by floods and weather, and he had learned his work from varied experiences and not just constructing new buildings by laying one brick or stone after the other.

From Mr. Jackson and the other skilled men, Michael had, in a short time, learned the basics in masonry, such as picking rubble or setting the foundation of a single or double drystone retaining wall, and he could dress building stones with fine or rough punch- drafted margins.

Working as an apprentice to such an accomplished mason, Michael had learned a wide variety of skills. He had built patterns in the fine rose, blue, and purple tones of limestone. He was familiar with granite and sandstone and several kinds of mortar. His last job involved the precision work of finely cut snecked gray stones native to his township. He was admired by Mr. Jackson for his natural craftsmanship and ease in personality. Mr. Jackson was considered one of the finest masons in the county, and he was sorry to see Michael leaving the village. However, he was aware that Michael's family needed his skills in America.

Michael slipped his tools back into the trunk, hoping that an employer here would recognize Mr. Jackson's name and would value Michael's experiences. As he focused again on their drive, Tim pointed out Lafayette's livery stable on Mulberry and then turned left and headed north. As Tim was talking to Joseph about Mr. Florentine, the stable owner, Margaret pointed out to the distracted Michael that they had turned onto Mott Street.

Margaret commented first on what a very narrow and busy street it was. They dodged a cart full of leafy greens and cabbages, one with crates full of live chickens, and a cart with pots and pans. There was shop after shop.

The thirteen-year-old Margaret had seen poor children walking aimlessly everywhere, and it seemed that Mott was the worst. She let the cows out of the barn before the milkin' started. She began worrying about her ability to take care of Charley and Ellen by herself during the day when Michael went to work. She wasn't sure what work Margaret did during the day and how they could all be in one small place at one time.

She looked at all those people on Mott and elsewhere, and those buildings. It was so crowded. She knew that the Quigley children needed work in a field—chickens or pigs to care for—the usual work on a farm that kept everyone busy providing food. She had also felt restricted by the boat. There were too many people in her space who weren't her family. She feared the same would be true in New York City. Joseph got into trouble on the boat because there was no work and no space. In her mind, she saw it all happening again.

Margaret knew Da expected Michael to take Joseph with him, but how could he keep Joseph occupied? Surely, unless he had a job, Joseph would be running in the streets with these other boys within the first hour. She couldn't imagine a space large enough to hold Joseph. Had it not been for the ropes and masts and Captain Lockhart, the ship would have been even more of a disaster for Joseph. After his experience on the boat and Staten Island, Margaret felt he would require fields in which he could be left alone with horses.

Margaret whispered, "Michael, me stomach is churnin', and me heart is thumpin'. What will ye do about Joseph here? Look at the number of idle boys in groups in the streets. Don't they go to school?"

Michael did not answer her.

Head bowed in total defeat, Margaret whispered, "I want to be a teacher." Choking, she said in a high-pitched voice, "Ma wants me in school." The tears welled up in her eyes and streamed down her scrunched-up, exhausted face. "How can ye pay for school for us, Michael, and how can we keep an eye on Joseph if he's not in school?"

Michael smiled and said, "Don't shut the barn door until the cows are out, me beautiful darlin'. We'll find a way for ye to become a teacher." Through his own choking voice, he said, "Things have a way of workin' out, lovely girl. Ye have to believe it. Dry yer eyes before we meet our cousin. All right then?"

Margaret felt a responsibility to step in for Ma when it came to schooling, cleaning, cooking—everything—but for Margaret, school seemed to be the most important. It overwhelmed her. She had thought that she might be forced to do laundry or be a servant to pay for Joseph's school before her own. It galled her, believing that she was certainly the better student and more deserving. Ma told everyone that the first thing she was going to do was enroll the children into an American Catholic school so they could grow up to be something other than paupers.

Margaret and Ellen were equally excited about school. Ellen wanted to be a nurse, but Ma thought Joseph was the most imaginative, by far the smartest and opinioned, and could be a lawyer who earned lots of money or could become a mayor or even president of the United States. She wanted Mary to become a nun and James a priest. Ma's dreams were grand with Joseph, but Margaret and Ellen had expressed their doubts between them regarding Joseph's ability to fulfill them.

Down each alley, women were hanging laundry out window lines that ran from one side of the narrow street to the other. There were men everywhere—standing on street corners, hanging out at shops. They were laughing, and some seemed quite happy, but it didn't look as though they were all employed.

Tim arrived at the Mott address, only a couple of blocks up from Canal, and waved to a man in front of Margaret's building who nodded and went inside. He would tell Margaret that the Quigley family had arrived. Instead of getting out, he suggested that since they were all in the wagon and cousin Margaret hadn't come out to the street, he could take them up through their neighborhood pointing out the shops and then show them the location of the church and the school before returning down Lafayette and back to Margaret's. Their cousin's place was only about two miles from the ferry dock. Saint Patrick's Church was on Mulberry, only a mile north of Margaret's. The Catholic school was right behind it and faced Mott.

The short trip up Mott, Broome, and Mulberry gave them an opportunity to get their bearings and grow more excited about their new city. The church was as grand as any they had seen. Tim told them that Saint Pat's served soup on Wednesday nights for immigrant families.

When they returned down Lafayette, Tim told them that the street stretched from south to north across the entire island of Manhattan. No matter if they got lost during the day, if they got on Lafayette, they could get back home by facing the sun. When they returned, Tim pointed out Margaret who was waiting outside the cobbler's shop, talking to a neighbor. Everyone knew everything about everyone else on this block—just like their villages back home. With each new family, the locals' hearts went out as though each child was their own. A little group of greeters had gathered. That's the way it would have been back in their village when someone new came to live there.

CHAPTER 8

MOTT STREET, NEW YORK CITY

Margaret's graying red hair was pulled up in back, and she was wearing a green skirt, a white apron, and a white blouse with billowing sleeves. Margaret immediately became "Cousin Margaret," so as not to confuse one Margaret with the other, but she told her cousins to call her Maggie like everyone else up and down the street.

Joseph reminded Cousin Maggie that his and Michael's mothers' names had been Margaret. "I thought all the Irish women were named Mary or Ellen, but I was wrong. There were seventeen Marys on the boat, but there were seven Margarets.

Amazed and laughing, Maggie said, "How many girls were named Bridgett?"

Joseph answered, "Seven."

"Well, aren't you a smart one, darlin'?"

"Yes," replied Joseph. "Ma and I talked about names. We decided that there were too many Margarets, Marys, and Ellens. Too many Bridgetts, Kathleens, and Catherines. There are too many Annes, Nancys, and Colleens. There are—"

"That's fine, Joseph," interrupted Ellen. "Stop now, one-of-a- kind Joseph."

Maggie laughed at Ellen's comment, but Joseph continued, "That's why Ma decided on Doroty for the baby's name. Ma wanted her to have an American name that no other Irish girl would have. How many Dorotys do you know, Maggie?"

She answered, "Only yer Doroty. Yer darlin' was also one of a kind then, wasn't she?"

Joseph replied, "Yes, Maggie. Like me."

When Maggie used the words "yer Doroty," Joseph whimpered and teared up without warning. He closed his eyes, lowered his head, and saw a vision of his tiny, blue-white, dead sister folded in the arms of a ma who never said goodbye. Embarrassed, he quickly ducked behind Michael's arm and stood with his head touching his coat.

Michael placed his free arm around Joseph's shoulder and Maggie, giving Joseph a moment, turned, and led them into her building through the bakery shop. As she proudly introduced her Quigley cousins to Mrs. O' Reilly, the smell of baking bread straightened Joseph up. Mrs. O'Reilly told the story that she had brought only her baking skills and recipes to America. She started with one borrowed pan and a coal stove in an apartment. Now she and her husband had one of the largest bakeries on the street. Two of her children were still in the school up at Saint Patrick's. Right off, she was an inspiration to Michael. If she could do it, so could he!

The smell in the bakery was remarkable enough, but Mrs. O'Reilly handed Margaret a fresh loaf of soda bread baked with buttermilk and without raisins. It was the first recipe she had ever sold. The children reeled with the thought of eating it.

Joseph told Mrs. O'Reilly that they had eaten plain white bread on Staten Island that melted or turned to paste in the soup, and they hated it. "It made all the Irishmen pop air biscuits we could hear and smell as we slept in the jail. It was terrible."

Maggie giggled as Joseph continued, "The butter on the island was wonderful, but I can't wait to taste butter on this!" The family hadn't had real bread for a very long time, and they couldn't wait to taste its still-warm, velvety, robust goodness.

Maggie told them that she had butter in her apartment and led them through a side door from the bakery and into the hallway below the stairs that led up to her second-floor apartment. There were "cubbies" up by the main door for mail. She told Ellen she could come down to get the mail every day, and Ellen was thrilled.

Another side door in the hall, across from the bakery, led into a shoe shop. Mr. Grandy was the cobbler, but their cousin did not fancy taking the children there. It was a wee space, and he was a very busy and serious man who did not like to be bothered. Instead, she poked her head through a side door into a tailor shop run by Mr.

Elliott. He came from County Cork but said that he was originally from Scotland. He lived up on the third floor.

Making conversation, Michael told him that his da had intended to become a tailor in America. The irony that there was a tailor's shop in this building did not escape Michael. Mr. Elliott responded, "That's what Maggie has told me. I'm so sorry for your loss. I would have employed yer da right off. I need a good tailor."

Michael thought, *Of course! Da had probably planned to ask Mr. Elliott for a job, or maybe Mr. Elliott had been looking forward to hiring Da, but Da didn't want to make promises he couldn't keep so he said nothing about it to us.*

Quite a number of letters had passed back and forth across the Atlantic, but due to difficult political and economic circumstances when he was little, and his mother's death, Michael was the only one of the Quigley children who was not taught to read, so he had no idea what the conversations had been—except that there would be a place to stay until they could "stand on their own two feet."

The brief thought of the loss of his parents nearly made Michael sick, and he felt himself, a grown man, melting as Joseph had done moments before. Even though he could see the opportunities that would present themselves, he also saw burdens added, and this would be a challenge. He'd have to get control over his emotions. James had warned his son not to "worry over spilt milk." "Just put one foot in front of the other," he had admonished. Michael decided he would follow that sound advice for the rest of his life. He was trying to take each thing as it came to him now and not "put the horse before the cart" as older sister Margaret had told him when he was a little boy.

The maintenance and apartment manager lived at the end of the hallway, at the back of the apartment. Tim and Michael lugged their trunk up to the second floor and turned left around the hall to the back of the building to Maggie's apartment, number 209, the apartment directly above the manager.

Maggie thanked Tim and offered a few coins, but Tim refused the money and said it was his pleasure to help.

Michael shook his hand and made a plan to pay him back some-day.

Joseph said, "Lafayette's me favorite horse in America so far—maybe I'll see him again."

Tim patted Joseph's head, laughed, and turned to leave.

Maggie settled everyone into her tiny space. Her lace curtains billowed in the cross-breeze of her kitchen area. Charley would sleep on a cot in the sitting room that was open to the kitchen and eating area. The bathroom was tucked in the southwest corner of the kitchen, next to the entrance. One girl would sleep with Maggie, and the other would sleep with a cousin named Honora Quigley, a sister to the older Maggie, and a daytime maid who would be coming home later. Both women slept in the same bedroom with a little curtain screen Margaret had fashioned. She had asked the maintenance man to fasten a rod diagonally on the walls across the room where Charley slept. Michael and Joseph would be sleeping in the hall.

The hallway to Margaret's apartment was on the north side of the building. Her apartment was in the northwest corner. The hallway where Michael and Joseph would sleep was on the west side, just outside the fire escape. There was an apartment across the hall from Margaret, but its door opened onto the south hall, so there would be privacy between Margaret's apartment and the hall where Joseph and Michael slept. Nobody else was forced to walk through their sleeping area. Only people who went out on the fire escape to cool off or smoke would walk past them as they slept on the hall floor.

The cleanliness of Maggie's apartment and the relative privacy from strangers was a relief. Cousin Margaret was family, so it was easier for them to relax. Before their evening meal, Maggie gave Joseph money and asked him to run across Mott to the butcher shop to buy bacon. "Tell the butcher the bacon is for Margaret Quigley—so you get the correct change." What a wonderful opportunity this was for him.

Joseph ran out the door of the apartment building as an older boy was entering. The young man lived in the apartment with his ma, Kate Mooney. After introducing himself, Jack Mooney said, "You need to call me McGee. Everyone knows me by McGee, so don't ever

100

use my ma's name if ye know what's good for ye." He then offered to accompany Joseph to the butcher shop.

Joseph said to McGee, "I don't know yer ma, so ye don't need to worry."

Joseph found McGee fascinating and frightening. He was profoundly different from any other person Joseph had known, but from their conversation, he seemed to be an independent young man who was earning money. Joseph agreed to join him the next day to learn the "ropes" of his "messenger" business. McGee laughed when Joseph told him he had already learned the ropes from Captain Lockhart.

The boys shared pieces of their immigration stories, and when they got back to the hallway of the building, McGee asked Joseph if he could tear off a piece of bacon to take to his ma. Joseph told McGee that it wasn't his money or his bacon so he wouldn't. "You'd have to fight me for it, McGee!" warned Joseph with a smile. Joseph had already learned not to be told by a stranger what to do, but to stand up for himself or do what is right—unless it was to his benefit. From his ma, he learned to smile and wink as he did it.

Michael was joyful to have heard from Maggie that Mr. Romaine, who owned Margaret's building, was engaged in a construction project down on Anthony Street, southwest of Mott and less than a kilometer away. Margaret had already told him about Michael's experience as a stonemason. He planned to walk down there first thing in the morning. Margaret reminded Michael to tell the boss that Mr. Romaine was expecting him.

Once the boys were settled in the hall, Michael asked Joseph to be prepared to walk down to Anthony Street with him early the next morning. Joseph explained that he couldn't because he was going to go with McGee to learn the ropes of a messenger boy.

Michael was amazed but worried that Joseph had jumped in so quickly. "I don't know this young man. Does Maggie?"

"What does it matter, Michael? I need to earn some money so the kids can eat."

"Ye are one of the kids, Joseph, and I need to keep ye safe." "Well, not in America. McGee says all the kids who are messenger boys are sometimes as young as Charley, and they're wealthy enough to send their older brothers through the seminary."

Michael expressed his skepticism and then added, "Charley and the girls are going down to the school tomorrow, and you should too—except that we want the school to still be standin' so maybe the others need to get established before we introduce you. You're coming with me, and that's it, Joseph. I'm following Da's orders, Joseph. We're to do what Da said."

Φ

The sun had barely risen on the horizon when Joseph woke up to a tapping on the window on the door of the fire escape. There stood McGee, finger upright and pressed over pursed lips in a "keep quiet" gesture. Joseph and Michael had placed their clothes in the hallway so as not to bother the ladies of the apartment. Quickly and quietly, Joseph dressed and slipped onto the fire escape with McGee, leaving Michael asleep and unaware of his escape.

It was a little cold, and Joseph was, again, used to eating, so his stomach growled as the boys rushed through the alley, heading north on Mulberry. He looked down toward the livery and saw only one horse that wasn't Lafayette. He wanted to go down that way, but McGee was on an assignment in another direction. He had messages to carry from Five Points up to Bleeker Street. They crossed Mulberry and sped down the alley to Orange. They turned south until they came back to Canal. Before they crossed, McGee told Joseph that he needed a "street" name so nobody he dealt with would know his real name.

"What about Mott?" asked Joseph.

"Joseph, I'm talkin' about a name other than yer real one when yer out of yer home. Ye don't want anyone to know yer real name. 'Tis not safe to share it. The Bowery Street B'hoys'll come right to yer home and beat yer mother. They'll run yer sister down with a horse if they know who she is."

"Horseboy?"

"That's no good. Nobody would believe that was your real name. You need a real-soundin' Irish name."

"How about McFee? We'll be McFee and McGee."

"What if some Roach Guard or Bowery B'hoy comes lookin' for ye, but gets confused between McFee and McGee and beats me to death by accident? I won't be gettin' killed for ye. McFee's no good."

Gettin' killed? Joseph thought. The gravity of the comment hadn't completely sunk in when Joseph asked, "How about McGuiness?" Joseph was thinking of Margaret or Ellen trod on by a horse as either sped to school up Mott. It would serve them right, but he couldn't let that happen.

"Did you hear me? No Mc-anythin'. They're too much alike. How about Blackie Collins?"

"I don't like it. A horse is called Blackie. How about Jackie Collins instead?"

"Jackie is fine. Hey, that's my name! I guess that's all right then. I'll remember it, and nobody else knows me real name anyway. Always remember, when we cross that street, we're in Five Points and with the Bowery B'hoys, so you're Jackie Collins—Jackie for short. Ye don't forget it. All right, then?"

"That's fine, then," replied Joseph, who practiced his new name numerous times while scurrying along. After crossing Canal, they walked into the smelly part of town, where dog carcasses could be found in the pond. On Beyard, McGee asked, "Hey, Jackie, are ye hungry?"

"Sure," replied Jackie Collins.

They came to a canvas-covered market with a cart holding something McGee called schnecken, a form of bread baked in a pan and covered with brown sugar, nuts, and on this sunny morning, honey bees. A very thin, brown-haired lady named Polly reached over and handed the boys two schnecken wrapped in a piece of paper. McGee asked for a tin of hot tea "for me little friend Jackie," which she handed over. Suddenly, she started yelling at them, "Git out of here, ye guttersnipes, or I'll call the coppers on ye."

McGee yelled, "Run, Jackie! Here comes Gino."

Joseph was terribly confused. McGee had paid for neither the tins of tea nor the bread, yet Polly had freely and cheerfully handed them over. Now she was yelling, "There's that brash boy again— and with his friends—them comin' around here for a handout. How dare ye!" The stocky man, Gino, had walked up to Polly and was casually talking to her.

The boys had run toward Centre Street, carefully so as to not spill their tea. With their backs against the warm stone, they sat up against a building on the sunny side of the street to enjoy their buns and tea. Joseph calmly asked, "McGee, who's Gino?"

"He's Polly's boss. Maybe he didn't see us pay," McGee said with a wink.

Joseph laughed. "He was probably tellin' her that he can't feed every Mick in the city!"

"I'm not a Mick. I'm a Collins, ye remember?" McGee laughed. "Didn't ye ever hear the name 'Mick' before? 'Tis a name for someone Irish."

Joseph answered, "No, I never did. By the way, how are we going to pay back Polly? I don't think she wanted us to take her sweet bread. I'm not sure. What do ye think?"

Laughing, McGee explained that he knew the "lady," Polly. To Joseph's astonishment, McGee revealed that "Jackie" might see her because she lived at the Mott Street apartment, but Jackie was never to tell anyone in any part of town about her at all. Not even his family at Mott was to know that Jackie knew her. If he saw her there, he was to ignore her, not call her out, especially not with the name Polly. If anyone ever asked anything, he knew nothing—whether he did or not.

Joseph was accustomed to expressing himself freely and often, but he believed that he was clever enough to live more than one life here. It was a whole new, bewildering world. So far, nobody across Canal Street was sweet and kind like the neighbors in his village back home and some of the adults in Margaret's apartment building. He didn't think McGee was sweet or kind. He was friendly, and charmin', maybe like Joseph.

McGee had taken Joseph to Polly's workplace so she could see who his new friend was, and she could sometimes say, "Help ye out, Jackie," if he were in danger. Joseph thought the sticky bread was a good start.

McGee explained, "She works on bread or fish carts for Gino. Once the buns are gone in the morning, there are no more. When fish arrives from the dock later in the morning, she sells that as well."

McGee had rarely seen Gino at Polly's breakfast cart that early in the day unless something was up. He said, "I don't like it if Gino sees me at Polly's cart. It's fine for him to bump into me if I'm runnin' in the streets, but not at Polly's cart in the mornin'. Since I'm not a seagull, he wouldn't see me in the afternoon around the fish. When ye run into a situation like that, ye have to change yer routine or be more careful."

Joseph hadn't seen "a situation like that" and had no idea what McGee was talking about.

McGee said, "Let me tell ye, I know things about Gino that Polly shouldn't know for her own good. Yer gonna find out a few things too, but don't ever talk to Polly or nobody about Gino or anyone else you meet ever on this messenger boy job. The only people who shares things is ye an' me. We're partners. Ye got that? The only thing we need to know is what is good for us. Knowin' too many things is bad for yer health."

Joseph asked McGee if he knew Polly's real name.

"I told ye, yer real name is whatever someone calls ye in the street—that's anythin' but yer real name. So what's yer real name right now?"

"Me real name is Jackie Collins."

"That's right. If yer somewhere on the street and yer family calls out Joseph, don't answer. Ye want nobody to know who ye are. You can talk to yer family later, but do not answer across any street or down any block. Don't never forget that the wrong man might be listenin', and yer family can suffer."

All relationships were to be kept secret if he was to become a messenger boy. It was a strange but critical lesson for Joseph if he wanted to earn money right away as McGee had promised.

When they had finished eating, McGee hid their tins behind a shrub. He'd get them another time. They then ran from one shop to another, in and out of buildings, all morning long through the alleys as McGee stuffed money and small papers into his many pockets inside his vest and trousers. McGee collected money from a very large number of men. Some were Italian, some Irish, one man a Negro. Another amazing fact was that McGee also collected numbers from them.

He had a small pencil and paper on which he wrote some things down—all in code. Many numbers he did not record. He had developed the ability to learn hundreds of numbers and various amounts of money in his head and not forget them. He called off numbers to Joseph and then tested him later. Joseph did a satisfactory job, according to McGee, though he needed to learn fast how to retain many more numbers. McGee gave Joseph hints on how to do that fast.

Sometimes Joseph was to be seen, and at others, he was not. It was up to McGee to decide when he was to remain hidden. McGee was trying to build a potential clientele for Joseph because he was secretly planning to move on in his job. He was beginning to think it was too dangerous. He trusted nobody, but he thought Joseph might be slick enough to remember numbers and keep the other "refinements" of the job straight and sorted in his head. Also, he was a newcomer who could be trained and knew nobody, so he wouldn't be snitchin' anytime soon.

The boys had worked their way down Orange Street to Anthony Street. Joseph suddenly froze when, in front of a large construction project, he saw Michael, his back to the street with a man pointing out what looked like directions. *Had Michael already gotten a job?* Joseph kept his head down and walked to the inside of the street so he could look outward, faced away from Michael while talking to McGee. When he was sure he had passed Michael, he didn't look back, so he had no idea if Michael noticed him. He doubted it and just kept going. Joseph had "run off," something he was not supposed to do, but he said nothing to McGee.

McGee declared that they needed to travel up Mulberry to the "office" on Bleeker where the money and numbers needed to be taken. The man on Bleeker knew McGee's name, but McGee didn't know his. It's how it worked. Joseph was a natural. He had already told McGee nothing about seeing his brother Michael. He was proud of Michael and wanted to share what a good brother he had, but he had already acquired some important skills. He would follow the lead of his new business partner, McGee. In the long run, it would pay.

Today, McGee could only walk up Mulberry to the office. Each day he took a different route. He ducked behind an unlocked door and moved all the money he had stuffed into pockets into a special cloth envelope sewn in his pants. If someone had watched him and grabbed his vest or a jacket, nothing would be there. When Joseph had to pee, they peed in an alley. While one peed, the other was lookout. McGee kept a constant vigilance so as not to be robbed. It required hard work and often resulted in heart-pounding fear.

When they arrived at Bleeker, McGee walked down a side alley halfway down a block. He slipped in a narrow door, leaving Joseph outside. Once it was clear inside the building, McGee motioned out the door with his hand for Joseph to go in. He whispered and pointed to the hallway where Joseph should stand hidden. Nobody used the hallway since the door was only a safe exit from the office. After a coded knock on the office door, it opened.

After McGee stepped in, Joseph's job was to listen through the door and remain unseen. If he heard footsteps, he was to slip back into the alley and out to Bleeker. He could sit down in the street next to a shoe shop as though he was waiting for his da in the store. That was his story. After McGee rattled off numbers and amounts of money and collected a few dollars, the man of Bleeker made a highly unusual request. He asked McGee if he knew someone down at Five Points with a wagon who could load it with dead fish or rotten produce up to Waverly late the next afternoon. McGee was a little stunned, so it took him a minute to think. Even though Polly worked in the market and knew most of the deliverymen, he couldn't see how she could help him. Gino didn't seem to fit in either, though Bleeker man and Gino obviously knew each other, he would not mention it, nor would he ask too many questions.

It needed to be delivered, on time, to a man's abandoned livery stable on Waverly Place near the Aston Opera House. The story went that there was some English "clown" named McCready who was going to act in a production of Shakespeare's Macbeth. Everybody knew that Edwin Forrest, an Irish actor, was better. A March performance had been canceled until rivals could cool down. All of New York feared the Irish gangsters who didn't want McCready to perform. One food fight had already broken out, and it was feared that the next time would elicit real ammunition—not just cabbages or fish.

Bleeker man said that the boys down in the Five Points needed to get supplies up north before the performance tomorrow night. It was a real emergency, and it needed to be done without suspicion. The delivery was to look as though it was a daily delivery—nothing out of the ordinary—even for the time or the day and the place. For the play, the military had been called out by the mayor of New York. He was taking every precaution to keep the Bowery Street B'hoys out of the fancy neighborhood and far away from the theater tomorrow night.

The huge payoff of fifty dollars went to whoever could pull it off.

McGee asked "Bleekerman" to give him two hours and he'd see what he could do. When he said, "Thank you, Mr. Bleekerman. That's a generous payoff for rotten produce. I'll be back."

Joseph ran swiftly out the door and sat at the cobbler's shop.

CHAPTER 9

SHAKESPEARE AT THE OPERA HOUSE

After talking with Jackie Collins, McGee decided that they could use Tim's wagon and give ten dollars to Tim, taking twenty each for themselves. Joseph knew Michael couldn't earn that much in a week as a mason. All McGee had gotten Joseph today was a sticky bun, half a tin of tea, and a lot of running around. Also, Joseph knew he was in for it when he got back to Maggie's apartment and Michael got home. Joseph assured himself that this delivery job would be his chance to break into business and become a wealthy man. Only later did Joseph think himself to still be a child. He liked the excitement of runnin' in a man's world, and he knew he was smart and slick enough to do a good job.

McGee was totally stumped by Bleekerman's problem. Bleekerman said his men couldn't do it because they would be recognized and would be thrown in jail by the military long before they ever got to the Aston Opera House. Joseph was certain in his mind that kids like him and McGee would never be expected to be involved in something like that, especially a little kid like himself. His voice hadn't even changed yet. They would never be suspected. He couldn't resist.

Joseph and McGee ran back to Bleekerman's door and knocked. "Who's this greenhorn Mick?" he screamed.

The diminutive Joseph held out his hand for a handshake. "My name's Blackie, er … Jackie to you, and I can drive your wagon and deliver the produce."

The short, bald man, whose suspenders looked as though they would pop at any moment and snap him in the face, dropped his gold folding lorgnette with its gold chain and then place it in his vest pocket. His vest, he wore flopping open over his suspenders. Joseph had the thought that he was probably unable to fasten it shut.

Though he was probably a man of means, he didn't spend his money on clothing. To Joseph, he didn't appear to be highfalutin though he was obviously a man with power and not to be taken lightly. Mr. Bleekerman didn't laugh at Joseph, and he didn't scold; he just stared at him intently and with a look that he wanted to ask many questions.

Joseph said, "I may appear to be a child, but I'm not an eejit, Mr. Bleeker Street, er ... Bleekerman. You haird me correctly. Me plan will work, and I'm a pitiful Irish lad who'll do it for McGee and me Collins family. We know a lady named Polly who'd love to go to the theater. Me horse is Lafayette, and I have a fancy wagon that holds a ton of things. We'll take Polly, all dressed up for a night on the town. She's never been to a play at the theater. Nobody will guess. Two young boys who look like Polly's children, in a dressed-up wagon, a night with the upper crust seein' Shakespeare? You got a ticket, Mr. Bleeker Street, or not? We'll need it now."

"Coincidentally, Jackie and McGee, I do have a ticket. I have a number of 'friends' who will also be attending and I haven't handed out all my tickets until I know the men get their fish loaded."

Φ

Very early the next morning, Joseph was sitting at Margaret's table. Michael was ready to leave for his temporary job filling in for a sick mason for three more days. Joseph still had red eyes from crying from his thrashing. It wasn't typical for the Quigley family to beat on each other as children or parents, but these times were desperate. The siblings kicked or pinched, but there were no harsh lickings as there were with some other families. This was the first ever, but Michael felt it was necessary for Joseph to get the message that they were good people—and New York was a dangerous place. Hadn't they lost enough family already? Michael had taken on more than he could handle, and Joseph absolutely had to quit running off. He would certainly get into terrible trouble that would ruin their stay at Margaret's and jeopardize whatever opportunities they had left.

Maggie was distraught and wondered what she had taken on. Joseph waited impatiently for Michael to go out the door. As he ate his groats and cream, he promised to stay inside, but he kept an ear on the fire escape. He needed to get to the livery stable now—and get that wagon down to Five Points and into the delivery shed before the people on the street began to show up for their fish. He'd have to hitch the wagon with help from McGee. Hopefully, he was standing outside the fire escape at this moment and would be ready to run. He had made McGee a believer and he would get Michael too—but only after he brought home the bacon.

In the late afternoon the day before, after they quit running their "messages," he had stopped at Saint Patrick's on his way home and then gone to the stable. Tim was just bringing in Lafayette for the day. Joseph complimented Tim and Lafayette in front of McGee. Joseph bragged about their success, Tim's business, the greatness of Lafayette, and on and on he went. Those compliments had elicited the response Joseph planned. Tim invited them aboard, and they jumped on. Once on, Joseph asked Tim if he could take the reins.

Like a pro, Joseph sat tall and proud behind the large horse. In Ireland, it had been necessary for him to drive a wagon as large as this, and in a muddy field, so this was nothing. He told Tim that back home, all the kids could rein a workhorse. They swiftly glided around the large New York city block on the hard brick stones of a beautiful May afternoon. Joseph sometimes stood. He talked to Lafayette the entire time. He told him how strong and beautiful he was. With each word of praise, Joseph believed that Lafayette grew taller.

When they had returned to the livery stable, Tim pointed out the special decorations used in parades and for special occasions. Joseph took note and found the long pole for releasing them from their anchors on the high walls. He and McGee also had an opportunity to meet Tim's boss, Mr. White. Tim bragged to Mr. White about Joseph's remarkable horse skills at his age and told him they had a good prospective teamster on their hands.

Joseph had everything set up in his mind for the next morning. He could get to the stables, prepare Lafayette for his big day, and he could return home safely. He could not wait. It would not be a handout, but earnings from a real job, a dangerous job that not just anyone could manage.

Φ

Polly, when she stepped on the wagon, was dressed in a remarkable gold dress. Joseph would not have been able to describe it, but she had gotten it from a lady who worked in a brothel on Anthony and Bowery. It had fringe that resembled some of the trim they had pulled down from the walls of the livery stable. Joseph didn't know what a brothel was, exactly, but he knew it was not good. As McGee explained and described, enough registered so that Joseph asked McGee to quit explaining.

As they began their journey from Bowery Street, Joseph took Bowery straight up until they got to Tenth. His plan was to turn south off Tenth onto Lafayette, and go down Lafayette to the theater, approaching from the north. If the military were there, they would believe that this wagon had not come from the south where all the trouble would originate. There were numbers of carts, coaches, and wagons carrying Macbeth audience members to the play. The military had formed them into a single, long line.

Lafayette and his wagon, though remarkably different in style, were festooned with everything from the livery stable. Polly had her theater ticket from Mr. Bleekerman in hand, and off she stepped in front of the theater. A policeman stepped forward. Tongue-in-cheek, he complimented the young boys on the presentation of the wagon.

Joseph proceeded a block more down Lafayette and then turned west. The police, who had their eye on the wagon, would expect him to not continue south, since it appeared he had arrived from the north. They were carefully watching anything that continued in a southerly direction, as they assumed some of these patrons were from the Five Points or Bowery Street gangs. Going north on Broadway, Joseph saw they were approaching Waverly. He had planned to turn west to arrive at the drop-off, but the street was, for some reason, blocked off. His heart sank, and he and McGee slowed down and asked the police what the problem was.

The policeman said that side streets above and below the theater had been blocked off by the military for safety, and nobody was allowed to travel or park on them. To continue north, they would have to travel east, the opposite direction from where they were expected to deliver their goods. He reminded them that this had been announced in the newspapers for days, and they should have planned appropriately.

Joseph told him that he hadn't been to school and couldn't read the newspaper. He said, "I just let off me aunt Polly; now I have to get me Ma, Josephine Collins, who is a maid on Waverly. What can I do? 'Tis an emergency!"

The policeman told him he'd have to continue up Broadway, passing by Waverly.

Joseph pleaded, "I have to get me ma on Waverly because me sister Ellen is sick, and Cousin Maggie thinks she might die. How far will we have to go out of our way? Will I get lost? I have to take Ma way up North Broadway to Ellen. This is me cousin Timothy who has come to help me." Joseph talked on, telling the most sorrowful tale about his cousins, uncles, aunt—on and on he went until the policeman could hear no more.

"All right, son, go ahead, but first, what have you in the wagon?"

Joseph answered, "I have produce I didn't get delivered. Ellen fell ill, and we had to take her to me aunt's house. We'll have to take care of the produce tomorrow. I must get movin' now, right now!" The policeman moved his long wagon forward and waved Joseph through.

Joseph said, "God bless ye. Christ beside ye, Officer. We have suffered so. I'll mention your kindness to the chief. If I had something to give ye, I would." Ma had been right. Joseph hid the truth behind his face and smile, and it got them the six blocks to the empty stable, where two men in caps were waiting. They swung open the wide doors, and Joseph drove Lafayette through them. Once off the wagon, they were led out the back door of the building and into the house next door.

As the wagon was emptied in the old livery, the boys sat in the house and ate a meal cooked by a lady named Molly. Joseph's face barely reached the top of the table. Both he and McGee seemed to be children playing the roles of men in a folly.

"Jaisus, Mary, and Joseph," said McGee, "they could have done better than to have an Irishwoman called Molly. Fiona would have sounded better. Molly is as bad as Polly!"

They both laughed.

Joseph said, "Her name is probably Mary, Ellen, Bridgette, or Margaret. Does it matter? It's the best meal I ever had." Being Jackie made Joseph feel like the upper crust, having just eaten fat chunks of spring lamb, carrot, and celery in a delicious sauce on which floated buttermilk dumplings. It was hot, steamy, and delicious. After their meal, Jackie and McGee tasted frozen lemon custard.

The men rewarded Lafayette with accolades, a big drink of water, and a generous serving of oats with molasses.

While the wagon was being unloaded, men were coming out of the woodwork to retrieve its contents. There were men in top hats knocking on Molly's door asking where to get their guns or asking if they really had to take a fish and a pistol as instructed. When they asked, she handed them a page of newspaper for hygiene and easier concealment. Nobody had warned them to keep quiet—that innocent children had delivered the goods and were filling their scrawny bellies in Molly's dining room.

Joseph was fascinated by the life of crime into which he now realized he had fallen. He had enthusiastically embraced the possibilities of it, though his intent was not selfish. Ultimately, he was doing this for his family; he thought he could make things better. He just liked the idea that it was he who had made everything possible and not Michael.

As they were eating their custard, Joseph asked McGee what the men were buying with all that money. "Where's it goin'?"

McGee answered, "It's buyin' hope, hope through numbers. Sometimes they're just choosin' numbers, and sometimes they're bettin' on horse or dog races or fistfights—Irishmen gettin' drunk and beatin' each other up. It just depends."

Joseph said, "Is that legal, McGee?" McGee answered, "Not usually."

"This custard is really great, isn't it?" responded Joseph.

In no time, the boys returned down Greene, circled east to Bleeker, and picked up their money from Mr. Bleekerman, who first checked the wagon to see that it was empty. Swiftly they returned to Mulberry where they were surprised that a glowering Tim was waiting. It wasn't a good surprise. It was dark, and Joseph would soon be in the worst trouble of his life for the second night in a row.

The boys had agreed not to lie to Tim. No lie could buy them redemption. Joseph knew sins of omission, so he explained to McGee that he would avoid the lie by not telling all the truth. Before Tim could ask questions, Joseph handed Tim ten dollars. Joseph and McGee thanked Tim, apologized, and told him that they had "borrowed" Lafayette for McGee's mother and, also, so Michael could keep their family together.

Joseph promised that Tim would probably never see him again because he was going to start school tomorrow to become a lawyer. As they helped Tim remove Lafayette's tack, brush him down, undress the wagon tassels and other fittings, and hang them quickly back up on the wall, Joseph begged Tim not to tell Maggie. He promised to go to confession and Communion and said that he would be in such trouble with Michael that nothing Tim could do to him would matter. Michael would kill him.

Tim thought it was a reasonable solution for the Joseph problem, but Tim would never allow Joseph or McGee near the stable again.

The boys told Tim that McGee's mother would recall this glorious night at the theater and the famous Mr. McCready on her deathbed. After all, this had all been for McGee's mother and her lifetime dream of seeing a real Shakespeare play before she died, and "never mind ye" where the money came from or what purpose it had been handed out. It was no problem, if not irrelevant. They would suffer any punishment to fulfill her dying wish.

Joseph had arrived back at Margaret's apartment as the curtain rose on the second act, but Michael had already arrived. Michael, fretting yet another evening, Joseph immediately laid his twenty dollars on the table and calmly announced that "he'd had a very good day at his deliveries."

At Maggie's apartment on Mott, Joseph realized that Bleekerman did not get "Polly" home safely. It was high entertainment when Margaret and the landlord found Kate Mooney pounding at the front door of the locked apartment building in the very early hours of morning, wearing a golden dress hanging off one shoulder, filthy tasseled trim dragging on the ground behind her. When the riot broke out, fish flying and guns blazing, "Miss Polly" had run for her life and then stumbled block after block in the dark through the drizzling night before she arrived home. Thank God she was still alive.

That was the moment Joseph learned that Polly was Jack Mooney's mother. Joseph did not tell Maggie she was also known as Polly. Joseph asked McGee if she knew about the guns. He could only tell Polly that it was all coincidental that he had chosen that evening for her special event.

The riot was reported in the papers, and she did not believe that her son or Joseph could have known what was going to happen. After all, Joseph had only been in town several days, and he was still a child.

CHAPTER 10

LEAVING MANHATTAN ISLAND, LATE JUNE 1849

It was very early on a foggy morning when the Quigley children climbed into a wagon for their ride to the dock. Tim was not the driver, and Lafayette was not on the two-horse team. With their vouchers—provided through charitable efforts of Saint Patrick's and the masons—and Margaret's sizable basket of travel-compatible food, they were headed to Philadelphia.

Michael had promised Da he would find his sister in Missouri. They had been told that on the frontier, the Irish Catholics by the thousands were building churches, schools, and roads, but Michael might have to get to Kansas Town, a large settlement on the confluence of the Missouri and Kansas Rivers, by working down the Ohio or Mississippi Rivers one job at a time.

From the masons and with help from the church, he was able to get vouchers for work on a seminary in Cincinnati. There was a very substantial outbreak of cholera in the city. German and Irish masons rushing to complete the many projects before winter were dying in great numbers. Irish masons willing to take the risk of contracting the disease were being sent there daily. Michael didn't think it would be safe for Charley and Ellen, but he and Joseph had been around cholera on numerous occasions before the Wave and had not succumbed.

Long before James Quigley's family arrived in New York, Margaret Quigley had already been in touch with her older widowed sister, Ellen Moore, who lived in Pittsburgh to discuss how best to help the new arrivals. They had expected ten family members. Ellen had also been in contact with James Quigley who had thought of the possibility of Michael becoming a miner in Pennsylvania if he experienced difficulty with becoming a mason in New York.

Ellen Moore's husband had been an accountant, and they had lived there for twenty years before his death. Ellen had a large, beautiful home, and she had been taking in Irish orphans. She had suggested to Margaret at one point that she might have room for Michael and Joseph temporarily, and maybe Margaret and Ellen for longer, if necessary. They thought Mary and James would need to stay with their parents—or at least their mother—if James went on to Pittsburgh with his older sons to also work in the mines. Together they waltzed through enough plans to provide for every possibility.

However, none of them had anticipated that five members of the family would die and that Michael would have made such a good impression that he would be paid to move on to Cincinnati with Joseph as a potential worker. At that point, it was a joint decision between Michael and the sisters that Charley and Ellen probably should not go with the boys into a cholera epidemic, and Cousin Ellen could easily take them for as long as necessary.

For the first leg of the journey to Philadelphia, Michael had money inside his new waistcoat. The coat had been made by Mr. Elliott for a man who never picked it up. Michael felt proper in his coat with its silk pockets large enough for his money. He planned to use the money sparingly for as far as it would take them. He had no idea how far that would be, but to keep it from being stolen, he would somehow claim to all within hearing distance that he didn't have a "pot to pee in nor a window to throw it out of," and it would be believed. He was one among thousands of "starvin' Irish" who had traveled the route they were on.

The Catholic church knew they were hungry people, so the vouchers included meals on all the trains and at inns where a full meal could be purchased along with a good night's sleep as well.

After boarding their ferry, the family steamed south, quietly past the north end of Staten Island. Michael had situated his little family on the deck so they sat facing the New Jersey coastline, backs away from Staten Island and the cold chill of the Atlantic breeze. Joseph had been exploring the boat since it rattled out of port. Because they were on the west side of Staten Island, the little ones hadn't realized that the island was behind them until they had passed the north end of the island—and Joseph felt everyone needed to know where they were. "The fog has gone, the sun is up, and do ye know what island is on the other side of the boat? I'm afraid we've gone too far to see where Ma, Da, and the babies are, but come and look."

Michael hadn't advised him not to talk about Staten Island, but from this point on, he tried to direct the conversation away from whatever thoughtless or irrelevant idea might pop into Joseph's mind. In order to ameliorate grief, Michael grudgingly ran to the portside of the boat with his family upon Joseph's announcement. Under Joseph's encouragement, they took one last look at the island that had swallowed their parents and three siblings. Sickened from being confronted by the harsh reality of their lives, Michael fell to his knees in grief, and the others followed. He pulled them together in prayer before returning to the New Jersey side of the boat.

As soon as they got out of the wind, Joseph asked, "Now what kind of miserable life are we goin' to have, Michael, leavin' poor, heart-broken Margaret behind us to live in poverty with the hungry nuns? She didn't want us to leave, Michael. I could have made money with you, and we would have done fine. We didn't have to leave her."

Michael's patience finally gave out. "Of course, she didn't want us to leave, Joseph. Don't act the eejit! Ye know very well that yer runnin' wild in the streets and becomin' a gangster in one day made it hard on Margaret at Maggie's. Makin' money by breakin' the law hurts yer whole family as well as yer soul. Yer older sister felt that she wanted to take care of ye three, but ye didn't listen or behave. Ye made it impossible for her and me, so don't be blamin' me, Joseph, for what ye couldn't do to 'help' our family. You're gettin' older, and ye should have enough sense at yer age to know what's right and wrong. Am I goin' to be keepin' ye out of prison for the rest of yer life? Were ye goin' to teach Charley to be a criminal through yer example? If I hadn't gotten ye out of there, that's what would have happened."

"Charley is a good boy. Ellen and Margaret are good girls and smart. They need good lives like ye do, Joseph. The Quigley family will not live off the profits of crime, so don't include any of us in any thoughts that what you did was fine because ye earned twenty dollars. In the process, ye hurt our cousin Margaret's reputation. What do ye think her neighbors think of her now? Do ye know that people were seriously hurt and a lot of damage was done by what ye allowed to happen? If it's a secret now, it won't be for long. Don't tell me yer just a kid and ye didn't know what ye were carryin' in that wagon. That's a lie, and that's what worries me the most, Joseph.

"Besides, Margaret wanted to be a teacher. She'll be able to graduate from a college, become a top-notch teacher, and she'll be safe from the hoodlums of the ghetto like McGee Mooney and his 'employees.'

"Let me tell ye, children, bein' Irish 'tis not an easy road, but ye have no choice but to take it. On it, God asks ye to rise above the problems—not make them worse. We need to dwell on the future, not the past. We need to stop talkin' about the past. It's over now; we loved our family, but they expect us to succeed as they would have. We have to go forward any way we can."

Michael knew the future was becoming a hollow place in the children's minds as they had seldom lived beyond day to day. However, they knew that Michael was asking them to be good people because they were Irish Catholics and, moreover, they were Quigley children. As he spoke, they believed him. He was the oldest, and all but Joseph nodded their resignation and agreement as he presented his case.

"Joseph," continued Michael, "don't ye want the people in America to look up to the Irish for the stone bridges, beautiful buildings, the roads, the canals, and the railroads? Think of the churches the immigrants have already built. The Catholics are already known for their schools and hospitals, politicians, lawyers, and cops. Look at me. I'm going to go build a seminary, a college for priests that will be standin' for decades, maybe a hundred years or more. Is stuffing yer pockets with poor people's puny amounts of cash, runnin' away from coppers, and getting intoxicated how ye want people to remember us, Joseph?

"There will be a day when you'll fulfill God's wish. You will serve the needy and provide comfort for others whose needs we're expected to put before our own. Our people, like our own da, have spun, woven, and tailored, doing simple things to bring warmth and comfort to others. They were to do what was best for God, family, and neighbors. We'll do the same. Do not weep for bein' a poor Catholic or Irish. Feel proud that God has saved ye for a better purpose. We'll find a place for each of us where life is better if we believe in God and we believe that we can."

The children were silent and still angry with Joseph. Michael hugged them all as their boat passed out of Arthur Kill and chugged on to dock at Perth Amboy, New Jersey.

Except for Joseph, their minds had moved on after disembarking. Joseph decided he was right and Michael was misguided. He thought, *Why does Michael think everything I do is wrong or bad?* Joseph couldn't recall all that Michael was tellin' them on the deck, but he knew that everyone was against him, and he felt they had no reason.

Joseph shared his reasoning with Charley. A lot of people gambled. It was their money. They made the choice. Some of those poor people got ahead, especially the guys like Gino or Mr. Bleekerman. Joseph knew he could have done what they did, only better, and never gone to jail. Gino and Bleekerman didn't really hurt anyone. They gave kids jobs that helped feed their families. Joseph couldn't see the harm, regardless of the riot at the opera house.

At their stop in Perth Amboy, the sun was high in the azure sky. Until they boarded for Philadelphia, they found a cozy spot behind a building, in the sun and out of the spring wind to eat a meal of Margaret's fried chicken and the heavenly bread and butter sandwiches donated from Mrs. O'Reilly's bakery downstairs. Michael regretted that he could not save the chicken for a day they might have nothing, but he did save it for a dinner that night, when they would arrive in Philadelphia around eleven o'clock.

Because it was so late and the day, like all of them, was full of emotion, they were exhausted by the time they arrived in Philadelphia. Coming from New York made for a very long day and evening. They found the train station where they would board their Philadelphia-Columbia train at six forty-five, which was only five hours away.

In the small station, there were several empty benches. Because they held tickets for the next train out, they were allowed to wait in the station through the night with several other immigrant travelers with tickets but nowhere else to go. Ellen and Charley were able to stretch out and fall asleep. Parked on their narrow bench, Michael tried to think of good things he could say to a very stormy and sad Joseph who had grown unusually quieter as the day progressed.

Michael, who had lectured them to look forward, not back, wondered if Joseph still had thoughts of Ireland in his mind, as he had heard none of them speak of home for some time. Ireland was a four thousand-mile ocean journey as well as a lifetime away. So much had happened that Michael could barely think of home; absolutely everything had changed.

"Do ye remember home, Joseph?"

With the prompt, Joseph turned his perfect face up to Michael and then glanced off to the side, trying to recall Ireland through his filter of exhaustion and anger. It took some time before the dancing gaslight sparkled in the tears welling up around Joseph's tired and defiant blue eyes. "I do remember, Michael."

"What, then, comes first to mind, Joseph?"

"Ma. I want me ma and da back. I want Margaret, Mary, and James … and tiny Doroty. We didn't even get to know her, Michael."

"I understand, Joseph. I have lost two mothers and all the same family you have lost as well as two older sisters ye never knew. I loved them all the same, but can ye think of somethin' else ye loved about Ireland?"

After a pause Joseph continued, "Men takin' the horses and cattle to the fair in fómhar / autumn. I loved seein' all the different horses and meetin' the men who owned them and the boys who rode them. Da startin' the spring plantin'. Singin' in the church with Ma. I remember when Ellen and Charley were born. Charley was a grand baby, wasn't he, Michael? 'Twas excitin' to have another smilin' boy, wasn't it, Michael?"

"Ellen and Charley are a joy, Joseph, and the thought of leavin' them both behind breaks me heart. Even if cousin Ellen is a fine lady, 'tis not what we are wantin' to do, is it, Joseph? But Cincinnati is not safe for them, Joseph. I told ye there is cholera, and people are dyin' like flies. Ye and I are stronger, but I'm not willin' to take little Quigley children into their deaths. We will go back to Ellen's and get them before we leave Cincinnati. I'll build at the seminary until it's done, and then we'll decide what to do. Maybe you'll go to the seminary. Maybe we'll decide to stay in Cincinnati or come back to live in Philadelphia. I still want to go to Kansas Town. It's a new world there, and there's lots of land and jobs. We can each have a farm of our own, and I think me sister is there."

"I hate it all, Michael. Our family's fallin' apart. I'm not sure we can go on without Charley and Ellen. See them sleepin' now. I'm glad they're able to sleep. I wonder if Margaret is sleepin' and gettin' along with the nuns? I hear they have to pray night and day. I hope she can be happy there and find friends. I don't want her to be alone and gettin' beat every day for nothin'."

Michael said, "Oh, I don't think they punish anyone who doesn't deserve it. Margaret would never do anything wrong. She'd be an inspiration for some young ladies. She'll make a splendid nun and a wonderful teacher."

Not even talking about Ireland was a safe topic, and family talk was too much, so they both stopped speaking. They still needed new and happy memories. Joseph looked at his younger siblings for a while, and then he looked down at the tiled floor of the station. Soon, he shut his eyes, slumped over, and leaned up against Michael to fall into an uneasy sleep. Michael closed his eyes, constantly shifting to hold Joseph upright, and he waited for daylight. He resisted an urge to walk out of the station and stay in Philadelphia. He was tired of a disrupted life, but he had a real job waiting for him in Cincinnati, and there was no time to waste getting there. From Philadelphia to Pittsburgh took only three or four days. In the past, by wagon, it would have taken them more than two or three weeks. Michael couldn't imagine how hard that would have been, and he was looking forward to the train.

They woke up and got in line as more passengers began to gather at the station for their early departure. The stationmaster's loud voice called out destinations and times, waking Charley and Ellen. They were all excited as they stepped aboard their first train. They were all smiles as they sat down on their first comfortable seating since they left Ireland. There was even ample room for Charley and Ellen to stretch out, giggle, and enjoy the soft velvety seats. The train was warm, unlike the deck of the ferry, and other than the clickety-clank of the rails, the ride of eighty-two miles was fairly relaxing and fast. Michael was, for the first time since leaving New York, able to nap easily. The children were tired as well, having traveled a day by ferry and slept a very short evening in the station, but they were peaceful and content for most of the trip.

The train made a number of stops during which the passengers were able to run to the strategically placed outhouses.

Along their way were signs for places with familiar-sounding Irish or Scottish names: McConnelstown, McVey, McAllister, Tyrone, Newry, Armagh, and Donegal. Joseph, and sometimes Ellen, read the signs aloud. Other immigrants were also pleased by the names of familiar places. It seemed to Michael that nearly every Irishman who wanted to stay alive was forced to leave Ireland at some point. Still, they were able to find a new place. It was obvious they wanted to take Ireland with them, so they named their new homes after their Irish homes.

While traveling, the Quigley family ate Margaret's lovely, raisin-laden New York version of oatcakes, and at a brief stop in Coatsville, Michael bought some wild strawberries for the children. They were fascinated and delighted by the large, juicy berries. They had only seen wild, small berries in Ireland. In all, the trip to Columbia only took them several hours, and they enjoyed the entire ride.

Φ

At Columbia, they began their more than 150-mile journey traveling the Main Line Canals of Pennsylvania. Passing from one lift lock to another, their little boat drifted past beautiful farms with tidy railings, well-fed dairy cattle, and scenic woodlands. More amazing to Michael and Joseph was the amount of engineering required to keep the system working. Between the train and the canal system, Joseph found things to bring cheer. There were aqueducts, side-feeding streams, dams, bridges, large sluice doors, stables, and piles of building supplies. Signs of excessive wear and flood damage were here and there, and Joseph incessantly pointed out all of it.

Small teams of workmen could be seen on bridges, dam walls, or roads. Mules or horses of every size, commonly led by Irishmen, pulled their boats and little barges until they reached a point at which a new team would be attached as passengers sat in a lock and the water dropped or rose.

Joseph was fascinated and would occasionally lean his head out the window and yell, "Dia dhuit / Good day, Mick! I like yer mule."

Ellen was so annoyed that she said to Michael, "Please tell the Irish riffraff, scaothaire / know-it-all, to stop yellin' out the window. Ye don't see the upper crust doin' that—even Ma would be ashamed of him."

People turned and looked at Joseph with a variety of expressions. When Michael did not respond to Ellen, she reprimanded Joseph herself. "Stop it, ye gobshite / incessant talker! Callin' people Mick is disrespectful, and yellin' out is rude. You don't see the upper crust yellin' this and that out their cakeholes, do ye now? Yer actin' like Irish riffraff."

Michael finally said, "That's enough, Joseph, Ellen."

When they reached Hollidaysburg, their first destination on the canal, they were able to find a room to spend what was left of the night. The day had been hot, but a cool breeze wafted down from the Allegheny Mountains, causing the fluffy curtains in the comfortable room to gently flap them to sleep. The room was clean and fresh. It was the best place they had ever been. They had abundant clean water, the bed linen smelled fresh, and they were peaceful.

Φ

The next morning, after the proper breakfast provided by the inn, they stepped aboard the most wonderful form of transportation imaginable: the Allegheny Portage Railroad. Built in the gaps across the Allegheny Mountains, a thirty-six-mile system of ten incline planes carried them up. Five tracks went up one side in a sawtooth pattern, and five went down the other side in the same manner. A canalboat, riding on rails, was pulled by a stationary steam engine. It was all part of the Pennsylvania Canal system. The little cars were barges with wheels.

When they reached Johnstown on the west, they continued in fairly narrow canals, via mule power, all the way to Pittsburgh. The system included the first train tunnel ever constructed in America.

Michael and Joseph imagined wagons hauling people over those many mountains. Traveling diagonally across their stony faces would have taken days. The portage cars were pulled straight up the hill. If the portage railroad and canals had not been there, it would have taken the Quigley family several weeks of arduous travel and not several days to get to Pittsburgh.

Michael and Joseph marveled at the engineering and were constantly in awe. Ellen loved it because there was limited talk of mules and horses around the steam engines. Joseph hadn't learned too much about steam engines before he got there. It filled his brain with new ideas, and he had to stop talking to think about them.

This amazing system of trains and canals also allowed goods to be moved to the Ohio River many times cheaper than it had been only two decades before. The combination of trains and canals was called the Main Line, and it provided tremendous fun and adventure for the family. There were places for passengers to eat and sleep in nearly every town. The family's food held out very well, because the Main Line voucher gave them an opportunity to eat things that they had never eaten before.

The Quigleys had learned about social class at birth. Their aristocratic ancestors had already lost their linen industry and their lands through the English-Scottish occupation that started with Queen Elizabeth I. Their schools, church, and language had been stripped mostly away as the rents, tithes, taxes, and famines settled upon them in grinding cycles. Steerage accommodations on the Wave left no doubt for these children as to what their poverty provided or how this generation of Irish were valued by those in power.

The neighborhoods in New York had differences that shouted, "I am this or that," but all immigrants wanted to be American. Within days, those of the Quigley ilk wove themselves into their niche with pride. In short order, the cream began to rise. On the trains, Ellen observed and practiced being a lady. She fell from grace only with the help of Joseph or when she had to set him straight. Charley giggled through every episode and foul word.

The inns and taverns of the Main Line were designed like all other railroads of the day. Service spaces were divided to allow for class distinctions. Upper-class clients were catered to. Highfalutin men wore top hats, and their women wore dresses of silk taffeta, making it easy to distinguish who was who. The rich or famous rode and paid for one car, and the immigrants rode in another. Bars were open to men only. There were separate doors and well- appointed rooms for wealthy men and single women. As they moved from situation to situation, the Quigleys adapted to what was appropriate to their class.

The food, however, was the same for everyone. It reflected a desire to attract those with high taste to the trains, but again, everything was available to those who paid. The Quigley family tried bits of an unending variety of custards. They even ordered brain sauce. This gave them a sense of freedom and allowed them to rub shoulders with those who were called the "idle rich" in Ireland. Here, the well-to-do class was envied, and people believed that hard work and time could bring them into the fold. The train and canals opened the Quigley family up to possibilities. They were going places.

The entire journey was an amazing adventure, though they were not looking forward to the end of the line. It finally came in Pittsburgh, where their canal terminated in the center of the city—and not far from Cousin Ellen's home. They were able to catch a small cart to Ellen's beautiful house and arrived sooner than they had imagined.

CHAPTER 11

PITTSBURGH, PENNSYLVANIA, JULY 1849

Meeting Cousin Ellen was as easy as going home. She was open and lovely, and she greeted them as though she had come from their township. Michael was immediately impressed and relieved to know where Charley and little Ellen would be living. He regretted the plan that the children should not be made to linger over the parting as it would be too difficult for them. For Michael, the time passed too quickly. He could not adjust to the idea, and it tore into his heart the entire day. For the children, he repressed his tears while showing compassion for their situation.

Eight-year-old Charley Quigley was a delight to everyone who met him. He was naturally a relaxed boy, but on this Monday afternoon, he was as distraught as he found himself on Staten Island. Michael and Joseph looked into Charley's tearful eyes and felt just as crushed. Standing on the steps of their elderly cousin's large wrap-around porch of her Pittsburgh home, Michael promised Charley and his nine-year old sister, Ellen, that he and Joseph would come back to get them when they had settled and could afford to take care of them.

Ellen had introduced two orphaned teenage girls who had already been living with her: Nancy and Jane. Joseph, one hand holding Ellen's hand and the other holding Charley's hand said, "I like Nancy and Jane. They're real clean. I don't think ye'll see any bedbugs here. I know those girls can help ye with yer lessons. Ye'll be wearin' real shoes and clean petticoats and goin' to school every day. Livin' with the girls will be like bein' with Ma and our Margaret. Ye'll grow up to be a nurse, maybe. Michael and me? We'll be out diggin' in the rocks every day. Yer better off here; am I right, Michael?"

Michael answered, "Yer right, Joseph, and we'll not be worryin' about you two if ye'll stay put right here with Ellen. She's family, and a fine lady, and that's what's best now. We'll be in Cincinnati as long as necessary, but don't forget, once Joseph and I get settled on our farm in Missouri, we'll come and get ye. Ye can be sure of it. Ye can have yer own chickens on our farm."

Some of Cousin Margaret's very young orphans had been retrieved by family members, but most had not. Few children were ever retrieved. Ellen knew that most immigrants were headed for the frontier or places where they knew they could not feed or care for their little children. Many parents died of cholera before they ever got to any destination. In the second half of the 1800s, thousands of Irish orphans were being scattered across the landscape from New York to California. These children represented the separation that often happened to the immigrant families. It had already happened to Quigleys in the past, including Cousin Ellen. She listened, but she knew the truth.

It was nearing the time when supper was served. Michael knew he and Joseph had to part. Soon, the children would be saying the blessing in the large dining room, and Cousin Ellen would be sitting at the head of the table, instructing the children about the rules at home and the world at large.

Ellen Quigley Moore, forever the teacher, seemed to have found a balance between uncompromising adherence to rules and grandmotherly cheerfulness. She was unbending in her standards because she, herself, had gone through the experience of being absolutely poor and separated from family too young. She had experienced the discipline and education of nuns. She understood the need for parental continuity and the love and dependability of an adult, but most of all, a family. She tried to make the boardinghouse of separate bedrooms and common bathrooms into a family.

She believed in the power of prayer, and she took all her children to church on Sunday. Ellen had eventually garnered the privilege of a reserved pew near the front. Painful consequences were Ellen's job as the adult head of the household, but her charges felt loved, safe, and secure. Anyone who was unkind or "unfit" by Ellen's standards was removed from the household and sent to the convent, a "found-ling" home, or off with a two-parent family. At eighteen, they were normally sent out into the world. She would only work with children who could form a secure "family" while being orphans.

The arrangement for Ellen and Charley, made between cousins, Ellen Quigley Moore and her sister Margaret Quigley in New York, seemed to be remarkably rich in opportunity and very good luck af-ter such grief. It was more than Michael could have ever wished for. He believed his ma and da would be glad it had turned out so well for these two little ones.

Charley still wasn't sold on the idea of being left behind. Sitting outside on the porch steps, he cried and begged, "Please, Michael. I can go with ye. I didn't get killed by the cholera on the boat. Joseph might be a bad boy sometimes, but he's me brother, and we get along fine, Michael. I promise, I can work and help ye both. The frontier doesn't scare me—not after the *Wave* or New York City!" Ellen had already made up her mind that she liked the house, and she didn't think it appealing to sleep under the night skies or work in the rocks with the boys. She recognized the wisdom of staying in Pittsburgh with Ellen, Nancy, and Jane, and she sat beside Charley and said, "What about me, Charley? Ye and I have always been together. Ye can't leave me. Ma wanted us to stay together and take care of each other. She said so. Do ye remember? Ma gave us that responsibility to form a bond that must not be broken. We have to do what Ma says."

As Michael was telling Charley to have a warrior's courage, Cousin Ellen saved them all by calling, "Charley, I have somethin' to show ye, sweet darlin'." She came down the long front steps of the large house in the late sun with a fiddle in her hand. "Look what I have, Charley. It's been hangin' in the parlor waitin' for ye, me love. I knew the minute I saw ye that yer soul can make that instrument sing as though it was Mr. Moore come down from heaven. Oh, how Malachi made our feet dance to the light! Mr. Shaughnessy from the church, a great fiddler in his own right, has been lookin' for someone very special, someone like you, Charley, who could make this fiddle liven our hearts again. Malachi Moore played this long ago, but won't Mr.

130

Shaughnessy be pleased to know that the angels have sent ye to us, Charley?"

With love in her eyes, Ellen stepped down next to little Ellen, in front of Charley, leaned in very close to him so their gentle eyes would meet, and whispered, "Yer ma must have spoken to the angels, Charley. I'd wager she knew how grand a soul ye have and how we were waitin' here for ye, darlin'. I truly believe Ma sent ye to us. Do ye think yer mother had somethin' to do with it?"

Charley looked directly at Cousin Ellen with his large, wet, gray eyes. A bright smile burst from his golden heart at the mention of his ma, and at that moment, Ellen Moore fell head over heels in love with sweet little Charley Quigley who, at that moment, decided that he would, indeed, bring back to life the heartrending Irish tunes for which she yearned. Now, he yearned for them too.

"Ellen, sweet girl, kiss yer brothers quickly so they won't miss the boat and trip immediately with Nancy and Jane inside. Charley, ye do the same. I'll try to play you and Charley me favorite little Irish tune. Before yer supper, we'll have Nancy braid up that thick Quigley hair or it'll be in your milk. Come, me dandy, lovin' Charley. You can sit by yer old Cousin Ellen tonight and for as long as ye wish. We'll move Nancy across the table with yer sister."

Little Ellen was thrilled to be between the big girls.

Turning their backs on Joseph and Michael, the children headed back into the house ahead of Ellen, excited to hear the fiddle. Nancy took Little Ellen's hand and led her across the porch and through the large, chestnut door. Little Ellen was attracted to its welcoming double-arched windows, and she stopped very briefly to rub a frame. Charley cast his last sad look at his big brothers and declared, "Ye shouldn't leave me, Michael. Me da would never leave me."

"That is correct, Charley. If our da and ma were here, they would never leave ye, me darlin' lad." Michael began to sob as he lumbered down the stairs, and Charley turned and walked into the house.

As she grabbed the front door and partly closed it, Ellen Moore turned, looked at Joseph and Michael, and said, "God has placed these sweet ones in me care. I will treat them as their own mother did. Críost bí tú, páistí / Christ be with you, children." She was fighting tears and putting on her good face. She had done this too many times before, and it broke her heart every time. She decided at that moment that these Quigley children would be her last refugees.

Mr. Lacy, waiting on the street, had taken the Quigley boys' single trunk and placed it on his little cart. The boys stepped on, and they were off to the landing. During the ride, sitting back-to-back, facing out from two sides of the cart, they did not speak. Each was silently searching for someone to blame for the situation in which they found themselves at such different ages. They were not fully aware that they were both victims. All Irish potato famine immigrants, regardless of their ilk, were experiencing these same trials of the body, heart, and soul.

After several miles of hearing only the clopping of the horses' hooves on the wet stones and a short ferry ride across the Allegheny River, the Quigley boys stood with their trunk and two carpetbags on the northwestern banks at the confluence of the Monongahela and the Allegheny Rivers that formed the great Ohio.

Φ

With other passengers, they sat on a short drystone wall along the broad, nearly water-level shoreline and waited to board the Amazonia. The steamboat would take them the 475 miles to their Cincinnati destination. Ellen's little meat pies comforted them. On their trip, they would again be fed through their travel vouchers given by the church. Not knowing what or when they would eat again, they keenly savored the chunks of pork and potato of a little stew sealed in the buttery crust—their second pies of the day, thanks to a generous Ellen. She had also stuffed fifteen dollars into one of Michael's empty front pockets. He was as grateful as if it were a thousand dollars. Michael had always been a boy who appreciated even the smallest thought, gesture, or gift. He was a generous spirit with nothing of his own to share but the shirt off his back and his kindness.

Joseph watched the steamboat's loading activity with his usual high level of interest. Leaving Michael to sit on the wall alone, he walked down to the boat to analyze every inch of the packet's side paddles.

Carts and wagons wheeled down the long bank to the large stage plank that was placed on the rocky beach by tall booms on either side of the bow. These planks transferred passengers and cargo. Because they would be headed downstream, the right stage was accommodating the busy loading activity.

Along the river, there appeared to be none of the docks the Quigley boys had become acquainted with on the Atlantic Ocean ports. The Ohio River was wide and swift, and the shorelines washed away in floods, making large wooden docks impractical. It was apparent that they would see none of the charming stone walkways, manor houses, and beautifully crafted stone walls graced by drifting swans that lined Irish streams or even the tidy canals.

These large and fragile American boats were driven right up on the beaches with their flat bottoms. Bulwarks rose only inches above the water line. Joseph could not imagine them in waves of any size at all. He worried that a single load of potatoes and three bags of barley could sink this boat. The crew might have to empty an entire barrel of whiskey to lighten the load and keep the packet afloat! In an adolescent fantasy, he hoped he might be asked to help them.

Along the edge of the water, there were many boats lined up, side by side and end to end. Some small boats were roped to the large boats. Roped to one packet, somewhat smaller than the Amazonia, was a sizable flatboat with oars. With its square ends, the tiny single-man boat looked like a barrel with a seat. That wee boat sat on a small skiff in the square-ended boat.

Joseph couldn't imagine how a boat, on a boat, on a boat would be put to use by the packet. *What fool would cross the Ohio River alone in a barrel that was swirled around by large steam-powered paddles?*

Joseph continued comparing and contrasting the large *Amazonia* to a smaller, wooden-hull stern wheel named *Eclipse* that was drifting down the wide Ohio ahead of the *Amazonia*. It had a small load of boxes and barrels. It seemed that the men were patting one of the barrels with satisfaction and laughing with anticipation. He tried to compare the load of the *Eclipse* to that of the *Amazonia* and determine what would be the difference between these two. *Will they be landin' in different places?*

Michael was looking east, behind his seat, and a distant late-afternoon shower cast a rainbow. The place was so different, but the golden light against the darkening sky reminded him of late-spring and early-summer evenings in Ireland.

Looking into the setting sun, Joseph didn't notice the rainbow. He couldn't wait to get on the *Amazonia* and see what tomorrow might bring. All the little kids, except for Margaret, had been left behind, and he was going with the men to work in Cincinnati. He felt like a man starting a great adventure.

Unlike Joseph, Michael was afraid to think of what the days ahead in Cincinnati might bring. He felt terribly alone and unprepared. The weight of the world was on his shoulders. It seemed to him that young Irishmen were always staring into the face of uncertainty or death. There were days when he wished death would come sooner than later, but he didn't share these dark thoughts with anyone. It was against his faith to think such things, and his optimistic and forward-looking da only spoke of such things on his last day when he was at death's very door.

Michael wondered, again, how he could care for his difficult and unpredictable little brother. He nervously felt for the vouchers in his pocket. The priest who handed them to him reminded him again that people in Cincinnati were dying by the hundreds from cholera, primarily German and Irish immigrants. He questioned whether Joseph should be going. Michael still had time to back out, but the church there needed good stonemasons. He would try to do work that would make his teacher, Mr. Jackson of Tipperary, proud.

Leaving Pittsburgh, Michael and Joseph were all that was left of a good and hopeful family only two months before. Michael wondered, What will become of us now? Before the rainbow had a chance to fade away, he looked back west, attempting to force the memories of the deceased and abandoned from his mind for a moment. Michael briefly shut his eyes and prayed for God to stand firmly beside him, to take away the fear and sickness in his heart, and to have mercy on his soul for leaving Margaret, Charley, and Ellen behind.

CHAPTER 12

DOWN THE OHIO, 1849

Michael's voucher from the priest at Saint Patrick's was good for passage on any packet from Pittsburgh, Pennsylvania, to Cincinnati, Ohio. The 470-mile trip was estimated to take about sixty hours, not including the stops at Marietta and Pomeroy and occasional stops for fuel. Once the Amazonia was underway, Joseph familiarized himself with the layout and operations of the boat. Being so oblivious of others, he was equally unnoticeable as he roamed freely about the boat. He normally didn't feel out of place because he gave himself permission to do as he wished or needed.

On the floor at the foot of the passenger steps, near the bow of the main deck, he passed several stacks of Pittsburgh newspapers. He could read, but he wasn't interested in knowing which steamboats had blown up or sunk. One stack was the Pittsburgh Daily Evening Post. Joseph wondered, Don't they have newspapers in Cincinnati? He sneaked around boxes of tools where only the crew was allowed to go. There were axes, saws, and something else whose label he couldn't make out.

He noticed some bags of grain. It was close to summer, but he didn't know what kind of grain would be in the bags at that time of year. It appeared to have been already milled, and he wondered if it was still good. He looked for moth holes but found none. Toward the stern, several boxes of books appeared to be going to the Common Schools of Cincinnati. In front of the books were the pervasive barrels of whiskey—something he would find on every supply boat on the Ohio, Mississippi, and Missouri Rivers.

The *Amazonia* was one of the boats that regularly made the three-day journey to Cincinnati, where Michael would immediately put his masonry skills to use. He was told that Joseph would pick rocks in a quarry that was not far from the church. Michael would use the cut limestone from the quarry to build a Catholic seminary on a hill. It was being built by two Irish brothers. The brothers were seeking highly skilled Irish stonemasons for the building that was supposed to be completed by 1851. The construction had begun in 1848, but the work had slowed in 1849, due to cholera deaths. Cholera was also being spread by passengers from the very boats on which the Quigley boys were riding. The lucky boys had already been spared from the disease in Ireland, on the Wave, and on Staten Island, but for many people around them, the disease remained their constant threat, and many had succumbed.

Cincinnati was booming with Irish and German Catholic immigrants. Unfortunately, the Protestant German majority was still celebrating the Reformation. Cincinnati Protestants did not see the Irish Catholic minority as democratic, or human, and there was considerable foment at the rapid increase in their population. The established residents were afraid the Catholics would be more loyal to the European pope than to America and would upset the fragile democracy.

Michael had been told to mind his manners around the dominant German Protestants if he wanted to keep his job. They did not want dissent. He was to silently repeat, "God forgive them as they know not what they do," but he was not to argue when he was outnumbered—and in Cincinnati, he was.

The new seminary was designed to improve the shortage of priests. The church was trying to ensure that the Irish would not convert due to lack of access to the sacraments, their isolation from other Catholic settlements, and intimidation. On the frontier, there were few places for the thousands of Catholics to attend Mass, so many were not practicing their faith.

The archbishop was also working at Catholic diplomacy to provide better acceptance of the growing Catholic population by the Protestant majority that was often openly hostile to both the Catholics and the running slaves on the Underground Railroad. Catholics were flooding down the Ohio, and slaves were fleeing up it. They often converged in Cincinnati. Churches were picking up the human "refuse" from both directions. Of course, Catholics were interested in caring for the sick, and the cholera academic was keeping them busy. Helping others was what Catholics did best, so they usually ran the first hospital in every settlement. Being the first to provide medicine and nursing was helpful to their religious- tolerance education campaign.

To entice more skilled Irish workers, Michael had been provided with boardinghouse lodging with the other skilled masons. He would have a bed and food. After arriving in Cincinnati, Michael was shocked to learn that Joseph, as a rock picker, would be living and working with a group of variously skilled laborers maybe forty miles northeast of the site of the seminary. Only four days after tearfully leaving their little siblings on Ellen's doorstep, Joseph and Michael were, themselves, separated.

The supervisor of the men was not happy to find Joseph among his new workers as they walked over the ridge of the steep shoreline to have their names called for their wagon ride. Nevertheless, Joseph was soon hauled away in a large wagon. It was at the approach of dark, and their shared trunk was with Michael, leaving almost nothing for Joseph to take with him for comfort. Michael took off his coat and threw it to him as Joseph, empty-handed, pulled away in the workmen's wagon. Michael did not see tears in Joseph's eyes, but he had them in his own, and he hoped that Joseph was finding comfort in prayer. It was all he had.

In discussions about his job, Michael had not revealed Joseph's age. When he committed to the job opportunity and threw his little brother's name into the agreement, he wasn't aware that Joseph would be required to live with rough, single, older men in a canvas shelter so far away. There would be several other young men with him, but none nearly as young as Joseph. Michael knew it meant trouble for his little brother. He knew that Joseph might suffer beyond his ability to cope or defend himself from abuse. His mind ran wild with disagreeable thoughts, and he felt as though he had betrayed and abandoned Joseph.

That evening, on his knees, Michael spoke with his father, "Da in heaven, I am truly sorry for what is happening. You trusted me, and now our Joseph has been abandoned as well. Christ, forgive me. I promise that I will do all that is within me power to reunite your family, Da. Mea culpa, mea culpa, mea maxima culpa." He pressed his fist over his heart and beat his chest three times.

Φ

The next morning was gray and cold, but Joseph pitched into his job with a man's enthusiasm. His assignment was to pick up the scraplings from the mason's chiseling. Once the rock was blasted or cut loose from the hillside, masons would chisel out appropriate-sized large blocks for stacking in buildings or walls. It was extremely heavy and precise work.

As he picked up his chinkers, Joseph marveled at the uniformity in the skilled men's workmanship. *How could all those different men carve limestone blocks, all the same size, from a mountain?* He had seen it in their Irish village, but now he noticed because he might have to learn the craft himself. His brother had already mastered many skills and was back in the city refining those very stones into a building that might last for centuries. Joseph felt proud that he had a brother who had that strength and ability. People could walk past a post office, a courthouse, or a church and know that the beauty of the building depended on men like his brother. He touched as many of the finished stones as possible, thinking Michael might pick up that stone, sense his touch, and know he was still alive.

Joseph spent his first two days exhausted. He tossed his rubble into various baskets that were then hauled by the older boys or young men into boxes, loaded onto wagons, and then hauled to the nearby Little Miami River. Joseph's rubble was used as backfill or road surface or crushed into mortar products. Because of his size and age, the work was backbreaking—and boring. The stones were rough, and they hurt his hands. He grew tired of lifting and stooping, and he wanted to drive the wagon instead. He had set about a plan to place himself into a position of driving a mule team. Unfortunately, driving the wagon meant unloading it as well, and he eventually realized that he just couldn't do it. He was a baby among these men. He wasn't in New York. His plan to commandeer a wagon was a fantasy that would have to wait until he was either a man or in a better place.

Joseph found that living in an oiled canvas bunkhouse in the wilderness was dirty, hot, and cold. The cool air dropped down on him in the evening, flattened him, and exacerbated his growing sadness and physical exhaustion. Pulling Michael's coat around his shoulders, he tried to dream every night of Ma holding him in her feather ticking in front of the fire of their cottage. He wanted to smell her and hear her sweet singing. He wanted to hug Charley and cuddle baby James or Mary. Instead, he smelled and heard dirty, drunk men snoring, complaining, or talking about things he didn't want or need to hear. Some days, their soup reminded him of the gruel used to starve the Irish in the workhouses or the mush of Staten Island. Only on days when there were meals of pork, venison, or potatoes in milk and butter did he have a sense of well-being.

He felt awful when the men teased him. He felt even worse when the older boys teased him. After about a week, he was given food infested with ants. One of the ailing men, who had gone out to relieve himself, refused to eat his food after he had accidentally set his tin plate among ants on the edge of camp. A German man suggested that "das baby" didn't need much food because he was a picker. An unkind older German boy suggested that because Joseph was one of the "starvin' Irish" who were used to "eatin' dirt," Joseph wouldn't mind a few tasty ants. The boy reached over and exchanged Joseph's plate with the one infested with ants. Then a man handed Joseph a cup of whiskey to help it go down. Everyone laughed.

Quietly, Joseph imagined what his ma or Michael would have done in this situation. His ma could have laid them all on their respective arses with her words. Even his sister Ellen could put them in their places. Michael wasn't a fighter, but he wouldn't let this happen to Joseph. The men would respect Michael; he had a strong mason's hands, a country gentleman's manners, and greater skill than even the bosses here. If Michael or their da were here, the men would not treat a Quigley this way. A Quigley was a man to be respected.

Joseph was a lonely child in the quarry who had to "mind his manners" until he could find Michael. He vowed that he would get a gun and shoot the older boy at his first opportunity. Nobody would weep for him; he was rotten.

The boss would normally step in to defend Joseph if he was in the mess tent or within hearing distance, but he was out of the camp, getting drunk with friends. Joseph hated them all. He needed to cry, and he wanted Michael, but neither was possible. He held in the anger and resentment as well as the physical pain. He learned to cry in silence. He cried with his stomach.

The next night, when he went to his bunk to retire, he discovered that one of his only comforts, his straw-filled batting, was missing. He ate his supper, and leaving Michael's coat behind, he quietly walked away from the mess tent. The men had shared the whiskey that was on the "menu" nightly. Cold, tired, somewhat drunk, and still hungry, Joseph retrieved his coat and then walked up into the woods and hid. He watched one of the boys look for and call him in the growing darkness, but he was well hidden and could see the Little Miami River from his vantage point on the hillside. The boy lost interest, and the men suggested that "das baby" Joseph would come back as he had no way out.

Joseph planned that he would walk south down the wagon road under the summer moonlight and follow the river to see where it led. He didn't care if Michael would be angry because he walked away from his job. He would go find Michael regardless. The thought had entered his mind that maybe Michael knew all along that Joseph was going to be sent to the quarry in the mountains—but didn't want him to know. If Joseph was angry enough, he could do that, but Michael wouldn't do that. Michael told people the truth. *Why would Michael treat me differently?*

If Michael didn't want him, maybe he could sleep someplace in the streets of Cincinnati as the Irish children did in New York. He would feel more at home with the boys who played craps than these filthy quarrymen. He would certainly have more opportunities on the streets of Cincinnati than in the Ohio woods. Since the food and "housing" were most of his income, he had no money in his pocket.

He had made more money in one wild night in Manhattan than he could earn there in half a year.

If he couldn't find Michael, he would go back north to Pittsburgh and stay with Charley and Ellen. He'd go to school and become a lawyer like Mr. Walsh, Ellen's first husband, or an accountant like her second husband, Malachi Moore. He was smart enough for either job, and he could have a horse or two of his own. He visualized himself a gentleman and relished the image.

After sleeping on a sandbar all night, Joseph decided to lie on his back in the river, under the hot morning sun, and let the cold river water carry him feetfirst downstream. It was a little too cold, even with Michael's coat on, so he would stand up with his back to the sun, and when he was sufficiently brave enough, he would flop back into the water. When he could bear it, he let the current move him quickly. At one point, he dashed out and hid behind some bushes as a wagon of stones was rumbling down the river road. As an Irish immigrant child alone, he worried what could happen to him.

Eventually, he came to a wide, shallow confluence of a fairly large creek. A boy on a small flatboat with some baskets tied together was dragging his little boat out into the main stream. Seeing that Joseph was in great need, he asked, "Hey, are you all right? Do you want to come along?" The boy waited until Joseph caught up to him. "My name is Bruno."

Using his New York sensibilities, Joseph did not tell him his name. Instead, he said, "What ye got there, Bruno?"

"My mother makes cakes and knits wool hats for the steamboat passengers downstream."

"Are we close to the Ohio River?" Joseph asked.

"We sure are. The Little Miami flows right into it. It's going to start getting bigger, so I need my boat. From the mouth, it's only about four miles to Cincinnati."

"What are you doing up here? Where did you come from?" Bruno continued.

Joseph told Bruno his story from Pittsburgh and said he was going to find his brother in Cincinnati if he could.

Bruno said, "Sometimes I float even farther down than Cincinnati—sometimes as far as Petersburg, Kentucky, or Aurora, Indiana. Once I float down and sell my stuff, I like to pick up vegetables, apples, or something to sell back up the river on my way home. Sometimes I sell one item at a time—or the whole load to a captain."

Although that sounded like a possibility to get to Michael and earn a little money, Joseph was cheered up when he discovered where he was. Michael might be only five miles downriver.

Joseph was grateful for an agreeable companion, and he was hungry. Once he began to dry out and warm up, the negotiations began. He said, "If ye let me eat one of the cakes to see if 'tis all right, I'll gladly help ye sell them."

The charming Joseph prevailed. Bruno agreed to give Joseph one to eat for every ten he sold. Once they reached the Ohio, they sold their way down the Ohio River and then into Cincinnati for the rest of the day. Joseph caught on to the poling and maneuvering of the boat like a natural. They would drift alongside another flatboat to sell. When they got to Cincinnati, Bruno talked with the captain of a large packet while Joseph stood at the end of the plank of disembarking passengers.

Including the eaten sample, Joseph ended up with two more cakes by the end of their afternoon adventure. Joseph couldn't cut a deal with the hats, but they weren't selling anyway.

Bruno told Joseph that a good salesman only negotiates prices down on things that might perish. The hats were too valuable. He always had to get rid of the cakes or spring and summer produce as quickly as possible. As food began to spoil, he could always make a deal. The hats and mittens, however, didn't spoil and if they fell in the river, they floated when they first hit the water. He could capture most of them and wring them out—none the worse for wear.

CHAPTER 13

CINCINNATI, 1849–1852

Very late that day, when Bruno deposited Joseph on the main beach of Cincinnati, Joseph hadn't recalled how steep and high it was since landing there with Michael. He could climb either a direct trail or walk up a much longer, diagonally cut road for teams, across the broad face of the waterfront. He felt as though he was walking as far back up in elevation as he had just floated down. He was anxious to see Michael, so he started the steep hike directly up the beach hill to the top of the cliff.

Obscured from view was the switchback of the less inclined road that met him at the spot where the trail ended at the top. There was a large, graveled pullout area where wagons could linger momentarily to off-load things they had carted up the hill.

An older man was driving a tinker's caravan. He had been going through a basket of carrots and dividing them into bundles. His beautiful large stallion was polishing off a carrot as Joseph arrived.

The horse looked up at Joseph, nickered, and shook his halter in greeting.

"Well, hello to you too, Mr. …?"

The man answered, "Gus … short for Gustav."

"Gustav doesn't seem friendly enough to me," Joseph said.

"I can understand that you feel that way. You seem like a friendly lad. Do you have a horse?"

"No, I don't have a horse, but I will someday. Right now, I'm a poor, starvin' Irishman lookin' for me brother."

The man asked, "Where did ye come from? I didn't see any small boats landin'. I just got a shipment of things off that steamer that's gettin' ready to leave. I delivered some clean laundry for the captain and picked up some cucumbers and carrots from upriver. I have some ladies getting ready to make pickles, but they need the cucumbers first. What's your name, lad?"

"Joseph. Joseph Quigley," he answered as he extended his hand for a handshake. "I love yer stallion. I just got off a flatboat where I was helping a friend sell hats and mittens."

"In summer? That seems unusual. I'm Laurence Kelly, at your service," said the driver. "Where is your brother?"

"I don't know. He's a stonemason building a seminary somewhere in town," he answered as he held the bridle and patted the neck, shoulder, and breast of the stallion. He breathed a little air into Gus's muzzle and whispered, "Yer beautiful, Gus."

Laurence pointed to another hill across a valley and said, "The seminary is that way, on that ridge. I follow this road, drop down in that hollow, and drive up the ravine. My farm is much farther out of town, but I'm leaving my wagon at the livery stable and taking Gus home. My afternoon deliveries are done, except for the cucumbers, but I'll start from the stable tomorrow. Since I'm going out past the seminary, would you like me to drop you off?"

"It's an answer to me prayers, Mr. Kelly. I was afraid I'd be walking all over town lookin' for him. He lives in a house, and I'd like to have a decent roof over me head and a dinner in me belly. I've been eatin' gruel in a quarry, so I want to catch him before he stops workin' and goes to his house. I have no idea where his house is."

Joseph stepped up and onto the wagon seat and immediately learned that Gus was a dapple-gray Norman-Percheron. As they rode along, Joseph explained how he and Michael happened to get to Cincinnati. The "street" rules here were much different from the rules in New York. Joseph felt as though he could tell Laurence everything—maybe as though he were a grandfather. After all the talking, they arrived in no time at the road that led to the seminary.

Joseph stepped off, thanked Laurence profusely, and said he'd like to drive Gus someday. He then headed along the road up the hill. The seminary grew in God's glory toward the sky as he got closer, having been obscured by trees, houses, and shrubs below the ridgeline. It was truly more than Joseph could have imagined. Massive in appearance, it looked as though it were destined to become a Greek treasure. He was awestruck with amazement and pride that his brother was fitting the large granite stones into this monumental and beautiful work of art. He did not see men working, but he heard the familiar clunking of stone falling when broken and the metallic pitch of stone tools being struck. It came from behind the entrance.

The entrance had many wide steps from the sides that went straight up to the wide floor leading to a cathedral-sized opening that would one day be graced with giant doors. There were massive white columns across the front and along a portico that ran the entire width of the building. Joseph walked around the far end of the long structure, and the men were working on a snecked-stone, creamy white and light brown wall that extended perpendicular to and directly behind what was obviously the grand entrance of a chapel.

As he drew closer, he saw Michael intently chiseling away at a stone Joseph might have already seen at the quarry.

Joseph shouted, "There's me lovin' brother Michael! Michael! I'm here, Michael!" He ran to him.

Michael turned, dropped his mallet, and extended his arms. "Thank you, heavenly Father. Me little brother is alive!" They both wept in joy, and Michael said, "I missed ye so much, deartháir / brother. I wasn't sure I could go on without ye."

After a prolonged hug and a kiss on Michael's cheek, Joseph extended a hand. In it, he held a small cake made with dried apple and cherries, a drop of molasses, and sprinkled with sugar. "This is what I earned today on the river. I've had mine already."

"What? On the river, Joseph? I sent ye into a quarry. What in God's name happened? Did yer boss tell ye about the letter Father Kauffman sent to the quarry to retrieve ye?"

"No, Michael, there was no letter. I heard nothin'. Perhaps I left before it arrived. It doesn't matter. I'm here now, Michael, and I've met a dear friend, Laurence Kelly. He dropped me off down the road from his tinker's wagon."

Michael exclaimed, "Yes! I've seen it. It is painted in bright blues, yellows, and reds of a gypsy wagon, and it has a round cover and high sides. I have seen him at Mass with his wife."

"That's Mr. Kelly," Joseph said as he sat in the dirt next to a pile of granite blocks and explained the quarry and how he was fed and treated and how they gave him whiskey every day.

Michael was appalled, but he was very proud that Joseph had the courage and intelligence to leave. "We'll talk to Father Kauffman. We'll try not to criticize the men too much, but I will tell him that we can't have ye drinkin' whiskey every day, mistreated and taken advantage of. I'll tell him I want ye in school. Maybe he can help me out. He graduated from the pope's college in Rome, so I'm sure he'll understand that a smart and active lad belongs in school." Michael took a bite of his cake. "This is quite delicious."

"I remember when ye bought us strawberries when we were goin' to Pittsburgh. I wanted to bring ye somethin' good."

Michael promised Joseph he would never let him go again. Michael ate his cake, collected his tools, and introduced Joseph to the other men, and then they hopped aboard a shuttle wagon that dropped the men off at their boardinghouses around the neighborhood. Some men walked.

Michael worked out a new housing arrangement with a cousin of the parish housekeeper, and at the end of the summer, Joseph enrolled in a City of Cincinnati school with about two hundred girls and fewer than fifty boys. Not wanting to return to the quarry, Joseph sang in the church choir to "stay out of trouble." He and Michael got through the winter of 1849 and into the spring of 1850 without hunger, disease, or familial loss.

Two of Joseph's friends gave Michael cause for concern, including Thomas, who had been living with family friends and had run away. The "errand boy" was living on his own on the river, and he was a serious drinker at the age of fourteen. However, Michael believed that the overwhelming number of girls would help Joseph behave. They would provide the moral equivalent of Ellen and Margaret, whom he missed, thought of, and prayed for daily.

Joseph was taken with the idea of going into business with Bruno and his drunken friend Thomas, but Michael refused. Thomas always had money—but no solid food, no coat, and no shoes that fit. He was not taken care of, and he was not able to care for himself.

In the summer of 1851, Joseph revealed his adolescent growing pains. Once school was out for the summer, Joseph assisted Laurence Kelly with his deliveries. From the riverboats to the little communities on the edge of Cincinnati, they delivered people's parcels or fresh produce he picked up along the way to or from a boat. He also loaded eggs on his wagon if he had room.

When the river was too low for boats to arrive, when the boats failed to arrive due to accidents, or when produce was sparse, Laurence sold soap, tea, scrub brushes, and kitchen items along with his deliveries. For tips, he would also pick up and drop off things for regulars around town. For a very small charge, he even returned books to the library or occasionally took stranded children home from school. He liked to travel around. He said his grandfather had been a tinker.

Mr. Kelly loved to sing, as did Joseph, and by the end of the first summer, they became known as having a "wagonload of songs." Laurence knew every Irish person in town and every Celtic tune from his childhood and the New York City pubs. Joseph learned them quickly and added his own harmonies—something that tickled the girls from school.

There were days when Laurence let Joseph take Gus's reins so he could catch short naps. This happened with greater frequency after they had delivered all their goods and were on their way back to the stable. Normally, Laurence did the driving and Joseph did the running up to the porches, to the back doors of shops, or out to the barns. It was hard work with so many hills. Laurence only took Gus home to his farm Friday nights. It was quite a way out. He would take him back to town early Tuesday morning.

On very hot or long days, Laurence dropped Joseph off closer to his house. Laurence was getting more tired with age, and sometimes Joseph rode the extra miles and helped old Laurence feed, brush, and bed down Gus. He felt affection and loyalty for the older man, and he felt it was to his advantage to build greater trust by helping him. Always with a motive, the trust was designed to provide Joseph with more time with Gertie and the girls from school.

Joseph had grown fond of Mr. Kelly's old mare, Gertie. She was a mix of the draft and common American riding horse, and she had birthed quite a few colts that Gus had fathered and Mr. Kelly had sold. As they rode throughout Cincinnati, Laurence proudly pointed to the progeny of Gertie and Gus and called many by name. It seemed that every large, beautiful dapple in town was born in Mr. Kelly's barn or pasture on the north side of town.

No mare ever had a sweeter disposition than Gertie, but she wasn't being ridden much, and Laurence thought that letting Joseph ride her in his "off" time was good for both of them. It became Joseph's joy to "help" Laurence keep Gertie fit and, consequently, find more opportunities to enjoy his feminine schoolmates. He could ride Gertie from the barn to his house and stop here and there on the way. Gertie found fresh grass and pretty girls everywhere they stopped. Joseph was learning by leaps and bounds about girls in general.

The young ladies generally agreed that Joseph was beautiful to look at—and his singing voice was thrilling. He had developed the art of "chumming" with several at once. As it grew later in the afternoon and each girl had to scramble home, there was always that one girl who lagged behind to flirt. These young ladies fed both Joseph and Gertie sweet treats like jelly beans, a new penny candy from the general store, or carrots from their gardens.

The sweetest of all treats was that delicious feeling that Joseph had when he looked into the liquid of a girl's eyes, glanced at a sweet kiss of summer sun on her freckled face, or realized she yearned to touch him. He loved it when a girl held on tight as he galloped Gertie across her field and down the road toward town. He would steal his kiss as he helped a girl slide off Gertie. Sometimes he would get off first, and then he would reach up and help her off, his hands landing about her waist. Riding bareback made close contact an easier trick.

The Irish girls were bold enough not to worry about sidesaddle etiquette, as the European girls from the Continent did. Girls named Murphy, O'Dea, Brown, or Allen straddled Gertie's wide girth, holding tight to Joseph as they showed him secret places along streams and amid gardens and parklands. In those private places, Joseph could explore his emerging interest in their feminine attributes, while maintaining his Old Country, Catholic morals. He mostly turned over rocks, poked at bugs in the dirt, or picked the girls bouquets of dandelions and daisies. They would stand by streams and skip rocks.

A particular Saturday proved to be a glorious late summer day. A small storm had changed the atmosphere, and the nights were cooler. The grass and shrubs looked ragged and brown, and the delicious smell in the air promised the arrival of autumn. The day was lazy. Sarah had lain down in the grass and asked Joseph to place his head on her belly. Sarah then told funny jokes and his head bounced up and down as they both giggled.

Along the broad creek, after "fishing," Joseph and Sarah discovered a sandy beach quite a way below a mill where Joseph again felt inspired to finally display his great performance, the same one he had shared with a snobby girl he called Princess Anna Svoboda. It had failed, but it was Anna's failure and loss, not Joseph's.

Anna granted Joseph "right of presence" with her. She would tease Joseph, asking if he could meet her this day or that—or this place or that. When he did, she treated him like a rotten potato. She wanted him to be jealous of her, but he turned the tables on her, forcing her to be jealous of Sarah Conroy.

When Princess Anna asked Joseph to meet her on Saturday, he said, "Sarah and I have something really special planned for Saturday. Besides, Princess Anna, Sarah Conroy—whose ginger locks dance in the sun, who smells like a moonlit rose, and has the smile of an angel—would insult neither an outstandin' Irish boy nor his fine and deservin' mare."

So, with special relish, he parked the fragrant and sparkling Sarah Conroy on the bank with their unused, whittled willow fishing poles and thought, *Today will be different—on this perfect summer Saturday with the lovely Miss Sarah Conroy.*

At one end of their little beach, he stood up on Gertie and commanded her to gallop to the other end. Standing sideways, facing out toward Sarah with one arm extended in the air and holding a fishing pole sword, the large mare took off. As Gertie had not received a command for a turnaround she normally received in the pasture, her long legs quickly ran out of sand. At the edge of the shoreline, she stopped abruptly, leaned her head down, and deposited Joseph headfirst on large polished river rocks and spent shrubs.

He was immediately rendered unconscious.

Gertie snorted in his face and backed off slightly, still standing over his body and looking for him to rise. He did not.

Φ

Sarah Conroy thought he was dead—or playing a trick. Throwing down the poles, she charged toward Joseph's limp body and screamed, "Stop it, Joe Quigley. Stop it right now. No more dirty Irish tricks! You're so full of yerself, Joseph Quigley."

Insults were of no use. Joseph was out, and she panicked. She tried to lift him, but being a slight fourteen-year-old girl, she was ineffective. She tried dragging his limp body to a different spot and rolling him, but nothing worked. Gertie just stood there protectively and pawed the earth. Sarah had to get help. Climbing aboard the mare she yelled, "Jaisus, Mary, and Joseph, Joe Quigley, please don't die— or I'll never forgive ye! I'm goin' to find Laurence or Michael. We'll bring Gus and the wagon up to get ye. God, I love ye, Joe! Christ be with ye. I'm goin' now. Do not die for me. 'Tis not winsome."

She turned Gertie about, kicked her flank, shook the reins, and off they quickly moved, returning from where they had come in the morning. Very quickly, however, Sarah realized that she didn't know where she was going. Although she knew Michael was a mason working on the seminary and she had known who Laurence was since she had arrived in Cincinnati, she had no idea where either lived. She pulled back Gertie's reins. Sarah's home was just north of the seminary, but it didn't make sense to take Gertie all the way there. For a moment, she couldn't decide what was best. The important divide in the trail was coming up soon, and she gave the solution up to Gertie.

Quickly, Sarah dropped the reins across Gertie's withers. Confused for a moment, Gertie stopped ten yards before the divide. She stood and bobbed her head up and down a few times, whinnied, pawed the ground a little, and turned her head to the left to peek at Sarah.

Sarah said, "Go home, Gertie. Either go home—or go find Michael. Do it now, Gertie, because my precious, beautiful Joe Quigley is dyin' in the rocks, and we can't have it. He was a boy showing off, and he got what was comin', but he does not deserve to die, Gertie. We have to get Laurence and his wagon." Gertie froze, and Sarah Conroy screamed, "Go find Gus, Gertie!"

At the sound of Gus's name, Gertie's ears perked, and she tentatively walked forward.

Of course, Sarah thought. *Gertie wants to go home and eat with Gus. Every fat mare wants to go home and eat.* Sarah made encouraging forward thrusts with her hips and said, "Go home to Gus and get yer dinner, Gertie!"

Gertie gingerly passed the turnoff that would have led to Sarah's house. However, once she had passed the turnoff and Sarah had not stopped her, she began to gain steam. In no time, she was rampaging through the bushes, taking a shortcut over downed trees, and stumbling over roots and rocks. For an old mare, she was moving at a terrifying pace.

Frightened, Sarah had bent down forward, flat on Gertie so a tree limb would not knock her to the ground. She had thrown her left arm about Gertie's large neck, and with her right hand, she held tight to a fistful of hair on the crest of her black mane. She closed her eyes, waited for whatever end was to come, and prayed to God to keep her on this powerful old girl.

Sarah eventually sensed they were out of danger and in the open. They had survived the woods and began crossing a field. Sarah could see crop stubble under Gertie's plowing hooves. She looked up and noticed they were headed directly toward a small barn across the field.

On the other side of a railing fence, Gus was peering up from a small pasture. He thundered the short distance to the railing, and Gertie stopped abruptly and muzzled Gus over the rails.

Knowing she would go nowhere, Sarah dropped Gertie's reins and ran the short distance to the cottage. Sarah was relieved that Laurence and Briona were at home. Because it was early afternoon and Michael was still working at the seminary, he suggested that they head directly out to the stream with Gus and the wagon.

Briona Kelly cooled down Gertie, and Laurence hitched Gus to the wagon. Gertie had a good long drink, a sizable portion of grain, and leaned up against the side of her stall to take a much- deserved nap.

The search for Joseph took them up the road along the creek. About half a mile south of the sandy beach, a weary and wobbly Joseph was dragging himself down the road in their direction.

Gus was a joyful sight for Joseph—who was considerably confused about what had happened. He hadn't remembered the entire fiasco and had no idea why Sarah would be with Laurence and traveling up the rough creek road.

As he greeted them, he asked, "I found meself battered and sittin' along the stream, but why are the both of ye here? Why am I here? Me head hurts. Have I died?"

"Ye should have, Joseph," replied Sarah. "Please don't be actin' the maggot. 'Tis not the time for yer teasin'. Are ye well, Joseph?"

"I am not well. Me shoulder hurts, and me head is thumpin'." Not understanding the nature of being "knocked out," neither adolescent was able to grasp the realities of what had happened. Sarah told Joseph about his "trick" on Gertie, and he insisted that he had done no such thing. He insisted that had done the trick with Anna and had sent her walkin' home by herself because she insulted him. But was that today? Did I fall off Gertie while taking her home?

"'Tis not true, Joe Quigley. It was I, not Anna, who sat in the sand and saw Gertie dump ye over her head."

The two continued to fuss over who was lying when Laurence suggested to Joseph it would be best if he sat next to him and drop the subject. It would give his head a little time to clear up. He told Joseph and Sarah that his brains had been rattled, and it might take a day or two for him to remember. "Please stop talkin', Sarah. Joseph's brain needs a rest—and so do I."

She sat in the back and bounced her way home without any trout and no more discussion. After stepping out, she said, "Yer trick is wonderful, Joseph, but ye shouldn't have done it for Anna! She always pokes fun in yer direction ye know? She doesn't like us because we're Irish. Ye shouldn't associate with the likes of them who hates the Irish! There's no respect in it."

Joseph decided from that moment that Sarah Conroy was correct. He had no time for any but sweet, smart Catholic girls from Ireland. Later, Michael agreed and reminded him, "Ge milis a'mhil, cò dh'imlicheadh o bhòrr dri / Honey might be sweet, but nobody licks it off a briar!"

CHAPTER 14

INTO MISSOURI, 1852

As the completion of the seminary approached, Michael's tolerance of Cincinnati hospitality grew less—and so did the demand for his special skills on the main buildings. He was forced to supplement his seminary work with jobs around the city. He repaired streets, built small dry stack walls, and did everything he could. Some jobs paid very well, so he and Joseph were able to save considerable money toward their next trip downriver. However, Michael felt that he would never go any further in life if he didn't leave Cincinnati. Land was more available on the edge of the frontier, and he wanted to find his older sister Margaret.

One day, as Michael was cooking yet another German sausage, sauerkraut, and potatoes, Joseph announced, "Michael, don't ye think it's time we bought a good flatboat and went into business on the river?"

Michael stabbed a sausage and turned it over. The escaping juices splattered up from the hot grease, and a bubble landed onto Michael's cheek. He splashed cold water on the burn and said, "I thought we had discussed that no time is a good time for buyin' a boat! I'd rather we run off to the circus. Ye must be kiddn' me, Joseph. Buy a boat? We won't be sinkin' our hard-earned money into a boat."

"C'mon, Michael, hear me out. Bruno offered a great deal on a boat he's tryin' to sell. He's done well and is buyin' a new boat."

"And how would ye know a 'good deal' on an old river boat? How long has Bruno been tryin' to sell his broken boat? How many have already turned him down? Where is the goodness in Bruno who is willing to sell a broken boat to a starvin' Irish boy who knows nothin' about the river trade? Did ye notice it is winter? Nobody's floating on the river in winter. They're choppin' themselves out of the ice. They're hopin' to bring somethin' in on their losses from the past six months."

"There can be no better time to buy, Michael. We can get it for ten dollars. It would cost more in just a month or so. 'Tis a large flatboat missin' only a few boards. We can travel as far as Paducah, Kentucky, tradin' things along the way. We can make a store on the boat and sell gloves, hats, coats—clothes Bruno's mother can supply us at a grand price."

"Really, Joseph? Ye think the spring is a great time to be floating into the tropics of the south and sellin' wool hats, coats, and mittens? Are ye not thinkin', Joseph?" Michael turned his golden-browned slices of potato over and dumped in another tablespoon of bacon grease. "Joseph, please set the table and make the tea." He handed Joseph the steaming tea pot and continued, "Joseph, I want to go find me sister Margaret. Maybe she knows where our sister Ann is. I'm a stonemason who wants to earn money enough to marry, own land, and be a farmer in the rich soils of Missouri or Kansas. That's who our people are. I will not drown or blow up meself and me only other family member in the Ohio River. Are ye anxious to meet yer eternal Father, Joseph? Ye can do that on a horse! Do you want to catch on fire or be encased in ice? What if yer rotten flatboat sinks and Bruno's mittens drown? Ye'll have to repay him for nothin' with nothin' or outrun all the Germans of Cincinnati who will be on yer trail. How clever is that for an Irish lad?"

"That won't happen, Michael. I'm quittin' school and goin' out with Bruno, and I'll learn how to avoid river accidents. A flatboat does not explode. Ye know nothin' about the business, Michael. I do. I learned from me deliveries and from Bruno."

"Bruno? Ye ran away from yer job, which was fine, and sold little cakes one afternoon with the first river rat ye met. The rivers are only good for delivering coal, steel, wood, or food on a grand scale ... and travelin' in the spring months to spread cholera among immigrants! Do you want to lose your only source of income on a sandbar and then fight with drunks to save yer britches? Ye'll not be quittin' school to become a drunken ignoramus river rat! If I had me wits about me, ye'd go to the seminary and become a drunken priest instead! Ma and Da would have been proud to have another Quigley priest."

"Michael, if I was to be a priest, I'd be a sober one. You know that. There's plenty of good sober ones. They go to the school to visit; they don't stumble through the door as they arrive. They are very proper." Joseph slammed the teapot back down on the back of the stove and went to the set table to wait for the food.

"Well, then, let's hope if yer not a priest, ye'll still be a sober and a proper man. It seems that you admire proper men of the cloth. There are no proper men of the river! Only over me dead body will ye be soaked in whiskey and floatin' on the river the rest of yer born days!"

Joseph missed the wagon deliveries with Laurence, and he yearned for a "real" man's job.

Though they were still relatively poor, Michael had proved his ability to find work where he could. He had also managed, for the most part, to obey his da and keep Joseph in school or with him to the extent that he could. His success provided him with confidence, and he felt ready to continue down the Ohio River— closer to his Missouri dream.

The two older sisters Michael loved and longed for had disappeared into the American frontier long before he arrived in New York. He thought that Margaret had drifted into Missouri— somewhere along the Missouri River just north of Independence. He had been told that hundreds of Irish were now knocking down the bluffs of the Kansas Town settlement and turning it into a city. There was a building and business boom led by the Irish Catholics—or so the Catholics said in their newspaper. The Cincinnati paper said a cathedral was going to be built in Kansas Town, and a new stone church at the old Saint Mary's Parish in Independence would be constructed someday.

Michael planned to arrive just as he was needed.

Φ

On Monday morning, March 15, 1852, when the higher water of the melting snows made the rivers easier to navigate, Laurence hitched up Gus early, placed the leaf garland Sarah Conroy had fashioned for the event around his ears, and picked up his favorite Irish immigrants in his open wagon.

After Joseph lavished many kisses on the seriously aging Gus, and they had said all their goodbyes, Michael and Joseph stepped aboard the *Gem*. Their departure from Cincinnati had a different tone from that of Pittsburgh. They waved to their dear friends who pulled away before the boat departed.

This time, it was Michael who was more relieved to be moving on. Joseph removed the garland from Gus's head and held it with a wistful expression. He would never see Gus, Laurence, or Sarah Conroy again. Joseph looked at Sarah and realized that she would become the standard against whom all others would be measured. Without a doubt, however, there would be some young Irish lad with access to whiskey on the boat, and he might get over his Cincinnati losses pretty quickly.

The *Gem* was a steamboat that had been launched from Cincinnati two years earlier. At 211 feet in length and capable of carrying 298 tons, it was headed for the great Mississippi River. The *Gem* would take them as far as Cairo, Illinois, about 550 miles to the end of the Ohio River.

The only thing fancy about the boat was the lettering of her name. As they stepped aboard, a banjo player, a fiddler, and a piper entertained them from the hurricane deck, creating a festive mood on the cold, breezy day. Because it was not a particularly fancy boat, it seemed a little out of place to Michael.

On this trip, he had $150 deeply buried in his pocket, in addition to the travel voucher he had arranged with the stonemasons. Cincinnati had given him further distance from abject poverty. Some of his fellow masons were headed out with him to the frontier to help build the cathedral in Kansas Town.

Standing on the upper deck next to Michael, a fellow passenger said, "Another boat named the *Gem* sank in 1840. I don't think it was the same owner or pilot who ran this boat. This captain might be Lewis Snap or Peter Hanger." The gentleman wanted to be somebody by dropping names of captains.

Michael didn't care—except that he was going to learn who this captain was, and if he survived, he would know who to sue. He had considered looking up Bernard Quigley, a distant cousin Ellen in Pittsburgh had named if he needed a lawyer. This motivated Michael to look him up for sure when they got to St. Louis.

The stranger continued to describe the everyday explosions and wrecks. Every person he knew had had a relative or friend run up on a sandbar, crashed into a tree, or been stripped by water or rocks into a sharply pointed pole that ripped up the deck to drown passengers, livestock, and cargo. Some had escaped a fire, often started by immigrant-class passengers on the main deck, or had been robbed by someone who jumped off the boat and drifted away never to be prosecuted for their crimes.

Michael thought of moving from his place, but he knew that regulars loved to relate important or historical horrors to unsuspecting immigrants and then watch their reactions.

Michael already knew that relatives often died of cholera only days after stepping on the boat. Every summer in Cincinnati, bodies or coffins with bodies in them washed up on the shores. A priest might be called down to bless the dead. Michael sarcastically thought it would be better to bless the living for having survived the truth and the stories about the truth.

It was not uncommon for deceased passengers to be placed in a coffin made by a carpenter on the boat. Having ready-made coffins allowed the captain to dispose of cholera victims immediately. As passengers drifted down or plowed up any river, they could look out along the banks and see coffins that had been washed into visibility by bank or riverbed erosion. Some immigrants might simply be thrown into the river to drift into mud or logjams or wash up on beaches, spreading the disease further downriver.

Unfortunately, a steamboat was the only conveyance that would carry Michael to his dream of marriage, landownership, and the perpetuation of his family line—an important consideration since he believed that his family was disintegrating. Other than months of riding wagons or walking, the river was their only way to Independence, Missouri. It would take him and Joseph only sixty hours,

158

about three days, to travel the 520 miles to Cairo, Illinois, if there were no accidents. This did not include spontaneous fuel stops, waits for other boats, stops for recalculating which channel to take, and an occasional stop to run off a thief. Because the life expectancy of a boat was about four years, Michael and Joseph could expect to be grounded or worse. This was an older boat that had clearly outlived its life expectancy.

Michael prayed at every bend, island, logjam, or widening of the stream. It was obvious to Michael that Joseph was more relaxed, and he was still enthusiastic about boat ownership. Michael observed him talking with all the "knowledgeable" regulars. However, when Michael casually asked him if he liked horses or boats better for transportation, Joseph chose horses.

Graced with high water and a sober captain, they arrived in Cairo when expected. The trip produced the typical number of close calls, illness among some passengers, arguments, and good food and bad, but they arrived in fairly good financial shape, having not been robbed. In Cairo, they were immediately able to catch their next boat heading up the Mississippi.

Φ

The Mississippi boat was overloaded with people. There were so many that Joseph wondered how one more could squeeze aboard. Other than several beautiful chestnut Morgans, most of the cargo was barrels full of pork, the last of winter apples, whiskey, and boxes marked "US Army." The young man caring for the horses told Joseph that the boxes had tools, tents, and other "classified" provisions headed to the US Army in St. Louis. When Joseph asked if he meant guns and swords, the young man winked with a broad smile and said, "I guess I mentioned everything else, but I can't tell you anything about weapons. Maybe there are—and maybe there aren't. Your guess is as good as mine."

At dark, after a soldier and a horse-handling friend had gone up to the boiler deck for libations and a Virginia reel with the pretty young girls, Joseph, unable to resist, slipped down to the main deck and climbed up on a hitching rail in the dark. Holding on to a trim board above the wall and floor-to-ceiling posts, he eased himself past the first two horses and headed for the biggest. He spoke quietly and stroked his dark flanks, calling the name of Major, a name he had already given him earlier in the day.

After sweet-talking and calling his name, Joseph slipped down on his bare back. "There's a good lad, Major. Yer feelin' strong, Major, and I bet yer steady and can run hard across the prairie. Too bad ye'll be in the army, lad, but yer a brave one to do it. Yer a fine horse and a leader—I can tell. I hope ye don't get shot through with a cannon. What a damned shame it would be. Some officer will be prancin' along on ye, noddin' here and there at the girls."

Major was muscular and had a long mane, and Joseph wished he had an open field. He closed his eyes and visualized himself galloping along in the grass of a smooth field. He imagined himself a soldier, a feather in his hat, riding on Major and shooting one bad robber after the other. He suddenly heard Michael walking toward the horses and calling his name. The nothin' horse on the end began to make a fuss, so Joseph slid silently off Major, patted him up on the rump, avoiding a possible kick, and thanked him for the ride.

The 180-mile trip from Cairo to Saint Louis was expected to take two or three days, and it was the most treacherous segment of the Mississippi. They saw wreckage here and there from the Ohio end to the Missouri end. Joseph saw the skeletons of ships sticking out of the Mississippi mud around a number of bends, and when he pointed them out to Michael, Michael asked him to stop.

The gentleman "historian" they had met on the upper deck passed on the information to Joseph that one Cairo boat explosion had killed 1,443 persons. It was more than had ever perished on a river, and in spite of Joseph's sense of adventure and admiration for the livestock on the boat, when Joseph passed on the information to Michael, he suddenly had a total cessation of joy on this leg of the journey.

Michael said, "Please stick by me. If somethin' happens, I don't want to lose ye. We have to survive or go down together."

Joseph said, "Michael, don't ye worry. I already have a horse picked out for me and one for ye. They're strong, and I can make them plow through the water as easy as that! I'll take the lead, Michael. Ye follow."

Michael responded, "Not every horse likes the water, Joseph. Ye have to train 'em. Ye won't have time to train 'em when we're sinkin'. The horses will be screamin' their own heads off. What about fire? Can ye get 'em through flames as well? What about explosion? Can ye piece 'em back together?"

Joseph replied, "We'll let God take it from there, Michael."

Φ

When they reached the Saint Louis Levee, Joseph counted sixty boats lined up along the narrow shoreline. There was no shore access for man or horse at St. Louis, and the landing was completely packed in more than one boat deep. They could hardly wait to get off the boat, but it took forever.

St. Louis was a large city that had exploded in population over the growth of the steamboat industry. Young dreamers like Michael and Joseph constituted the majority of immigrants. Those planning to continue on to Independence, Kansas Town, Saint Joseph, or any other landing took horrendous risks. The Missouri was recognized as one of the most turbulent and muddy rivers of the West. However, that's how people usually got to the Oregon, California, and Santa Fe trails.

Michael decided that the population of St. Louis consisted of those who had lost their courage to travel farther because of their Mississippi experience and the legends of the Missouri.

Even though they had four hundred miles more to travel on to Independence, Michael decided they needed a break. They would look for Bernard Quigley, eat an authentic French meal, and could go to church before stepping on another paddle-wheeled coffin on the Missouri.

In St. Louis, along the shoreline, the newly arrived pioneers hustled and looked for locations to join up with relatives who had come before them. Some were searching for work, and some were negotiating with or running from predators who took advantage of immigrants like themselves. Nearly all had a piece of paper on which was written the names of people who had come before. It reminded Michael of New York.

Michael felt fortunate that he had been able to make connections to jobs or know of specific opportunities ahead of his arrival, through either the church or the stonemasons, and usually both. That first job in New York—obtained with the help of fellow parishioners and Irish Catholic neighbors of Margaret's township back home—had resulted in every opportunity he had been given so far. The reputation of his teacher and mentor, Mr. Jackson, counted immensely. Michael felt blessed and needed to rise to the expectation to keep going. At each place, he had a plan before arriving. He believed in the priests who assured him there was a need for his skill as he moved on—even if it started out as hard labor. Eventually, his talents would be discovered, and there was always a need for them because of the growth on the frontier.

The age and diversity of St. Louis's residents was immediately noticeable. There were the long-established Spanish and French. Most immigrants who had arrived in the past decade were German. The Irish had only recently begun to pour into the region, but most were moving on into Kansas and western Missouri. There seemed to be freed African slaves going about their business, which was more like New York City than Cincinnati. Maybe they weren't free but worked for masters who ran the shipping industry or agriculture, especially tobacco. Michael didn't know the situation in St. Louis, but since slavery was not allowed in Pennsylvania, all the dark-skinned people he saw living there were probably free.

In Cincinnati, slaves were streaming across the river at night and then skirting up through towns running north. He had heard it called the Underground Railroad. There were stations along the way—homes and churches and tunnels—where people could hide them until they were with family or in Canada. Oberlin, Ohio, was a well-known town where slaves could get help as their masters were chasing after them. Corrupt locals would often trick adolescent slave males with offers of work and then snatch them for a hefty fee.

162

In Oberlin, there was also a university that had professors and administrators who were sympathetic to the slaves' freedom, and they were highly involved in helping the slaves. Unlike the progressive Ohio Michael and Joseph had discovered, Missouri was behind in its modern development and racial attitudes. Michael was warned repeatedly that Missouri was different from states in the North.

There were many more Catholics in St. Louis than in Cincinnati. Michael and Joseph saw French nuns, schoolchildren in uniforms, and other signs of familiarity everywhere they looked. Most immigrants in St. Louis had arrived either as Michael and Joseph had—down the Ohio—or had come up the Mississippi from New Orleans. These long and difficult migrations wore people down. Joseph and Michael needed to walk off their exhaustion and get away from the stress of being confined on the boat for many days amid the poor hygiene and closeness of too many needy, greedy, and often intoxicated strangers. They tried to avoid densely crowded areas and restaurants where they might catch a disease.

St. Louis had interesting stone architecture and shops, cobbled streets, and beautiful churches and parks. The metalwork attracted Michael's interest, but he noticed that Joseph was still commenting on the horses and carts. There was good food and the peace and comfort of sitting out of the roasting humidity in a cool and quiet church with high ceilings. They entered a Spanish-looking church where the windows were open, and there was the usual small scattering of people in quiet meditation or saying their rosaries.

Michael made sure they attended Mass in one of these attractive churches before departing. They attended the daily Mass where they believed Bernard could be. Attending Mass regularly was impossible during their steamboat journey. The recitation of the lauds and chanting of the nuns were beautiful.

Joseph was discreetly humming to himself—as though he knew the music. He could pick up a tune in an instant, and his voice carried and was a beautiful complement to the lighter voices of the nuns.

Church had always felt like home to the Quigley family. Here, the brothers felt the comfort and familial closeness of a large church—something not experienced since New York. They liked the European feel. Mass was always the same, and everyone always knew the responses in Latin. There were complete families starting their days there, which brought the feeling that Michael wanted to have in his life: comfort and a sense of close family, community support, and hope.

Michael wanted to contact Bernard Quigley, and he decided to ask the man whom he'd seen keeping the grounds at the cathedral the day before.

Yes, he did know a Bernard Quigley—he was well-known in the church community—but he was away, possibly down in Cape Girardeau where some of his family "might have" land. He wasn't sure.

A priest walking across the grounds suggested that Bernard Quigley might be on business since he had already been gone for a number of days. He was an usher and had notified the others that he would be gone. Michael and Joseph had been to Neely's Landing near Cape Girardeau just days ago. It was a few miles north of Cairo, past interesting rocks, and they had seen slaves out along a rich delta, probably in fields of tobacco.

Bernard was a lawyer and a landowner, and Michael wondered if he owned slaves. As a good Catholic whose family had been subject to the tyranny of the English—including many soldiers and children snatched and sent into slavery in Barbados—Michael didn't know how Bernard could be both a lawyer who protected people's rights and a slave owner. It was troubling to him that an Irishman could own slaves. Michael's strong opinion was generally shared by his generation of immigrants. It seemed that there should only be one side to the issue—to love one another and follow the example set by Christ—but that wasn't the case as they traveled farther south and west toward Missouri.

The longer the Irish had been in the country, or if they had landed in the South, the more likely they would be proslavery. Maybe they had purchased slaves that came with the land. Slave ownership was somewhat dependent on wealth. If you had no love in your heart and

164

wanted someone else to do your work, you had to pay for the advantage. Slaves were expensive. Michael had learned on the *Gem* that on the frontier, if you had slaves, you were more likely to be a doctor or lawyer, like Bernard, but they didn't think he had them because his home was in the city. They didn't know who his family was in Cape Girardeau. Michael wasn't really sure how he was related—except that Bernard had the same last name and Ellen said he was a cousin.

German immigrants were more likely to be abolitionists since they arrived later than the early Irish and Scots, and in greater numbers, and Michael was told there had been no slavery in Germany.

In Pennsylvania, Michael had learned that immigrants who were Quakers were outwardly against slavery. It was mostly German Quakers who had landed in Pennsylvania and the Scots- Irish Presbyterians from William Penn's colony who were behind the abolitionist movement in America. That's why Pennsylvania was among the first states to abolish slavery in the late 1700s.

Michael also knew that the Quakers came to Ireland to help the hungry Irish during the famine. Michael had been reminded by Ellen to thank anyone he might meet from the Navajo Nation for their generous donation to help save the Irish from the English- caused famine.

Michael and Joseph decided that Pennsylvania was best on the issue. Ohio and Illinois were welcoming runaways and helping them flee farther north or settle, so that was good. Kentucky seemed to be mixed. It was mainly slave free in the north, but not in the south. Missouri was also mixed.

Michael and Joseph were warned that Missouri had large parcels of land that were conducive to growing cotton or tobacco, and slavery was common there. These were places in the north and northeast and fairly close to Independence and far to the south of the Missouri River, and closer to Arkansas. It was these early, well-established landowners, many from the South, who were proslavery. Michael and Joseph were reminded that there was much conflict, and because the wealthy people did not want to lose their free labor, some Missouri slaves were being taken into Texas by their owners. Men with more than forty acres required a hired man if it was more than a single family could handle. Slavers sometimes owned up to one hundred slaves in order to become wealthy. They depended on others to do their work for them. They had a lot to lose. The move for abolition caused civil divisions and conflicts that were increasing daily along the Missouri-Kansas border. It was rapidly getting out of hand.

Φ

After their short break in St. Louis, Michael and Joseph boarded their first stern-wheeler and headed up the river toward the confluence of the Missouri and the Mississippi. There was no banjo player or other form of entertainment to add a celebratory touch as they had seen in other places. To Michael, the mood was very somber. He immediately began to feel apprehension. He took a position leaning over the rail of the upper deck, and Joseph joined him.

"Can ye believe that here we are, Michael, seasoned steamboat travelers?"

Michael replied, "No, Joseph. I think we're lucky travelers. The seasoned travelers are the ones who end up in the river or require rescue at one point or the other."

"Maybe so, Michael. Look at the color of the water. The Ohio and Mississippi water looked a lot cleaner. This water is turnin' yellow-brown and muddy. What do ye suppose that means?"

"It means that high water somewhere or meltin' snow is pulling dirt into the water. Maybe there was a large slide that's bein' washed downriver."

Joseph looked out at the bank and said, "The land around here looks pretty solid; it must be comin' from farther up the river. Maybe a packet would be better than this paddle wheel. Listen to the scrapin' and clunkin' and the strain on the wheel."

As they agreed it was churning as much mud and gravel as water, the paddle wheel suddenly ground to a stop, and they found themselves stuck just offshore.

The seasoned traveler standing beside them said, "Welcome to Fort Belle Fountaine." He sounded like a tour guide.

166

Michael said, "I can't see the structures well through the trees, but it looks like the Spanish style I saw in St. Louis. I see that they're stone rather than the wood I'm seein' everywhere else but the city."

The knowledgeable passenger informed them that it was something that was built to defend the new Louisiana Purchase, and it had been active until after the War of 1812.

Michael said, "I thought that war was fought around the Great Lakes. I had an ancestor in Pennsylvania who fought in that war up North."

"Just because someone comes to fight you at your front door doesn't mean he won't try to come through your back door. Some of those Indians who fought for the British had been sent into Kansas on reservations along the Kansas-Missouri border, up the Missouri River, and they were on the side of the English to defeat the onslaught of immigrants. The US government has a lot of land, and it had to start defending it all after the Louisiana Purchase. They needed fortifications all the way down to the gulf, where the Mississippi drains into the Atlantic Ocean."

Joseph said, "How long do you think we'll have to wait here?"

The man laughed and shrugged his shoulders. "We'll wait for as long as it takes. It could take five minutes or five hours."

Michael said, "Joseph, let's go down to the livestock. I need to talk to ye privately." The two moved down to the livestock deck and leaned up against a box of geese.

Michael said, "Ye know, we're about to step off into a ragin' battle we know little about when we get to Independence. Since we've been told slavers are everywhere, how are we goin' to handle the situation? We need to stick with the same plan, Joseph. I think that since I'll probably be workin' with the Irish Catholics on the church, there won't be disagreement like there might be with you at school—unless it's a Catholic school where there won't be two sides to the issue. The Protestants might be English, and they will feel differently. I don't know about the Indians. We might find ourselves outnumbered when we buy a farm."

Joseph, now fifteen, gave what Michael thought was a good answer: "There are ways to protect yerself that I learned from McGee. Ye keep yer ears open and yer yappin' Irish mouth shut— but ye keep yer ears shut too if there is somethin' ye don't need to know. Only ye and yer partner need to share some things, and nobody else needs to know. That's you and me as partners, Michael." Joseph tried to pronounce you in the proper way he had learned from the corrections of Princess Anna. "Ye heard what the Irishman said when we were eatin' in their charity house. We go to no gatherin' or meetin' where slavery or votin' is the topic. Ye leave when the subjects of slavery or votin' come up—or we excuse ourselves to go feed the pigs, milk a cow, or weed the corn. It's that simple, Michael. We just tell 'em we can't vote yet."

Michael said, "When we're naturalized, we'll go vote for the abolitionists—but we'll tell nobody and sign no oaths or agreements. Every time Da signed somethin' in Ireland, we lost somethin' in the exchange."

"That's right, Michael."

The discussion came to an end.

As in all groundings, they sat and waited. There was a lot of traffic on the river. Michael was told that the water was apparently somewhat low on this day for the time of the year, though that could change after a large storm. Michael leaned his head back against the wall of the furnace room and tried to nap with the cattle lowing off his right shoulder.

Eventually, another large boat appeared from the west and halted. Soon, a small barge appeared from behind. After some forward and backward maneuverings of large poles, situated on the bow that pounded along in the gravel, a push from the small barge forced them out to the midstream, and they were on their way. After passing another ahead, they sped up considerably. However, it was half a day in which they had gained only half a dozen miles of their four hundred-mile journey.

Rivers frequently changed course. One year the midstream went to the right of a bar, and the next, if trees or stumps lodged on a bank, the midstream went left. A captain had to look at charts, but most of all, use his expertise and wisdom to know how to read the current and power through a turn. It demanded intelligence, experience, and courage, especially carrying all the people and precious cargo under explosive steam power.

They pushed past two large bends before stopping to load fuel. The crew dropped the loading plank and handed out tools to those with vouchers—mostly immigrants. The sturdy men, like Michael, were given saws, axes, splitters, and mauls. The straps were given to young boys to hold together limbs or chunks. The higher-class travelers would volunteer out of boredom, but they were not approached directly as were the immigrants.

Though Joseph and Michael had felt annoyed on the Ohio at being asked over and over by boat hands to become porters of cargo or fuel, it did provide exercise and relief from the boredom or stress of waiting for potential calamity. Most immigrants felt a need to oblige without complaint.

The boats burned a lot of wood, and the banks of the river showed the results of constant chopping. Some sections were nearly devoid of forests. After hauling many cords of wood aboard, they resumed upriver to a spot a crew member pointed out as Pinckney Bend. By this point, they had not traveled far and were still about three hundred miles from Independence. The boat was intentionally beached, and a flatboat was sent upriver to check out the channel on the bend.

As the flatboat rounded the bend, it appeared that another steamboat was stuck sideways in the main channel up ahead, with a sizable gravel bar and shallow water to the right. After resuming passage, the passengers again saw wreckage from previous trips and felt grateful that their grounding had not resulted in a catastrophe.

The next day, when Michael and Joseph mingled with the paying passengers, the storytellers who had traveled up and down the river for twenty years shared the horrors. One tale was that a boat had recently been abandoned by the captain after passengers and crew began dying of cholera. An adolescent boy from the town had happened upon the ghost ship with crew all gone and passengers strung along the beach unattended and some still dying. The captain and crew had landed and fled for home—and they all died from cholera within days of leaving their dying passengers on the riverbank.

Φ

Joseph had drifted toward the many livestock on the steamboat, and there were no passengers left on the main deck. Mingling among the horses, one of which reminded him of the great Lafayette, he introduced himself to eighteen-year-old Joshua McCollum.

Joseph asked, "Joshua, I think ye look like a cowboy. How is it yer stayin' down here takin' care of so many animals?"

"I'm in charge of horses, mules, hogs, and chickens—anything my outfitting company hauls from St. Louis to Westport Landing. My job is to keep them from jumping off or being taken off. I'm called a handler since I work with every kind of livestock. Passengers call us cowboys or cowhands."

"So, which of these are yers?" Joseph asked.

"Today, I have two oxen, four mules, a box of chickens, two team horses, two heifers, and a very valuable Holstein bull calf that came upriver from Kentucky. He's the one standing in alfalfa."

"Yer in charge of a farm!" exclaimed Joseph.

"Yes, I am, but my boss, Mr. McCoy, doesn't trust regular deckhands. He says that paying my wages saves him money in the long haul. Deckhands occasionally lose a rambunctious horse in the river or let one be stolen. Sometimes it's more than a handful, but the deckhands help with the loading and unloading. At the landings, they put up the fences and rails to direct them, especially with the bulls or oxen. At Westport, McCoy's experienced men come out and meet me—or the people who are heading out on the trail will come out on the beach to get their own livestock. Sometimes I'll help them hitch up their team right there on the beach—and then off they go."

"Where's the Westport Landing?" Joseph asked.

"It's just upriver and around a bend from Independence. West Bottoms is on the water, and it's easy to land a steamboat and get the livestock off the deck."

Joshua told Joseph that one time, when a ship ran aground, he had a lot of cattle aboard. He had taken his Morgan along to St. Louis to be sure they all got on and off. "The river was pretty low, and we were up on solid ground. I ran the herd off the boat down the loading ramp and herded them all the way into Independence, then down the creek, behind the bluffs, back on the beach, and into the Bottoms. The trail was great because the weather was good. The cattle had plenty to drink, and I got them all home. It was fun because a gentleman who had his horse aboard decided to go along. It was a real adventure—lots of fun. I don't think it's happened before or since."

Joseph hung around the animals enough that Joshua was able to get a helping hand from him. Joshua said that he lived in West Bottoms right where the Westport Landing was. It was below the Kansas Town bluffs, at the confluence of the Kansas and the Missouri Rivers. It was the center of action for young wagon drivers and cowhands who worked for the Oregon, California, and Santa Fe Trail outfitters.

West Bottoms was a collection of shacks and shanties where the very impoverished Irish families settled. They provided the labor for leveling the bluffs and building the roads, and they supplied skilled and unskilled sweat for the growing city of Kansas Town, above the bluffs. Though Westport Landing was on the shore, the town of Westport, headquarters for his outfitter, was uphill and south of the bluffs. West Bottoms was partially mudflats and had been farmland that flooded annually. Westport was high above the river level. The enterprise of livestock down between the Missouri and the Kansas River was growing into an export business for beef going north.

Life in West Bottoms was typical for the stress-ridden, impoverished immigrants who settled in the only space available and close to their point of arrival and jobs. Overcrowding, poor hygiene, cholera, bad nutrition, prostitution, moonshining, and the cheap labor required for a boomtown all bloomed in West Bottoms. Potato plants also bloomed in the muck of the "streets" and were carefully protected by their owners, especially by those who made poteen. Such settlements were allowed to grow haphazardly, and West Bottoms

171

had been exploding in population for several years with the tidal wave of Irish.

Places like West Bottoms were where immigrants planning to go farther west often planted themselves. They even camped alongshore until they obtained their wagons, gathered their animals, and purchased their provisions. All up and down the riverbanks were families in transition or crisis. All who planned to go farther west to California or the Oregon Territory had to follow the Santa Fe Trail across the Kansas River until they arrived at the point where the "Road to Oregon" veered off to the right, heading north.

Even with such problems as deadly illnesses, Joshua assured Joseph that West Bottoms was a place for an ambitious and hardworking young Irish kid to begin building his life. Joshua was "mostly" living with a family named White. More recently, he had found new places to flop at night. Francis and Abigail White had a new baby. Francis, a leatherworker, had taken Joshua under his care on the boat to help him negotiate "difficulties" when he was in trouble or needed help. Josh tagged along with them on their way to Missouri. He told Joseph he would have starved without Abigail White's biscuits, and he invited Joseph to visit them in their shack and eat the "best biscuits in the world."

First, he would have to ask Abigail if she could have a visitor. She hadn't fully recovered from her baby, but she had resumed sewing for an outfitter. Also, Joshua needed to round up something to gift the family. He never went empty-handed. He would like to have bought something for Abigail in St. Louis, but he didn't have an opportunity this trip. He bought useful things for the family: nice soap, something to eat, tea, or maybe new heavy-duty needles. Of course, he casually added that he could always find something to steal off the boat that he could trade for what he needed. He winked, but Joseph, knowing several young men from boats in Cincinnati, understood it was part of the culture.

Apparently, two men ran the show in Westport Landing, which was where the hotel, bank, shops, saloons, and general and outfitting stores were located. Joshua worked directly for Mr. McCoy. John McCoy had started the Town of Kansas Company, which outfitted the pioneers who started from Westport on their journeys to the California gold fields, the Mormon settlement in Utah, down the Santa Fe Trail, or north up the Oregon Trail. Independence, Wyandotte, Fort Leavenworth, Weston, Saint Joseph, Council Bluffs, and other landings provided entrance to the trails. Independence or Westport were the first places to disembark close to the trails.

At Westport, longhorn beef cattle were driven up from Texas, but the other livestock for outfitters came from Iowa, Illinois, Kansas, Kentucky, Tennessee, or any other place they could get what they needed. Suppliers were sprouting up from the newly settled local breeders as well as the states to the north or east that had been "in business" since the late 1700s. He told Joseph that pork, however, usually came from Iowa, Illinois, and even from Ohio in barrels.

Joseph said, "I know that pork barrels left Cincinnati. The Germans make and eat sausage every day, so there were hogs at every German home in town and out—and breweries."

Josh did haul live hogs, but the barrels provided a large part of affordable provisions for the pioneers as well as the military.

In St. Louis, Joseph, fascinated by the military cargo, saw a lot of pork and beer barrels rolled off the decks.

From the first day, Josh seemed impressed by Joseph's skill with the livestock, especially mules. It was not typical for a fifteen- year-old kid to form a relationship with an unknown or unfamiliar mule. Joseph had grown partial to Elizabeth's beautiful eyes, which followed his every move. Joseph believed that Elizabeth, like Princess Anna of Cincinnati, silently loved him. However, here, he would attempt no tricks to woo her. He smiled and called her name in her ear. One time, she reached her head up and nudged him.

Because Josh always felt at odds with the mules, they didn't tend to trust or obey him. He told Joseph that he had once suggested to his immediate boss, Ciaran, that he needed a "bossy" mule to take with him to St. Louis. The bossy mule could meet any mules that were to be brought back and encourage them to behave. Ciaran ignored him and told him that it was Josh's fault and not the fault of the mules that he didn't get along with.

Joseph said, "Didn't anyone tell ye the names of the mules ye were meetin'? If ye'd known their names, ye could have become friends right off. If the mule doesn't have a name, like me friend Elizabeth, ye have to name 'em, especially if they're lookin' in yer eyes. To love ye, they need to know ye! They have to be wantin' to be near ye—or they won't do as ye ask. Remember that, and ye'll be doin' a fine job. Yer askin' 'em and not tellin' 'em what to do. There's no trust between strangers, only between friends."

Josh looked at Joseph and laughed. "Where did ye learn that, Joseph?"

"In Ireland ... from me ma and da. That's what they do in me township. I don't know about the rest of Ireland."

Josh recommended that Joseph get off at Westport Landing, go directly into town, and talk with Mr. McCoy or McCoy's partner about a job. Josh could put in a good word, and if Joseph got a job, he could stay somewhere with him for a few days in West Bottoms.

"Would they let me drive a team?" Joseph asked.

"I've never seen a young lad be given that much responsibility. Teams and wagons are expensive, you know? Young boys who have no families sometimes work for bed and board. They often ride from the shore where families are preparing to depart on the trail into Westport to buy the right harness, butt strap, or hitching item found missing when families hitch up for the first time. The boys get good tips for those errands—sometimes as much as a dollar for the day."

Because Joseph was so "charming'" and his "hair and teeth were handsome," he would be good at the job, especially if he had a horse. "Too many families start their ventures without knowing much of anything, so we're always scrambling to get the animals out of Westport fast, before anyone gets hurt—people or animals. You'd have to prove yourself before becoming a driver—"

"Joshua, have ye ever worked with a Lipicán?"

"A what?" asked Joshua.

"A Lipicán horse. It's spelled L-i-p-i-c-á- n. I knew a princess in Cincinnati, and her family owned them in Czechoslovakia. It's a big, fancy horse. Men do tricks on their broad backs."

"I never heard of the horse or the country." Joshua laughed. "How'd a kid like you get to know a princess from Chicklowbaka?" Joseph answered, "Through trial and error. It's Czech-o-slo-va-ki-a. Think lo-slow, but there's no l. I nearly busted me cranium, and I made an eejit of meself for the girls in Cincinnati. Never again. They need to come after me—like the queen, our beautiful Elizabeth here! Look there, Josh, she loves me."

After laughing, Josh said, "Actually, ye can get a fancy horse from Tennessee or Kentucky. I'm serious, Joe, do ye know about the horses from Tennessee or Kentucky? Every once in a while, a horse comes along that is used on the plantations in Missouri. They're very showy. You'll see them when they arrive. The wealthy slavers use them in the fields down to the south and up north along the Mississippi. They make the masters look important and strong. On large plantations farther to the south, the overseers can always see when the master is in the fields because he's the only one with that horse.

"Tennessee horses are pretty fast, and they trot real pretty. Some of them are large—up to seventeen hands. There's a man in Strother who has a beautiful horse from Tennessee. I saw it come in. It's called a Hanoverian. It was seventeen hands—and shiny black with white socks. When it ran on the sand, it was the most beautiful thing I've ever seen.

"You like the fancy horses, Joe? If you do, I have a good Morgan I take hunting. He's small, but he's strong. I got him about two years ago from a man who decided to go back to New York. He didn't want to take the horse with him, so he sold him to me. There are a lot of Morgans to be had. If you worked for the outfitters, you could get yourself a Morgan at a good price. You're right there where people need to sell livestock as well as buy it. They'll get rid of a small American rider for a sturdier horse. A Morgan's a great horse, and you'd have a place to keep him for sure. There's lots of barns and stables, and your feed would be cheap—especially if ye steal it! I borrow feed now and then from Mr. McCoy. I think he knows, but I work hard and make up for it. If he knows, he's never pointed it out."

Joseph thrilled at the idea of having his own horse and cheap feed in a few years. He would get one from Tennessee or Kentucky if he could. The idea of working with horses and mules excited him. Even though the oxen were probably the most reliable animals on the trails, Joseph was not as interested in them. They were heavy and dull. They just did their jobs—plodding on like his brother Michael. He thought he could tolerate oxen because they were more reliable, but he'd never love them. He tolerated and often admired Michael's sober, down-to-earth personality because he loved and needed him. *But I could never be like Michael. I'm more like a Hanoverian or a Lipicán.*

Josh also said that there was a lot of fun to be had in Westport. "Boys get together on the beach and drink whiskey around fires from barrels occasionally rolled off the boats or broken barrels that have been emptied into buckets. In the summer, there are lots of girls who meet them from West Bottoms. They come out to drink. There are lots of women who work the saloons in Westport." Josh laughed. "You can learn a lot of good tricks there because those women are not shy at all. There's a bunch of 'em in their own cribs—each with her own specialty—but they do cost money."

Joseph said, "Are those the circus women in Westport? I was workin' on handstands on a friend's mixed draft mare. I'd love to learn new tricks."

Josh laughed at the nice boy from Ireland. That would likely change fairly fast in West Bottoms, but Josh wouldn't be the one encouraging him.

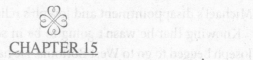

CHAPTER 15

BECOMING A MISSOURIAN

Independence, Missouri, provided Michael and Joseph immediate employment. Within days of arriving down the five-mile, mule-drawn railroad from the river into the town, Michael was handed a shovel and asked to join other Irish immigrants in knocking down a great bluff for a road north of town. Independence had been bustling since the 1840s, busily growing westward into Kansas Town. Now, having lost some of its Santa Fe and Oregon Trail "overlanders," its importance was waning. Many pioneers were beginning to bypass the cholera of Independence and head upriver for Westport, which was closer to the trails.

Avoiding Independence also eliminated the Blue River crossing and a polluted fork that had been a common but deadly route to Kansas. However, in 1852, Independence was still far from dead. It still led in the number of outfitters, and it offered jobs for immigrants like Michael and Joseph who were still disembarking daily on the Wayne City Landing directly north of the town.

Some Irish crews west of Independence on the south Missouri River bank were leveling ground for buildings. Though "laborer" was the listed occupation of most Irishmen and boys, Michael immediately set his goal on becoming a true mason and not shoveling shale or carrying hod. The sandy-colored bluffs running east-west on the south shore of the Missouri were literally mountains, but the Quigley brothers joined hundreds of hungry men with families to feed. They, too, began chiseling and digging large access openings as much as ninety feet deep from the riverbank to the plateaus above. Joseph shoveled beside Michael. With men of all ages, they dug or picked away in the limestone, shale, and dust throughout their first summer.

Unfortunately, there were no public schools in Independence— to Michael's disappointment and Joseph's relief.

Knowing that he wasn't going to be in school, from his first day, Joseph begged to go to West Bottoms. He hated digging, but Michael was content to do so because he believed his persistence would pay off with a mason's position and not a laborer's. Joseph had no such options, and he knew it. He was a handler or a wagoner at heart. He didn't even look like Michael. He was lean like a cowboy, but Michael wouldn't concede.

Michael could not agree with Joseph's desire to live in West Bottoms and work for men in Westport. He feared he'd become part of the permanent riffraff class of the slum. Michael insisted that Joseph stay in Independence with him. He told Joseph he needed to get settled in before they could make plans later. He argued that Joseph would find extreme hardship in Westport without a means of support from a working adult.

Michael planned to have Joseph in school by the end of summer, and he could work in Independence until then. Hod carriers, the next job up from digger, earned a dollar or so a day. Joseph had grown to be more muscular in his fifteenth year, and his opportunities for carrying heavy loads were better than they were in Cincinnati.

Michael wanted them to become true gentlemen farmers, like some of the Irish descendants in Pennsylvania. He knew that a person could come to the expanding country, buy beautiful farmland cheap, work hard, and do well. Michael saw himself a proud family man with an upstanding reputation in the community. He pictured himself in church on Sunday with a row of Quigley children sitting quietly beside him in the pew. That's how he saw Joseph as well. He would say to Joseph, "We need to make Da proud. I don't know if ye can become a lawyer, but ye need to be in school for Ma."

Joseph would say, "We need to eat. I don't need to be a stonemason or lawyer to make Ma or Da proud. I have more personality—a better voice—and I plan to have a better horse than most stonemasons."

In his heart, Joseph knew that he would be a better person if he stuck with Michael and obeyed, but it ran against his passions. Nobody could contain him and get away with it. He could hear their da's favorite admonishment: "Water seeks its own level."

Joseph knew Michael thought Joseph was the proverbial bad apple in the Quigley barrel. Joseph, on the other hand, decided that it meant that Westport was calling—and he needed to be where he belonged.

Joseph saw himself doing handstands on a Tennessee trotting horse seventeen hands high, if they got that tall. He saw himself a handsome sharpshooter as he galloped past the bad guys. Maybe he'd be driving a team of fine mules in a parade. Maybe he would invent the horse boat. Often, he saw himself on the beach with Josh, drinking whiskey and singing for the girls to woo them into misbehavior. He was going to be independent and enterprising like the river rats. His possibilities were endless, and he pondered a new one nearly every day of his teenage life. Sacrificing himself to a hill of sandy dirt was not how he imagined he would get ahead in life.

Φ

Michael's aggressive solicitations of clergy to enroll Joseph somewhere, his faithfulness as a volunteer in Saint Mary's Parish, and his high ambition won him recognition and secured him a solid job in masonry with the other Catholic men in Independence. Grinding pertinacity and sacrifice were at his core. He could dig dirt until the mountain was gone if he thought something better might come along as a consequence.

Using the immigrant Irish Catholics to construct the first buildings and roads in and around Kansas Town was the idea of Father Donnelly. Donnelly attended city planning meetings and became recognized as a visionary. This was not typical for a priest, but the Irish priests had thousands of Irish immigrants who needed more than the usual amount of support. Because the priests sent to America were all well educated—many with architecture, engineering, law, and teaching degrees—they had skills and talents they put to work. Father Donnelly had become a savior and a celebrity among the Irish Catholics. Known for his brilliance and skills as a degreed civil engineer, he recruited families from New York and Boston, employing an entire Irish village as cheap labor. He settled them along the bluffs and not far from where Immaculate Conception Church was later built. The Kansas Town area of Connaught Town absorbed more than three hundred impoverished Irish families originally from Connaught, Ireland. As the limestone and shale bluffs of Kansas Town began crumbling under Irish hands, a vibrant city was spreading like prairie fire from Westport across the Blue River and into Independence.

Michael and Joseph had luckily arrived in the midst of a boom. Not since leaving Ohio had Joseph or Michael entertained the thought that Joseph was lawyer or priest material. The full reality of opportunity versus ilk on the frontier of the new country had set in. The Quigley boys—who had arrived in America without their ilk—now competed to rise above abject poverty. Famine, disease, prejudice, and refugee status had brought all these Irish Catholic neighbors to the same level: impoverished laborer with hope but rarely any schooling.

Though their beginnings were fraught with privations and strife, the goal of being a farmer was realistic. Being a farmer meant possibly owning hundreds of acres. For Irishmen in the city, becoming a politician seemed to be a Catholic calling, and they fought their collective ways up into power, notoriety, and sometimes corruption. Farming men usually converted their meager laborers' savings into forty- or sixty-acre plots and then expanded. For the Irish, who had been diminished by the English to one-acre plots of rotten potatoes and famine, the promise of Missouri and Kansas farms was an amazing prospect.

Unfortunately, Michael continued to harbor guilt over not fulfilling Ma's wishes that her little children would become educated and, perhaps, famous. Michael thought that his little sister Margaret, being in the convent, had the greatest chance of becoming a nurse or teacher. His worst fear was his inability to rein in Joseph's appetite for alcohol and high-risk adventure. Joseph required the application of intense influences of Ma, school, or stern clergy to force and direct his talents. Michael realized that he did not possess the attributes or resources to form Joseph into the son Margaret Quigley desired. Joseph was described by one priest as "incorrigible," and he gave Michael a "pass" on his effectiveness. Worse, Michael dreaded the possibility that it would always be his job to pick up Joseph's pieces when he disintegrated into drinking for reasons beyond Michael's understanding.

On a Friday afternoon late in the summer of their arrival, Mike was digging and directing what should be dug versus cut out for masonry when a coworker who hauled loads got off his team momentarily and walked over to tell Mike that Joseph had disappeared from work.

"Disappeared?" Mike asked. "What do ye mean?"

"Well, he and his friend Will got their checks and apparently put their shovels down and walked away. Another young lad said they were going over to West Bottoms to check it out—or maybe to the steamboats there."

Michael answered, "Well, I have work to do; apparently, he doesn't! I certainly didn't give him permission to leave his job. Thanks for lettin' me know. I appreciate knowin', but I don't know what I can do about it right now."

Michael finished his work and walked to the bank with the other men to deposit as much money as possible. So far, Joseph had put his money into the same savings account with Michael for their farm. The men who did not normally walk straight to the bank were the ones who imbibed and caroused. Many were single men, but certainly not all. Michael was single, but it was not like him to place himself in harm's way. He always went directly to the bank to buy his dream of a farm for him and Joseph and a family of his own. Then he stopped at the store and went to his room at the boardinghouse. He expected Joseph to follow his example, but it was hopeless.

As he walked along and reached the bank queue where men were lined up, tired but talking and laughing about the day or financial affairs, Michael thought about the day Joseph arrived at Margaret's apartment with his money. Though he surely would have become a criminal in New York, his heart was in the right place. Joseph wanted to make his contribution to the family. Part of that money got them successfully to Pittsburgh.

Here, Joseph was apparently losing his feeling of belonging to family. Michael thought Joseph might believe he was giving money to Michael but providing nothing for himself.

Michael thought Joseph felt perfectly at home with the adolescent males who were contemplating visits to prostitutes in town or getting drunk in back roads and fighting their way out. Sometimes, Joseph laughed about it and said it was normal because it's what his friends did. Michael thought maybe that was what was happening with Joseph at the very moment in West Bottoms. He was so young to be acting so badly.

Michael questioned whether or not he should go looking for Joseph, but he had to work the next day. Maybe Joseph would get rained on in the middle of the night and would come home. Looking for him might be a waste of time. West Bottoms might not be where Joseph ended up, anyway, so where would he go look? Unfortunately, Joseph did not return. The sun was shining on Saturday morning, and Michael approached the men on Joseph's digging team. "Have ye seen me brother, Joseph, or his friend who left with him on Friday afternoon?"

One of the older men said, "Are ye jokin' with me, Mike? Ye and Joseph don't look alike, and ye sure don't act alike. So he's really yer brother?"

Michael answered, "Yes. We're not much alike because he's me half brother—the bad half!"

The man laughed along with the others who had heard the comment and responded, "So, he's the one in the Quigley barrel rottin' the rest of the apples?"

· "Not exactly. Yer now speakin' to the only one left in the barrel. It doesn't look like he's gonna jump back in the barrel with me— unless I can go get him," quipped Michael.

Another man added, "Maybe that's not a good idea. Maybe ye need to let him rot on his own. I can tell ye, the lad he's with is not fine and upstandin'. He's one I'd throw out of the barrel for sure." The first man laughed and added, "I bet ye neither is 'upstandin'' right now!"

Again, the men laughed, but it made Michael feel sick inside. *What would Da think of me now, lettin' Joseph run off with undesirables? He is not in school, he is out of control, and I am sick of the whole thing. If we had our farm, Joseph would have a team to drive through the fields, and things would be fine.*

The man who started the fun added, "He's a good worker when he gets goin', and he sure can sing. He gets a song goin' now and then, and it's fun for everyone. He's a boy with two sides to him, wouldn't ye say?"

Michael answered, "Yes, I would say that. It's like he knows better and wants to be good, but he loses his senses and goes off followin' someone who drinks. And ye haven't seen the boy who went with him?"

The man answered, "No, but I don't think he'll come back. The other boy, an orphan, said he didn't like diggin' and thought that workin' on the steamboats would be more to his likin'. He and Joe went off talkin', and before I know it, I looked up and their shovels was lyin' on the ground. Another boy told me Joseph was going to West Bottoms to find a lad named Josh."

Michael thanked the gentlemen and went back to his own job: riding on a load of material to the building site.

At the end of the day, Michael spoke with the supervising priest, Father Steven, to tell him that he was headed to West Bottoms to find his brother and that he planned to be back on Monday—no matter what. The priest told him that he was doing what Christ would have done: to go find the errant son and return him to the fold.

Michael left after work in a cart from the livery stable. Because it was late summer, and the sky was still light at eight o'clock, the trip was quick. Michael had not been to West Bottoms before, but he was appalled by the squalor. There were people and livestock and shanties that would put New York City to shame. There was water running down the fetid streets and boardwalks barely reaching above the water level. There were intoxicated paupers and crying babies. Michael couldn't believe that Joseph would choose to live in West Bottoms. *It would be like choosing to stay aboard the Wave. Why would Joseph, regardless of his age, choose to be here and not with me in the cozy, clean room provided by the church?*

Out on the vast beach, there were groups of young people and bonfires. Michael decided to walk through the groups and search for his brother and Josh McCollum. If Josh had lived in West Bottoms for some time, someone might know him.

It was a good idea. At the main bonfire, Josh was holding center court and talking with another young man. There was no whiskey in his hand. Josh was clearly not intoxicated. He seemed to be a regular young man, and not so bad.

Josh said, "What a surprise to see you! You're Michael Quigley, right?"

"Yes, I am, Josh, and do ye know where me brother Joseph might be?"

"Yes, he's here. I was with him earlier today. He came here with a boy named Will. I was unable to help him because he and the other lad got very drunk, and I could not introduce him to Mr. McCoy that way. Mr. McCoy is a minister who does not agree with drinkin', and he will not hire a man who has a drinkin' habit. It was not a good time for Joseph, so I didn't tell McCoy he was here—drunk. I'm sorry I could not help him. I did not know he was afflicted. He is so talented. Maybe this was a bad mistake, and he can come back."

Michael answered, "Well, he is occasionally afflicted and always talented. He made a bad mistake with the help of his friend Will, but I need to get him home now so I can get him back to work. We're wantin' to buy a farm. Neither of us can afford to be sent away from our jobs, so I need him now."

Josh exclaimed, "I understand, Mr. Quigley. I'll help you find him. Will went off on a steamboat to St. Louis, but Joseph can't be far. He's probably on the beach or in a shanty."

It had just turned dark, but the stars were beautiful in the sky and the night was calm. There was much laughter, but Josh told Michael it often turned to fights and violence as the evening wore on.

Michael and Josh went from bonfire to bonfire and person to person, breaking up romantic alliances and inebriated conversations until they came upon a body lying facedown and alone in the muddy sand. It was Joseph. The sad, sad, charming lad everyone loved had held out as long as possible, but he could not control his grief, anger, and addiction.

Michael rolled him over to be sure he wasn't dead. "Joseph! Joseph, it's Michael. I've come to take ye home with me, dear boy. I love ye. Please, Joseph, I'm here to help ye. Try to stand up, and I'll help ye to get home."

"Joseph, it's Josh. Get up, Joseph, so your brother can take you home. You can meet Mr. McCoy next time—when you're feeling better."

Joseph growled and said, "Take yer filthy hands off me. Go away! Leave me be, mister!" He reached up, grabbed Michael, pulled him down, and began punching at his ribs. "Go away! I'm stayin' here until Ma comes!"

Michael wrestled Joseph down, sat on him, and held his arms. "Stop it, Joseph. Ye don't know what yer saying or doin'. 'Tis yer brother to take ye home. I'm doing this for our da, Joseph. This is what our da asked of me. This is what Ma would expect of me. This is what Christ asks of me. Father Steven told me it was right to come and get ye—to save ye until ye grow up a little more and can think better about this on yer own."

Joseph began to cry and said, "Yer not takin' me home. We have no home, Michael. Home is with Ma, and she's not here. I want me ma, Michael."

Michael answered, "I know, Joseph. We both lost our mas. I lost two mas, but we're goin' to put ye in a cart and take ye to our house where you can sleep until ye feel better. Yer right. Yer ma's not here, and me ma's not here, but we have each other. That's the one thing we will always have, Joseph. Ye have a brother who can help ye grow up. Ye still have a family, and it will get better in time."

Joseph passed out again, and a group of young people carried him up to the settlement and placed him in Michael's carriage.

When Joseph returned to work on Tuesday morning, all the men wanted to know if he'd had a "grand time" in West Bottoms. He did not answer, and he did not talk about it to them, due to the humiliation.

However, it was not the same with Michael. When the subject came up that Joseph wanted to go to try it again, Michael would try to reason that Joseph might let his feelings reel out of control again in West Bottoms—and he would destroy himself. He needed to grow older and learn to discipline himself before trying to deal with the challenges of such poverty and competition.

Joseph disagreed vehemently, saying it was Will's fault that he got hopelessly intoxicated, and he assured Michael that Will had gone off on a steamboat and probably wouldn't be back.

Michael said, "Will has nothin' to do with this, Joseph. Ye just have to be strong and grow up without drinkin'. Ye can be yerself and become successful at anything ye want to do, but not if yer goin' to drink whiskey. Alcohol ruins it all. Ye can't be a drunk husband or father either. Our da didn't drink, did he?"

After numerous, nonproductive arguments, Michael eventually let go of parental obligations by removing himself emotionally from the idea that Joseph was his failure. He told Joseph that he would no longer be expected to give to their farm savings, but if he saved enough money for a horse, Michael would let him go in the spring, when he was sixteen. He promised he would not go after him if he didn't put down his shovel and run, but he'd be there to take Joseph back anytime he needed him.

To some extent, he quit caring about what happened when Joseph misbehaved. Sometimes Michael wanted Joseph to suffer the consequences of his actions and learn. Throughout the winter, Michael would say, "Nobody starts the trails west in winter snows—maybe yer horse can feed ye until ye drown in the bottle," "The devil will welcome ye to the winters and the saloons of West Bottoms," and "Maybe ye can sleep with the winterin' hogs. West Bottoms has no cozy room with a little stove like we have here. Ye'll starve or freeze before spring. Maybe ye need to suffer more to understand, but I surely don't favor yer dyin', so ye have to stay here with me for now."

However, he quit disagreeing that Josh McCollum had opened the door to Joseph's future, and it was waiting for him in West Bottoms and not on the limestone or shale roads of Independence. One spring day, Michael said, "Go ahead then. I can't stop ye." Joseph

186

said, "Maybe I'd be more like ye if I stayed here and learned to be a good boy. But ye'll see, Michael. It'll work out fine.

I'll make ye proud to be me brother."

Before Joseph left, Michael repeated another of their da's favorite admonishments: "Don't climb in the barrel with the bad apples or ye'll rot in the barrel." Then he kissed his weeping sixteen- year-old brother and let him go.

Joseph caught a ride to Westport—the more civilized and established town above the cliffs where Mr. McCoy lived and the churches were located—and walked down to West Bottoms. He hadn't bought a horse, but he had enough money in his pocket to get one when he arrived—thanks to Michael, who had actually saved most of the money.

Φ

Through it all, the diligent and thrifty Michael had met a girl at Saint Mary's named Rose. She worked as a daytime servant in one of the big houses not far from the town square. Her family lived close to his boardinghouse, and he saw her at church and at her home. Rose came from a good and faithful family with a hardworking father who provided well in the meat industry. Michael saw himself as he saw Rose's father: sober, dependable, and faithful. Rose proved to be an ambitious girl, but she seemed to be complicated in her needs. She had many close family members in Independence, and Michael fit easily into the rhythm of more concrete members of her family.

In the spring of 1853—at now twenty-three years old—Michael was considered an upstanding young man and an adequate, if not exceptional, catch. People saw his and the other Irish stonemasons' fine work about the town. It was a great source of pride, and the people of the region appreciated the families who were realizing the dream of the brilliant and progressive Father Donnelly. The Catholics were beginning to thrive.

That summer, Michael began to understand that Rose was overly fascinated by the gentry class. It became clear to Michael that she didn't want to lose her city job in the fancy home where there were holiday parties and big dinners with special punches and little cakes. She couldn't wait for the "seasons" to come, and she talked incessantly about decorations, desserts, and guest lists. Michael eventually fretted about how to move on from Rose.

As luck would have it, Mary Murphy, a distant cousin of the Boyle family, arrived into the picture. Rose introduced the two. She thought she was shifting Michael's interest toward Mary, but it had already shifted without any help from Rose. Mary did not look down on maids who milked cows, or the job of hoeing weeds. Unlike Rose, Mary never would have driven a horse for miles in search of silk or something that smelled good and would cost an unreasonable price because of the shop it was in or the company it kept.

Mary shared Michael's vision of stepping out on a hot summer morn to see acres of corn, barley, or flax and a wide-open horizon. With Michael, she visualized daughters hanging laundry and sturdy boys in the field with their da. She saw herself helping her husband in traditional and expected ways. Mary Murphy was ready to accept the challenges of weather and weeds on the prairie.

Once Michael met Mary, his destiny was set. Mary was lovely, spiritual, and motherly. She greatly loved and admired Michael for his kindness, faithfulness, and honesty. She was grateful that he—like her father and unlike Michael's brother—did not have the "Irish weakness." Mary was familiar with the ethnic tendency toward excessive drinking and didn't want to have it in her and Michael's family.

On January 24, 1854, at their beloved Saint Mary's in Independence, Michael Quigley and Mary Murphy were married by the great priest, Father Donnelly. Joseph rode his horse to Independence to participate in the wedding. He was proud of his brother, and he thought Mary was the perfect wife.

By the time he married, Michael had nearly saved enough to purchase his forty-acre piece. For a time, when there was no work in Independence, he and Mary moved out to Big Creek to work as farmhands for a Mennonite couple. The little house in which they lived was sparse and cold, but Michael was handy. He repaired the fireplace and wind-proofed it as much as possible. The land was lo-

cated east of Pleasant Hill in Cass County. While there, he found the
farm he planned to buy.

In downtimes, Michael would stay with Mary's family in Independence and complete masonry jobs to supplement their savings.

Φ

Still a kid of sixteen in the spring of 1853, Joseph struggled to put a
roof over his head. There were plenty of other boys in his situation
who worked, got paid, and then drank and caroused. It was their
whole life.

Through his early childhood, Joseph had created plenty of concern, but it did not match the misery that had been dumped on him
in Ireland and until he and Michael got settled in Cincinnati. His
ability to survive it all gave him resilience, but it also sometimes
made him hard-hearted because he was learning to feel indifference.
Now that he could make significant choices, his desire to live freely and independently placed him among the single male riffraff of
West Bottoms.

Kansas Town officially became Kansas City in 1853. It had only
2,500 people, but it had its typical number of degenerate youth of
both genders. Fortunately, Joseph wasn't one of them, as Michael
had predicted. Because he had come from a spiritual family, he
knew right from wrong. Though he entertained girls of all persuasions, he preferred intelligent and decent girls. He simply crossed
the Quigley behavior line with women because he could. He adapted
immediately to the culture of his single male companions of West
Bottoms. Respectable Catholic girls from thriving and stable families of Westport were not generally accessible in his life. As soon
as the solid Irish families could, they moved into Westport to join
a less impoverished and better educated class, but as a single youth,
that didn't include Joseph. Fortunately, his talent led him to work
and learn from some men of good character and influence.

Very soon after his arrival in West Bottoms, Joseph was assigned
by Mr. McCoy's outfitting company to work with Mr. Martin Hayes.
Martin was a middle-aged wagon driver and expert. When he performed work for McCoy, Joseph was his assistant and learned ev-

ery way to properly match up and hitch horses, mules, or oxen in a team. Joseph could identify and use every piece of equipment by the time he was seventeen. Martin had worked his whole life with outfitters, traders, and suppliers in the business, and then he began transporting independently. He appreciated Joseph's special talents and often hired Joseph to accompany him on important trips into Independence. By 1854, Joseph went by himself. Joseph had not been intoxicated in front of Martin Hayes who didn't drink at all.

When he could, Joseph rode out to visit Michael and Mary. He liked proving to Michael that he was still alive, and he enjoyed seeing family. In May of 1855, Mary and Michael had a daughter, Ellen, and she reminded Joseph a little of his sister Margaret. She was smart, pretty, and a good, good little girl.

When Joseph went to pick up yokes outside Independence, he often stopped by the Murphy family to pick up Ellen and sing and dance around with her. It fired his own desire to have a family. His task at this part of his life, however, was to pick up oxen yokes and other equipment made by Hiram Young.

People took notice of the handsome, diminutive Irish lad singing and smartly driving the giant wagon with the large team along the busy streets from Kansas Town to Hiram's well-known collection of barns in Independence.

Hiram was a former slave who had bought his freedom. He started out making handsome and sturdy wood products like ax handles and yokes for the outfitters. He first had purchased the freedom of his wife, so their successively born children could be free. It was from the wood objects that he purchased his own freedom and began building large wagons for the trails. Mr. Hayes spoke highly of Hiram and made sure Joseph was aware of Hiram's fine work and reputation. Joseph admired Hiram's handiwork, but he also loved to talk with him.

Hiram was measured and quiet, at least with the white folks he didn't know but did business with. Some of his responses came after considerable deliberation. Not possessing social correctness, Joseph had no end of questions about how a slave lived, how Hiram felt as a child being separated from family, and how it was to buy your own or someone else's freedom. Joseph felt comfortable asking questions anyplace or anytime of anyone, so he asked Hiram a lot of questions others might think inappropriate. People were shocked at how brash Joe Quigley could be. He seemed unable to notice that the conversations were usually one-sided.

As Hiram worked on a yoke for McCoy, Joseph asked, "Mr. Young, is yer mother alive?"

Hiram answered, "I'm not sure."

Joseph responded, "I know me mother is dead because she died on the boat comin' to America. She died the day we arrived, after traveling six weeks. I don't know when me da died. When we arrived at Staten Island, we were quarantined. They took him away, but he was almost dead when he left, so he might have died the same day. We had a baby that died right after she was born. Her name was Doroty, but not even me ma got to know her. Did ye know yer ma, Hiram?"

Hiram answered, "I think so, but I may have been sold off when I was an infant."

"Did ye say sold, Hiram?"

"Yes. We were all bought or sold—like I sell these yokes and wagons or an ax."

Joseph continued, "Three of my siblings probably died in the same week. Me brother Michael and I had to leave me sister Margaret behind in a convent so she could go to school to become a teacher."

Hiram asked, "Do you think she was blessed to be able to go to school—or would you rather have kept Margaret with your family?"

"Families are supposed to be together, don't ye think? She might have died goin' off with us, or maybe we couldn't have fed her. I don't know if anything we did was right. Our da told Michael that he should have stayed in Ireland so we could all die together lyin' in a field with the sheep, but I'm glad if she'll be happy bein' a teacher. It sounds like your family was broken up because of how bad slavery is. Mine was broken up by illness and bein' too poor and havin' no place. We had no place to be together. We had no money for food. I guess ye had no place to go either. If ye did, ye'd have to be able to hide—or they'd come and take ye back, right? I guess it's still that way now. Ye didn't have yer own money either, did ye?"

"That's right, Joseph. No place, no father, no money. I had nothin' of my own until now, and that doesn't mean I'll get to keep it unless I keep fightin' for everything I've ever made of my own."

"What about brothers or sisters?"

Hiram answered, "My brother is free. So is his wife. He works here with me in one of the barns, and we're fixin' to get more of the family freed when we can."

Joseph said, "Stepbrother Michael lives in Independence. He's older. His ma died when he was seven, so Da married her cousin Margaret, who was me ma. I have a younger sister and brother in Pennsylvania. We had to leave them with a cousin, but we told them that when we get a farm, we'll send for them. I really miss me brother Charley. Ye'd love Charley. Everyone loves Charley. He's the nicest person in the world.

"One thing I can say, Hiram, is that being free is a wonderful thing. In Ireland, people have always had to fight unfair laws and the heavy hand of the English. There were laws that didn't let Irish Catholics go to their own church. Irish parents couldn't send their children to school or teach their own children. English soldiers buried priests and nuns in the sand up to their necks and left them to face the rising tides. It's better there now.

"Here, I'd say the slaves never had any laws on their side. For some people, life is so unfair that I don't understand it. Makes me wonder why God made things the way they are. For someone all-knowin' and all-lovin', it doesn't make sense to me. What do ye think, Hiram?"

"I think it doesn't matter. It is just the way it is. We can fight to change those who have power over us or try to change the circumstance—even if it kills us. I also think we're done fixing the adjustment on this yoke."

Joseph knew Hiram could be trusted and would listen, but he knew Hiram wanted to be done with him now. Even if Joseph talked on, Hiram would continue to work or talk with his men as Joseph talked away, totally ignoring Joseph until he caught on to shut it.

With Joseph, no idea went undiscussed. Hanging about older men who possessed special skills and who were engaged in work was where he spent most of his time—whether he was getting paid or not. As Hiram worked on broken or replacement parts, yokes, and other things for Hayes, Joseph incessantly asked, "Why" or "What does that do?" or "Have you ever tried?"

Martin Hayes and Hiram answered all Joseph's equipment and livestock questions.

There was only one day Hiram did not talk with Joseph. Joseph had been drinking, and Hiram knew it. He made Joseph sleep in the barn overnight before he would send him back with Martin's wagon and his load, and he didn't feed him. He offered food if Joseph was hungry—but not if he had been drinking. Joseph learned that in one event.

From their conversations, Joseph formed an even stronger opinion about the slavery questions. It robbed people of their lives, and when it came to family and livelihood, it was cruel and unfair. He couldn't imagine Hiram making beautiful wagons or yokes of wood and someone else getting paid for them. It would be worse if someone else got the credit for making them.

Hiram's wagons were made for mules or oxen and were designed to be especially sturdy for the beasts and the trails going to the West. They were highly reliable, and they were thought to be better by "insiders" than wagons other manufacturers from the region made. Each wagon carried Hiram's signature when it was complete.

Joe admired how Hiram learned how to go after everything he deserved. He refused to let others, white or otherwise, rob him of his pride or dignity. He had good lawyers, and he used them. Joseph especially respected that Hiram did not scoop or bow. He was a short man who stood tall. Joseph felt the same way about being Irish.

One day, Joseph asked, "Mr. Hiram, someday I'm going to start me own business. Do you suppose that you could build me wagon?"

Hiram answered, "Of course, Mr. Quigley. When you have the money saved, I would be proud to start my woodworkers on your own Hiram Young wagon—unless you come here and have been drinking. I'll sell a wagon to anyone with the money, but I don't like to build a beautiful wagon for a person who would go out and kill himself or an animal pulling the wagon. If a man has been drinking, he will not leave my barn with an animal or the wagon." From that moment on, Joseph discussed with Hiram the custom design of his future wagon, but he never drank when he would be around Hiram. Every time he discussed cost or asked for another special feature, Hiram would raise the price.

One day, Hiram turned to Joseph, looked him straight in the eye, and stated, "Son, have you ever heard that you have to put the horse before the cart?"

Joseph replied, "Mr. Hiram, I have thought of such a thing, but seeing yer beautiful wagons and wantin' one so bad, I never planned for it in that order."

They both laughed, and Joseph never discussed the wagon again. Instead, he started to save for his horse and a proper team. He wanted his first wagon to be a horse-driven one, and he hoped Hiram would see it his way.

As spring of 1855 approached, Martin Hayes had business with Hiram. On the day after Joseph bought his first draft horse, they hitched her up to the team and took a ride over to Hiram's farm so Joseph could show off his new horse.

"Yes, it's a nice horse," Hiram noted. "Congratulations on the start of your business. The horse goes before the cart, Joe, but oxen or mules go before my wagons, so when you bring me four mules, we'll hitch up your wagon together."

Mr. Hayes also helped Joseph set high standards for running his wagon business. He taught Joseph how to acquire good jobs and get the money he was worth. Everyone respected Martin's knowledge, and Joseph realized that when he acted like Mr. Hayes, people treated him like they treated Martin. Joseph always referred to Martin as "Mr. Hayes" when speaking of him to clients. It brought both of them dignity and respect. Teamsters were not paid well, and they often got cheated, but Mr. Hayes was so respected that people who knew who he was didn't try to cheat him.

Joseph was grateful for and proud of the work he did for Hayes, and as he developed his own business, his reputation with Martin spilled over into his own business.

CHAPTER 16

WESTPHALIA, KANSAS, 1857

When Joseph was nineteen, in 1856, he moved out of the West Bottoms shanties and into a boardinghouse above the bluffs. It was a few blocks from where the new Catholic church was to be built. The boardinghouse represented a significant move up, and it changed his world. It was his first room alone, and he wasn't bouncing from place to place in overcrowded and often chaotic conditions among young males competing for resources, girls, and opportunities. In West Bottoms, people were always arriving, moving on, or disappearing. Things got decrepit quickly.

In Westport proper, he could depend on a decent meal from his landlady when he was home. He had a difficult stomach, and the elderly widow, Judith O'Neill, cooked with lots of potatoes and other root vegetables from her small garden. It was well worth the cost. They filled him up and, along with fresh eggs, quieted his fickle gut.

Judith treated Joseph like a son. Friends came to her door to hear the personal concerts he "practiced" the night before in the pub. Judith really had no idea how old Joseph was, and neither did the men he worked with. They more or less treated him like he was an adult, but they thought of him as a kid because of his personality.

Judith most often requested "The Voice of Joy," "The Lullaby," and "The Fair Hills of Eire Ogh." When there was a lady friend present who Judith especially liked, Joseph would spring "O Judith, My Dear" on her. She would giggle, swoon, and say, "Oh, Joe." Sometimes, she would cry with joy from his attention and missing her own family.

Living in Westport, he was closer to the nightly action in the friendly pub and the big hotel. In 1854, a grandson of Daniel Boone, Albert Gallatin Boone, had built the building adjacent to the pub that became the general store. Westport's noted pioneer and entrepreneur, Mr. McCoy, a Baptist missionary to the natives, owned most of the surrounding land and was credited for developing Westport into the center of commerce. He sold his land only to those who would develop responsibly. Solid buildings of stone and brick became the norm, and Westport was booming from a settlement into an attractive major city. The steamboat business was still supporting the growing meatpacking industry, the making of saddles and other leather goods, and breeding cattle and horses. Ground for the first train far east into St. Louis had been broken in 1851, and everyone knew that the train was on its way, sooner or later, to what was called Kansas Town. It was only a matter of time before the slow and dangerous steamboats would be obsolete for carrying cargo and passengers. Joseph couldn't wait to see what a train would bring. He planned to greet it as a wealthy man when it arrived.

With his young peers, Joseph constantly honed his driving, riding, and shooting skills. He was doing financially as well as could be expected. In spite of his appetite for being the life of the party, he diligently worked and saved money for his Hiram Young wagon so he could fully run his own business. He still worked jobs for Martin, but he also did some of his own jobs. They shared equipment and animals, which was an unusual arrangement, but they worked well together and seldom had disagreements.

Back in 1853, in his preparations for his own company, Joseph's first thought was to acquire Elizabeth to be his lead. Mr. McCoy agreed to separate his ownership with Elizabeth when Joseph proposed a deal to "work out" his debt for her. He was only a kid, so Mr. McCoy was amazed when—with that twinkle in his steely eyes—Joseph told McCoy that Elizabeth had fallen in love with him at first sight. He said, "I have to have her. We belong together because she loves me."

Joseph had used her while employed by McCoy. He had already demonstrated for McCoy how Elizabeth trained her eyes on only him when he was in her presence. Elizabeth wanted to follow him and nobody else. He had, on occasion, had to persuade her to move for other drivers. Joseph believed she begged to demonstrate her love for him in front of others.

The day he approached McCoy, he had McCoy stand next to him, both directly in front of Elizabeth. He draped her reins over her neck and asked McCoy to walk forward, asking Elizabeth to walk forward with him. She refused to budge. When Joe walked forward, Elizabeth, without a command followed him—and her nose was practically sitting on his shoulder after two steps.

McCoy and Joe shook hands, and he handed her over to him for practically nothing.

Joseph said, "Elizabeth, say thank you." He pulled gently on her reins, and she kicked up her heels, cuddled her head under Joseph's armpit, and acted like a giddy bride.

In 1856, he had been able to acquire a perfect companion for Elizabeth Quigley and named him Jack. He would tell people that Jack's last name was Ass—until people quit laughing. Elizabeth and Jack, with two of Martin's mules, made a great team, and he and Martin prospered with them.

Φ

Unfortunately, in 1857, though the railroad had not yet reached Kansas City, the financial and banking crisis had. The "Great Panic" was the first international financial crisis. It hit Joseph broadside because he couldn't imagine such a thing could happen in such a prosperous place. Many blamed it on the railroads or the governor, but it was affecting the world.

Kansas Town had grown three times its size in the short time he had lived there. Money was hard to come by in the panic, and Joseph's outfitter jobs were becoming diminished. He hauled limited livestock for the very few who were going west, and he generally hauled anything he could get his hands on.

During hard times, Michael worked on road construction to supplement his farming and its crashed product prices. As Joseph was having difficulty in the panic, Michael was doing stonework over a bridge crossing in a newly platted land in Kansas that would be called Garnett. It was to become the county seat of Anderson County, and he hoped to step into the job of bricklayer on the courthouse. There was road construction in progress to access Garnett directly from Ottawa, thirty miles north, and Westphalia, about fifteen miles to the west. The revenue had already been collected by the county for the initial work, so Michael got there the moment the surveyors were to start on the roads.

Michael recommended Joseph as a hauler of the surveying equipment from Kansas City to Garnett and out to Westphalia. Westphalia was near another town to the north called Emerald where a predominant Irish settlement had recently been established.

Φ

On a crisp autumn Friday, a group of young ladies was riding a substantial carriage into Garnett. Joseph needed to pull over to allow the girls to pass on the rough, narrow road into town. He got off his wagon, doffed his hat, and bowed for them as they passed. Instead of continuing on their way, they stopped to find out who the uniquely polite gentleman was.

It was not unusual for men to display chivalrous behavior when yielding right-of-way, but this young man was so handsome and keen to flirt that, as they were "women of good will and quality," it was incumbent upon them show a special level of gratitude—and they did.

Once the ladies passed, two of them stepped from the carriage with a small, decorated box.

The older girl said, "My name is Agnes McManus."

The younger girl stated, "And I'm her sister, Mary McManus. We're on our way to a birthday party in Garnett, but you are so demonstrative in your politeness that we'd like to offer you one of our petit fours. Would you like lemon or sassafras?"

"Sassafras?" exclaimed Joe. "First, let me introduce meself. I am Joe Quigley, but I've never heard of sassafras in a petit four—let alone have I heard of a petit four."

Agnes said, "Then ye must try it, Mr. Quigley. It's French for little oven. When yer hot oven begins to cool, ye put in the cake so it will bake—but not burn."

Joseph replied, "I feel me own oven is burnin' right now."

Mary blushed, handed him a one-inch frosted square of sassafras cake, and cocked her head to one side.

Joseph knew she felt a desire to touch his hand again. If he liked it, she would give him another.

He ate it, declaring it the most delicious thing he had ever tasted.

Mary handed him a lemon cake. As she slowly pulled her hand away, he followed it for a brief moment.

She emitted a little "Oh!" and giggled.

Agnes placed the lid back on the box, and Mary helped her retie the bow.

"How can I ever thank ye, ladies?"

Mary's hair was piled up and fixed with pins and a claret ribbon. With sparkling eyes and a little flirty twist of her shoulders, so that the little curls bounced about her face, Mary said, "We came from a farm outside Westphalia—so maybe ye'll see us again."

Joseph looked directly into Mary's clear eyes and said, "I will pray for it. In fact, I'm on me way there now to unload these construction materials. I unloaded some in Garnett earlier. I'm from Westport. Some of this came off a steamboat there, and it is being used to help Garnett grow with several large buildings and improved roads. This road to Westphalia needs work as well, so I'm hauling things to both Garnett and Westphalia. Some of it will be used to survey this road. However, before ye go, please let me sing a little song in repayment for yer delicious petit fours."

Joseph cleared his throat and broke into his spontaneous and dramatic version of an Irish tune called "Till We Meet Again." He used it often, merely changing the words to fit the intended audience.

May the sunshine kiss ye on yer cheek,
May it rest within yer soul,
Ye are the sweetest ladies that I'll ever get to know.
May the wind propel ye into town,
So ye can meet yer friends,
May luck and love be at yer call, till we meet again.

Agnes and Mary blushed and cooed, and Mary fell into her pattern of very nervous chatter, an Irish trend she had practiced to perfection. She told Joseph that they would be at Mass at Saint Patrick's, a little cabin in Emerald, on Sunday after next, and if he were there, they would be sure to see him again. He could meet Agnes's boyfriend, Frank Drumm, and their little sister, Bridget, who was nine.

Mary took a breath and continued with the history lesson. "Me older brother, Daniel, is twenty-four, but our sisters Kate and Teresa are just little ones. Our sister Margaret Groves is married and twenty-one. She won't be there. I turned seventeen last month. I'll let Agnes tell you how old she is if she wishes. Of course, you can see that she is older than I since she's getting' married. However, Ma and Da will be there, and the Drumms, Fitzgeralds, Agnews, Magraths, and possibly Grants, our grandparents' family. They're all family and friends who settled the village of Emerald. Ye'd love our family. They're very charmin'. Ye can't miss the church; it's on the top of the very prominent hill—the only one ye'll see."

Joseph took a deep breath and acted grateful, but he was overwhelmed and terrified of meeting so many persons of apparent great ilk in one place. He decided to not visit Saint Patrick's on Sunday. *Who made French petit fours on pioneer settlements on the Kansas prairie? Not the starvin' Irish to be sure. Many lived in dirt caves dug into the side of a hill—with a face made of mud and grass surrounding a window or two and a framed-out door. Fancy for his family was fried prátaí / potatoes, but not petit fours.*

As Mary McManus spoke, he discerned that these were not people like he and his brother. He had not met the likes of these girls before, and he might not be properly dressed, hauling dirty equipment and stone blocks with mules. These girls wore fancy dresses and carried a cedar chest with more dresses of silk or taffeta.

Agnes said, "I think it would just be lovely, Mr. Quigley, if you could join us at church, but we must get to Henrietta's, Mary, don't ye think? We don't want to miss supper with the Magraths."

Mary added, "Tomorrow, I'm playing the piano at the party. Too bad yer goin' in the wrong direction, Joseph Quigley. Ye could sing, and I could play. Yer ridin' in the right direction to the church. Ye'll have to turn north when ye get to Westphalia. Westphalia is left; the church is right. We live on the way to the church—"

"That's fine, Mary," Agnes said. "We'll be sayin' our goodbyes, Mr. Quigley. It's been lovely, then." She smiled genuinely and added, "Till we meet again!"

Before Mary stepped her sixteen-year-old body into the carriage, she turned around and glanced at Joseph with a look that said that her heart was being ripped from her body at saying goodbye to the most handsome man and beautiful voice she'd ever encountered. She yelled, "Again, Joseph, where do ye live?"

Joseph pointed north and said, "I live all the way in Westport."

She answered, "I may go there to teach. Perhaps I'll see you then."

Joseph thought, *'Tis unlikely. She's so young she'll probably get over that thought by the time she gets to the party.*

Mary climbed into the carriage, and Agnes climbed up to take the reins. Mary waved out the window and turned and blew a kiss. Joseph's heart skipped a beat, and he suddenly felt significantly taken by this sparkly girl.

Mary and Agnes were different from the girls he was accustomed to meeting in West Bottoms who worked in saloons and restaurants. They washed laundry and hauled it in baskets up the long hill to the nice homes that lined the streets above the bluffs.

The wealthy girls of Westport were the kind of young ladies who had been living in a different world from Joseph. He drove past them without speaking. He thought those girls to be standoffish and disinclined to share their *petit fours*.

He didn't know of a place where kids went to school in Westport. None of the children in the West Bottoms slum had money for school. *Where in the world would Mary McManus be teaching?*

Mary was someone different. Even though the McManus girls seemed to be highfalutin, they had no reservations about stopping to talk with Joseph. They did not make him feel less than they, something that would not happen in Westport. They were more like the Irish hometown girls or farmer girls like Mary Murphy. Irish parents in Kansas City warned their daughters not to talk with the boys from West Bottoms, let alone hand out little cakes. They were trying to be more like the English-style American in Westport—keeping themselves separated from the riffraff.

Mary seemed to be a better educated and seriously wholesome version of Sarah Conroy, but Joseph had decided to forgo Mary's invitation because it was very inconvenient—and she was very young. Also, he lived nearly a hundred miles from Westphalia. If he weren't so desperate for work, and it hadn't been for Michael, he wouldn't have been in Westphalia in the first place. He felt out of his element.

Unfortunately, as he rode on, he began thinking of possibilities: If he settled a little north of Garnett, like Wea or Pottawatomie, he could haul for these new roads until the town was finished, and maybe he would see Mary again. However, he couldn't take care of a team and live in two places. He would not move out there because of an attractive young girl he didn't know. Besides, he wanted to work in a place that was booming.

After leaving his load in Westphalia as directed, he decided not to take the same route home. He spent a night in his wagon. He tethered his team of mules in a harvested field of corn stubble a couple of miles north out of town near a stream, a little Protestant church, and a cemetery. He was glad he had mules. They were easy to feed and rest. Tomorrow he would ride through Emerald and then catch the main road straight into Westport.

Hauling large loads so far out and back took most of his week. It was risky because it was more difficult to care for his team and repair broken equipment. He also decided that if he didn't absolutely have to haul gravel, he wouldn't. Hauling gravel, he'd need to board with the working crew in Garnett and have a permanent job in construction, perhaps leaving Westport altogether. Once he returned home, however, he checked on his biggest-paying contact, John Miller, and he tried to get the fascinating young Mary McManus from Westphalia out of his mind.

One good turn of luck for Michael and Joseph was the construction in 1857 and 1858 of the Immaculate Conception Church. It was northeast of West Bottoms—and on the way to Independence. The brick was made by the immigrants of Connaught, Ireland, who constructed the factory and used the limestone located from the bluffs very close to the cathedral. Joseph hauled materials to and from the site regularly for several weeks. The company provided the rock wagon and paid for Elizabeth and Jack's livery since they did not provide the mules with the wagon. Michael gave Joseph additional leads from his church connections.

Φ

By 1858, the Jayhawkers of Kansas and the Border Ruffians of Missouri were running wild and mean along the Kansas-Missouri border. Cargo Joseph carried outside Westport or Kansas City had become fair game. People had clearly chosen sides in the abolitionist or proslavery camps, and it was beginning to boil over into Joseph's life, livelihood, and stomach. Though things got tough, Joseph got tougher. When men tried to swindle him, Joseph went immediately after his money with his gun if he couldn't settle in trade. He had bought or traded for horses, his Sharps rifle, and his special revolver, and he had gained a reputation as a sharpshooter as well as a highly skilled teamster.

He went hunting with Josh and another acquaintance, Billy, but it usually evolved into target practice, shared tales, and serious preparation for violence on the roads. When he was around Billy, he watched his back. Billy looked for any excuse to turn on a mustard seed, and he was secesh for sure.

Joseph had come to rely on shooting accuracy when transporting things on long hauls around Jackson, Cass, Johnson, Lafayette, Pettis, or Saline Counties. On some of his deliveries, he was given forewarning to take a partner to ride shotgun. Sometimes Josh or another friend would drive Joseph's wagon as Joseph rode guard. He was a better shot, and he carried both weapons, which he practiced shooting with both hands. He earned more money when the job would be especially dangerous or when the military hired him. He charged for the security. Joe bought bullets first— before livestock food after every paycheck—and he found himself shooting at men more often than he ever told Mr. Hayes. He shot to stop and not necessarily to kill. He had not missed all his targets on the road, but a robber didn't go to the authorities to complain about their wounds.

Joseph was staying on the right side of the law, and he had not been charged with wounding or killing anyone. He didn't know if he had killed anyone yet, but it seemed inevitable to him.

Learning to kill made him less charming but more in demand. The fact that he had a reputation as a marksman and had good weapons gave him a level of power he enjoyed. "It's how ye become a man to be reckoned with and looked up to, if yer not afeared of losin' yer biscuits," he would tell the ladies.

During the worst of the slack period, in early spring of 1858, Michael told Joseph to go back out to Garnett, because they had just taken out a large workforce. Michael was present when the men were loading up, and the boss in charge of the project was looking for a large wagon to haul supplies to Garnett and then load up an unusually large piece of equipment that needed to go from Garnett out to Westphalia.

Michael had spoken up for Joseph and had the name of the supplier for Joseph. Joseph jumped on his Morgan, Cúramach, and rode to the supplier who told Joseph he was needed to haul to Garnett as soon as possible. They were expecting their load within the week. The load was mainly food and tools, and it paid very well. Donald, the supplier, told him to take a rifle in the event he ran into thieves, which was becoming a regular event. It was also wet, and hauling his heavy wagon in mud worried him.

However, Joseph was glad to finally have an excuse for going back out toward Westphalia. His heart beat a little faster when he thought of the prospect of meeting the McManus girls again. It would work out because he had spoken with John Miller from the leather factory who said he had some big business deal coming up and might need Joseph's help later in the month. John was secretive and asked Joseph not to share what he had been told, but he gave Joseph money to commit to the jobs.

Unless he had a reason, Joseph didn't tell other drivers— other than Martin or Josh—what his jobs were because he didn't want anyone else cutting in on his work opportunities. If a driver told someone else where he was headed the next day, another driver might get there first and take his job. Competition was tough during the panic, and political division was growing more dangerous. No road was safe on the border.

It seemed that half his friends and acquaintances went one way, and the other half went the other way on the slavery issue.

He could trust no one, and it was growing nearly impossible to either remain outwardly neutral or to sort out who was on which side without asking. His potential client, John Miller, seemed a little disingenuous, but Joseph knew there was money in the jobs.

On Joseph's way out to Garnett, he had no bad encounters. Once his team was unhitched for a good meal and the load was discharged, the workers began to load up the equipment for Westphalia. The load turned out to be a large metal contraption with wheels that was disassembled so as to fit in a wagon. It had a large rectangular paddle like a plow that could be dragged down a road to smooth it out level. It was pulled by a team behind a crew of men shoveling down rock. Joseph had seen the smaller wooden version of it before—but not the metal version. It weighed a lot. Because the weather was excellent, Joe's team could probably handle it, but maybe not with ease.

He was going to stay the night to rest and feed his mules, try to find an additional mule, and start fresh early in the morning. He asked around about anyone with mules. A crew boss had picked up mules from a farm north of town, so Joseph rode out with him to take a look at a possible addition to his team. He saw a number of mules out in a field. There was a little dog sitting next to one who looked like the mule's companion. Joseph inquired of the farmer if the mule and dog were friends.

The owner said, "Yes. The mule's name is Santa Fe, and he is partial to the dog."

As Joseph guessed by his appearance, Santa Fe had experienced a career of hauling, but he still seemed healthy, strong, and not too old. The man said he was all right with selling him or renting him out.

Joseph was skeptical. "Have ye ever rented out a mule before?"

"Yes." The man laughed and shook his head. "This very mule has worked a few times in Garnett this winter. I can guarantee he's had more than one driver, and he's worked out fine. He's a pretty easy spirit. Whoever rents him has to feed him."

Joseph was always concerned about strangers, and he knew that a mule didn't go for a lot of ridiculousness. They also didn't like change. As Joseph took time to think, the man stood by and waited for a decision.

Joseph went up to Santa Fe, called him by his name, and talked with him quietly without touching him. Joseph then stood in front of him, turned, and walked away. The mule did not follow. When Joseph turned around and looked behind him, Santa Fe was looking back at the dog. Joseph said, "What's the dog's name?"

"Sandy."

Joseph patted his hands on his thighs and said, "Come on, boy. Come on, Sandy."

The little dog went to Joseph and was petted.

"That's a good boy, Sandy." Joseph turned around and started to walk away again. Soon, he turned back to the mule and said, "Come on, Santa Fe. Come with me and Sandy. Come on, Sandy. Santa Fe, I have something in my pocket if ye'll walk with us." Joseph patted his pocket.

Sandy walked along with Joseph. As the distance between Joseph and Santa Fe got greater, the mule couldn't resist. He trotted forward, braying loudly. As soon as Santa Fe matched strides with them, Joseph produced an apple slice from his pocket and offered it.

Santa Fe immediately took the treat, and as long as Joseph walked forward, Santa Fe followed.

Joseph picked up Sandy and set him on Santa Fe's back. Confused, Sandy and Santa Fe stood still until Joe pulled Sandy's front legs down and held him on top of Santa Fe. Santa Fe brayed and sniffed Joseph's pocket for a second slice. As they walked along, Joseph held Sandy steady, and Santa Fe kept walking.

Joseph reached up and took Sandy off. "I'll only need Santa Fe for a day's work, but I want to take him to the stable tonight to meet his new girlfriend, Elizabeth. There are two men who are riding with me tomorrow who can bring him back within the next day or two. Can I take Sandy with us? He can ride in the wagon part of the way.

He won't run off if Santa Fe is there, and Santa Fe will like a friend with him—someone besides me."

They shook hands, and it was a deal.

In his wagon, Joseph had a basket for personal items. For the ride home on Santa Fe, Joseph fastened a strap through slits in the bottom of the basket that would hold it to Santa Fe's back. He sang a new song about Elizabeth, Santa Fe, and Sandy as he rigged the basket. When he tried the basket bed out on his back, Santa Fe was completely agreeable to it. For the night, Joseph flung the basket down into the straw in their stall. In the livery stable, Elizabeth, Santa Fe, and Sandy slept in the same stall overnight and got along perfectly.

When Joseph hitched his team back up, he placed Elizabeth alone in the lead and Santa Fe directly behind her, next to Jack, and took his load without trouble to a waiting crew in Westphalia. The two men who had ridden behind to reassemble the machine returned leading Santa Fe and Sandy, riding home in his basket or trotting along beside.

Joseph had already decided that he would return home the same way he returned on his last trip, riding past the McManus farm and the church in Emerald. This time, he asked directions to the McManus farm since he had passed it by not knowing for sure which was theirs last time.

When he saw Mary out hanging laundry for her mother with two younger girls, he knew he had arrived. He also saw three men carrying a wardrobe out to a wagon. There were other boxes, a barrel, two chairs, and a desk sitting next to the wagon.

He drove his team all the way around a circular driveway and faced it to the road in front before he stopped. As Mary dropped what she was doing with her sister Bridget, Joseph pulled on his brake and hopped down to greet Mary.

Mary was far more restrained in the presence of her parents than she had been on the day they parted—when she threw her secret kiss—but her blushing cheeks revealed her feelings.

Joseph saw their large barn, a carriage house, and two other large sheds. He wondered how long they had been in Kansas and decided they must have come to America in better financial and physical shape than Joseph's family had arrived.

Mary greeted him and took him back toward their wagon to meet her father, two other men, and her brother.

"Da, this is Joseph Quigley, whom Agnes and I met on the way to the birthday party. Do ye recall?"

"Of course, I recall, Mary. Mr. Quigley, I'm John McManus, Mary's father."

The two shook hands, and Joseph said, "It looks as though someone is moving in or out?"

John McManus asked, "You don't know anything about this, do you?" He was suddenly curious as to why Joseph would happen to show up at this moment. He noticed his daughter's self- consciousness and rosy cheeks.

"No. I just left a metal road grader off in Westphalia for Anderson County to put back together and use, and now I'm on my way back to Westport. I met your Agnes and Mary when I had to stop and let them pass on the road a while back. They told me about your farm and the church in Emerald. This is a more direct route and a better road home, so I thought I'd stop and say hello when I saw Mary hanging laundry. Your daughters were so nice and gave me samples of their petit fours. This is not a social trip for me—or else I might have brought a gift of me own."

Mary said, "I know what ye can do. Ye can sing for us!"

John said, "Probably not right now, Mary." He turned to Joseph. "Now that she's seventeen, Mary has decided to accept a job teaching in a new and very small private school. We need to move her into a boardinghouse in Westport. Students will be tutored in her apartment, so she's taking everything she owns. We don't have quite enough room, but it looks like we might have struck some good luck in your sudden appearance."

"This is Mary's brother Daniel, Agnes's fiancée, Mr. Drumm, and a neighbor, John Keyser."

The men shook hands cordially.

Daniel said, "Joseph, are you goin' to pick up another load on yer way back?"

"No, actually. I brought supplies into Garnett and then the grader out here. Me wagon is empty."

Mary pressed her fingers together as if in prayer and exclaimed, "'Tis divine providence! Now I can get all me books, me desk, and me chair as well."

"Don't ye think we should ask the gentleman first if he is in the mood to carry yer things a hundred miles? He is a workin' man, Mary, not yer willin' servant."

Mary said, "Well, Mr. Workin' Man, could we hire ye to haul me wardrobe and desk to Westport if it is not out of yer way?"

"'Tis exactly on me way. I live in Westport, so yer family will not have to turn around and come back with an empty wagon. I'll ask for water and a good meal for me and me mules in exchange. Also, I was going to sleep on the road tonight. Perhaps I could sleep in yer barn?"

John said, "We can easily feed yer team and better than the barn, ye can sleep in the farmhand quarters. We have one worker there now. Do ye mind?"

Joseph agreed, and the deal was struck.

Daniel and Mary McManus rode along, and she became Joseph's Westport neighbor.

CHAPTER 17

WESTPORT, MISSOURI, 1858

John Miller had a condescending way and always dressed to make the best impression. He acted more important than he actually was. He started out too friendly with Joseph. He should have treated Joseph like everyone else in his position did: respectful, to the point, and socially superior. Miller wanted to take Joseph for drinks.

Joseph thought, *As though a middle-aged businessman had anything in common with a young Irish mule driver.*

When Miller moved the conversation toward the slavery issue, Joseph would say, "I know nothin' about politics. I'm a wagoner and a handler, and I haven't been here long enough to be a citizen." To Joseph, it became obvious that Miller wanted more from him than merely carrying something from one place to the other. Miller was seeking loyalty. He was manipulative. He sought ways to compromise Joseph and his limited loyalties. For conversational purposes, Joseph conveyed the impression that he was the only person in his family.

Joseph knew that nothing would be learned about him from his real mentors, Hiram and Martin, and they actually knew Joseph. However, Martin had Quakers in his background. If Miller thought Joseph's partner was a Quaker, he could have assumed Joseph was a Union sympathizer. Because Mr. Hayes stayed neutral by not dressing, speaking, or attending meetings as a Quaker, Miller probably could not have guessed.

John Miller was thought to be high up in the leather business. Joseph's impression of Miller's job was that he managed the products in how they were shipped from the factory or where they would go. Regardless, Miller acted as though he owned the business. He was clearly considered the leather boss around the employees who loaded, transported, or directly delivered the goods from the factory's warehouse.

The factory was near the cattle yards and slaughterhouse so the storage and distribution building was also on the flats near the boats. Mostly immigrants lived in West Bottoms, but men went "uptown" to Westport to rub shoulders with Miller. Josh and others had recently seen Miller associated with important men of money in the hotel and the pub. Well-dressed men usually received preferential treatment in private clubs and parties.

After two jobs with Miller, the businessmen began to nod toward Quigley, or say, "Good evening, Mr. Quigley," if they saw him eating at the hotel or the pub. Even though Joseph was rough around the edges and went into the pub with the other young men smelling like a mule more than a finely rolled cigar, he was increasingly recognized. Joseph felt like he was growing in importance for the men who made deals in back rooms and paid well. Joseph realized they probably hired him for his youth, skills, toughness, and dependability. It also became apparent that they were secesh developing trust, and Joseph did acquire a taste for the cigars they offered.

Among teamsters, rumors began to emerge that the Confederate rebels were stealing from the Union Army directly from the steamboat shipments that were off-loaded for Sedalia, Fort Scott, or Wyandotte, Kansas. Joseph had a front-row seat and was loading goods from the boats almost daily. In his position, he adhered ardently to the St. Louis advice to listen more and talk less. He was also constantly watching and looking for patterns.

One day, a wagoner looked at Joseph and said, "I'd bet me arse one of us is carrying secesh goods, and we don't even know it." Joseph never talked about what he carried, whom he carried for, or anything he saw or suspected, but the haulers knew who had the best clients. The best were, of course, the steady customers who paid the most. Men were also careful not to share how much anyone paid them or how they paid them.

If the rumors were true, Joseph intended to stay clear of such dealings that the wagoner had suggested. The leather company was maybe the biggest in America, and thousands of people across the country used their saddles. Most of the teamsters who carried large or heavy loads had carried things for John Miller or the leather company at one time or another, so Joe wasn't unique. However, to Joe's knowledge, none of them received up-front money for getting things to their destinations as Joseph did. He had never heard of such a thing until he became the recipient. It was hush money, and his secesh alliance, as far as he knew for sure, didn't exist. He had nothing to say about anything.

Jobs for Mr. Miller usually took Joseph to Strother, Warrensburg, or east of Independence—as far as Sedalia. The contents he carried included a range of things: bags of horse feed and surveying and other construction equipment in heavy wooden boxes like those he had seen in St. Louis on the Gem. They were loaded first and topped off with grain after other haulers had left the beach. There were saddles and leather fittings for horses and other basic goods a military operation might need. Not being in the military, Joseph supposed that both the Union and Confederates might use the same things from these heavy boxes, though he seldom delivered things to a Union fort other than horses in his earlier days. He couldn't—and for a long time didn't—speculate on exactly who ended up with the contents of his loads.

Nobody his age would turn down a well-paying job. However, after several large hauls, it became obvious that he probably wasn't working for John Miller alone. It made no sense for a leather merchant to be hauling boxes and boxes labeled surveying tools east toward Sedalia under a layer of oat bags or flour, and sometimes no leather at all.

After five jobs, Joseph decided he was working for a clandestine organization of powerful men building an arsenal. If they were supplying the slavers with arms, he was their stupid Mick pawn. Though his only link to them was through Mr. Miller, he knew Miller's associates. Miller was friends with secesh river pilots and boat agents who had unusual access to and knowledge of cargo. The willing and corrupt agent would mark cargo with a black smudge of charcoal for the deckhands. Miller had marked Joseph's wagon with the same smudge. Joseph didn't ask why, but he decided he had been drawn into a secesh theft scheme in which everyone kept their mouths shut.

He had carried goods from nearly all the regular stern-wheelers or side-wheelers that landed on the Jackson County shoreline, and he knew that some captains were passionate Confederates for whom cotton, tobacco, and other slave-produced crops were their livelihood. Many were born and lived in the South and were rich and powerful men. Joseph knew they would do whatever they could to preserve slavery or fight for the secesh cause. Their wealth depended on it.

He was unwittingly acting as a traitor might, and he would need to get out before he was destroyed. He was now in a matrix of slave owners, economics based on slavery, rich men protecting their wealth, and other corrupt men optimizing their opportunities to ride on the coattails of someone else's success or misery.

Φ

He had recently carried farm equipment out to Big Creek and visited Michael. Ellen was three years old, and their son, John, was several months old. Mike and Mary seemed happy and were holding their own. There had been thefts and other growing pressures from the border conflict, but Michael's farm, which he now owned, kept them alive. Now adult siblings subjected to new pressures, he and Michael were able to talk about their lives and discuss the future. Things looked promising for the hardworking Michael, but Joseph could feel himself becoming squeezed and threatened. His surroundings had grown more dangerous and unpredictable.

Recently, he had hauled a plow and other equipment and cattle feed out to a farmer toward Sedalia. Just as he came to a ravine that opened out to a wetland, then back up to higher ground, his big mare's ears started twitching. She did a little halting step, and the other horse, one of Martin's geldings, joined her. Joseph stopped his wagon and checked his guns. He should have brought Josh, but he didn't earn enough from small farmers to justify the cost of paying another driver as he rode shotgun. The weather looked ominous as dark clouds roiled up ahead on the horizon toward the Missouri.

He sped up as he dropped down toward the creek in the ravine, and he heard a rifle and felt a bullet whiz past his right ear and barely catch the right flank of his mare. Wrapping the reins around a special bar installed on his seat, he turned from where the shot might have come and began shooting. He saw the man run up the right wall of the ravine and another man on a horse above him. As his team rushed the wagon down the rough road without his direction, he trained his rifle on the horse at the top of the hill and shot. The horse fell to his knees, and the rider fell off. He hadn't killed the horse, but he knew he had caught its left knee. As the runner cleared the top, Joseph shot him—and his rifle flew out of his hand.

Joseph thought, *Good! They're goin' nowhere soon, and me horse will be fine.*

Once out of the ravine, they didn't have far to go. When they arrived at a road that turned left, they drove up it to the man's farm. Joseph felt terrible, and he told the man that someone had shot his horse. He didn't reveal, however, that he had shot back and won! He didn't know if it might have been one of the man's neighbors.

They emptied the wagon, Joseph washed out the short, in-and- out superficial wound on his mare, and he immediately headed back, his stomach grinding all the way.

Going out past Independence was getting tough, and he decided that he would always hire someone to drive out that way. The secesh were growing in strength in certain areas, especially where future railroads would run.

It disturbed him when a horse or mule was wounded or when he had to shoot animals or people, and he began to consider the advantages of shoveling shale in the streets as Michael had frequently done.

The day his horse was wounded, he pledged that he would murder any man who shot Elizabeth—whether she died or not. Elizabeth was his first purchase and his second love; Gertie was his first.

Martin Hayes was never approached for jobs by Miller.

One day, Martin said, "Joseph, don't use anything of mine— ever again—for a Miller job. I don't trust him, and neither should you. I think I know what side you're on, and it's not Miller's or his cronies.

You know that what you're carrying doesn't normally belong on a farm. If you were taking hay or grain, it would make sense. No farm requires multiple loads of uniform-sized wooden boxes of hardware—and you know it. You can get hurt bad, Joe." Joseph agreed, watched every step he took, and kept looking over both shoulders. He didn't fraternize with the enemy as some drivers wanted to, and he guessed he wasn't the only one helping the wrong side.

Φ

He had gone for several walks, checking in on Mary to see that she was settled and safe. They went to Mass together. Mary seemed thrilled when she stood next to Joseph in church and sang.

People would turn around, look at the handsome couple, and smile.

Joseph had, with Mary's help, bought a new suit, and when in Mary's presence, Joe acted as appropriate as he looked. He never drank in front of her, and he had never gone to her apartment intoxicated. He stayed away from Mary when he was drinking.

He thought of Mary as he thought of his mother and his sisters Margaret and Ellen. They would have liked Mary and her sisters and brother, and she would have fit perfectly with his family as they were in 1848. Mary was exactly the person they would have approved of for him, but they would expect him to rise up to her standards. Joseph wasn't sure he could do that, but he would see how it went. Maybe she could reform an "occasional" drunk.

She was teaching several mornings a week, and privately tutoring students in her apartment as well. Several wealthy clients sent carriages to pick her up. Some people had a piano on which she could give lessons. Overall, she was doing very well. Mary was in high demand—as there was no school yet—and she was happy to afford her own place and have money to buy her own food and clothing.

In spite of her apparent social class, she was modest and didn't require much more than she had, though it was substantially more than the girls in West Bottoms had ever had. In that regard, Joseph believed she was a perfect fit with Michael's wife, Mary Murphy. Joseph wanted Michael and Mary to eventually meet Mary McManus, but right now, his life was complicated. He was too busy hiding his demons and dodging bullets.

Φ

As he prepared to enter the pub one night, he noticed, through the window, his bar hostess acquaintance Jenny who was holding in her hands, something in common with Mr. Miller. It appeared to Joseph that Mr. Miller was handing her money in what might be a "payoff " for some kind of service or favor. Joseph stopped and peeked over the top of the bar curtains in the window as he backed away, down the outside walkway, watching Jenny discreetly receive her small wad of cash as she nervously looked around her and slipped it into her apron.

He had seen plenty of men handing money to girls, but not Mr. Miller. Miller wasn't loose with the women who worked around the bar. He seemed to be a family man. Joe walked back around the block, turned his back to the pub door, leaned up against the building, and bent over in the dark as though he were sick until Mr. Miller walked out of the bar and past him.

Joe walked into the bar and sat at a back table. Jenny walked directly to his table, and he recognized himself as her obvious target. He had not spent time with Jenny other than when she waited on him in the establishment. She did not interest him— and even less so since he had met Mary. "So, Jenny, how are ye on this fine evenin'? I'm having dinner, so would you like to keep me company?"

Jenny said, "I'd love to, Joe, but I'm workin'. I need to keep circulatin' to keep the drinks movin'. Maybe we could have a nice long walk when I'm done here, Joe. It would be lovely to spend some time conversatin'—just the two of us. It seems that all the boys are here when we talk, so it would be nice to have just you and me, wouldn't it?"

"I don't believe you, Jenny. Ye know I have nothin' to share with ye, so what is it yer needin' to know?"

"Let's talk later, Joe. This is our busy time right now, but I'll be done after the dinner hour tonight, and I'll have all the rest of the evening just for you."

217

"Tell yer boss that ye and I have important business that can't wait. Tell him it won't take long, and he'll get some of Miller's money if he obliges. I don't think Mr. Miller spends good money for nothin', but that's what I'm thinkin' he's gettin' tonight. Pay for me meal and give a cut to yer boss. Miller will be gettin' nothin' out of me for his efforts. Ye know what nothin' is; that's what ye are: nothin'."

Jenny was only seventeen, and many girls who were in her line of work got hurt or ended their lives facedown in the Missouri River. She went to an office door at the side of the bar, told her boss that she wanted to take a "break" to spend a little time alone with Joe Quigley, and returned to Joe's table.

What might have been a flirty moment and good business for Jenny had turned sour. Her face was flushed. She no longer looked like a highly dressed woman soliciting a good time. She looked more like a frightened child in makeup who had been stretched beyond her capacity. She wasn't born to be a spy or a harlot; she was an impoverished immigrant teenager doing her best without parental guidance. She said, "My boss told me to do my business fast."

"Would ye like to sing to me, Jenny? I want to hear a tune called 'A-Spillin' of the Beans!'"

Joseph could tell Jenny had no idea what he meant. There would be no point in trying to be clever with her. He decided he would just be mean to her and get whatever it was over with. "Here's me order: I want yer fried chicken dinner, a whiskey, and I want to know what ye plan to say to Mr. Miller about me. Why did you go from Mr. Miller's money directly to me?"

"What do you mean, Joe?"

"Are ye that dumb, darlin'? Ye can't recall what Mr. Miller asked ye to do? If so, ye need to go back down to West Bottoms and work in yer crib. That requires no thought."

Without another word, Jenny ordered Joe's dinner.

Joe downed his whiskey, grabbed Jenny by the wrist, and discretely directed her out to the street. He pulled her back to the alley, slammed her face against the building, and grasped her hands tightly behind her back. "What does Mr. Miller want you to do for the money? I'm sure he prefers information over a fast trick. He's not yer type either."

Jenny said, "He wants you to tell me how you earn such good money being only a young teamster. He's wondering if you're stealing things off the boats or from his warehouse. Things are disappearing from the leather warehouse, and he thinks it might be you. People have seen you over there. He also wants to know if you're a Yankee or a Secesh."

Joseph answered, "So, Jenny, you can tell Mr. Miller that I earn me money by knowin' me business. I learned how to hitch me teams from Martin Hayes and Hiram Young. I learned how to manage money from me brother—who got us here from New York with nothin'. If he wants to know why I'm so smart, tell him I'm an Irish Catholic Quigley. We're born that way. Tell him me sister Ellen and me mule Elizabeth might be smarter than he. But be sure, Jenny, to ask him why he's not smart enough to know who's stealin' from his company. He might ask his workers before he asks the likes of you and me. Ye can tell him ye know for sure it isn't Joe Quigley who's stealin'.

"Do ye think Mr. Miller should stop sharin' his shortcomin's with the likes of us? Do ye think, Jenny, that Mr. Miller might be the one stealin' from his own company? Do you think he wants ye to spread rumors for him by pointin' the finger at me and handin' a wad of money and whisperin' in the ear of a stupid crib trick? Tell him for me it's his business to know his business, but not my business. I take care of me own business, and I don't like someone tryin' to set me up. He's usin' ye to put me in the spotlight so he can set me up. He thinks we're two stupid Micks." Joseph tightened a hand about the nape of Jenny's neck. "Do ye know how to swim? We don't expect to hear about this conversation again, do we, Jenny? Forget this moment—or ye might have an eternal float in the river. Now it's between you and Miller!" Joe loosened his grip, shoved Jenny toward the pub door, and walked behind her.

Jenny cried, turned toward Joe, and said, "I'm sorry. I might not remember everything you said. I won't repeat a thing to anyone; you have my word. I promise not to tell on ye."

"Yer word, is it? Ye've nothin' to tell on me for, darlin'. Just pay for me fried chicken as well as me whiskey—I'll have another, please— and give the rest of Mr. Miller's money to yer boss to pay for yer alley time. Yer no spy, child. Take up sewin' or prayin'. Ye'd do better with either."

Φ

The next afternoon, Joseph stopped by Mary's building to say hello. He had recently tried to stay away because of his entanglements and had lost his confidence. He didn't really believe he was good enough for her. She was so different from all the other girls who had once attracted him—but attracted him no more.

As she talked about her family or her work, he knew they lived in two different worlds. However, he knew he could love and trust her—and he knew she'd be a wonderful mother with high aspirations for their children. Maybe they would have a lawyer if they had a family. He would see to it that they had a child named after him— and he would become the lawyer his ma wanted in the family.

"Oh, Joseph!" Mary exclaimed with delight. "I almost forgot to tell ye that a lady from the Presbyterian Church who plays the organ is wantin' to give away her spinet. My poor landlady told me that I can have it if I can find someone to go pick it up. The young man who lives down the hall is a bookkeeper at the leather factory. He can help us carry it. My landlady's health is very poor. She's losin' weight daily, so I don't want to ask her to find help. I think she may have consumption. Do ye think ye could find someone else to help me pick it up?"

Joseph answered, "Please don't ask the bookkeeper, and I'll find plenty of help to get it for ye."

Mary asked, "Why wouldn't ye ask Mr. Lander? He's quite young and strong. I teach Johnny Miller, the son of a man who works in the leather office with him. Mr. Lander learned I was a teacher and recommended me to Mr. Miller. I was very grateful to him."

Joseph nearly gasped. "Have ye had any reason to mention me name to Johnny, his father, or Mr. Lander?"

Mary responded, "Of course not, but why do ye ask that? Do ye know them?"

Joseph knew that Mary liked to talk. She wanted everyone to know and love everyone else, so she was inclined to rattle off names in her every sentence. She was the middle child with considerably older siblings to look up to and whose expectations she wanted to meet. Then she and Agnes had considerably younger siblings for whom she was responsible as the oldest children left in the home. Mary seemed to be the cog of the wheel around which everything else revolved, but she was a little impulsive. When Joseph was at a party singing, he was the same way. He loved to have fun, and he saw that quality in her the day he met her.

"When is Johnny Miller scheduled to come here again, Mary?" "He's comin' tomorrow afternoon at two o'clock. He stays until three, and he'll be here the day after that at the same time."

Joseph asked, "Mary, don't ye think these rooms need new wallpaper and paint? I think it's too dingy in here for students, don't ye? Before we get yer piano, I think ye should have all yer students stay in their homes and ye go to them. Also, ye would have more privacy, don't ye think? If ye were brightenin' up yer place, they couldn't come anyway. We'd have to move the furniture all about. Because yer teachin' in the mornin', yer workers would have to come while yer students were here. Workers couldn't be hammerin' and such while yer tryin' to teach."

Mary looked at Joseph for a minute. She appeared perplexed. "So, Joseph Quigley, what's the situation with John Miller Sr. and the leather factory?"

"Oh, sweet, darlin' adorable Mary." He bent toward her and planted a perfect kiss on her cheek.

She reached up and very slowly kissed Joseph on the lips.

He asked, "Why is life so damned difficult? How does it get so complicated?"

"There's nothin' complicated about it at all, Joseph. Yer just so beautiful that I can't help meself."

"Is anyone on their way here now?" Joseph asked. Mary answered, "No. Why?"

"Let me ask ye, Mary. How do ye feel about slavery?"

Mary looked at him, again perplexed, and answered, "I abhor slavery. Many members of my mother's Grant family were sent into slavery in Barbados. Like many Irish children, they just disappeared. As you know, many Scottish soldiers and little Irish girls were sent there by the English to work in the cotton and make mixed slave babies. It's part of our history we tell every generation. Did ye not know that Irish girls who travel alone on the road have been lookin' over their shoulders for centuries?

"Think of the misery, Joseph, of all the families torn apart, workin' for nothin' and bein' mistreated and without rights. Slavery needs to be abolished once and forever and people let free. The New England company that helped me family purchase land in Emerald sent the Irish here to settle and keep Kansas free. They encouraged well-educated and stable families with the resources to build free schools, churches, and towns. That's why I'm here. In part, Irish bein' in Anderson, Kansas, has to do with Northerners tryin' to stop slavery."

Joseph answered, "I'm glad to hear ye feel that way. Do ye know that people who are fightin' to keep slavery can be very mean and corrupt? Did ye know they can be involved in sabotage and will kill people if it serves their cause? What's worse, Mary, is that ye don't know always who they are. They can be yer neighbor, yer landlord, yer student's father." Joseph looked at Mary to see if she was putting "your student's father" together with Mr. Miller. "They can be all kinds of people if ye know what I'm sayin'. They also cannot be trusted. Ye have to keep yer mouth absolutely shut about yer politics, the names of yer friends, who ye work for, and who ye know.

"Out on the farm, ye can trust all yer Irish neighbors who came together to settle, but outside that, here in Westport, it's not always safe. Right now, it's not safe for me because of my work, but I'm goin' to fix things in time. It will take time, and I don't want us to get hurt. I don't want to tell ye how I'm goin' to fix it, but I think we could have a life together, don't ye?"

Joseph kissed Mary again, looked directly into her eyes, and said, "Promise me, darlin', I don't want ye to teach Johnny Miller at yer place. I don't think it's safe. John Miller knows me. I have hauled loads for him and the leather company. We all have, but we didn't always know the details about what we're haulin'. I can't tell ye any more than that, but I don't want Mr. Miller, his son, or the bookkeeper in yer place. I also don't want them to see me in yer place. I don't want ye to mention me name. Can ye do something about that? Promise me that ye'll find a reason, like remodelin' or yer spinet didn't fit so ye had to move—anything ye can think of, so they cannot guess that it has to do with me or their politics.

"When I come pick ye up for Mass, we can meet someplace within walkin' distance, but I can't come here because I don't want to be seen by yer neighbor in this building or anyone on this street. Don't make friends with anyone where I go to pick ye up. There are a lot of people in Westport who work in that leather factory. There might be things happenin' there that ye don't want to know about. If ye know, then someone will try to get it out of ye. Do ye understand? If they blame me, they'll come to ye, and we can't have it happenin'."

Joseph took a piece of writing paper off Mary's desk and wrote down his address. "I need to go now. Here's me address. Ye can come to me boardinghouse or mail me instructions for meetin' ye somewhere—like the ends of the earth. That's how far I'd go for ye, Mary." Joseph wrapped his arms around Mary and sweetly sang a new and more tender version of "Till We Meet Again."

Mary cried as Joseph sang into her ear.

Initially, Joseph wondered why Mr. Miller's group of Confederates didn't send some of their boxes and barrels directly to landings near the destinations where he was carrying them. *It made no sense that they were shipped all the way to Kansas City and then hauled by land back in the direction from which they had come. Why not off- load things in Jefferson if the destination was Sedalia? When I go to Sedalia, men haul the cargo north across the Missouri by ferry and into Chariton or Carroll Counties. Maybe it depends on the agent. There are more in the city of Kansas than anyplace along the river—and they probably needed to work with a corrupt agent.* Joe decided he would learn which agent in West Bottoms was corrupt.

And these secesh men trust me? Where and who are their guards? Joseph began to run through the list of everyone he knew. At the top of the rat list of bottom-dwellers was Billy Davies. Billy talked a lot. Maybe Joe could learn more.

When Billy was drunk and bragging about his friends, Joseph learned that Miller and James had recently met at the hotel with a steamboat captain, a well-known secesh sympathizer, and a steamboat agent for the *David Tatum*. Kansas's governor, Andrew Horatio Reeder, a proslavery advocate, had made his escape to Pennsylvania on the *David Tatum*. It was no secret at the time. The whole state knew.

Joseph also learned that even though Mr. Miller lived in town, he owned a large farm east of Strother. He was a friend of Mr. James, the owner of more than a thousand acres and a small group of slaves he had brought with him from Kentucky. *Maybe Miller wants to sell or rent his farm to James.*

Billy seemed interested in running straight to Joseph when the theft rumors started.

Joseph really had no idea what Miller's gang had planned for him in the long run. He was getting nervous, and he recalled a priest in Cincinnati who advised the boys that they probably could get away with a mortal sin once. A single act of redemption experienced in the confessional was only a test of their character and faith. It should serve as a warning. They might die before they got back to their confessor or had an opportunity to make their Act of Contrition to God to ask forgiveness. If they hadn't resisted temptation the first time, what might they do the second or third times? The second or third times could be their last, and their sin was likely to be repeated many times after the third time.

Joseph had progressed well past his third opportunity at redemption. He needed a plan to extricate himself before it was too late. Now he wanted to be with Mary, and he didn't want anything to happen to her. She was in the wild "cow town" of Westport on her own, and Joseph could endanger her.

However, Joseph had pride. The gang of secesh could not expect him to haul their weapons of war without a substantial payoff. His business sense, arrogance, and Quigley sense of fairness kicked in. He needed to show them; he needed to negotiate. He believed that they were able to give Joe more. They probably thought he was stupid and didn't know he was working for chaff in their world.

Joseph thought Billy Davies was a natural-born criminal, and he could be cruel and unpredictable. He didn't know right from wrong, and he liked to steal. Mr. Miller, the steamship captain, Mr. Howard, and Mr. Neumann rubbed shoulders in the hotel and on the landing, and Billy acted as though he wanted to be one of them. Billy spoke about the likelihood of being a hired gun for the secesh who might be stealing. If Billy showed up in the wrong place at the wrong time, Joseph hoped he was sober and could draw first. It wouldn't matter to Billy if Joseph was a friend—he was a stone-cold killer.

Fortunately, it wasn't long before Billy disappeared. Joseph hoped that he had been shot, but it was said that he was working in Kansas after deciding to travel with a minister preaching that slavery was a divine institution ordained by God. That, thought Joseph, would allow Billy to justify, as an almighty proslavery Christian, murder, stealing, rape, and any other spontaneous violence in which Billy would willingly engage. He gravitated toward true evil.

Φ

Before his second dangerous trip to the Strother farm, Joseph surprised Mr. Miller in the leatherworks warehouse. In his first excursion into the warehouse, Joseph hid in the darkness and watched Mr. Miller. This time, he came upon Mr. Miller as he was moving things from one box into another. Joseph couldn't see what Mr. Miller was handling, but he didn't care.

Joseph quietly startled his target. "Mr. Miller? John?"

Miller jumped and swung around, tent pegs or something else in one hand. "This is me first time in here, right, John? I hear yer suggestin' otherwise, but I'm not here to talk about that. I'm here to tell ye that I need very much to speak with Stone Neumann."

As Miller gave himself time to ponder Joseph's request, Joseph took his pistol from his hip, pointed it through the darkness at the corner of the warehouse, and asked, "Well, then, Mr. Miller, I ask ye, can you arrange a conversation with yer friend Stone?"

Stone Neumann was a well-known businessman and Confederate sympathizer from Strother. Josh had told Joseph that the Hanoverian had gone to Strother—and so had the loads. Joseph determined that this whole thing was Stone Neumann's operation—and Stone Neumann owned the most beautiful horses he believed he had ever seen.

From a quiet and discrete conversation with an Irish farmhand at their last transfer of goods, Joseph learned that the farmhand had seen Stone Neumann's Hanoverians. They kept them in the indoor paddock during deliveries so they wouldn't get caught in a firing exchange. He knew, also, that Josh McCollum had escorted several of these very horses from Tennessee to the Westport Landing where Mr. Neumann had come, himself, with a couple of his young German ranch hands to retrieve the horses.

Joseph wondered: *Do these men not know that outfitters, stock hands, and deckhands all know each other? They hang at the same bars, talk, and trade, and most are recent immigrants who support and defend one another. They share tidbits about the businesses and the men who owned them. Besides, I pay particular attention to all the fancy horses that come off the boats.*

It dawned on Joseph that the people at the bottom knew those at the top, but the reverse wasn't necessarily true. Those on the bottom layer of society strove to be like the upper crust—to have what they had. The truth was that other than a favorite bartender, barber, or driver, those at the top paid little attention to the riffraff at the bottom who served them. One immigrant was no different from the other. The "high and mighty" might know individual names here and there, but they knew little and cared little about them as a whole. The slum dwellers, like Joseph, had the values of servants who helped make others rich. People at the bottom were often loyal, dependable, and even friendly, but they didn't rub shoulders with those at the top. Miller would not know that Joseph was so savvy.

Joseph, his pistol now pointed only feet away from Miller— but not at him—said, "Tell Mr. Neumann that I need something from him before I can continue to do his work. Tell him I want a bigger reward. I'm just a lowly Irishman, but I know me value. I'm needin' a beautiful bay Hanoverian gelding, all his leather tack, and a wagon of feed. I'll pick it up at his farm on our next gathering. Why do ye look so surprised, Mr. Miller? We Irish don't always have money or position, but we know how to put our brains to good use. Perhaps yer thinkin' we're blind and foolish as well. 'Tis not true. We are not blind, Mr. Miller. I know all yer friends. I know what yer friends do.

"It doesn't benefit ye to know all me friends, Mr. Miller. Yer often actin' like me loyal friend. We've shared whiskey and cigars. Is that not a loyal friend? I'd like to see ye keep up the appearances and be me pretend friend so I don't have to betray yers. Yer not way up there, Mr. Miller, but yer friends are. I don't want to rat them out— and neither do ye."

Φ

On his third job from the David Tatum to the Strother farm where he made his special drop, John Miller insisted on riding behind the wagon with a bandanna tied around his face and his hat dropped low. Two men fell in behind Mr. Miller about ten miles out. Joseph had not put blinders on Elizabeth, and he noticed the two men after Elizabeth tipped him off. She could hear and sense things Joseph couldn't. She was also sensitive to the other mules who might get spooked when the dynamics in the group changed. Joseph watched her ears, the position of her head, and her gait. Without blinders, she never failed to warn Joseph—with a head turn, a nod, and a snort— to look around behind him.

All three of the men riding behind the wagon looked like cowboys who drove up the longhorns from Texas. However, the setting was wrong. Maybe they were new German immigrants who didn't know how out of place they appeared. It felt uncomfortable for Joseph, and he tried to sort it out. *Could one of these men be someone I know from one the landings? Are they plannin' to get their goods and then shoot me? Will they be able to tag me as a treasonist against the Union? I have no bandanna, no mask. Maybe that's better. Maybe I look as though my wagon has been commandeered. Jesus, Mary, and Joseph, this is Hiram's wagon. Will God ever forgive me? Hiram must never think I am consorting with the enemy.*

After a few more miles, Joseph was directed to drive his team into a large barn where two thrashing rigs were parked outside, making room for the load. The doors closed, and Joseph was given a horse to ride, escorted by Mr. Miller, to accommodations where he would spend the night. He spoke not one word until they arrived at the farmhouse where he was to stay.

The next day, he found himself still alive. He rode back to a designated spot, picked up the empty wagon and team, and returned to Westport. *Had they decided to kill me and then changed their plans? Are they waiting for someone else to come along? Is Stone still thinking over what to do—or had he been gone and when he returned to learn of the plan to shoot me, had he stopped it?* Joseph had no idea, but he thanked Elizabeth for being a very good girl throughout it all. He would never ask her to do this again.

This trip unnerved him for a few days, and he decided for certain that he would not use Hiram's wagon. He would not use Mr. Hayes's wagon either. He would "borrow" one from another hauler—maybe one from a secesh recommended by Miller. To keep themselves in business, Joseph's group would trade and borrow livestock and equipment, but he'd do what he needed to until he got his Hanoverian—or he was shot.

Φ

On a rainy Saturday afternoon, as Joseph was preparing to go out, Judith O'Neill came knocking on Joseph's door. "Joseph? Joseph Quigley, I have quite a surprise for ye."

When Joseph answered his bedroom door, Judith announced, "There is a lovely young lady downstairs come calling on ye. I have never seen her. Where have ye been keeping her? Do ye know her? Don't keep her waitin', darlin'."

"Thank you, Judith. This is a surprise—and a very good one." After putting on his boots, Joseph went downstairs to greet Mary.

She was flushed and slightly out of breath. "Oh, Joseph, I am so glad you're here. I'm afraid I have terrible news. My landlady suddenly died, and her son has taken over. I asked, but he will not let me have a piano because of the noise. I must find another place to go. What will I do? Ma and Da got that apartment for me through a banker friend, and it might be the only one like it in Westport."

Coming into the room with tea and a few biscuits, Judith said, "A little treat for ye two. And your name is?"

Judith already had learned her name, but she wanted Joseph to learn how to properly introduce a lady.

Joseph answered, "Mary McManus."

Judith embarrassed Joseph by demonstrating a proper introduction: "Mrs. O'Neill, I'd like to present my friend, Mary McManus. Mary, this is Judith O'Neill."

Mary did a little curtsy and answered, "Very pleased to meet you, Mrs. O'Neill."

"So, Miss McManus, I overheard yer plight, and I know many ladies with places. People in Westport come and go often. We'll find somethin'. It is a piano that troubles ye?"

"Yes. I have a piano waiting to be picked up, but now I have no place to take it. I also have a desk and chairs that will have to fit, and I need to be able to have students come to me apartment. A single boardin' room like Joseph's here isn't quite adequate. I need at least two rooms. Also, I'd like to be able to do me own cookin' so I can save me money."

Judith said, "That is a little more difficult, but let me have a few days. I have an idea about a much larger place, but it comes with a companion. Could ye have a companion? Also, could ye live on the other side of Westport?

Mary answered, "Yes, I could live on the east side of Westport, and a companion would depend on who it is."

This sounded great to Joseph. A new place would solve their problems, but he wasn't sure about the companion part.

Mary would be living in a house, and the companion was a little brown pug. The house belonged to a lady who had moved temporarily to Washington with her husband, an officer in the Union Army.

He had a desk job and was older, and they would be there for some time.

Φ

After several days, an unhappy Stone Neumann walked into the hotel bar to meet Joseph. Josh McCollum, Malachy White, and Michael Tracy were there with Joseph when Mr. Neumann walked in.

Joseph said, "Oh, what a grand surprise! First, me good friends and business partners show up unexpected—and then we are honored by the highly regarded? 'Tis a great day to meet you, sir. Stone Neumann, it is then? I heard you wanted to speak to me about horses. Perhaps ye could procure these men a round of whiskey, and we can find a bit o' privacy. Ye perhaps know someone who can direct us to a better place?"

"Ya, dat would be a good ting." Mr. Neumann did not seem enthusiastic about buying whiskey for a group of young, rough, arrogant Irishmen.

"Perhaps privacy isn't necessary, Mr. Neumann. You do know Mr. McCollum, is that correct? I believe he's escorted many a fine horse from Kentucky and Tennessee out yer way.

"Ah, Mr. Neumann, yer givin' me a look like me sister Ellen. That Ellen always knew exactly what was in the works. She's in Pennsylvania now, but I still understand the meanin' of that look." Joseph had been told explicitly to come alone, but he made it clear that the presence of his friends was purely coincidental and they knew absolutely nothing. He believed that Neumann had learned his lesson: he couldn't easily toss about this young lad who was in for getting his fair cut from risky business.

Malachy said, "So you're a rancher, sir?"

Joseph said, "Regardless, Malachy, we'll be discussin' me teamster business. That's what I do! So, then, we'll be excusin' ourselves, but don't count me out of a whiskey at the conclusion of our business chat. It won't take long, boys."

Φ

It was a bitterly cold autumn day before Thanksgiving in 1859 when the *David Tatum* again arrived for another job. The cargo went on a wagon behind a team of familiar and not-so-familiar mules. Joseph acted indifferent and relaxed as they loaded the stolen Union weapons.

After the group left Westport, two Neumann guards in bandannas fell into line behind the wagon well outside town. However, about five miles from Neumann's farm, two men came up from nowhere and followed the entourage about a quarter of a mile behind.

One of Neumann's guards lost his nerve and grabbed his rifle. "I make a couple of warning shots, ya?"

Miller stopped him.

The nervous guard said, "We need to scare them, ya?"

Miller said, "Stay calm, FT. We don't want to draw attention. They might be my neighbors going to their farm. I can't see that far, so how would you know? Do you want to tell the sheriff or a judge where you were going and what you were doing when you turned around and shot one of my neighbors? Stay calm. You have things to learn. I thought you were better than this."

When Joseph arrived and drove the wagon into the barn, his team was taken to a different barn.

The nervous man said, "You are excited to get your fancy horse, ya? Da Irish Yankee as corrupt as the secesh, ya?"

Miller said, "FT, please stop talking. Follow the rules—even if you are the golden nephew."

Joseph walked with Mr. Neumann into a separate, splendid stable and saw Fitzgerald, standing tall and looking toward Joseph. "Did ye tell him his name like I asked ye?"

"Ya, he knows he is Fitzgerald."

Joseph walked up to Fitzgerald, patted his head, breathed air in his nostrils, and said, "Dia duit, mo chapaill / Hello, my horse, Fitzgerald."

"This cause, Joseph, is greater than your youthful desires. You are a greedy and impudent man-child. I hope you understand you have placed yourself and all of us in an unusual and dangerous position. We will always know where this horse is."

Joseph answered, "Please don't worry about me position. Worry about yer own." He tied Fitzgerald to the back of the wagon and rode to a place between Westport and Strother.

There, Joseph outfitted Fitzgerald in his new saddle, thanks to Miller, and traveled east, away from Westport and Independence. Malachy White, who now owned Joseph's Morgan, took the wagon and team back to the stable Joseph's group shared in Westport.

As he and Fitzgerald hustled down the road, he finally picked up on two men just north of the turnoff to the Pleasant Hill Road. He had expected company, but he hadn't noticed them until now. He believed they were Neumann's hired assassins. Joseph felt outnumbered and maybe outgunned, but he was going to lead them to a place where he felt confident he might have the upper hand. It might be his turning point between manhood and death. He could not turn back.

About four miles out of town, he headed northeast, running through brush, tall grasses, and trees along a stream. He hoped he'd be hard to track and might arrive at a good vantage point. He stopped only to give Fitzgerald drinks and never drove him across mud, dirt, or sand. He turned east, up onto a ridge behind—but a distance away from—the farm where Michael and he had lived before the raid by Lane's men.

Above, a flat stone clearing beyond a primitive and rugged trail from the east was hidden behind yellow pine trees that continued to give good coverage even in November. The spot was high above the dwindling road on the prairie bed—where the men were always traveling—and Joseph had good visibility.

When he once again spotted the men, still and conversing on the main road, Joseph realized they correctly assumed he would head for the only ridge in sight. They were experienced, and their weapons were as good as Joseph's. He saw one of the men hired to kill him pointing in his direction with his rifle, outlining the ravine Joseph had chosen. Joseph had scouted this area as a shortcut to their ransacked and burned-out farms. He hoped the men had not scouted it themselves. This side of the plateau had revealed to Joseph a narrow Indian trail and perfect hideout for a small party. From miles away, the pursuers could see the plateau, the ridgeline, and as they got closer, the tree line that revealed Joseph's chosen ravine, though he was sure they didn't know exactly where he was. His rugged trail led to the place where he and young John Murphy chose to safely hide his Hiram Young wagon.

From their gestures, Joseph believed he had accurately predicted their course. They likely believed he would stay on his fast and sturdy horse in an attempt to outrun and outride them up the ravine where the road turned off. Though he was shaking and nervous, Joseph had confidence that they believed he was running scared and had no idea where he was or what he was getting himself into. Maybe they thought he had more confidence in his horse than was justified, but Joseph planned that it would be they, not he, who would run out of navigable animal trails in the ravine. He was not going to be trapped. Joseph prayed that Christ would stand beside him, the horse thief, against the assassins.

Joseph left some tracks at the mouth of the stream, and then he turned Fitzgerald gently over rocks and upward through the trees onto the trail the men would not see unless they continued north, well past the ravine. From the top of the ridge, Joseph dismounted, removed his bulky coat, and quickly dropped down into the steep ravine through the thick brush and trees. He found a temporary vantage point. As he observed the men carefully examining the hoofprints where the road ran out, the sweat dripped off his brow and his heart pounded in his chest. The men were carefully examining the hoofprints where the road ran out.

After convincing themselves they were closing in fast, the men continued gingerly and quietly on, up the ravine, focusing on the ground and the trees. Joseph had struggled up a large oak above the pines, at a point where the ravine narrowed dramatically, making passage impossible for a horse. The shooters continued on until they heard the crack of a rifle. As the sides of the ravine echoed with the shot, the man in the back tumbled from his horse, shot through the head by Joseph's first shot.

Joseph took another deep breath. As soon as the partner realized what had happened, Joseph saw him panic and attempt to turn his horse back. His way was blocked by his dead companion whose horse was trained to stand over his wounded rider. The trees and brush hugged the stream, moving Joseph's target in and out of the light as the partner tried desperately to gain passage. He finally got his horse turned downstream, but he should have dismounted immediately instead. Before he had an opportunity to dismount and take cover, Joseph shot him in the back, between the shoulder blades, at heart level. As the man fell into the stream, Joseph climbed, slid, and jumped down the oak, walked the short distance down from his tree, and shot both the men's horses with his rifle. Then, he shot both men again at close range with his Navy Colt revolver, and he quickly scrambled back up to Fitzgerald.

He did not continue up to the settlement or return to Strother or Westport. Exhausted, he rode Fitzgerald almost due north into a small settlement east of Independence where Michael was presently living near the Murphys while completing a masonry repair on a bridge. Joseph wanted to avoid any of the local farmers of Big Creek who might know him and would likely be secessionists.

At the Murphy farm, he relaxed and hid out for a few days.

He told them nothing about the event, saying that he wanted them to see Fitzgerald. He also planned for them to meet Mary at the farm in the near future. Joseph told them that if they felt about her as he did, he was going to marry her.

Michael was happy but leery. Mary sounded wonderful, but they knew Joseph's temper and drinking problems and wondered if he was doing the right thing. As he described Mary, they wondered if she could straighten him out or if he would drag her down. They prayed for the former, but they were anxious to see if she was what he thought she was.

Φ

As Joseph rode Fitzgerald back to Westport, he reflected on the past few days and felt justified. What he did to the men was in self-defense, but he knew in his gut that revenge from the Neumann family

234

could still catch him. Like the loss of a mother, such things never went away.

He also thought about the Cincinnati priest's lessons on redemption but wasn't sure how extortion fit with being justified. He was confident about the shootings; Neumann's men would have killed him. Then he decided to put it out of his mind. None of it was his fault in the first place. The seceshes deserved it.

He also wondered if the several drunken episodes in which he exposed his propensity to drink and get angry had soured Mary to him enough that she would say no to his proposal. The last time he saw her, he had arrived intoxicated, had vomited and passed out, and then spent the night on her floor. She went to teach, exhausted, the next day. He cleaned up his mess before leaving, but they hadn't spoken for days.

During another episode, she had questioned what he was doing to get into such a bad position with Mr. Miller. She began to lecture him from a religious point of view as though he were doing something wrong. He wasn't going to tell her anything, and he had been drinking. He became so angry that he got rough and pushed her up against the wall and told her to never tell him what to do or not do again.

After sobering up and staying away for a few days, he promised to never do that again, and she had relented. Joseph now thought he might not be able to keep such promises. He knew that once they married, they could not reverse their promises. There was no such thing as divorce in the Catholic Church, so he'd have to promise himself things as well when he made promises to Mary.

After leaving his refuge with Michael, Joseph rode Fitzgerald to a livery stable and then walked to Mary's little house and asked if she would go to Independence with him in a few days. He told her they were going to the Murphy farm to a little Unionist- sympathizing farming community to take his new horse very early in the morning the day after tomorrow. It was Thanksgiving, and they would be there with Mary's family. He also told her that he was going to move to a farm in Big Creek, and he wanted her to become his bride and go with him.

"Oh, Joseph, I'm not sure that I should do that. We haven't gotten along too well. I think I might not be the right person for ye. I love ye, but I'm afraid I might be makin' a big mistake. Do ye understand, Joseph? I don't live like ye do."

Joseph said, "Yer wrong, Mary McManus. I'm a better person than ye know, and I can prove it to ye. I won't drink again. If I go live on a farm and not with the riffraff, me life can be like yers. I want ye to meet me brother Michael and his family. Ye'll see that I come from a decent farmin' people. At least, come along and meet me brother, then ye can think about it after knowing who I really am."

However, Joseph turned right around, casting doubts by telling Mary she was to tell no one where she was going and should leave a message in her window: "School canceled due to family emergency in Topeka."

Mary asked, "Why Topeka? Ye never mentioned anyone in Topeka. Why would ye be tryin' to throw people off?"

Joseph wrapped his arms around Mary, kissed her, and sang a song about a wild country meadow. "I have to go. I'll be back to get ye on Wednesday mornin'. I love ye, darlin'."

With the little pug tied in a gunnysack in his rented cart, he rode to Judith's.

The next day, he went to the stable to settle up his business with Martin, Josh, and Malachy. He loaded up his Hiram Young wagon and paid Judith, and in the morning, he said goodbye to his Westport home. Josh added one of his mules he would sell to Joseph's team and came along to drive. As Judith would have nothing to do with the pug, it was tucked in the hay under a horse blanket in a corner of the wagon to be hauled back out to Michael's. Joseph could take him out to Big Creek.

Φ

When Joseph arrived at Mary's, she was ready. He introduced her to Fitzgerald and lifted her onto a small blanket he had prepared for her to ride on behind him. She was astounded by the magnificence of the horse and fell in love with Joseph all over again. She wondered if this was the kind of man who owned such a magnificent horse.

She had never seen anything like him. It was cold, but Fitzgerald was muscular and warm. Joseph wrapped a new wool blanket around Mary's body.

Not many days after the Murphy Thanksgiving dinner, Mary and Joseph announced their engagement during a party at Saint Mary's Church. They started to prepare for their December 21 wedding, which was only a month away.

Mary sent a letter to her parents and asked if they could wire her some money for a gown and flowers. Her parents were not happy. They had already decided that they were not wild about her plans to marry. They thought she had not known Joseph long enough—and that he was not of her ilk. However, they decided to support her as she was going to marry in the Immaculate Conception Catholic Cathedral in the city of Kansas, and Father Donnelly would be the officiant. They were very familiar with the church, having attended Mass and baptisms on numerous occasions.

Margaret and Agnes arranged for a special milk cow to be shipped to Independence. Margaret's husband, a veterinarian, had purchased several through a friend from Europe for their herd. They loved her and thought it would be a wonderful investment for Mary. Mary Murphy's brother, a teenager, took the cow, which Joseph had named Sunshine, out to Michael's at Big Creek to be there when Mary arrived after her wedding. Michael and Joseph had returned to the farm and did not go back to Independence until it was time for the wedding.

Under a beautiful, clear sky in snow-blanketed Kansas City, Joseph and Mary married in the midst of the McManus, Quigley, and Murphy families. It was December 21, 1859.

Joseph had received a bottle of whiskey from Josh and Malachy for the occasion, so he was, regretfully, not yet completely recovered for his own wedding. Mary was humiliated and hoped her family had not noticed. Unfortunately, they had, but they pretended for her, as his behavior was not terrible, and it was not uncommon for a man to imbibe with his male friends the night before his wedding. It was not something that a McManus, a Grant, or Michael Quigley would do. Again, in their eyes, Joseph had lacked the character necessary

237

to rise to Mary's ilk. Uncle Terrance felt especially concerned for his niece, and in a moment of compassion and generosity, he gifted her one of the prized little books of his collection. Each Magrath and McManus girl who married received a special book, but Mary's was the most special of all.

After marrying, Joseph and Mary moved to Big Creek to live in the farmhand's cabin on Michael's property. Joseph rented the farm next door. He could keep the profits from the farm, but he had to pay rent for the pastures and the use of the barn. Michael owned the farmhand's cabin, so Joseph and Mary were not charged rent, but they were allowed to repair it as they wished while they lived there.

In 1860, when they were burned out of their Big Creek home by Jay-hawkers—as were Michael and Mary Murphy—Mary fled straight to Westphalia to live with brother Daniel. After a short time with Michael, Joseph went to Harrisonville with his beloved Fitzgerald to join the Missouri Home Guard. They did not lose the Hiram Young wagon or Fitzgerald, but they lost Sunshine, Elizabeth, and an unborn baby.

CHAPTER 18

JOSEPH IN THE CAVALRY, SEDALIA, MISSOURI, 1862

Though he was granted permission by Alexander to go to the blacksmith in Strother, after capturing his would-be assassin who killed Matthew, Joseph gathered a good piece of intelligence for his company.

With Frederick's horse, Lucky, hooked to a decrepit cart driven by a German boy, Joe rode Fitzgerald into the hay barn at the Neumann ranch, on the edge of dusk, to have a little chat with Henry, the Irish farmhand the Neumanns thought was German. It was Henry who quickly filled Lucky's cart with feed and a large can of molasses. From this very brief and confidential encounter with the farmhand, it seemed that the major Confederate players, Captain Shelby, Colonel Cockrell, Colonel Coffee, Colonel Hays, and others had begun a diligent campaign in laying down a permanent Confederate foundation in the area. This continued for the spring and was to continue in Jackson and Cass Counties for the entire summer of 1862. The Neumann's Irish farmhand had met quite a few secesh. Most had gone to the Neumann barn to attend to their horses. One officer had just gotten a new horse from Stone.

Henry warned Joseph that his unannounced visit with Lucky might prove suicidal, and he told the boy in the cart to get ready to duck or stop his cart and dive off. Henry had heard what happened to the men who followed Joseph and promised that he would amble into Herman's shop if he heard a ruckus, so Joseph wouldn't be attacked. Unfortunately, Henry couldn't promise any real defense because he had no gun. He was there to clean barns and feed horses, and he didn't want to tip anyone off that he was abolitionist until he had money enough to leave, which would be soon. Everyone assumed he was a secesh; otherwise, he would not have a job. It was getting harder to remain quiet, and he planned to go back to his family in Ohio as soon as possible.

Joseph, riding Fitzgerald, quietly presented himself and Lucky at the half-opened doorway of Herman Neumann's blacksmith shop and barn. With a smirk on his face, he brazenly announced, "I brought back Lucky as a favor to Frederick. I'll drop him off with a farmhand for ye for ninety dollars."

Herman defiantly replied, "You get a bullet before any ninety dollars."

"Then I'll sell Lucky to someone else. Would ye be surprised to know that Frederick was—somehow—in me MSM company? Would ye believe that he murdered a soldier in our detachment, me own fine Irish friend Matthew? I come to tell ye poor Frederick has been taken to the army in Butler for a court-martial for treason. Lucky's still worth somethin', so I'd like to sell him back to ye." Joseph slightly let back his coat and showed his hand resting on his pistol. "No? If I don't get the money, he gets to go back to the militia to be a cavalry horse again."

Herman stood momentarily frozen, and then he lifted a large hammer and hurled it at Joseph's hand. "You filthy animal!" he cried.

Fitzgerald danced and pawed the ground until Joseph commanded him to steady himself.

When the hammer fell to the ground, the normally quiet and unpleasant blacksmith unleashed bitter and grief-filled language on Joseph.

Joseph never suggested how he came to know that "Frederick Schmidt" was actually Frederick Neumann, but he didn't need to explain. When Herman saw Lucky, he probably guessed that Joseph had either been told by someone they knew—or had managed to figure out who Frederick was on his own. Maybe under duress, Frederick had admitted who he was. "You greatly outnumbered, Yankee dog! Frederick did not have to kill you, Mr. *Quickly*, but it won't be long until your kind will be trumbled into the earth. My Frederick, he give life for cause. We know you already kill two goot men doing der jobs. A shame it was over Yankee scum like you! You are tiny, drunken Hibernian criminal on a large, stolen horse, and you are

240

as goot as dead. When I can, I kill you myself mit mine own hands! You watch back leaving dis barn. Watch back on useless scouting trips out Big Creek, Rose Hill—anywhere—you might run into more trouble den you tink.

"Independence already taken from Yankee. Slaves going back home every day. Confederacy's growing every day, and rabble cavalry can't stop it. Rebels are coming from South too. Arkansas not out of dis war, ya? There are more Neumanns on the way. Dey all goot hunters mit Union guns, ya? You remember who give them Union guns, ya? You carry dem; we now turn you in."

Joseph replied, "No, 'tis too late. Frederick told the army about the guns your family stole to save his skin, but it didn't work." Then Joseph told a lie to keep Herman busy: "A US Army troop is right behind me, on its way here, Herman. They want to talk to Frederick's da. They are very polite and intelligent, bein' mostly tiny Hibernians.

"Would they really believe that an Irish kid would steal Union guns for a family of secesh, a steamboat captain, a leather merchant, and who knows how many others in Westport and then serve in a Yankee cavalry for two years killing secesh?

"Do ye remember last time ye sent ridin' companions along with me? It seems they got lost, ya? If companions follow me today, I will deliver them into the hands of me cavalry that's comin' in the very direction I'm goin'! The army's comin' in one direction and me Company C in another.

"Tell me then, Herman: You become secesh so ye can fix fancy horse hooves? Ye can't do that, man, without someone else's slaves workin' fer nothin' in a field over there? If slavery's yer cause, ye haven't thought it out well. Your son, Frederick, did not think either. He was not smart enough to outwit this skinny, drunken Hibernian. Neither can you, so, as my sister Ellen used to say, shut yer cakehole, then. Yer days are numbered, secesh!"

Wasting bullets from his pistol over Herman's head, into the other end of the barn and another near the feet of Herman, Joseph put his pistol away, turned, stood in his saddle, and with the barrel of his rifle, reached over and closed the door of the barn. Following the boy in the cart behind Lucky, Joseph was off, reins in left hand, rifle in his right, and pistol at the ready in his belt. It seemed there was nobody over his shoulder but his farmhand informant, running toward the shop as though he were running to help Herman, who was no more the wiser about his Irish farmhand who yearned to be in Ohio.

Φ

Straight back to camp in Harrisonville, Joseph shared his intelligence: the names of the secesh officers who were obtaining support out of the Neumann ranch in Strother. The molasses was used sparingly to boost Fitzgerald's enthusiasm for practicing moves that made him beautiful to Joseph. When they "practiced" on Sundays, Fitz got his molasses over his oats. Joseph was also able to trade some of the molasses for whiskey in which he was now imbibing on too many days.

Nevertheless, Joseph had been given the special assignment to escort President Lincoln from his boat into Independence with the cavalry. Lincoln also planned a parade in Independence to visit the troops and demonstrate the Union presence in Missouri. He was going to recognize the cavalry volunteers, in particular, for their courageous and effective service. The officers had unanimously chosen Joseph to be Lincoln's escort and the leader of the parade.

Φ

On August 10, 1862, a small detail of Joseph's company was sent on a routine scouting mission to Independence. There was a rumor that Cole Younger and his gang might be hiding out in the area, waiting for a large gathering of other secesh gangs. There were always so many rumors that the militia and regulars risked the danger of dismissing them. It wasn't always the most popular rumor that was correct, but Joseph's tips—given by the farmhand and inadvertently by Herman Neumann—were credible in the big picture from their start, months ago.

The men weren't sure if Younger would be on the northeast side of Independence or coming from the southeast. Herman had mentioned to Joseph that Arkansas was not done with the war. It would be very likely that some forces being built were riding north, along the border out of Arkansas, and traveling into Independence. Strother was directly south and a comfortable distance away, so they may have gotten reinforcements or supplies there for their Independence attack.

However, there had been a "signature" bank robbery to the east the day before, not far west from Lexington that had the attributes of a Younger job. Joseph's detail, already small in number, decided to split just south of Strother.

One trio rode from the west, then diagonally on a northeast trail across the Blue River, and the others circled around, across the Little Blue. When Joseph's group got to a gathering of trees in the rolling hills, just east of a cemetery south of the city of Independence, they saw a gang of at least a dozen men, saddlebags bulging with goods, rifles in hand, heading almost due north on the main road toward downtown.

As Joseph and the other two men watched, they determined it was Cole Younger's gang. Younger's gang ran right past Hiram Young's barns, shooting off a few rounds, and then continued up the hill to town. People began to gather, so the men spread out and blended with the local population of other men on their horses. By the time they got to the road where Saint Mary's Parish was located, the church Joseph and his brother once attended, people were lining the streets and cheering Younger on! Joseph hoped that few parishioners were in the crowd. Not wanting to be recognized, he held back. The other two men saw him, turned to follow, and faded out of town, all three having made the same, correct identification of Younger.

They decided to take a better road to their reconnaissance by heading south to the main road that led east to Sedalia and west to Kansas Town, when off a heavily wooded side trail came a gang of a dozen riders firing in their direction. They abruptly ran west, toward their reconnaissance site on a ridge east of the Blue River, each man heading off across the prairie in a different direction. After about

243

half a mile, only half of the gang was in pursuit, and because the secesh had nobody to fight, they turned around.

Hiding behind tall grass on high ground, Joseph saw through his binoculars the gang turn north toward Independence.

On their ridge, the men decided it could have been some of William Quantrill's Raiders, but they were never close enough to properly identify any of them. However, the gang had all the markings: they were not far behind Younger, they were on the same trail, and they were organized and well outfitted.

The scouts uniformly decided that their best course was to assume there were secesh in every direction, and they rode carefully on at night through Peculiar, bypassing Strother, to share the bad news.

As they returned early in the morning hours of August 11 to tell their commanding officer that Cole Younger's gang was being cheered in the streets of Independence, the First Battle of Independence began. Union deaths from the attack reached well over three hundred men. Captain Breckenridge had found no Confederates in Independence days before and had disregarded previous scouting reports to the contrary, including Joseph's news from the Neumann ranch. It was believed by some in the following days that the overconfidence of Breckenridge resulted in his need to quickly surrender to the Confederates. The First Battle of Independence was a great disgrace, and it was believed that Independence, for now, was gone to the Union.

Φ

Two days after Joseph's return to Harrisonville, he was told of the cancellation of his presidential parade escort assignment. Joseph was sent first to Lexington—north of Sedalia on the Missouri River—and then to Sedalia, in Pettis County, in the District of Central Missouri. It was two days' ride from Big Creek. He was sent with a special, permanent detachment of Missouri Militia Second Battalion Cavalry men to remain there in the support of regular army personnel. The Second Missouri Volunteer Cavalry, also known as Merrill's Horse, of the regular army, had already been sent to Sedalia when the railroad opened in 1861. The army had decided to locate a

244

federal post in Sedalia in January 1861. Sedalia officially became the Pacific Railroad's terminus with the first arrival of passengers. Military men and materials could now be moved quickly into the heart of Missouri. The route was west from St. Louis, passed through Jefferson City, Missouri, about sixty miles east, and then went west into Sedalia. It was going to become the first railroad into Kansas City, and it was the responsibility of the army to keep it functioning between St. Louis and Sedalia.

The other railroad now usable by the Union, the Southwest, had come south of Sedalia, as far as Rolla, Missouri, also in 1861. It supplied the army facility at Springfield, a distance of 120 miles over terrible roads. It was rumored among brass that Schofield begged to move the Springfield location nearer to the source of supplies in Rolla. The wagoners of Springfield suffered terribly in the mud, and men and materials were wasted on the arrangement. There was limited talk of sending some of the Sedalia wagoners south to Springfield.

Schofield had prevailed upon his superiors, General Curtis for one, to allow him to relocate. It would have improved the movement and security of men and supplies, and he felt it would have facilitated developing a railroad line down the Mississippi to the Gulf of Mexico, a goal of the Union. Deaf ears and vacillating voices were turned on Schofield.

By 1862, Joseph's detachment permanently replaced Merrill's who went on to Alabama, Arkansas, Tennessee, and other locations in the South to carry out their effective mission of defeating guerilla warfare using guerrilla tactics of their own. Only cavalry had the mobility necessary to fight guerilla-style war, and Merrill's was known as the best among the regulars.

Merrill's Horse was raised by Major General John Fremont and organized by Captain Lewis Merrill. The men had established a reputation for controlling the northern part of Missouri, a region with a significant population of slaves and secesh along the Mississippi River. It was also the destination of many stolen weapons from the boats in Kansas City. The cavalry's recruits came from all over Missouri and were highly trained. They had been very busy, but as far as Joseph was concerned, the town of Sedalia was a dead end full of constant conflict. There were nearly daily attempts to slow down or bring down the railroad, and the town had been nearly cleaned out of businessmen and residents due to the war. Once the train arrived along with the Confederates, not one more building had been constructed.

Knowing Joseph was a professional wagoner and could work with mules, he was given the additional assignment to help haul supplies from the Missouri Pacific to Harrisonville and beyond. Joseph was part of a small detachment who were to stay in Sedalia. Eighty-one of his battalion, the rest, had remained in Lexington until all of those men were sent east to Lone Jack in Jackson County, located between Cass and Pettis. Joseph was not among them. Joseph did not know if his health had deteriorated to the point of being detrimental to his fellow soldiers or if he was greatly needed on the highly dangerous job of hauling in the long lines of wagons going west from the train.

Joseph could not recall one trip out or back that didn't include a load tipping over or getting stuck in the mud while being shot at by the many secesh or looting gangs hungry for livestock feed, ammunition, boots, winter clothing, and anything else the military needed throughout Missouri, Kansas, or places west. Dozens of times, Joseph sat in his wagon with shooting men coming at him from one side or the other—or both sides at once. When they came from one side, he could jump down behind the wagon. He found himself shooting at the horses from behind his wheels—when he couldn't see the men. It was effective, but it made him heartsick.

Losing his escort assignment and then being separated from the rest of his company had a further debilitating effect on Joseph. What made him sadder still was that on August 15 and August 16, the Battle of Lone Jack ensued. Its location was just north of Pleasant Hill. The Union forces that participated in the Lone Jack battle included the Seventh Missouri Cavalry, the single largest group of only 265 men, the Sixth and Eighth Missouri State Militia, the Seventh Missouri State Militia Cavalry, the Third Indiana Artillery of only thirty-six men, and his Second Battalion Cavalry of eighty-one men. During the battle, it was reported that the men of Company

C had remained hidden behind the trees, but under the leadership of Captain Long, they poured a steady crossfire against the rebels. For a time, the action forced the rebels back. Joseph's Company C, without him, was said to be the most powerful Union display of the battle.

The Confederates who participated at Lone Jack were from the Confederate Missouri State Guard, mostly the recruiters who had been heavily infiltrating the area, and a mixed contingent of guerillas and volunteers up from Arkansas, the area where they had been sent in May, and a region vital for acquiring intelligence.

Joseph was disgusted to think of their useless mission in early May. It was consumed by the death of Matthew, and days, miles, and resources had been wasted on the unlikely traitor Frederick. Had they been able to attend to their task, they might have helped disrupt the organization of the Confederate attack in Lone Jack, which was their mission.

Joseph was nearly consumed by hatred and anger at the thought of it. He felt like a failure, and he never understood the motives of the Neumann family. They were so unlike the other Germans who hated slavery as much as his Irish companions. How could the family feel the financial need to rub elbows with wealthy horse owners who owned slaves? Like many others, they apparently thought the South had better odds over the Union, and they wanted to be on the winning side.

Frederick had come face-to-face with his God in Butler. There was some justice in the end for Matthew's family. Matthew's mother retrieved her son's body. She lived not far from Harrisonville. This was unusual during the war. Most men were buried not far from where they fell, hundreds of miles away from family. Then they were dragged and carried by cart to large graves like those of Joseph's parents on Staten Island, never to be found again.

Φ

Joseph seldom saw battlefields of dead soldiers and horses, but when he did, he silently dreaded the day he might lose Fitzgerald. In his condition, he thought he was more likely to get sick and die than his horse was. A shocking number of men had fallen ill and died in the regular, and an alarming number of horses had been killed at Lone Jack. The men in the cavalry knew the horses as well as they knew the men who rode them. Each horse had a personality and worked in a unique way with each man. Loss of either partner was a loss felt by everyone. Every horse lost required a readjustment by its rider. No two horses were alike any more than the men were.

He felt guilty that he had not been with the rest of his fellow cavalrymen in Lone Jack. That his beloved Fitz was still standing was remarkable after reflecting on all the horses that had been shot down in his battalion. It had happened over and over to all cavalry soldiers and team drivers. He had heard that thump of a bullet entering a horse's muscle many times. Some horses remained standing and fighting, and the ammunition stayed in them—many until infection caught up to them. Some had bullets in them for months before a new bullet found its target: brain, heart, lungs, or another vital organ.

Unfortunately, at Lone Jack, even though the Confederates wanted for ammunition, they greatly outnumbered the Union. The attack was not the complete surprise it was meant to be, but the numbers were staggering: Union eight hundred men versus between fifteen hundred and three thousand men for the Confederacy.

It could have been different had the timing worked out. More than three thousand Union soldiers had been sent to Lone Jack. Sadly, they did not arrive in time for the battle. Also, the Union might have won with more artillery. They needed the army canons that were on their way. The Union did, however, disperse additional enemy during a skirmish after the battle.

From August 17–19, Joseph was on the march from Georgetown, north of Sedalia, and then on for about 140 miles to Springfield. The troops marched day and night through Osceola, across the Osage to Camp Schofield. There they chased and scattered the many guerrillas and recruits in protection of that camp until the evening of September 21.

Φ

Joseph hadn't heard much about Sedalia until he moved out to Big Creek in 1860, but he had learned about the Missouri Pacific line being built. However, by the time he arrived, he soon realized that once Merrill's Horse departed, Sedalia was going to be rough duty. The railroad and Union camp made it a target under constant attack. There were a lot of troops to feed, and they would go without when necessary. The Confederacy wanted the town and the railroad, so only the very resilient citizens prevailed, and they did so under constant fear.

In his travels up to Lexington, Independence, and then south to Springfield and back, Joseph had experienced serious bouts of sickness. He had a perpetually burning or cramping stomach, diarrhea, burning in his chest, and bloody vomit, and he was occasionally passing out. It was a combination of his accelerated drinking and food that did not settle well. Because of it, he cut back on his food. There wasn't much fare to begin with, but when he could, he ate eggs and went fishing in the Pearl River. His favorites, like thick cream and butter—something he craved to add weight to his body—made his stomach sick and gave him diarrhea. He didn't have much fat on him before, but now it was all gone. The dysentery and loss of weight made him weak and scrawny. He needed to do something, but he wasn't sure what he could do. In Sedalia, he was caught in a downhill cycle with his health.

Φ

The locals of Sedalia were in a potentially excellent financial location if they could last through the war. Rod Gallie, a Scot, owned a freight company and a grocery. He was the local butcher and was heavily depended on by the town. Joseph visited his shop when he thought the military food might kill him. Gallie had a golden secret in his shop: smoked fish. It was softer than the jerky that tore at Joseph's gut, but it was rare and expensive. It became Joseph's payday medicine—along with the candied ginger Mr. Gallie handed him from time to time. Ginger beer was common in the Northeast, but not candied ginger root. Mr. Gallie obtained the root, and Mrs. Gallie candied it in her kitchen or brewed it up in her root cellar. It was the parading Fitzgerald that made Joe Quigley's name familiar around the army town and brought him the advantage of treats like fish and ginger candy.

As far as Joseph knew, the best-known house in Sedalia belonged to Thomas W. Cloney of the Cashier Sedalia Savings Bank. Thomas, whose family hailed from Cloney Township in Ireland, and Mr. Crawford, had a small mercantile business in the village, and when Sedalia became a target of the Confederates, their properties were watched carefully. Though Mr. Beck did some small merchandising that catered to the soldiers in town, there were few permanent homes in town. Most people were farmers who lived outside, but the military watched over the local businesses as though they were a branch of their operations.

None of the businesses in town were yet made of brick or stone, which Joseph thought marked a civilized and proper settlement. The buildings were typically made of wood and could easily be burned, always a concern along with all the other wood structures supporting the railroad. The war would sort out whether or not the train line could continue on to Kansas City or south to the gulf. Had the Confederates prevailed, and Union businessmen given up, the train could have become a dead end in a ghost town. Sedalia had an unusual feel that Joseph labeled "uncertainty with great vigor."

The cattle traffic from Texas was beginning to circumvent Kansas City, Westport, and Independence because of the trains that rendered obsolete the steamboats of the Missouri and Mississippi Rivers all the way to Chicago. As a consequence, men from nearby cities with big visions and fistfuls of money were poised to move or resettle their businesses in Sedalia. They had thoughts of dominating commerce with the military, livestock, and meat transport, as well as with the railroad operation itself. However, it would have to wait for the outcome of the war. The army now controlled the railroads as well as the river transportation, but it was difficult.

On January 31, 1862, the Railways and Telegraph Act allowed President Lincoln to take over the railroads. Prior to the act, Confederates had left the railroad in shambles shortly after the Fort Sumter, South Carolina, attack. The railroad officials showed attributes of excessive greed over Union welfare by trying to benefit from such occurrences rather than throwing in their support for the Union. Therefore, the act was implemented. Lincoln had appointed Thomas Scott, a railroad tycoon and industrialist, the position of assistant secretary of war. It was through his leadership that the railroad kept the Union Army supplied and connected through incorporating the telegraph lines and bureaus. The army, therefore, was able to maintain a close eye on the telegraph as it watched the railroad.

Freed slaves were able to find jobs working on construction and maintenance of the railroads. Slaves had built many of the American railroads. The line to Sedalia was mostly built by the Irish—some of whom settled temporarily in Lincolnville with the freed slaves and runaways. North of the post and the railroad in Sedalia, these "contraband" Irish and freed slaves built a shantytown made of scraps of wood and discarded railroad materials. The army and militia cavalry got help from Lincolnville residents who built trenches, latrines, and forts—dirty and heavy work that had to be done to support the soldiers. They survived on the largesse and protection of the military.

When the trains began to roll, Sedalia was a constant target. On his first scouting assignment north, as Joseph's troop passed the little shantytown settlement, a young Irish immigrant, maybe not twenty years old, hollered, "Irish, I like yer horse. He's a fine specimen. He looks like somethin' ye might see back home, not out here on the frontier. He looks like a Connemara pony or maybe a Britain—big, strong and athletic one he is."

Being a show-off, Joseph directed Fitzpatrick into his dressage. "Will ye look at that, Daniel?" declared the younger lad to his brother.

Joseph introduced himself. They said they were the O'Boyle boys, Daniel and Connor, from County Kilkenny, by way of Pennsylvania. They started out miners but had decided to go down the Ohio for something "aboveground." After drifting across Kentucky and Tennessee, they grabbed their first railroad construction job in the swamps of South Carolina. They had been working with slaves from

251

their first job there, but they decided to get out of the South as well as out of the water.

"Slavery is evil. The men who own other men are evil. It made us sad to be around it," stated Daniel. "They treated us all bad, but in different ways. The slaves couldn't leave, but we could, so we ran off. We traveled with a freedman who wanted to journey to Oregon to paint pictures of the West. He was a ginger, named Aristotle. 'Twas lookin' for a free-spirited red-headed freed slave girl to love. We taught him how to win his lass with Irish love songs. No more handsome or talented man could ye meet. We regretted partin' with him in St. Louis. We came here by train, but Aristotle, a man of great wisdom, indeed, went up the Missouri by boat, to Saint Joseph, and is likely well on his way to Oregon. Here we are—two ignorant Irish lads in yer fine village, watchin' our backsides from injury by secesh!"

Joseph laughed. "So am I! That makes us all eejits!"

Connor, the younger O'Boyle, said, "We're makin' a plan to be naturalized before we're dead, but fer now, we're livin' in the shanties. Maybe we'll see ye in the saloon before we move on—"

"Or in hell!" Daniel shouted.

Joseph agreed while falling back into line with his fellow scouts.

Though Joseph's main contribution was protecting the railroad, or doing extra duty as a wagoner, scouting for secesh with Fitzgerald was more to his liking. He would do the best he could at anything. He realized that every job was important. Unfortunately, Joseph was growing sicker, and he was tired of soldiering. Though he was dedicated to getting peace back to the farmers of Cass County, he was increasingly missing Mary and Michael. Michael was his family, and although they didn't always agree, Joseph loved and admired him. Joseph called Michael a "good, good man."

Φ

Only days from hearing the final news about Lone Jack, the Sedalia men from Company C decided to hit their favorite saloon to commiserate. They had received their pay, and as was customary, they were given the night out on the town. The army could not stop the routine of payday drinking. Rather than waste time and valuable man resources disciplining men, the army just turned men loose on the occasion and hoped for the best. It made Sedalia a very tough place—not one where people would settle to raise their families. There were few single women in town, but the ones who were there were busy building a special reputation for the bordellos of Sedalia, which would grow throughout the war. The railroad helped to label Sedalia as a place where women could easily access quick money, especially on army payday—and then make a quick escape.

Before the men set out for the saloon, all but Joseph ate fairly well in camp. They traveled the short distance to the saloon by foot. Joseph never took Fitzgerald where he wouldn't take his sisters. He left him safely in the barn.

The bar was crowded, and a fight broke out about two hours after the men arrived. It was not unusual for an altercation to occur. There was always conflict over drinks, women, soldiers who shirked duty, or the politics of the war. On a local level, the War Department stepping in and taking over railroad regulation irritated some local businessmen and railroad personnel who felt prevailed upon by the Union Army, especially those secessionists who hated Lincoln.

Unfortunately, the town was split about fifty-fifty on the slavery issue. The cavalry or regulars could expect that a significant degree of displeasure would be directed at military personnel by locals. The importance of the complaints loomed larger with each shot of whiskey served. Once the first punch was thrown, the fights could grow in intensity until a shot rang out or a man lay bleeding on the ground from a stab wound. Soldiers saved bullets and liked the quiet, less obvious approach of a knife.

Joseph had been standing at the bar with a single whiskey and an empty stomach. There was an altercation occurring next to him, but he couldn't hear what they were saying or see what was happening. He wanted to be alert and ready for a fight, but he felt as though he was in a dream of being in the bar.

Suddenly, he realized that he was on the floor, but he couldn't talk or get up. He lay there as a blackness grew around the frame of his eyes until there was nothing.

Joseph briefly came to an awareness as he felt himself dumped into a wagon. He thought it might be the empty one that was parked in the street, but before he could decide what to do about it, the blackness came back—and he disappeared.

It wasn't until Joseph began retching that he woke up again. His stomach was in such pain, and he was so miserable that he forced himself to call, "Padraig." He realized that he was too weak to call loud enough to be heard.

His friend Padraig and others had left him in the wagon to "sober up." It was somewhat mystifying to them because nobody had seen him finish a single drink. Normally, he wasn't so noticeably intoxicated so soon. Joseph had a reputation of a large capacity for a small man.

When the men returned with a lantern to check on him, they immediately noticed that his vomit was rusty. They believed it to be blood. They hadn't noticed that from a man who wasn't dying, so they hitched up the wagon and got it back to camp.

Back at camp, when they removed him from the wagon, they noticed that he had serious diarrhea, and because he still had not "sobered up," it was decided he might not have been intoxicated at all. He didn't smell good, but it wasn't alcohol they smelled. It was sickness. Furthermore, they saw no face wounds or head damage and no bullet holes or knife wounds that might have initiated his collapse. They cleaned him up and placed him on his cot.

An officer was immediately informed. It was decided that they would leave him alone to see how we was in the morning. It was a typical procedure. If there was no wound, and a man lived to the next day, then he was attended to medically.

The next day, he did not respond to reveille and was unable to rouse himself. Thought to be a tough man of high energy, his behavior was highly unusual and indicative of a very sick individual. After a proper daylight inspection, he was left to cook up a temperature that might indicate dysentery, typhoid fever, measles, smallpox, or pneumonia. He did not have many of the classic symptoms. It was decided he might just be a worse alcoholic than anyone had thought. After a few days of spuds, no whiskey, fish from Rod Gallie's store, and greens that one of the O'Boyle's passed along to Padraig, Joseph was returned to duty as a wagoner.

Through the summer, Joseph drove supplies from the railroad to Harrisonville or Independence. His loads were varied, but he liked hauling the lighter loads that did not tip him over and bury him in mud. Some of the attacks had lightened up as the secesh temporarily left the area.

Φ

In late September, 1862, a drizzle met Joseph's patrol out to the northeast of town. There was a report of smoke not far from a trestle that merited attention. Joseph had the shivers, but he had not drunk any coffee or whiskey for several days. He also hadn't been eating much and felt extremely weak; therefore, he decided to hang back a bit to avoid causing any problems for the other men. It was not his typical position. He tried to conserve his limited energy and dismiss the stabbing pain in his gut. The scouts had divided into two groups and were approaching the target area from two directions. He could barely hear his orders through his foggy mind.

Joseph's unit would ride south and drop down into a ravine that led to a creek in the bottom. They would then continue slowly in the northeasterly direction of the ravine. The others planned to move quickly east to circle wide around the area—on the outside of a wooded area that outlined the edge of a large hemp field. They would then ride along the creek to the trestle area, approaching Joseph's group from the opposite direction and pinch off a secesh escape.

These maneuvers would sometimes cause men to fire on their own if they started firing before they should or if they miscalculated direction or distance. They assumed the enemy would not escape east or west and would possibly cross the stream, turn north, and continue up toward Marshall or Boonville. Both places were heavily Confederate. The scouts stayed close to the railroad, avoiding being "drawn off" to leave it exposed to attack.

Joseph was at the back of the scouts, barely hanging on and still confused. He was completely spent of energy, and Fitzgerald knew it. Fitz stepped easy. The others had traveled about a quarter of a mile ahead of him when Joseph was startled fully conscious by a group of four secesh charging ahead of him from the woods, westward down the brushy bank of the shallow ravine. They were unloading their weapons northeast, in the direction of the rear of Joseph's cavalry companions, not noticing Joseph behind them as they charged through the trees and bushes of the lowland trail running along the stream.

Joseph kicked Fitzgerald's sides, which sent him charging within shooting range of a young guerilla at the back. Joseph shot with his pistol, but the young rebel, rifle in hand, looked behind him. Joseph felt a stabbing pain in his gut and looked down as he attempted to pull out his rifle. The secesh turned in his saddle, his horse holding steady, and began shooting before Joseph could grab his rifle.

Fitzgerald stopped charging and turned a full circle around on the trail. Then facing the young man who was shooting, he immediately reared up his full height, hooves pawing in the air toward the shooter. In the same moment, Joseph's failing body slumped, right shoulder down and off Fitzgerald headfirst with his right boot twisted in his stirrup. Simultaneously, his rifle flew off into the thorny undergrowth. The second time Fitzgerald reared up and twisted, Joseph's foot came out of the stirrup. Somehow, he flopped over onto his face, body crumpled inward.

From his second rise to an upright position to paw the air, Fitzgerald suddenly crashed to his front knees with a crackling thump, then pitched over and hit the ground on his right side with mangled legs attempting to flail the air, his great torso just missing Joseph's body. Fitzgerald's broken front legs continued thrashing loosely by his side in an attempt to rise. His nostrils flaring and eyes protruding from their sockets, he lifted his head up and over attempting to look back toward Joseph.

Joseph woke up enough to hear the air escape from his beloved horse's lungs. He knew Fitzgerald's heart would be pumping in its last powerful attempts to feed his body, but the blood would be pumped out through the holes in his lungs—and Fitzgerald would be gone soon.

Joseph called out, "Slán, capall maith, me deartháir / Farewell,- good horse, me brother. I have loved you more than meself." He then passed out from illness and a broken heart.

The young secesh and a companion who rode back saw two large holes through Fitzgerald's pectorals. One bullet probably went into his lungs, and the second, maybe six inches lower, may have entered his heart and maybe his lungs for a second hit. Fitzgerald appeared to be still alive, so the young man lifted his rifle, shot Fitzgerald in the head, and said, "I'm sorry, great steed." There they both lay, horse and soldier, as the young rebels realized that their three fellow guerillas were making an escape from the onslaught of seven cavalrymen riding in their direction. They quickly turned north and plunged back through the brush as Joseph's peers arrived down the narrow trail from the trestle.

Up ahead, five men from Joseph's troop patrol took off after the other secesh, but two others rode back to Joe and Fitzgerald. Padraig jumped out of his saddle and immediately ran to Joseph. Seeing no blood, he and another skirmisher gently rolled him over. They saw nothing. There were no holes in his shirt or pants that they could see. They opened and loosened his clothing. His heart was beating, and he appeared to be breathing. He was passed out similar to how he passed out at the bar. He had not been shot!

They slapped him and called his name.

When Joseph came to, he immediately vomited blood. He was completely exhausted, his complexion and eyes were yellow, and he was skin and bones. Joseph briefly came to and asked, "Is he gone?" Joseph spoke to Fitzgerald so he would know he was loved and then passed out again at the thought of it.

When he came to again, he wondered if Fitzgerald had been turning to run, trying to protect him, or standing up to fight. In that moment, Joseph's rifle was gone, and he could not will himself to his pistol; Fitz would have to do the fighting. Joseph just tried to hold on.

A Celtic warrior's horse won his respect by dying in battle. Joseph was proud that Fitz had stood up and taken the bullets for him, but he regretted that he hadn't run when he had the opportunity. If Joseph had been in control of his body, he might have saved the great

257

horse. Joseph was embarrassed that this event wasn't a true battle like the one the men in Lone Jack had endured. He thought that maybe men would think he was drunk and had needlessly squandered Fitzgerald's life. Regardless, Fitzgerald died acting the warrior, and that's what helped to console Joseph. He was so proud of Fitz, but he was not proud of himself. He felt unworthy of the horse he had been given.

When Joseph regained consciousness he began wailing deliriously. "Jaisus, Mary, and Joseph! The secesh devil killed me Fitzgerald! Michael, Ma, precious Charley, he killed me Celtic warrior gelding! Jaisus, Mary McManus, now what? What will I do in this damned war without Fitzgerald? I've lost me heart, dammit! O, Christ beside me now! I've lost me best friend a man could ever have!"

Padraig lifted himself on his Morgan, and the men tossed the feather-light Joseph on behind him. One of the men said, "Don't worry, Joe. We'll come back and get Fitz as soon as we can. We'll have to get permission and a wagon."

Joseph remained slumped against Padraig, barely hanging on the entire trip back to the camp.

Joseph was the color of yellow chalk, and his return created a stir in camp. Even the commander was stunned. It was as though Fitz had been the invisible and magical horse, and taking bullets to the heart or lungs and breaking both of his powerful front legs seemed unimaginable. The fact that the secesh who shot him had attempted to put him out of his suffering was respected. Joseph was grateful that he hadn't needed to do it himself, but his heart was broken.

It was Friday afternoon, and the men immediately began to discuss not wanting to leave Fitzgerald out on the trail where animals might get to him. With that suggestion, many exceptions began to fall in place on the post at every level. As Joseph burned with fever on his cot, the many Irishmen among them thought it was normal and right for the Celtic warrior gelding of mystical status to have a proper burial. Eventually the officers went along with the men's plans—as long as they knew it was not a military-sanctioned ceremony, and it happened on their free time outside the camp. It was to cost the army nothing, it was not to interfere in any way with the operations or mission, the men were not to become intoxicated, and they were not to miss call to quarters.

The men took their oldest, most decrepit wagon and an unusable three-wheeled wagon from the junk pile and fashioned them together to carry Fitzgerald back. A sizable number of men had gone out to pull Fitzgerald's giant form up their makeshift ramp and onto the bed of what they called their "Irish horse hearse." They dug a sizable pit and put in as much fuel from the prairie floor as they thought it might take. Men from Lincolnville came out to help lay down the fuel in preparation.

It was late Saturday when the men came back from retrieving Fitzgerald. The drummer had gone about a mile down the road on his horse and waited to play a dirge for the entourage. As the body was returned to its resting place, the men could assemble and stand quietly around. The bugler played an original call, and the return of Fitzgerald lasted ten minutes from just outside town. Fitzgerald lay in state just outside the cattle corral, around the south end near a cornfield. Joseph stayed in his tent—too sick to look up or admire the parade into town.

On Sunday, after roll call and the assignment of limited compulsory duties, the men were free. Normally, soldiers would clean their guns and other equipment, write letters, catch up their journals, attend church services, or play cards. On occasion, a priest or minister would go to the camp to administer to the men who voluntarily attended their service. They would listen for the bugle for church call, which was also used for funeral escorts.

After the men were dismissed, Joseph was helped out of bed and lifted out onto Padraig's horse, and he and his contingent of mourners ambled out around to the side of the corral where Fitzgerald had been placed.

The men gave their last salute to the great Fitzgerald—Celtic warrior steed of Company C—and the funeral pyre was lit.

The next day, the commander notified Joseph that he would be sent up to the hospital in Lexington, hopefully for a short stay. Joseph's "short stay" lasted throughout November and December. Before Christmas, he was sent to the Benton Barracks in St. Louis.

Letter: Westphalia, Kansas, February, 1863
To: Joseph Quigley, St. Louis, Missouri
From: Mary McManus,
Westphalia, Anderson County, Kansas

My dearest Joe,
I cannot tell you the joy of receiving the letter from the army
last Thursday. It has been so long since I have heard from you
that I wasn't sure we'd see one another ever again. That you
will be mustered out at the end of March is most wonderful
news. So many wet, cold months have filled your illness that I
feared you might be dead by now.
   When you come home to Kansas, I promise you I will return
you to a state of complete health. Hopefully, through your illness, you've learned not to be drinking so much. However, I
hear it's very common among the soldiers.

Joseph turned to the nurse and said, "Kansas isn't home.
Fitzgerald was me home, and he's gone. I can't learn not to drink. It's
like ridin' a horse. Ye can't unlearn it. Drinkin' got me from Staten
Island through the war. Goin' from one drunken state to another is
how ye can stand livin' this life such as it is. She knew I was drinkin'
before I became a soldier."
   The nurse replied, "All the soldiers who have survived are afraid
that they won't be able to regain their health. Your wife sounds wonderful, and I think you might do better than you think. If I were you,
I'd let your wife take care of you and hope for the best."

We have been planting our early summer crops, so there has
been much work. Daniel and everyone else has been introducing more winter wheat, and we're going from 150 acres of corn
to 100 acres of corn and 60 acres of wheat. Of course, we still
have 60 acres of oats. The wheat takes much less water, but
who can judge the weather? The rest is alfalfa he sells to sister

Margaret for her Jerseys and now Guernseys. Nobody else has them, so she is very proud and feeds them well. We've been guarding them against the raiders.

Margaret and John are expecting their first child. I don't know when. I am sworn to secrecy.

Daily, I feed my chickens, milk several cows, and play my piano. Joining me in these homely chores will help you regain your strength. It's a good thing you do not have to drive a team again. Now you can become a real farmer. Our best years are ahead of us. I cannot wait!

Again, Joseph interrupted the nurse, "She'll have to hold me up to be workin' 150 acres of corn and sixty acres of wheat. I can't get on me pot without help, and I'm lucky I still have me legs. Drivin' a team is all I can do."

He could hardly listen to what the nurse was reading to him. Mary went on and on telling him how great everything was going to be. *Does she know what's goin' on? Has Mary been on holiday in France the last two years?*

He felt like dying right then. He didn't want to feed chickens. He wanted to eat a meal that didn't result in pain. He wanted to be clean and sleep warm, and he was trying not to die—even though he would have preferred it at the moment. But Mary McManus went on making decisions about his future as a farmer and remaking him in the image of her da.

I have a new riding horse, Da named April, as he gave it to me last April, and she was born in April two years before. My nice old Isabella h ad to be put down after the terrible rains of last June. Her hooves got thrush, and she just couldn't get over it. We soaked linen in hydrogen peroxide and tied it around her hind hooves, but it had little effect. The stable roof leaked spring and summer, before the drought, and she had the stall on the end. We ran out of straw before the rains stopped. Sometimes Daniel and I would trade stalls, but it didn't help. He doesn't think the rain had anything to do with it because she never stood directly in water for days. Only one side of her stall was wet. She was limping so badly that I couldn't ride her. Her hip started giving out because of her poor walking and probably her age. I miss her; she was a gentle lady. I love my April, but she is quite different from Isabella. She's very light on her feet, moves quickly and is smaller than Isabella. One might think, at times, that she is an Arabian princess.

Joseph said, "Isabella got her hooves wet? The cavalry horses stand over their dead riders for days in the rain to protect them. They stand until they drop dead. Fitz traveled hundreds of miles in heat, snow, and flood saving me arse and Missouri farms. He got shot and lived for me. He got shot and died for me. Isabella had her hooves wrapped in white linen? Her horse had a roof while mine had the sky? What did her Isabella do for anyone?"

The nurse said, "Mr. Quigley, would you love your wife more if she had been fighting in the cavalry or if her horse had gotten shot out from under her? Would she be more to your liking if she had dysentery or cholera?"

Joseph said nothing.

The nurse added, "Like all the other wives, she cannot be insulted or belittled for keeping the home fires while you were away. She stood by you and did what she could. Many wives take care of the children and are running the farms by themselves. Why should a wife be blamed for telling her husband about their horses? Would you like me to stop reading the letter? Perhaps I could read it and tell you if there is something from it that you need to know." Joseph thought, *How will Mary understand how things have changed for me? It might as well have been a hundred years since we married, and things weren't that great then. Maybe I'll die and not have to face another life. I'm tired of this one.*

"Mr. Quigley, did you hear what I said?"

"'Tis unfortunate, but I have heard ye. Go ahead and finish the letter."

I cannot wait to see the great Fitzgerald. Who has been caring for him throughout your illness? You haven't mentioned him, so I was a little frightened to ask about him. I hope that he wasn't forced to fight on without you.

If he is gone, you must know I shall always have a place in my heart for him. He took such good care of you all these many years.

I pray our worst days are behind us.

I'm not sure I want to go back to Missouri ever. The land is good around Big Creek, and I love Michael and Mary, but maybe it would be easier to stay nearer to my McManus family. Hopefully, we can get our own farm here as soon as this terrible war is over.

My dear, please let me know what needs to be arranged to get you home. I cannot await your arrival, my darling.

Love,
Your faithful and adoring wife, Mary

"Mr. Quigley, Do want me to write back to your wife and tell her how you're getting home?"

Joseph answered, "Yes. Tell her I'll see her when I get there."

The nurse said, "That's not nice, Mr. Quigley. She has been waiting faithfully and is anxious to see you. You'll make her a nervous wreck if you don't answer her letter like a gentleman. Maybe she'll fear you have abandoned her. Do you plan to abandon her, Mr. Quigley? Should I tell her that so she'll be prepared?"

Joseph didn't want a discussion on abandonment with this woman. She was probably a mother herself who had a daughter waiting for a soldier. She was certainly old enough—and was obviously on Mary's side of the fence.

"If you love Mary, you must learn how to be kind again. It may take a little time, Mr. Quigley, but you want to be happy again. You were kind once, were you not? If you are not kind, you will not be loved, and if you do not love or you are not loved, you will not find joy."

Joseph said, "Please tell Mary that the army owes me a little money for Fitzgerald who is gone. I'll buy a good horse and get off the boat in Independence. Pleasant Hill isn't too far from Independence, so I'll go see Michael and Mary. Tell her to look for me in April. Sign it, 'With all me love, Joe.'"

"Mr. Quigley, my information here says that you can read and write. Can't you write the letter yourself?"

Joseph answered, "If ye don't write the letter, it won't get written. I can't bring meself to do it."

CHAPTER 19

WESTPHALIA, KANSAS, 1863–1865

Mary McManus's family had not lived in Anderson County a full decade, but by 1863, they felt they were at home on their farms. They and their neighbors arrived in the same wave from Ireland. The sons and daughters had married within a handful of families who had jointly become recipients of land purchases supported by the New England Emigrant Aid Company. At remarkably good prices, they were invited to flood into Kansas and shift the population away from becoming a slave state. They built a library, a school, and a church, and they cultivated the prairie in short time. They developed for themselves a tight-knit Catholic community that supported each other through every hardship.

Conflicts and atrocities of the Civil War continued around them, but they had been spared some of the Missouri-style looting and burning of their community that Mary and Joseph had encountered in 1860 at Big Creek and Order 11 in Cass County and had chased Joseph into war, sent Mary back home, or kept them from thriving.

After mustering out on March 31, Joseph had arrived from Lexington to Daniel McManus's farm in Anderson County. He rode a Morgan named Cara and had twenty dollars to his person. While Joseph served in the war, Mary lived in a little house next to Daniel and his wife, Mary, regularly milking cows and doing other chores. She also taught local children piano lessons from time to time and attended the church dinners, box lunches, and family parties that kept the community bonded in spite of the apparent chaos in the region.

For three long years, Mary had imagined Joseph attending Mass and neighborhood parties with her. She wanted to hear him sing. She wanted to dance with him and hoped he would enjoy her family and community. Mary could not wait to show him off; she had been married for more than three years, but she had only lived with Joseph in Missouri for about a year before he joined the Home Guard and then the Missouri Militia Cavalry. She also hoped he would not drink and would control his temper and mean streaks—at least in front of her family. It embarrassed her, hurt her feelings, and helped reinforce their belief that she had rushed into a marriage she would not have considered had she been more mature. They didn't think Joseph was capable of being a good husband or father. Hearing very little from him had made her fret for nearly three years.

From the moment Joseph moved in, Mary began suggesting and practicing songs they could perform together, but Joseph was not so keen on becoming the life of the party. She was trying to make up for lost time. He was sick. He had eaten too many worm-infested or moldy squares of hardtack and drunk campfire- boiled coffee on a stomach that rejected both, even when the food was in fairly good condition. His Irish famine experience had hardened him against cholera, but he had suffered stomach issues and chronic dysentery, the symptoms of which he had tolerated to some extent since being a teenager in West Bottoms. It had, with his alcoholism, gotten worse during his service in the cavalry. His skin had turned sallow and his mood was not so effusive or charming in gatherings as he had been. For Mary, it was dramatic. She wanted to start over as they had been when she was seventeen, but Joseph could not regress to the happy-go-lucky youth he had only been in Cincinnati, which Mary only imagined lay somewhere within him now.

Feeling better by May, Joseph decided that he really did love Mary, and he wanted to make her happier. She needed to be patient in return. They were absolutely dirt poor, but in June, only three months after Joseph was mustered out, Mary became pregnant. Throughout 1863, and in spite of Joseph's roller-coaster bouts of illness, they enjoyed the freedom of honeymooners, riding about the farming community to visit Mary's sisters, cousins, and their new babies.

Because Mary was expecting, she especially favored Mary Drumm, her sister Agnes's baby. She was only six months old when Mary began to experience bouts of nausea and fainting, symptoms that confirmed her own pregnancy. Since Agnes lived only a short distance away, Joseph could hitch April up to a little buggy of Daniel and Mary's, and off Mary would go to rock her niece, take little bouquets of wildflowers, and otherwise dream about her own little baby.

It was that summer in which unrest palpably festered in Joseph. Joseph did not enjoy being on display at another's pleasure, especially when he did not feel approved of. With her family, Mary hadn't openly discussed Joseph's embarrassing drinking issues she discovered in Westport. There were no men in her family who exhibited the Irish disease.

However, her family first saw it surface at Mary's wedding in 1859, and Mary had written things to Agnes when she lived in Big Creek. Agnes shared episodes that disturbed the family. Joseph would occasionally go out with the other Big Creek men who got drunk, and when she asked him where he had been, he had slapped her and told her it was none of her business. When she wanted to talk with him about how he should be, he would tell her to "shut it," and they had gone days without talking. Joseph told her he loved her, but his drinking made him morose for days. She was not so happy, but she got support from Mary and Michael Quigley, who did not drink at all.

Now, in Westphalia four years later, Joseph's drinking and mean streaks had crept into the forefront of conflicts on several occasions during the busy summer months and become a barrier in his relationship with Daniel.

Daniel had grown his large farm into an enterprise that required employees to maintain. Mary and Joseph were living in the place where Daniel usually had a sober, hardworking farmhand or two who were reliable.

Joseph did as well as he could, but he required months to recover from his dysentery and his cavalry experience, and he and Mary were dependent on Daniel. When he fell off the wagon or was unkind to Mary, the family would step in to get things back under control. Though he could be fun and charming, they generally didn't like him before he married Mary—and they found him less tolerable now.

However, tensions lessened as the crops were harvested and the winter months set in. Finally, in March, Mary and Joseph's son, John, was born. Family gathered around on the birthday to help, but from his birth, they became troubled. John was very small, and when first born, he did not want to breathe or cry as a robust baby would. His body was blue, and they rubbed him and bundled him. The grandparents, Mary and John McManus, made sure that the infant was raced within a few days to the Immaculate Conception Church in the city of Kansas for his baptism, where the Quigley, Murphy, and Grant families rallied around to give support.

Michael and Joseph quietly agreed that the little boy's big gray eyes and brown curls made him resemble Charley, and they fell in love with him. However, he didn't have the vitality or robust features of the sturdy little Charley.

Mary and her mother fussed John into June, and then he seemed to come into his own. However, his lips were always a little blue, and the doctor told Mary and Joseph he had a heart problem that might make him succumb early. He possibly could outgrow it, or if it did not heal on its own while he was less than a year, it could be a problem until he died at a young age.

While Mary was pregnant with John, her sister Margaret had birthed twins who died, so Mary and Joseph felt blessed and remained quiet and humble about John's condition. Everyone prayed that he might grow out of his problem. If God took John, they believed that he would be with Margaret's babies in heaven, and that would be lovely. Other than love and prayer, it was in God's hands, but Mary spent nearly every living minute looking and praying over John. She visualized fairies and angels watching over him as she slept, and she was afraid to lay him down alone in his basket.

As a farmhand throughout the rest of 1864, Joseph became more dependable and healthier. Besides a few milk cows, Daniel had a large team of oxen and several great workhorses to haul his farm equipment. He had beef cattle on a portion of rangeland and large fields of wheat, barley, alfalfa, flax, millet, or corn, depending on the season or year. He changed up his crops, but he tried to keep things growing as close to year-round as he could on more than three hundred acres. It required a lot of work and luck, and Joseph's skills with the work animals helped immensely. Joseph was good with repairs and creative solutions. He taught Daniel new ways of tying knots and improvising broken connections on straps. Equipment and animals did not stay out of commission for long with him around. Throughout the summer, Joseph did not drink—and the friction between Daniel and Joseph diminished.

Daniel had several other farmhands who worked for him, but it was inconvenient that they did not live on the farm. It was more difficult to hustle them up in an emergency, like getting the hay in before the rain, and Joseph sensed that Daniel wanted him and Mary to get on their feet and move so he could better utilize the farmhand quarters. Joseph knew that money was the issue, and he could not earn enough from Daniel. Daniel didn't expect Mary and Joseph to pay rent, but he did want them to save enough to move. It wasn't always Joseph's fault that they were not saving.

In July, Mary, without a discussion with Joseph, had taken a cart into Westphalia and purchased an expensive, hand-carved dark walnut rocker with hand-stitched tapestry in vibrant colors of red and green. It replaced the old, unupholstered pine rocker her da had dug up for her that she set outside on the little porch. Mary wanted to rock her sick little boy in a chair that was beautiful and comfortable. The old chair squeaked, and it was stiff and hard on her back. It made her feel poor. She wanted something quiet, soft, and elegant.

The new chair became everyone's business—something Joseph despised about the closeness and dominance of the large family. Nobody knew why she needed such a fancy chair, and everyone but Joseph discussed it with her. She cried and said that she wanted to rock all her babies in the chair. Joseph agreed that it was beautiful and something a proper lady like Mary should own.

Her ma said, "Mary, here ye are, a girl who has married a low- class driver, and yer buyin' somethin' only the idle rich would own! Don't ye know ye don't have a pot to pee in nor a window to throw it out of, darlin'?"

Joseph walked in on them and heard her.

Her ma didn't admit to being rude, and she didn't back down.

Joseph said, "Don't ye at least know that I love me wife? Mary deserves fine furniture as much as the rest of her sisters. I'm not an older, wealthy man like their husbands, but if I hadn't given me health to the Union, I'd also be a wealthy man by now. Ye need to wait a few more years before ye call me a low-class pauper."

Ma answered, "Joseph Quigley, I did not call ye a pauper, but when ye spend yer money on unnecessary things, Mary's da and I have to step in and help ye with the things ye need. And don't try to kid yerself or me. Ye've given as much money to whiskey as ye have to the Union. If ye fought to save yer farm, where is it then?"

Mary said, "Yer bein' unkind and unfair yerself, Ma. Ye'd be angry if I said that same thing to either Margaret's or Agnes's husbands, and ye know it. Joseph didn't invite in the raiders, did he? He didn't strike the match or steal the cattle."

Joseph added, "Don't worry, Mary. We'll be fine, and yer mother will get over the damned chair. She'll have to; we're not takin' it back. It's only a rockin' chair. Ye've had a difficult time, and this is the chair ye and John deserve. I don't care if we have to eat dirt, darlin'; it's stayin' right where it is!"

Her Ma, always needing to have the last word, added, "And without yer family, ye would be eatin' dirt."

Following this altercation, Mary said to Joseph. "I am so proud of ye to hold yer ground. Me ma isn't as inclined to unfairness as she is to thinkin' she's correct. She's also honest, and she says what she's thinkin'."

However, Joseph was frustrated with their living situation, and he was feeling a need to earn more money as he once had. He told Mary they would have to move from Anderson County to do so. He certainly could not afford to buy a farm at this stage of their lives, but he had to do something more than be a farmhand for Mary's brother. He was tired of the insults to himself and Mary, perceived or otherwise.

Returning to Westport appealed to Joseph, but by the end of summer, it was overrun by Confederates and not safe. Eventually, Major General Sterling Price marched into Independence with his Confederate Army, and in two days of October 1864, he won his biggest battle—the largest ever fought in Missouri. Though he had a huge victory, Price immediately marched out, and the Confederates never returned. Though it turned out to be the Confederates' most decisive victory, it also turned out to be their last battle fought in Missouri. It was too costly in soldier deaths for the Confederates to sustain their position.

Joseph heard that Paola, in Miami County, was booming. It was a base for the army, and there was a big market for transporting goods and outfitting teams for the Santa Fe Trail. Because the war was over, people were flooding into Kansas. Joe was sure he could make more money there, but Mary feared that Joseph might lose control over his drinking if she moved away from her family—and she made him promise that he would never drink again or strike her if they moved.

John cried from the summer heat. Mary let him lie naked on a wet towel with a loose modesty diaper resting atop his privates, and they often stood over his basket, monitored his temperature, and watched his heart beat as rapidly as a little bird. After such a spell, he was often lethargic, slept hard, and had very bluish lips. All the McManus women came and gave advice when it was too hot or too cold or when John had a bad spell.

They would talk as though Joseph were somehow responsible, so he either left the house or did not go inside when they were there.

One day, Mary's sister Bridget said, "If ye'd married a lawyer or doctor, ye'd have a nurse here to help ye."

Mary responded, "Yer a little sister sixteen years old and unmarried. I love ye, but where did you acquire yer expertise on marriage? From gossips? Where do ye suppose I would have met a wealthy lawyer? Watch yer tongue. Yer da is a farmer, and so is yer brother. Would you criticize Da for not marrying a princess—like yerself?

"Be gracious and act like a princess if ye think yer a princess, and don't be talkin' down to people as though ye were above them all. Don't forget yer an Irish refugee. We'll see how well ye do marryin' the idle rich out here among the immigrant Irish on the edge of the frontier. Due to luck, yer only one step higher than West Bottoms

271

girls, yer Highness! The next time ye talk to me like that, I promise to slap ye across yer cakehole!"

Bridget helped herself out of the little cabin.

Mary yelled, "Don't forget to share yer evil comment in confession this Sunday. Those waitin' in line would love to giggle."

Joseph wanted to appreciate the family's concern, and because he was so outnumbered, he sincerely tried to stay calm and charming. He was able to recall the sometimes-fussy relationships between sisters. However, when it came to John, their opinions about Joseph being unable to provide better were mean-spirited and unjustified. Joseph felt always to be under their suspicion and scrutiny. Their speech was punitive, and they could not forgive any of his transgressions. However, he could not leave until he and Mary were more secure. At times, he was resilient.

Once winter set in, Joseph lost some of his sense of urgency. Also, Mary's fears and refusal to take their sick infant away without a home or source of food gave Joseph pause. Mary was sure John would die if he were uprooted under harsh and uncertain conditions.

In January, Mary's sister Agnes had another baby girl, and her sister Margaret had a boy. It took much of the attention and pressure off Mary.

However, just days after John was counted as a one-year-old in the 1865 Kansas Census taken in May, Mary was holding her listless boy in her rocker. It was a cloudy, but warm day, and lightning was striking in the distance. She opened the cabin door to let in the breeze. Looking down on John, she said, "Me sweet, baby, are ye not goin' to nurse today? Ye are me sweet darlin', so ye need to keep up yer strength." She stroked his cheek. "Wake up, me angel, and smile at yer ma. Then I want ye to nurse for me."

John did not open his eyes for his ma as he normally would have.

Mary began to sing her lullaby, moved him into an upright position, buttoned up her bodice, gently placed his head on her shoulder, and patted his back.

He was as listless as a little cloth doll.

"Dear one, stay with Ma, baby. Do not let the angels take ye, John. I have hold of ye, John, and I will not let ye go. I need ye as much as the air in me breath, darlin'. Yer da needs ye too." She began to cry.

Mary laid him back down in her arms, and she watched John surrender to the angels. His breath stopped, and Mary's eyes closed. She visualized the angels and fairies as the thunder crashed nearly over their cabin, and the rain began to fall in large, rapid plops on the ground outside. John had slipped from his peaceful sleep into eternal rest, and she could not stop it. She continued to hold and rock him for time she could not count until Joseph walked into the house to get his coat.

Joseph took one look at Mary and sunk to his knees. "Mary, the look on yer face. John, John!" He placed his face on John's damp, blue-white cheek, heard no breathing, and could not feel or see his failed heart working. He lay his head against Mary's chest, below her chin, and looked down on John. He reached both arms around Mary and John, and they wept.

They stayed like that for some time before Daniel came knocking at the door to see why Joseph had not returned.

Φ

Three weeks later, in June, Mary became pregnant again. Now she was sick with grief and pregnancy, and she grew silent and as sad as a woman could be. She told nobody about her pregnancy because she was afraid. She grieved and milked Daniel's cows with her head propped up against the cow's flank. She grieved and walked through the summer fields, despairing and wondering how God could be so cruel. She wondered if her life would improve. She galloped on April across the corn and wheat fields to her parents' home and ate her mother's food. She prayed and asked for God's help, and she listened without speaking to Joseph talking incessantly about Paola.

After Daniel paid Joseph at the end of September, he rode out on Cara with a couple of farmhands and did not come back. He was absolutely gone. Mary later noticed that Joseph had taken his pistol, his rifle, and his saddlebag with him. He had planned to leave and had not told her! They had been doing so well, but maybe he could no longer tolerate her quiet, all-encompassing grief.

One of the farmhands told Daniel that Joseph had gotten drunk in Westphalia, got on his horse, and rode toward Garnett without saying anything.

She told her family that he had gone to Paola to find work in the hauling or transportation industry where he believed he could make good money. Because she was so unhappy and could provide few details about his whereabouts, Daniel and Ma decided that he had abandoned Mary.

Bridget was the first to say, "I told you so, Mary. Just because a man is handsome and can sing doesn't make him a good man."

Mary replied with a broad smile, "Yer right, Bridget. Just because a man is handsome and can sing doesn't make him a bad man. There are other things that do that. I canna wait until ye marry."

CHAPTER 20

PAOLA AND WEA, KANSAS, 1865–1870

One day, John and Mary McManus went to Mary's cabin to talk. Ma said, "Yer da and I have decided that ye should move in with us. Ye can stay with us as long as ye need to. If Joseph has abandoned ye, and he doesn't come back in a year, ye should file with the courts to be granted abandonment rights. We should talk with the priest and seek an annulment through the church. If ye get an annulment, ye can marry a better man and be happy."

Mary looked at her mother as though she had just been slapped across the face. "Did I not tell ye that he has gone to Paola to get a good-payin' job so we can move out of Daniel's cabin and be on our own?"

John McManus took Mary's hand and said, "Mary, maybe ye should think about how realistic it is that yer goin' to have a good future with Joseph. He's a man with talents. We know there are things about him that ye love. We know that he loved his son and that he probably means well. We don't doubt that, but yer ma and I don't think yer bein' realistic. Ye do real well on yer own. When yer with Joe, there is always unhappiness—and yer not being well provided for. He's had plenty of time to do better.

"Yer ma and I want our daughters to be happy. Look how well Margaret and Agnes are doin'. Their husbands are solid and sober. If they need somethin', they can get it. Ye'll be havin' trouble with food—not furniture or carriages. I'm afraid ye'll have a houseful of babies ye cannot feed."

Ma said, "Yer lucky ye don't have any more children. If Joseph doesn't come back, at least ye won't be havin' a baby without a father. Ye can marry another man if ye want children. There are plenty of fine men who go to church every Sunday and were born on a farm in the community."

Mary began to shake and cried out, "Ma, I'm havin' another baby. Joseph's baby. He is me husband. Stop! I need Joseph. I told ye, he's in Paola, and he will come back. He will take care of us. You'll see.

"If ye hadn't been so mean to him, he would not have gone off like he did. Ye hurt his feelings. Ye always hurt his feelings or insult him. Maybe ye don't mean to, but that's what ye do. He stays nice to ye and says nothin', but it insults him as a man. Do ye not realize what the war has done to him? He came back to me to face another barrage of hurt from me family. Daniel might get frustrated with Joseph's illness, but he doesn't say mean things like ye and Bridget. Maybe ye should try to be nice like Da, Margaret, Agnes, and Daniel.

"Did ye not remember that I waited years for Joseph to come back, and then I lost me precious John—and now Joseph is away again? Please. 'Tis not helpful what ye are sayin'. Maybe ye should all go back home for the evenin' so I can sit in me lovely chair and weep by meself."

Eventually, the entire family realized that Mary was pregnant again, and they decided to be more sensitive.

Mary stuck by her story that Joe would be back to get her and would have a job and a place for them to live. October passed, and November arrived. Then a telegram came through at the Garnett office for her.

The good father, John McManus, put his obviously pregnant daughter in the family carriage, and feeling as hopeful as Mary, he rushed them both to Garnett to pick it up.

Mary. Have house in Irish settlement, South Paola. Good job, livery. Holy Trinity Church near. Bring chair, baby basket, piano. Need food. Please come as soon as possible. Love, Joe.

Before Thanksgiving could arrive, Daniel loaded his wagon and tied April on a lead, and they were off the sixty miles to Paola. John McManus rode behind with a wad of cash hidden in his boot.

Daniel found the tiny cabin where they were to live, but only by luck. Before leaving for Kansas City, Joe had told people in the settlement, particularly Cecelia Riley, the lady in the first house entering the Irish settlement, to be on the lookout for Mary. Cecelia had told people who lived closest to the church and had told the priest, Father Francis Wattron, that Joseph might be up in Kansas City when his wife arrived in Paola.

The settlement area was very poor, and most had recently arrived. During the war, Paola was highly dangerous and complicated, but it was bustling now with hope, if not resources. The streets were laid out in a very regular grid, and nearly all the streets going east and west were named after Indian tribes that had been resettled there over the past twenty years.

The dusty house had cobwebs and filthy windows, and it smelled musty. There were several rotten boards off the kitchen and the back porch.

John McManus and Daniel took matters into their own hands. While Daniel and Mary swept, dusted, and washed down surfaces, John went out and found a man in the neighborhood who could reglaze the windows, cover rat holes, rehang a door, and add locks.

Cecelia Riley saw the activity and pitched in. She brought a strong teenage son, a sturdy scrub brush, and sweet lavender- scented soap for the bucket.

Daniel and Mary had packed brooms, a bucket, and rags, and John had a saw and a few other repair items. In the livestock shed, there were several hay bins with a few good boards among those that might have been kicked loose. John removed the good wood from the bins to reinforce old stringings under parts of the floor. Mrs. Riley and Daniel rummaged through a neighbor's lumber pile to grab a few new floorboards so Mary would not fall through and be hurt.

That Joe hadn't already accomplished this task before Mary, now five months pregnant, moved in was another argument in the McManus arsenal used to reinforce their opinions about her husband.

Mary's da shook hands with the repairman, and they brought in the furniture and other housewares. As a surprise, her da magically produced a carpet that the family had carried west from Philadelphia. It was constructed of wool from India, fit well, and was attractive in the room where the spinet and rocking chair sat.

Mary was especially touched that her lovely da would pass on such a wonderful gift, and she said, "Tell Ma how much this means to me. I'll have a little piece of me childhood adventure of comin' to America under me feet in the cold weather. Please tell Ma how grateful I am. I know how she loves this carpet. It must have been difficult for her to give it up. It will remind me of family while I hold me new baby. I hope she's a smart, sturdy McManus girl."

It was cold, so they put April's blanket over her before they tied her in the little livestock shed behind the house. John had redistributed some boards on her bin so the alfalfa would stay in it and she could still get at it. John cleaned out an old tub in the shed and filled it from the hand pump.

Daniel had started a fire in the stove when they arrived. It helped dry out the dampness of the newly washed floorboards, walls, and cupboards. Once things were more comfortable for Mary, Daniel and John McManus went to the inn for the night. It was now dark, and they planned to leave early in the morning.

Mary cried to be saying goodbye to her father and brother. She thanked them for all they did for her that, again, her husband didn't do. She expressed love through her tears, but she felt trepidation and thin hope. Also, she quietly promised her da that if something went too wrong, she would get word to them and possibly return home for good.

After everyone was gone, she made a pot of tea. She had a little jar of milk from home that she set out on a porch shelf. Da had brought a slab of salt pork wrapped in newspaper that she was afraid to set outside, as she thought the mice or rats might come along and have a feast. Mary nibbled on her ma's cheese, bread, and a winter apple, and she felt very alone. Other than the reassurances of Mrs. Riley, she had no idea where Joseph was or when he would return.

The cold night wind howled, but she stayed warm under her down. She listened to trees scraping, the cabin creaking, and things in the close neighborhood banging into sheds, houses, and posts in the night. It was not like the open farmland she was used to, and it took a very long time for her to fall asleep.

The next day, the handyman showed up to begin work on his repairs. The first things she asked for was the locks on the doors.

Mary was to pay him from the money her da gave her—but not until each job was completed.

Just as she was putting tea on, Joseph came through the door. He looked very rugged and had a beard, but she melted in his arms. "Oh, my husband, Joseph."

He held her and slowly waltzed her around in a circle, "Oh, me wife, Mary, so happy am I to see ye. How different the house feels! Did this happen because ye walked in through the door? Yer magic, Mary. Yer the best gift in me life, and look at that belly, me beautiful girl!"

Then the workman walked out of the bedroom where he had just reglazed a window.

Joseph apologized for the house, but he said he was busy working and had been sleeping in wagons in the hay until he had enough money to get the house. He was still riding to Kansas City and hauling furniture back to a place up north, too far away to always come to the cabin.

She was proud that he was so able to endure hardships, but at the same time, it was sad. She asked, "Are ye feelin' well, Joseph?"

He answered, "No, Mary. I have been lonely, cold, and hungry. I have missed ye and me baby, John. Do ye know how much I have missed ye? I was thinking about John when I came here today. I want this baby to do better and have a happier mother. I am so glad that God is goin' to let us have another baby. I promise that this place will get better—and we'll be happy. Ye can rock in yer chair, play the piano, go across the street to the church, and make friends in the neighborhood. I know ye met Mrs. Riley. Father Wattron sent me over to Mrs. Riley's house as soon as I found this place. It's not great, but we can make it better and get a better place by the time the baby comes along. Maybe ye can write a letter tomorrow to tell yer family how grateful I am that they brought ye to me and did so much to clean things and fix things up when ye got here."

"The workman will be back to finish several more jobs before the baby arrives. The wind blows through the house, so we have to finish that first." Mary suggested that Joseph should write the letter himself because it might sound more genuine coming from him instead of her. She didn't suggest, however, that he should have taken care of the filthy cabin before she got there, not leave it up to her family to fill in his gaps for him. *Did he expect me to show up and do all that work alone, a pregnant woman traveling all that way to arrive at a filthy shack where I could fall through the floor? If I were Ma or Bridget, I would have expressed my displeasure with him.* However, she was so happy to be with John's da and their new baby's family all together that she wanted to be gentle like Agnes or Da, and she had nothing to gain by appearing unloving or ungrateful, justified or not. She swallowed her disappointment and put it in the past. She would start over. Again.

She wanted to forgive Ma. Ma was generally right. That's why she had married John McManus. She was a Grant—ambitious, educated, and proper—and she made sure her family was provided for. She wanted the same for Mary. Bridget was just following Ma's good example. Bridget was smart and disciplined, and she would do as well as Ma. She was just young now, but she was correct in maintaining the standard.

Φ

Paola was very different from any place Mary had been. Miami County had been a campground and common hunting grounds for the Kanza and the Osage Indians. The first half of the century was very hard on every tribe on the frontier from the Great Lakes to the Southwest. Those who hadn't died of cholera, scarlet fever, measles, alcoholism, or other white man's diseases kept being moved around through the government's removal policy, various treaties, or reorganizations of tribal associations. As each tribe grew smaller, it lost power as well as land, and the smaller tribe was placed with a larger one, whether they had anything in common or not.

Miami County became a relocation site of reservations of various sizes for the Shawnee, Delaware, Iowa, Wyandot, Wea, Kickapoo, Ottawa, Cherokee, Plankashaw, Pottawatomie, Peoria, Kaskaskia, Miami, and others. They were often voluntarily moving there, as well as being forcefully moved. There they would stay until Oklahoma was ready to receive them all.

The various reservations were of very different sizes, ranging from small parcels of twenty acres for a family to several hundred to accommodate all the families of the tribe. In the center, at the town square, was the common area. People gathered there to hear a band that had formed or to watch the Indians race their horses around the track outside the square.

For the most part, everyone got along fine; the major law enforcement problem was alcoholism. The daily paper notified the general public of who was arrested for supplying Indians with alcohol. It was against the law to serve Indians, due to their intolerance and the death toll, but there were saloons hidden in houses and the backs of stores, and it was a constant problem.

For several years, the Oklahoma reservation was being prepared, and all Indians in Miami County who didn't have their own land were scheduled to leave their Miami County homes by the end of 1867. All the Indians on the reservation lands were removed to make room for the whites who were going to be sold their land. By the time Joseph and Mary arrived—and during the previous twenty years— many natives had established farms around the lands outside the city. Mixed families often had titles. From Joseph's cavalry days, he knew of Indian farms east of Paolo, in the Wea reservation. Because many of these people would be leaving, Joseph had several small farms in the back of his mind that he might be able to purchase if he could save some money.

For now, the Catholic church was the center of Joseph and Mary's community. The Holy Trinity Catholic Church was a rough stone building located across the street that served the Irish and the Indians. When Joseph was gone to Kansas City, Mary walked over in the snow for daily Mass or the rosary until Ellen was born in March, almost exactly two years after John had been born. Ellen was baptized by Father Francis Wattron, a French Benedictine priest ordained in Leavenworth who had only been in Paola a year.

When it came time for Mary's baby to arrive, Mrs. Riley arranged for two women from the church to go to the little house. On her way to the church, Mrs. Riley would routinely stop by to check on Mary's progress. On Saturday morning, March 17, Mary was building the fire in her little sitting room stove. It was a cold, rainy day, and Mary was aching.

Cecelia rapped at her door and said, "Good morning, Mary Quigley. Are ye ready to have yer baby yet?"

Mary laughed and said, "I'm certainly ready, but I'm not so sure about the baby—though me back is hurtin' a lot."

"Ah, good then," answered Cecelia. "Do ye have a kettle of water on the kitchen stove?"

Mary answered, "I still have hot water in me teapot. Would ye like a cup?"

"Surely. I've had one already, but I got a little chilled comin' over here," Cecelia said. "I swear it feels as though it might snow today."

Mary fixed Cecelia's tea, set it on the side table, and lost her balance, landing on the too-low piano stool. The moment she landed, she felt the warm spring of water gushing. She and Cecelia stood until the water stopped, and Cecelia quickly rushed across the street to call her friend over.

It wasn't longer than ten minutes later that a third lady joined them. She was the sturdy and healthy daughter Mary had prayed for. She had a very round face, large gray eyes, and giant dark curls.

Mary thanked Cecelia and suggested that she come visit exactly at the right moment if there was going to be a next time.

The lady from across the street and Cecelia cleaned up, washed Mary's petticoat, hung it in the kitchen to dry, and settled Mary and baby into the clean bed.

Joseph rushed in with a package in his hands. "Oh, Mary, ye've had our baby! She looks like a girl. Is she a girl?"

"Yes, Joseph. She's a girl who looks a little like John, does she not?"

"Oh, yes, darlin'. She does."

She was asleep, but Joseph asked if he could hold her. "I would hope so. She's yer daughter," Mary said.

Joseph took his baby and said, "I think yer an Ellen. Me sister Ellen would love it if ye were. Can we call her Ellen, Mary? We'll call the next girl Mary. Is that all right?"

Joseph cradled Ellen, handed Mary the package wrapped in string, and went to Mary's rocker to hold her. He smelled her head and kissed it. It reminded him of Charley's birth. His ma asked him to smell the newborn smell that she said he would recognize as Charley all the rest of his life. His baby Ellen smelled the same as Charley, his sister, and the infants James and Mary. He had not smelled Doroty, but Ellen was, at that moment, everything he had ever wanted, and he felt happy.

"Oh, Joseph," Mary called from the bedroom. "I love it. 'Tis beautiful. I had Ma keep John's baptismal gown because I didn't know where I could keep it here. This is perfect. Maybe ye can talk with Father Wattron tomorrow. We'll go to the train station and telegraph Ellen's grandparents when we know her baptism date. Also, tell Michael and Mary. We'll need a sponsor. Maybe Mary will stand for her—or Agnes or Margaret. Mrs. Riley would be happy to, but we need to have family members for godparents. I insist."

Father Wattron, who conducted Ellen's baptism, had a beautiful singing voice. Though they had an organist at Holy Trinity, Mary volunteered to play the organ when the organist was not available, which was fairly regularly. In fact, Mary played for Ellen's baptism. It was fun for her to do so—and unusual.

Mary and Joseph could not afford to immediately start giving to the church, so Mary played for funerals and weddings and special Masses at holidays as often as she could until the regular organist moved on. This was her first baptism.

Everyone loved it when Joseph came to Mass, when he held Ellen while Mary played, and when he and Father Wattron sang. There were plenty of Irish tenors in the congregation, and Joseph and Mary both enjoyed attending services with robust singing.

Joseph's first job had been driving carts and buggies for the livery in Paola. However, by the time Mary joined him, he was earning more by occasionally working for a freighter's team until it became his full-time work. He hauled goods, mostly furniture, from Kansas City to Twin Springs, a small town ten miles north of Paola, which had a large furniture store. The store attracted patrons, wealthy and poor, from as far as Fort Scott, Garnett, and Olathe.

Joseph, being gone often, gave Mary and baby Ellen peace. She could focus on her piano students, and she had time for sewing and rocking in her beautiful chair. She knew Joseph was probably drinking at night with the other drivers, but when he came home once or twice a week and every Saturday night, he seemed fine. She would regularly pray herself to sleep, deciding that there had been enough grief. She would put his drinking out of her mind.

Joseph earned enough to feed them, and he told her he was saving for a farm in Wea when one came available, which he thought could happen by the next spring. Mary was thrilled.

It was not long before Mary acquired a few beginning piano students. Ellen was such a good baby that she took her nap or entertained herself when Mary's students came for their lessons. The house was tiny, a little irregular in balance, but it was cozy and conveniently located near the school for students. Mary allowed one family to pay in fresh butter and eggs. She decided that she could do the same when they got their own farm. She missed milking a cow and feeding chickens.

One April afternoon in 1867, when Ellen was one, Mary became very unsteady on her feet. She thought she might be fainting—until her chimney began to lose its bricks and the house rattled about. She grabbed Ellen, and they ran outside to see dust rising from the chimneys of other houses. The shaking was so profound that she and Ellen had been thrown to the ground. Mary had never experienced anything like it before in her life, but she realized that it was an earthquake. Everyone had some damage, and she learned that the newspaper office had lost an entire wall.

The first day, Mary took the bricks from the chimney outdoors and constructed a makeshift stove. She made a box of bricks with four walls. The face and top were open, and the backs and sides each had a brick missing for a good draft. She then laid an old oven box her neighbor gave her down on three walls of bricks and built a fire on the bottom layer of bricks. With the oven on top, covering the fire, the light rain did not affect the fire or the food inside at all.

Joseph rode home the next day to find his girls doing well. He knew Mary would figure out how to work around any problems the earthquake would cause. She was a clever woman. In the oven, she heated bricks that she brought inside, wrapped in cornmeal sacks, and laid on the floor under Ellen's crib. She laid wrapped bricks on a board under her feet at her chair and stayed warm until bedtime. For the most part, the weather was mild, and the homeowner eventually fixed her chimney.

Φ

Every Irish family invited the priest to visit and bless their home. Because Mary did not have a proper parlor chair, she was a little embarrassed to invite Father Wattron to their little house. She had mentioned this several times to Joseph to explain why she had not yet invited Father Francis. They could not afford to buy a set of parlor chairs, so Mary, recalling the fuss over her rocker, let it drop. She didn't want to push Joseph into making an unnecessary purchase, and she didn't want to have Father Francis sit in her rocker while she sat on the piano stool. Of course, he would offer the chair to her, but she didn't want him sitting in a plain chair or the piano stool. She wasn't sure Mrs. Riley hadn't told him what had happened on the stool, so she would be embarrassed if he knew. Because she didn't want cheaply or poorly made chairs in her home that dissatisfied her, she chose nothing.

Normally, Joseph rode Cara home, leaving the wagon and team at their livery in Twin Springs or Paola. One cold Friday night in November of 1867, Joseph rode up to their house with a small carriage, carrying something bulky and large under a tarp. He ran up to the house and called, "Mary! Ellen! Come outside and see what I have for ye. I have a surprise!"

Holding Ellen, now twenty months, Mary was stunned to see what was under the tarp. "Joseph, I cannot believe that ye have found these! They nearly match me beautiful rocker. They must have been made by the same company."

From under the tarp, Joseph produced two tapestried parlor chairs. Joseph held up his lantern to see Mary's expression and asked, "Are ye happy now, Mrs. Quigley?"

Mary answered, "Yes, I am, Mr. Quigley. I am very happy. We can invite Father Francis here for Christmas, and ye can both sing carols. Also, Mr. Quigley, 'tis not only the chairs that makes me happy. We are expectin' another baby. Let's hope it is a big strappin' boy."

Joseph said, "We'll be needin' a farm for him first, but for now, ye have a rocker for the new baby and a beautiful chair for Ellen to sit by ye, and the priest to come and bless yer belly!" Joseph gave her a giant hug and kiss and sang a silly song.

Mary was joyful. She had a tiny room full of beautiful furniture that might belong to a very proper lady. She felt like a McManus woman, and she was havin' another baby.

Men who hauled furniture from Kansas to a store in Twin Springs would often see something they wanted to buy for the women in their lives. Some men were thieves and would occasionally steal things. Joseph didn't tell Mary, but her new chairs had been bought for a woman who did not want them, so the driver had to get rid of them since the lady was not his wife. He placed them in the office of the livery for a couple of days so he could take them back and try to get his money back as well. In the meantime, another man came along and stole them.

Joseph watched and waited for the man he had seen steal them. "Ah! There ye are. Do ye know that I saw ye take those chairs?"

The thief said, "Those were my chairs to begin with! How dare you accuse me of stealing?"

"I know yer not telling the truth because the man who bought them in the first place did not buy them for his wife. It was for another woman who is trying to relieve herself from him. His gift was

286

a bribe to get her back, but it didn't work. So yer tellin' me that yer the tall, handsome man who had the mistress? You know that is a lie, and I've caught ye.

"Let me give ye two ideas about the chairs: I can reveal to the actual owner who ye are, and ye can lose yer job for stealin' from the office—or I will buy them from ye right now for a very reasonable price and get the problem off yer hands. But ye have to promise it is our secret, ya?" Joseph patted and flashed the pistol under his coat, smiled his beautiful and charming smile, and extended his hand for a handshake. Then he gave the man two dollars, one for each chair— far less than they were worth.

Joseph knew that Mary would be outraged if she knew how he had come by them, but he didn't worry because he was not the one who had initially taken them. Each man in the chain had done something wrong, but that's what the freighter business was sometimes like. He had learned his negotiation skills with stolen goods in Westport. He didn't take things himself, but he knew how to work with those who did. They paid Joseph for their sins— just like they had with his beautiful and beloved horse, Fitzgerald.

After giving Mary her chairs, Joseph did not return the carriage to the livery. He unhitched it in the backyard and led Cara into the little livestock shed behind the house. The next day, he wanted to take Mary and Ellen over to the Wea reservation to see a farm. It was located about ten miles northeast of their location, only about five miles west of the Kansas-Missouri border. It was a perfect size for pigs and a field of corn. It belonged to a Wea native who had decided to move to the reservation with family. He could have stayed and declared his citizenship, but then he could not have lived on the reservation.

On scouting missions, Joseph had ridden often along that border and had found the land very attractive. He passed through on his way to Osage while scouting Confederates enroute to Camp Schofield.

The land was lightly cultivated because the Indians had still been hunting and left the land natural—unlike the big Kansas and Missouri farmers who cut every tree and burned all the grasses.

Joe knew that the Paola tribes were scheduled to move to Oklahoma by the end of the year. Every tribe had its own reservation borders, but there were large numbers of mixed-heritage people who had lived in the area for several generations. This included white people of predominantly French background who had moved with their Indian families from the Great Lakes states and black people as well who were with their Indian families from the South or local regions where they had moved onto the reservations and intermarried during and before the Civil War. Paola was a small town, and with many tribes in a small region, they intermarried. Women usually went with their husband's tribe. White husbands would go with their wives' tribes, but they more likely owned sixty-acre parcels of land.

There were Indian agents and missionaries who were responsible for looking out for their welfare, but they were usually more interested in individual religious and cultural conversion than they were for the good of the tribes. By 1867, families were deciding whether to become American citizens and live off the reservation or to stay with the tribe and be forced to move.

Most were moved involuntarily, but some were "free" to make their own arrangements. Unfortunately, large numbers were still dying from measles, smallpox, and alcoholism. Shortly after Mary arrived in Anderson County, a missionary priest who was visiting Catholics in the Emerald settlement, told the story of the Pottawatomie who were marched under terrible conditions to their deaths from their reservation to Topeka. By the time they arrived in Topeka, most had died.

Father Wattron was a missionary priest. The Holy Trinity Church was first erected by the Indians in 1846, but it had been used for stables until 1863. The stone church that Mary and Joseph attended was repaired in 1866, the year that Ellen was born. A bell tower and a new pipe organ were added.

Mary was satisfied enough with the land in Wea, but she thought it needed to be a bigger piece. It also seemed very wet— and maybe too near the creek. Joseph reminded her that she was having babies, and Joseph was not as healthy and strong as he had been before the

288

war, so they needed to start small. She didn't disagree. Maybe she needed to not overestimate what they could do. The dream she had for land was that of a community of healthy men—not a Civil War survivor. She would be patient until it was available.

As Mary and Joseph were entering their third winter in Paola, Joseph announced that he was riding up the next day to Wea to revisit the Indian, Billy Durand, whose farm he was now ready to purchase. Joseph surprised Mary by saying said he had a contract in his saddlebag.

Mary wanted to read it.

As he got his saddlebag and pulled it out, he said, "I got in touch with the Wea agent, and he knows that Billy will be glad to be selling his property. It's not a very big piece, and he was afraid he couldn't sell it. His two sisters own the forty acres next door, also on the creek, but they're planning to stay put. There was originally sixty acres that the family divided up. The agent got a description for me, and the clerk at the Miami County office wrote up the contract."

Mary asked a lot of questions Joseph couldn't answer: "Why are they so excited to get the tribes moved out of their homes? Would ye move to a reservation where the property belongs to hundreds of other people? At Holy Trinity, the Indians are still converting to Catholicism every day. Will there be a church for them on the reservation in Oklahoma?"

"I don't know, but here's the contract. All Billy has to do is agree to me cash price and sign his name. The agent said I was doin' the man a favor."

Mary looked at the contract he had pulled out and handed to her. She checked the acreage, the name of the township, and other details about which she wouldn't necessarily know right from wrong. She wished she could show it to her da or Daniel. They would know if it was on the up and up. She reached over, lifted the flap of his bag that was sitting on a chair, and saw a money pouch and a new, unopened bottle of whiskey. "Joseph, why do ye have a bottle of whiskey in yer bag? Are ye hidin' it from me? I won't have it in the house."

"Of course I'm hidin' it, Mary, but before ye get yer knickers in a tither, darlin', it's not mine except that I bought it for Billy."

Raising her voice first, Mary asked, "Joseph, do ye expect me to believe that it's not yers? You promised. Do ye know how much better we're doin' now? Ye break me heart every time ye fail."

"But that's the deal Billy and I had. He asked me to throw in a barrel of whiskey, but I told him I could only buy a bottle for him, and he agreed. Do ye see that it's not opened? It's not mine."

Mary said, "Ye can't sell a drink to an Indian, and here ye are buying a whole bottle. Are ye tryin' to get arrested? If Billy drinks it, his sisters might turn him in, and bein' drunk, he'll tell on ye. Why do ye not understand it?"

"Who says I don't understand it? I understand full well, but it's not goin' to happen that way—and ye'll have yer own hog farm in a week."

"Joseph, give me that bottle. Now!"

Joseph said, "No, I will not."

Mary reached into the bag, grabbed it, opened the door, and threw it out into the yard, thinking she would break it. Had Ellen not been standing at her feet, she would have whacked it with the frying pan.

Joseph said, "Good, Mary—it did not break."

She ran out the door, leaving Ellen crying in her wake.

Mary and Joseph arrived at the bottle at the same time. With both their hands on it, Mary lost her temper and tried to lift it up to crash it over Joseph's head.

"Now there ye go, yer high-class Irish lass bashin' her adorin' husband over the head with a bottle of fine whiskey. The wealthy pay plenty for it, Mary, and yer fixin' to smash it and kill me at the same time. If only yer da could see ye now, Mary."

Ellen was screaming with fear, and Mary ran back to the doorway to pick her up. "Everythin' is fine, darlin'. We're fine, Ellen. Don't cry, baby."

Joseph twisted off the lid of the bottle and began drinking large gulps. He drank half the bottle and said, "If ye hadn't had such a fit, Mary, I would never have drunk a drop—and I'd be ridin' off tomorrow, a happy man, to seal me deal with Billy and get ye yer precious farm."

Mary yelled, "Ye can't blame me for yer alcoholism, and ye can't bring that bottle back into this house. I don't care who's payin' the rent!" She slammed the door.

The door immediately reopened. Joseph stormed in, put on his coat and holster with his pistol, grabbed his rifle, slapped Mary sharply across the face, and knocked her against the doorframe.

"Ye better care who's payin' the rent—or ye could be out in the cold beggin' for a better provider." He grabbed his bag and was gone, slamming the door behind him.

She felt sick. It seemed that her Paola honeymoon of more than two years was probably over.

Joseph came back several days later with the contract signed and the title recorded. Joseph had planned to give Billy cash, but he didn't have it all by the time he got to Wea, so Mary and Joseph had a small mortgage of several payments to make in three-quarters of the coming year.

The sisters had an argument of some kind before Billy moved out. Apparently, Billy, fully intoxicated, had gone over to his sister's farm and broken the gate so the horses could get out. He then rode to the neighbors, who favored the sisters, and started a fire in their barn. It caused quite a stir, a lot of damage, and he was arrested for intoxication and the destruction of property.

It wasn't until the first day of May that Mary and Joseph could move into the farmhouse. It was actually a better house than the one from which they moved, but it was especially dirty and smelled of smoke as the chimney was in need of repair, something to which Billy had not attended for more than a year after the earthquake.

Mary loved the property and living by the creek, but she missed the church. She could no longer walk over to daily Mass or the rosary. She couldn't practice on the new organ, and it was harder to play for the funerals or weddings that brought her donations. She also missed the money or food received from music lessons.

After the Billy episode, Joseph didn't promise to never drink again, but he kept working at his hauling jobs to pay the extra mortgage payments he might have spent on a barrel of whiskey for the faithful Billy Durand—who did not tattle—and Joe started buying hogs. He got an excellent price by borrowing a cart at the livery and picking up two pregnant sows in Kansas City a month after they moved.

He rode into Pleasant Hill to see if Michael still had the Hiram Young wagon. Joseph thought about selling it because he had no team. He wanted to check on its condition. Michael was using it, but he had kept it in excellent condition in case Joseph moved to a larger farm and wanted it back. Joseph decided to wait.

Mary was working hard on house improvements, and she wanted a milk cow and chickens. Joseph asked her to wait until the sow had some piglets he could raise, and she remained patient. She hired the man in Paola to fix the cracked chimney in Wea, so they breathed easier, and she was able to keep the house cleaner.

On July 28, their strappin' boy turned out to be a very dark- haired, but healthy girl they had already named Mary.

Ellen, a toddler of twenty-eight months, squealed with delight and jumped up and down at having a little sister. She stood over the little basket that had held both John and herself and stared at Mary.

By August, Ellen could not wait any longer. She said, "Ma, I want to hold Maywee. I love Maywee. Maywee my baby too."

Mary agreed, "Yes, Mary is yer baby too. Come with Ma and sit in me chair. Are ye secure, darlin'? Put yer arms out—and let's have ye hold yer baby."

When Mary placed little Mary into Ellen's arms, Ellen sighed and said, "Oh, me Maywee." She looked into her sister's face, kissed her nose, and said, "I love ye, Maywee. Ye are me baby too."

Mary smiled at Ellen through her happy tears and said, "Ellen, you are the best sister in the world. Ye and yer Mary will be such good friends forever—like me and me sister Agnes. I do miss me dear sister Agnes, but I am so happy to see that ye and Mary will be the same good sisters as Agnes and I. Agnes, like yerself, Ellen, is very good and kind. She will always love me—no matter what happens in the whole world. Agnes married a very kind and lovely man. I hope the same for ye both, Ellen and Mary."

Φ

Joseph continued to haul furniture and whatever else he could until his sow had her piglets. Everything was fine until the rain came and didn't leave. The little creek rose and rose until it was in the hog shed. Joseph let the pigs out, and they ran about the yard. As the water rose, it covered every inch of field and yard around the house. The little piglets would have drowned had Mary and Joseph not invited them into the house. Mary hated it, but it had to be done. She did keep them away from the good furniture.

After Joseph sold the pigs for slaughter and saved two for breeding, he bought a rather average Holstein who had dried up and had not been bred. Joseph paid nearly nothing as they would have to feed a nonproductive cow through the winter. However, she eventually had a beautiful calf the next season. She became quite productive, which made Mary happy. A good spring of piglets allowed them to pay their second of three payments, and they were doing great—until the rains came again.

After the rain had fallen exceptionally hard for nearly a week in June, Joseph went into Paola and came home with a small covered wagon he had borrowed from the livery stable. He missed a hauling trip into Kansas City, but he knew the streams would be flooded. The Kansas and Missouri Rivers were also rising to dangerous levels. He stole boards from Billy's sister's junk pile, which she hadn't touched for two years. Using other boards from a broken- down fence that probably belonged to the sisters, Joseph built up the sides and a back on the wagon. He made a gate on one end. He then made a narrow ramp, and he and Mary either lifted or forced all the pigs into the wagon to wait out the flooding.

They couldn't move, but up came Wea Creek, a lake, a couple of ponds, the Marais Des Cygnes River. The water was everywhere. The water came up under the floor of the house. The pigs were safe, but the Quigleys were not happy that they had nearly been destroyed by flooding twice within eight months. Those living on the Kansas and other rivers were wiped out. Joseph learned that many families in West Bottoms were just washed away. They felt lucky to have skimmed by the crisis, but that was not the worst of their problems.

When Joseph and Mary went to Paola to make their last payment in September, Joseph was called into the office of the manager. Mary had come along with Ellen and Mary, and she sat out in the lobby of the bank with the girls.

The manager made small talk, and then he dropped the bomb: "I really don't know how to break this to you, but it appears there might be a problem with the title of your property. It may not really belong to you."

Joseph, in shock, replied, "It does. I signed a contract and paid for it, and we have lived there since May of 1868. Wait a moment—I need to get me wife in here." Joseph walked back out into the lobby. When he returned, the manager had pulled up another chair.

Mary sat in her da's lap and Ellen in her ma's lap to hear the bad, bad news.

Joseph said, "Now please explain this to the both of us."

The manager said, "The property you purchased was part of a sixty-acre parcel that belonged to the parents of Billy Durand and his sisters and a brother, Phillip Durand. The Durand mother was of the Wea tribe of Michigan. When the tribe was relocated, the French father, Jacques Durand came here and bought the sixty acres for three of his children: Josie, Claudette, and Phillip. The parents then returned to Michigan. They left, but Phillip moved into Ohio. He married a white woman, and they settled in her hometown of Chillicothe. The Durand parents did not give land to Billy because they knew he was often afflicted with lunacy, and they did not trust him to live beside his sisters without killing them. For a time, he was in an asylum, but there was nothing for him here, and on the property, he was fed by his sisters when he could not feed himself.

"The agent made a terrible mistake in believing Billy, who told him that he was the rightful owner of the third piece. The original title was damaged by water, and only the *ill* and the tail of the *p* were visible. The agent thought it was Billy's name and never verified it with the family or signer of the contract, who is deceased. They may not have known who Phillip was since he lived in Ohio. The sisters were quiet and never shared the truth because Billy needed a place to be. It was only when the Ohio Durand brother expressed a desire to sell his property that Billy was caught in the squeeze. Phillip didn't know that the sisters were not in the house you now occupy. They were at one time, but their husbands built the home they now live in. The husbands refused to move here, and the sisters would not move there. It's very strange.

"Billy misled the agent when he moved onto his brother Phillip's property. The girls had used the pasture for their horses, but they stopped when Billy moved in because they didn't want to deal with him. The agent who wrote your contract placed the name Billy where the name Phillip had been. He did not commit the fraud. It was Billy's fault, but he's not sane. Now we know it still belongs to Phillip though you are living there—and you have been defrauded.

"Phillip Durand has agreed to give you one year to move, and you can sue the agent or Billy Durand for the money you have given him. It was placed into a bank account for him. Phillip Durand received nothing, though he did learn that Billy fraudulently got title for the property through the agent and sold the property to you. I am going to return the last installment on the mortgage you paid today, and I will see if Billy still has an account here with money. If he does, I think I can take your other two payments out of his account with the agent's approval. The original down payment, I'm not sure, but I'll keep you informed."

Joseph and Mary sat there with their mouths agape until they returned to the carriage.

Mary said, "Joseph, we need to get yer money back from Billy."

Joseph laughed and said, "And he owes me for a barrel of whiskey."

"Oh, Joseph. Ye bought that poor man a barrel of whiskey? If anyone finds that out, ye'll be in jail, and then what will we do? That's certainly why he went on his rampage."

"They'll do nothin' if ye keep yer mouth shut. Still, we can live for a year, rent-free, and try to get our initial payment back from the agent or Billy, so we can save money for a larger farm. I'd like to return to Big Creek and live near Michael in Pleasant Hill. I'm sure Michael can keep an eye out for somethin' in Cass County."

In August, Michael Quigley—the son of Mary and Joseph— was born at the home of Michael and Mary Quigley in Pleasant Hill. On October 21, 1870, Joseph handed the Hinshaws, their new neighbors, four hundred dollars for the farm a mile away from Michael in Pleasant Hill, Cass County, Missouri. John and Mary McManus had loaned them the money for the farm. Joseph and Mary had not been able to save anything.

CHAPTER 21

FARM OF MARY AND JOSEPH QUIGLEY, PLEASANT HILL, MISSOURI, AUGUST 1874

Letter: August 1874
To: Daniel McManus, Pottawatomie, Coffey County, Kansas
From: Mary McManus Quigley, Pleasant Hill,
     Cass County, Missouri

Dear Brother Daniel,

Can you please share your advice? I hear that you were struck as well by the locusts, though perhaps not to the same extent. They came as a large black cloud swarming across the horizon out of the northwest. It looked to me like the end of days was coming, and it has left us in that state.

Joseph says he's going to shoot the last starving milk cow, Patches, who has now eaten the last twig off the trees and the last blade of greenery that could poke its head back above the dirt since July. We do not know if we should eat her or keep her. She's had two wonderful calves and has been our salvation.

There is no corn for the pigs and no grain for bread. We had potatoes, carrots, and cabbages in the root cellar, but the locusts ate the door off and got into our few winter stores. We already had too little— again. Not all the potatoes had finished growing, but the hoppers ate the last leaves off all the crops.

We had such a lovely spring, but then the drought hit. The corn was havin' a time of it anyway, but we would have had some. Now we have nothin'.

Nobody has horse tack, clothes, bedclothes, or shoes. Some women took their batting and laid it over the crops, poking stakes around to keep the hoppers out. The locust covered the bedding many inches deep and ate through it. Women set fire to their bedding to kill the hoppers, but in the end, they lost the plants and the bedding.

It seems that cousin Ulysses could step in and help us out once he learns we're all starvin'. Can Ma write to him and explain how destitute we are? There's a meeting at the church in Holden. People will be taking things they can share with neighbors. We have nothing to share, so Joseph's not going.

The new manager at the bank came around to those of us who are behind in our mortgages. Can you believe it? And I have a baby coming in two months—if God doesn't take him away to be with his brother John. Tell Ma I'm feeling strong enough if we can find enough food to get us through the autumn and winter months ahead.

We need help, Daniel.

Your desperate sister, Mary Quigley

Φ

Letter: September 1874
To: Mary McManus Quigley, Pleasant Hill, Missouri
From: Daniel McManus, Pottawatomie, Kansas Dearest Mary,

Hang on darlin', any way you can. The locusts have been a scourge from the Rocky Mountains to Texas, so President Grant knows. The states of Iowa, Kansas, Virginia, Illinois, and Minnesota have not been so badly affected, so they are presently sending food, hay, seed, and leather goods to the Dakotas, other parts of Kansas, and Missouri. Be sure to go to your Grange, if you have one, or the railroad station. Help is on its way, and it will continue as long as needed, though times will be hard.

Of course, you have always had hard times, but you prevail, don't you? You're the strongest and smartest woman I know.

Tell my nieces and nephews that the McManus and Grant families are praying for them.

You must have some neighbors who are good farmers and have been able to prepare for these events. Tell them you have children in need, and perhaps they can help you. Go ahead, swallow your pride, and ask. They might say yes.

More importantly, have Joseph hook up your plow and dig up the eggs. They cannot hatch if they are lying on top of the soil either drowning or drying up. Get them on top of the ground. Have the little children stomp them with their feet. The birds and chickens can help. Here, they were paying people for hatchlings, though I doubt you'll find a single hatchling now. Unfortunately, they'll be back in the spring.

Agnes now has beautiful new Jersey cows from Switzerland, and we will get a young one to you if we can. We'll breed a heifer and send her. So far, I believe we are the only people in Kansas who have them. They came from Philadelphia only a few months ago, but we don't know how they got to this country, and I don't think we can get another.

That's the absolute best we can do, as we have lost a lot ourselves. One good remarkable cow and some hay will save your children.

Christ beside you; we love you. Agnes, Margaret, and Bridget send all their love. Bridget's baby Kate is doing very well. It's so difficult for you women who are pregnant during the plagues.

Love,
Brother Daniel and Mary

On a Thursday morning in April 1875, glorious sunlight poured through the window of the Quigley children's bedroom. It jabbed Little Mary's eyes into a squint that forced her to turn away. Michael's restless feet instantly annoyed her senses, so Mary rolled toward Ellen's feet, which now touched her chest. The trio of Quigley siblings, two in one direction and Mary in the other, had settled at night like tired puppies. Now crowded in daylight, they squirmed awake to their ma's noisy return to the house. After milking their lanky old Holstein in the chilly dawn, Ma allowed doors to slam, the kettle to plop heavy on the metal stovetop, and the latch of the firebox to squeak and clank shut after adding kindling to the dwindling fire—just enough to boil tea water. When six-month-old Thomas began to cry, Ellen's feet hit the floor and headed toward Joseph Jr. Mary bolted from their bed with Michael following.

Little Joseph slept on a mattress on the floor in the corner. Not yet three, the older Michael wouldn't sleep with him because Joseph still peed in the bed. It was Ellen's job, now that they had their baby brother Thomas, to take care of Joseph's morning routine. She was nice to him even when he got cold, did not cooperate with his clean-up, or when he complained or cried. Once he was dressed, he stood in front of the firebox. That was usually the signal that the children were dressed and ready for their day.

As the girls did their chores with the boys, Ma sat down in her rocker to nurse six-month-old Thomas. After they had eaten, the girls rode off to school: Ellen in her little saddle and Mary holding on behind. This was a fairly cheerful family on this morning.

By Saturday, the cheer had changed to dread. Ma was daily refilling her washtub with clean water in preparation for another great catastrophe: the arrival of more locusts. Because the girls were at school, she compelled Joe to help her do their laundry two days early.

In 1860, before Joseph and Mary were burned out of their first Big Creek farm, Ma had enjoyed the chore of milking her cow, Sunshine. Among the Irish communities, milkmaids were common, so milking was something that Little Mary's da did not routinely do, especially when he was sick in bed. For as long as Little Mary could remember, her da got spells of sickness left over from being a soldier, and Ma milked. Even when she was expecting or carrying a baby, she milked; except for some weeks before Thomas was born in October, the girls took pride in going out with Ma to help her. They did all that Ma asked, including taking turns at milking Patches. In the summer, the plan was to get another heifer to replace the one they had lost to the locust plague, so each girl would become responsible for a cow. The Quigleys hoped to again afford a farmhand they had hired to help when Mary was pregnant with Joseph. Mary wanted to rebuild a small herd.

On this beautiful Saturday, Da arose with his wife and fed his horses their last meager portion of donated feed. Since early March, Joe had been moving horses from here to there across Big Creek in the neighboring fallow fields that had wild, nutritious stalks struggling to reclaim their place after the locusts of last summer. In the past, and recently in Paola and Wea, wild and Indian horses did not eat harvested grains. Their horses ran free or were tethered to thrive off nature. They were as strong and healthy as farm-raised horses. Joe thought his horses could do as well. It met with poor to mediocre success because they hadn't been raised on the grasses and didn't know what to eat. They were used to grain and alfalfa.

Patches was the only milk cow left after the plague and drought of the summer of 1874.

Joe slaughtered another cow, which had succumbed to starvation, and two of his hogs. Mary, using Elizabeth Collins's grinder, spiced and ground them together and made sausages that she hung in their smokehouse. With little else to eat, the sausages had been stretched throughout the winter.

Joseph gave two piglets to Michael in exchange for a chicken, but he suggested to Michael that they could level out the exchange when normalcy was restored after the plagues, droughts, and rains. Even though Michael had brought down livestock feed or food on occasion—and he alleviated the feeding stress off Joseph by exchanging the piglets for a hen—Mike's help was gifts and not a part of a long-standing negotiation. Joseph personally believed, because the hogs would grow to productive sows in short time, that Michael still owed him more, though he said nothing about it in the midst of the locust crisis.

Michael didn't think he should feed the piglets and then repay Joseph the value of a grown sow which could produce. He was already sacrificing for Joseph. Mary agreed that he should not have to pay for something that might exist in the future.

Patches had occasionally stripped the bark off trees through the winter. Uncle Michael and other parishioners at the Saint Patrick's Church in Holden had continued to receive help feeding both essential livestock and family from sporadic donations of Illinois hay and oats. Though about 60 percent of farmers were ruined in Cass County, some neighbors had escaped the worst of the attack of the 1874 Rocky Mountain locust. In the hit-and-miss pattern, generous neighbors who had been spared had willingly shared with the less fortunate. However, by winter, even the wealthier farmers' stores had seriously dwindled.

Most milk cows were dried up to save the meager feed for one or two top producers. Those that were dried up had already had their calves, and many were slaughtered. Patches had a male calf before the locust invasion in the summer of 1874, so Ma had milked her until she dried her up around the New Year. Unfortunately, the calf Patches had in March drowned in the swollen creek. However, Mary's children had become the beneficiaries of her lactation. Despite her scrawny condition, Patches poured forth enough milk to make adequate cream for butter, and on this Saturday, the creamy, salted butter was appreciated.

Φ

After their milk, tea, and corn bread, Ellen began her Saturday piano lesson. Leaving her little brothers, Michael and Joseph Jr., behind her, Mary hopped her skinny frame down the kitchen steps, jumping over the last one, to enjoy the Missouri morning. She first turned her face and then her back to the promising sun that soothed her spirit and gradually eased her breakfast shivers. She could smell the fresh greenness on the last evaporating dew.

As she walked out to greet the chickens, grabbing one of the new bantam Rhode Islands, she glanced across the farm toward the creek that wound itself around the edge of the pastures. Beyond the barren fields waiting for corn seeds, she was astounded by some fully matured green leaves. The trees had been stripped bare by locusts last year, and the entire landscape lain brown and lifeless from summer throughout the winter. The numerous dead trees that had not recovered stood as reminders and symbolized what would lie ahead. A few heavy spring rains had brought green hope on Thursday, and Mary had begun to anticipate the arrival of a better summer. By Saturday, hope was thin.

She released her restless chicken into the grass under the fence rails to pick at the pale little grasshopper hatchlings crawling in the occasional weed below. They made her fearful as she recalled how they killed crops and trees and caused the deaths of livestock and people. Farmers had been warned by a Thursday telegraphed message from Nebraska that the grasshopper plague was on its way. And since it was April, nothing would have a chance to be planted in the most important months of all.

As Little Mary put out clean water for the chickens and gathered the eggs in her tattered apron, she heard Ellen at the piano. It would be Mary's turn as soon as the tiny grains of pure white sand trickled through the pinched glass of their ornate brass timer sitting atop their spinet. She wasn't looking forward to practicing. It seemed like a terrible time to be practicing the piano. She would be sitting next to a pile of straw in her ma's lovely parlor. Her grandmother's lace had been removed, and grain bags covered the floors to protect against chicken waste. It made their house already smell like a barn.

Ellen loved to play and played well. Mary could always hear in her head how the song should sound, but her fingers didn't cooperate with her ears. Correcting mistakes by repeating something over and over made Mary yawn. Last year, she would practice ten of her thirty required minutes then hop off the little adjustable stool her grandmother had sent with the piano, spinning it the short distance up too high or down too low until she asked her ma if she was "done" now.

When Ma was occupied with a brother or had gone outside for a moment, Mary sometimes draped herself over the turning stool and dragged her feet and hands along on the floor to watch the seat winding up and down the large wooden screw. Mary kept track of the hairline crack in the center, hoping for its expansion and the stool's collapse. Unfortunately, Ma could hear that the piano was not playing. Ellen would call out through the kitchen door, "Ma, Mary's not practicin'." Ma would eventually return to the house, say nothing, turn the timer over to start anew, and say, "Should I tell yer da?"

Today, Mary had decided she would practice as she was expected. She would not hop off that stool. However, before she was called in on this sunny day, she squatted down to inspect a little grasshopper crawling out along the railing of what they called the "near pasture" where the milking shed stood.

The kitchen door opened, and her ma called, "Mary, darlin', where are ye?"

Mary heard her da talking to Michael in the empty cornfield. She saw the little puffs of dust as the two crossed along at the end of the unplanted rows. In his hand, Da had an old pitchfork to scratch up soil and stab grasshoppers along the way. All the farmers had planned to get their corn in very early, praying the plants might get a healthy head start before the grasshoppers showed again. Their millet would be mowed clean. Now they would be planting their corn seed very late and would pray for weather that was warmer and wetter than usual, months later.

As Michael stepped on the hatchlings, Da asked, "Are ye seein' a few buggers here and there? If we keep smashin' 'em, we should be able to be in pretty good shape, right, Michael?"

Everything was a challenge, but Da knew there was no way to be in "pretty good shape" by July's summer heat. He was being uncharacteristically positive.

For the past few days, Da and Ma had expressed between them concern over the recent lack of rain and the alarming news of locusts on the way. As Ma and Da hauled empty pork barrels partly full of water to be topped off in their bedroom by bucket, they bickered less frequently than usual about corn, millet, and the bank. The Quigley children read Da's tired, scarred face and knew he was brooding. Earlier, he had gone into the house and gotten his pistol. The walk across the empty field with Michael had done nothing to alleviate his concern, but Ma's interventions and the reality of impending disaster might have worked.

On this Saturday morning, Mary took her eggs, placed them in a green bowl on the small kitchen counter by the sink and said to Ma, "I've been lookin' at the locusts that are hatchin' along the fence. The hens are pickin' at them."

Ma said, "Ellen has nearly finished. We'll go out, take a look at the field, and talk with yer da. We'll see what he wants of ye—after yer done with yer piano lesson."

Mary added, "The cabbages are too small, and they'll be eaten by the locusts before we can eat them. Will the spuds grow back? Do ye think that we should pick the pigweed before the locusts get it?"

Ma looked back at her little girl with a sad face. "I think not," she replied.

Young pigweed leaves had been eaten to supplement poor diets in the past, and some women made tea of it. Too much, however, was neither good for people nor livestock, so its use was not common. However, in the warning that had been telegraphed, and pigweed being the Quigley family's only thriving plant, Ma understood her daughter's thinking: Pigweed is all there is. If we eat pigweed, we might not die.

Ma said, "Mary Stinkweeds, ye gave me a great idea. Let's gently pull up the vegetable seedlin's, wrap them in flour or gunnysacks, and store them in the root cellar. We'll cover the door with dirt so the locusts don't eat it. When they're all gone, we'll try to replant and water the seedlin's. Maybe we'll do better than we think! Let's do it."

Mary, Little Joseph, and Ma, holding Edward, headed out past the shed behind the pigpen to join Da and Michael and talk about stored seedlin's, weeds, and locusts.

Lying askew by the equipment shed, Mary saw her broken, child-sized loy, which had been made and given to her by Lawrence Collins. The sight of it made her decide not to go out to hear Da's assessment. Lawrence had made the loy for his own children, now grown. It was her tool, and she liked how it had felt before it had been broken in her da's pointless fit of rage last October, six months ago. It happened when her brother Thomas had just been born.

On Thursday, Mary could not wait for the potatoes and cabbages to grow in those beds she and Da had made with their loys. Already, on this Saturday, the sun had forced plants to poke their leafy heads out of the ground, and there were almost no grasshoppers hatching there. But on this day, the sight of the broken handle stabbed to the back of her heart, a loathing she too often felt for her da. Last autumn's painful incident had forever changed her feelings of love for her da to a conditional and ever- cautious state. The thought of impending doom increased her sadness over her garden, which would probably become as pathetic as the loy.

In the cool October before, she and her then-beloved da had built two rows of a lazy bed on the edge of the pasture. Trying to gain an advantage, Pleasant Hill farmers decided to get a little jump ahead of locusts. They built their beds in autumn instead of spring, smashing eggs as they went. Mary had loved working alone with her da. Sometimes they would harmonize together, and he would laugh or be funny and lighthearted. They had even danced down the bed's first trench when it was done. The day had started as one of the best.

As other farmers had also done—and as Uncle Daniel suggested—after last summer's devastation, the Quigleys plowed over the soil under their ravished fields, exposing locust eggs on the surface. They hoped to kill the tender eggs in the August sun. In the lazy bed, Little Mary and Da prepared the sod for planting their cabbages in March and their spuds as early as possible after the frost. Drought and devastation from locusts had lasted from spring to October, killing people in Nebraska, Iowa, Kansas, and Missouri. It seemed that everyone was barely holding on.

On that gentle October day, Joseph's loy turned rectangular sections of sod up that could be flipped over to rest on top of the ground. He sliced deep into the soil, lifting all the roots from three sides around and under the rectangle. Mary came beside him with her tool and helped him fold the sod sideways and upside down, so that its grassy top was now on the bottom, lying atop the untilled ground below it. She had just turned six in the middle of the plague, but three months later, she was working as hard as any child could to help her family have spuds by next May or June.

Eventually, they completed two topsy-turvy rows of dirt between two trenches. To keep planting soil at least two feet in width and depth, Da dug what they needed from their trenches, leaving a high dirt bed between two furrows.

As Mary removed several larvae and smashed them along a furrow, she said, "Da, we didn't turn over the sod next to our bed. Don't you think we should dig it all up around the garden?" Mary would never forget his reaction to her question.

"'Around the garden' is the whole farm, child!" His face flushed, his eyes narrowed, and he instantly blew up. She thought he was going to be funny and tease her, but he surprised her with rage, something he did when he was drunk. "Should we hand-dig every damned inch of the farm, little beansidhe? Jaisus, yer like yer uncle Mike and yer ma. The useless advice directed at me by ye persistent yappin' peasants never stops. I canna make God stop the grasshoppers. Can ye, Mary? Can ye keep them from eatin' the whole of Missouri and Kansas? What we are doin' on this farm right now is worthless, and we're worthless when it comes to abatin' the sufferin'! As long as we live, it will not stop. We're Irish; the sufferin' can't stop."

Mary said, "We have to do somethin'! What if they come back, Da?"

"They're not comin' back, Stinkweeds. They're here already. They're hatchin' right now under yer damned nose. Ye might as well go practice the piano instead of diggin', so ye can entertain at the McManus parties—if ye live that long. If ye keep on the way yer goin', ye'll dig till ye drop dead. A little girl like ye and her sick da canna keep back the plagues."

"I don't want to be one of the 'starvin' Irish,' Da!"

"Yer already one of the 'starvin' Irish.' Choose starvin', workin', or drinkin' yerself to death for nothin'! Irish are cheaper to hire than mules and expendable in war and famine. I've seen it me entire life—in all of us. Ye and yer ma are askin' me to squeeze blood from a turnip. 'See if the Irish Quigley mule can do the impossible at the bank so we McManus girls can hold our royal heads high.' Regardless, yer ma's family will blame 'drunken Joe Quigley' for losing the farm, not the locusts or the weather! The bank owns us, Mary."

Mary witnessed, again, the rage that Ma said "always boiled just beneath the surface." It broke their hearts. Mary would not be drinkin' herself to death. They were trained to recognize the rage and told when to run. Mary's parents were fighting over losing the farm to the bank every season of every year. The bank and the drinkin' were the two things that ruined their lives.

Da yelled, "It's like peein' in the ocean, child, and a damned waste of time. Give me that peasant loy; we're done with it!"

Mary's firm grip held tight as Da wrestled the little spade from her, causing her to fall in the dirt. She started to cry and wailed, "We're not done. We have to smash the eggs!"

Da bashed both tools into the ground, and the light handle of Mary's loy crunched in two. "Yer such a McManus! Shut it, child. We don't want yer ma out here supportin' the cause. I'm sick of ye all."

Mary was proud to be a McManus; a McManus woman was strong, smart, and proud. Da hadn't yet hit Little Mary, but he might hit her now because she was like her ma. If she had been inside, she and Ellen would grab the boys' hands and flee behind the pigs' shed or somewhere along the creek bank under the shrubs where he was too drunk to walk and find them. Screaming sometimes brought neighbors who would come to save their mother from Da's drunken slaps that knocked her to the ground. It was usually too late, however.

Da said, "Me life is dictated by meddlin' women and yer pairfect uncle Mike. When he falls on hard times, he has older sons so he can go into Independence and build somethin' from stone. Ye all forget I saved our farms during the war, so don't ye ever tell yer da what he should do again! Yer a baby, Mary, who knows nothin'!"

As he was growling his grievances and holding his gut, Mary remained motionless and stone-faced.

Da saddled his sorrel mare, Fiona, and plopped Ellen's small saddle in his lap. Only five months before, in an attempt to save the saddle from devouring locusts, Ellen and Mary had struggled away from the shed to the security of the house, ankle-deep and hair tangled under a black stinking sky of falling locusts. Once in the house, they covered the saddle under their feather-stuffed coverlet.

They daily swept out the invaders as the saddle lay under Joseph's mattress. In their beds, they had achieved a grand victory: the beautiful little saddle had survived. For more than two weeks, Ellen, Mary, and Michael slept around it while Ma and Da slept amid their own tack and Da's precious gun holster. He kept his gun on the bureau until he could safely hang his holster back up in the corner without it being eaten.

Before Joseph set off down the road toward town, he ambled Fiona over to the garden where Mary sat. Facing her, he said, "When I'm gone, little McManus gossip, go tattle this to yer Ma: Only an eejit Irishman like Joe Quigley woulda fought so hard to keep this place. Yer all goin' to lie in a pile and die here under yer ma's direction. I will not. Me own ma shoulda stayed in Ireland where we belonged. She woulda lived, and I'd a'been a lawyer and a gentleman with her. The Irish in Ireland are eatin' just fine now, but we're sick and starvin' here, after winnin' the great war in the promised land. Be proud and strong, Mary Quigley. When I'm dead, the bank will sell the farm to some other fools, and ye'll get a new English or German daddy from the bank."

Those last words shot through Mary's heart, and she sobbed as soon as Da was beyond earshot. Without a single word of love or kindness toward his broken little girl or about the rest of his family, he trotted arrogantly down the road with the children's saddle that Uncle Daniel had gifted Ellen when they moved to Missouri. Uncle Daniel would never talk to Little Mary that way. He and Michael were proper and real men. She picked up her broken loy, cradled it, and felt as sad as a little girl could feel. She didn't want an English or German daddy. She was a proud Irish girl who wanted her da to stay home and love her, Ma, and her siblings. She hated him when he was like this.

Trying to be an adult, Mary sat looking at her hard work beside the field and thought about what she could do to fix things. Everything looked dead, but in her mind's eye, she had imagined perfect, fat cabbages and dark green potato leaves, and she imagined the taste and smell of little salty hot buttered spuds rolling in cream. She looked out toward the road and moaned. "Oh, Da. Why would ye do this? Come back. I was helpin' ye. We'll be fine."

Growing chilled from fear, hunger, and the cool October breeze, she thought, *Da loves his dead ma better than he loves us. I don't like her. I'm glad she's dead. She didn't have to live with him like we do. I hate him; I wish he were dead.* Anger was winning the battle over her sadness, as it had with Ellen. She looked up, but she could no longer see her Da. Through her tears, she shouted, "Yer ma didn't love ye! She left ye behind because yer a mean boy.

I hate ye too, Da!"

Φ

With her memory of last October's tragedy, tears falling, and the sight of the today's smashed locust hatchlings, Mary returned to the house to relieve Ellen who had forgotten to notice the sand at the bottom of its glass triangle. Mary hadn't walked out with Ma and the boys on this Saturday morning to listen to her parents' talk about weeds, insects, and food. Her enthusiasm for the summer just around the corner was gone, but she held to her determination to practice the piano with more enthusiasm. She asked Ellen for help, telling her that she wasn't interested in the garden since the locusts would eat it anyway. Ellen felt the same sadness as Mary.

However, Ellen kissed Mary and told her that everything would be fine, and the two of them pulled out a duet to practice. They would help prepare for the siege and stick by Ma like good McManus women.

For now, they would practice their duets for a McManus party. Like their da, they were retaliating against him, and they knew it. It was how they could fight back and win. The more he complained about the goodness of the McManus clan, the more they were determined to be what he prophesized: "to be just like 'em." They had only been to a McManus party once, but they loved the idea of going in the future.

Ma had described the cakes and the fun. They would spend time planning for the dresses to wear and the duets they would play to impress the family. Also, they would marry grand men who were educated, like the McManus children in Kansas were becoming.

Φ

In the previous afternoon in October 1874, Joseph had turned up the road that led to the Heller farm. Heller's little black and white dog performed his obligatory barking. Outside their feed shed, Joseph dismounted Fiona and fixed his reins around a fence railing. As he grabbed the nicely tooled saddle, the Heller dog growled and reached up to nip at his pant leg. Joseph growled back and gave him a swift kick in the head. Carl Heller heard the exchange and walked out of his barn to see who his visitor was. He didn't call off the dog.

"Oh, it's you, Joe Quigley. What do you have there?"

"You know how we're all on hard times, Carl. I have to tell ye, Carl, we're at the end of our food, and this is all I have to trade. I'm lookin' to sell our saddle for cornmeal, maybe sorghum, tea, scratch, and a little cash."

After a second, Carl said, "Is that your children's saddle, Joe? I've seen your girls on it. It's very nice. Do they know you're fixin' to sell it? Getting what ye want in exchange for a saddle is a tall order, Joe."

"Me girls are near starving', so it doesn't matter what they think. Havin' a meal is more important than havin' a saddle, Carl. They can't eat the saddle; if they could, I'd keep it! 'Tis all I have left. It might be devoured by next summer anyway."

Carl answered, "Even if someone buys it, what's your plan for the next meal after that? You can't sell the farm now, but you can call it quits and go back to Kansas. You're not the only one in trouble, Joe. I don't have to tell you that more than half the town cleared out last year."

"We're nearly done in, Carl."

"Sorry, Joe, I ain't givin' up nothing for nobody right now. We're all in the same fix."

Joseph said, "Not my family, Carl. We're too far behind on our mortgage. I can't wander the prairie under a cloud of locusts with four little children, a nursing infant, and a sorrowful wife. I can't wander around on me own either."

"That's too bad, Joe, but I can't buy no saddle. My family comes first, and this saddle ain't going to get you or me through the next six months. Besides, the truth is, you might be looking for a little whiskey money, right? I ain't giving no money for no whiskey, especially not no Irishman as yourself. I've seen that Irish disease: whiskey first, family last. Find somebody else."

Joseph said, "God bless ye, Mr. Heller, for yer unnecessary comments. Enjoy yer beer!" Resisting his urge to kick Heller's dog again, Joe abruptly turned on a heel and headed out, the dog barking after him.

Joe felt humiliated and thought, *I can't wait to hear from Mary how I've embarrassed her. Once Mrs. Heller opens her mouth after Mass, it doesn't close till she's the last lady talkin'. 'Tis none of their damned business how I run mine, but the ladies will be in a tizzy, ditherin' around the Quigley gossip and makin' Mary hurt and angry!* He decided it would be better to head straight to Mr. Quinn's store to face the music. He might get lucky.

Saddle in hand, Joe walked into the store. A few regulars were sitting around the unlit stove comparing notes about whether they would get their winter wheat seed as promised. They had already gotten some autumn millet from Illinois, but Mr. Quinn had not heard about winter wheat coming in on the train. Sometimes things came when expected; sometimes they didn't. If it had been telegraphed, he would know.

Conversations among the men here and at the saloon included the growth of their millet, concern over locusts, next spring's corn, oats, seed potatoes, and everything else. October was a long way from spring planting in normal times, but there was no end to the anxiety caused by the last year's locust and weather disasters and the knowledge that it would hit again before the crops could grow. They felt that planting was an act of feeding the devil.

As Joe walked toward the group, Mr. Quinn asked, "What ye got there, Joe?"

One of the men said, "The leprechaun Mick's looking for a handout—as usual."

Joe was certain the comment came from the skinny, tall secesh sitting on a stool along the back counter behind the conversing men around the cold stove. Joe recognized him, but he didn't know him. Along with other Confederates, some of his family had gone to Texas with their small group of slaves before the official outbreak of the war.

There was just enough snickering for Joe to know that about half these men were secesh, even ten years after the war. He had brought his pistol, but he didn't want to shoot the hand that might feed him. Even in the midst of their drought and locust miseries, the emotions from the war had not subsided as they should have. Today, there were plenty of disgruntled men in town sharing stories of loss from multiple causes.

Without looking in the direction of the secesh, Joseph replied, "The war's over. Ye had yer chance to run with the scoundrels. There's still time to run south before the locusts come back to get ye. Things will be tastin' much better in Louisiana where the locusts aren't welcomed. It's God's country there; the devil watches over us here."

Some of the men laughed. The brown water from dead locust and their waste had tainted every drop of liquid and every morsel of food for months. They were facing another bout.

"What's yer name, boy?" Joseph asked.

Someone in the store yelled out, "It's Dennis ... Alden Beau Dennis. He's known as ABD or AD for short." The men refrained from chuckling out of respect for Mr. Quinn, who was growing nervous over the growing tension.

After a steely glance at AD, Joe said, "Mr. Quinn, may I speak with ye?"

When Joe walked over to the section of the counter where Mr. Quinn stood and laid down Ellen's saddle, the secesh slipped out the door. Maybe he sensed that Joe had his pistol. Another man went with him.

Quinn knew that rehashes of the war came without resolution. Joe's humorous attempt was meant to stir the pot, and Quinn was relieved that Joe had decided not to draw his pistol. He could never tell about Joe's mood. A few years back, he had drawn it in the saloon to everyone's surprise. He sensed that the animus today was the thought that Joe Quigley was selling his children's beautiful saddle for whiskey money. The town assumed he had missed mortgage payments or not fed his children in favor of whiskey. It was a growing reputation.

"What can I do for you, Joe?" Mr. Quinn said in a hushed voice so the others could not hear the details.

"Me family needs cornmeal, sorghum, tea, chicken scratch, and cash. Could I trade this saddle—or would ye buy it outright?"

Quinn replied, "Well, Joe, first I need to check yer invoice from the last time ye were in here. I'm not sure you don't owe me some cash already."

After a quiet exchange, Mr. Quinn eventually gave Joe a small tin of tea and a large advance of five dollars in cash for the saddle. He said, "I hope yer headed home, Joe. AD will be in the saloon, you know. He's fixin' for a fight; let me sell you some cornmeal before you go home."

Joe immediately stepped toward the door, leaving the saddle in Quinn's care. Outside, Joe placed the tea in his saddlebag and defiantly led Fiona down the short hill to the saloon, looking back over his shoulder with a smirk. *Quinn is a decent enough fellow, but he has no business telling me how to live.*

Φ

At the farm, Ellen was taking Little Joseph out to the garden to see the lazy beds when she saw their sister Mary whimpering in the dirt. Mary was looking at the broken loy. It took effort to break the loy; it was no accident.

Ellen said, "Where's Da?"

Mary looked at the ground and said, "I don't know, but Da told me not to talk about it."

Mary thought, *Did Da think he could sell our saddle and Ma, Ellen, and the boys would never know that it was missing from the shed?* Mary said, "Ellen, should we tell Ma that Da has gone to town—or should we just wait?"

"Maybe he went to see Uncle Mike or went into town to get tea or more cornmeal."

"No, Ellen. He took our saddle to sell. I think he wants to drink. He's mad at me."

Ellen said, "He took our saddle? That's my saddle. Why would he sell my saddle? You use it. Michael and Joseph have been usin' it with us. We saved it from the locusts just this summer. He knows how we love that saddle. I'd bet Da's not sellin' his gun or holster. They're worth more than our saddle!"

Mary said, "Da needs the gun for the farm. He can't sell it, Ellen."

Ellen ran to the house to Ma. Without permission, she came storming out with her coat on, put on the bridle, and climbed bareback on Da's large blind mare. Before Ma became aware, the mare charged her tall, lanky frame down the long, straight road with Ellen flopping dangerously toward Pleasant Hill. Their destination was the nearly five miles to Quinn's store or Da's favorite saloon.

By the time Ellen had ridden the first leg of the journey, she had thought through what could happen and lost some of her courage. At the T on the main road, she turned right and rode the short distance toward Uncle Mike's farm. She would get his help. Learning from his niece that his sick and impossible brother had taken the children's saddle to sell, Uncle Mike—burdened by yet another of Joseph's shenanigans since he had moved there—hitched his cart and headed toward town to investigate. If he was just selling the saddle, it wouldn't be so bad, but selling it for whiskey when everyone was going hungry was selfish and unforgiveable.

Michael told her to go home, but rather than obediently turning down the road to home as she normally would, she hid and waited as he passed at the T. She followed Michael at quite a distance into town. He did not stop and look back for Ellen. She thought, *Maybe he hasn't noticed me. Maybe he doesn't care. Maybe he's going to stop Da. Maybe I'll find the saddle and take it home myself.*

It had been a very long time since Joe had spent days drinking, but it was Michael's thirty-seven-year obligation and promise to his father to watch over the thorny Joseph. Michael had come to believe that God expected it of him, but he resented it. He had given up on Joe, but he interfered in his bad behavior only to help Mary McManus and the children.

Φ

At the saloon, Joseph had one whiskey he savored and a second that was gifted by a concerned neighbor who thought he was helping.

Unfortunately, Joseph decided to have a third for the road. The secesh he had encountered in Quinn's store was sitting at the far end of the bar. Joseph didn't want trouble, but he deserved a few drinks to help obliterate his predicament at home. He told himself that any man would have done the same. He felt no obligation to go home at any particular time. Most of the men in the bar would have agreed with him. He didn't need combatants. He had precocious daughters, a stern wife, and an interfering brother to fight with at home. His plan was to leave soon.

Joseph's empty glass had been retrieved by the bartender, and as he was saying his goodbyes, he heard a jovial and familiar voice. "Joseph Quigley, me dear cavalry friend, what are ye doin' here?"

The tall, graying man walked quietly up to Joe and whispered into his right ear, face away from AD. "I just bought yer saddle so ye could feed yer family—and here yer sittin'! I thought things was better, man. Quinn said ye'd be here, havin' a few whiskeys and not-so-friendly words with AD. I see no glass, friend. We'll have a drink, and I'll ride out aways with ye to keep ye out of here." Then he laughed in an effort to keep Joe on the positive side.

The friend was one of the Hayes men who had served with Joseph a decade before in the Guard and Cavalry. He said, "Whiskey, bartender, for two old soldiers of the Blue."

Looking down past patrons to the end of the bar, Joseph added, "And a pint for Mr. ABC, the secesh at the end there, in honor of John and me grindin' his arse in the Great War!"

Joe's robust companion released another hearty laugh, and others joined in.

The laughter subsided when AD said, "After Joseph Quigley drinks up his children's food and farm, y'all won't think it's that funny—so have a laugh at AD's expense. Go ahead. Y'all be weeping later over the dead bodies of Joe Quigley's children. Y'all be wishing the Grays had won because the country's been left to the drunken Micks." The secesh hurled a sturdy ale glass that landed aside John's head and crashed with a thunk on the bar, unbroken. Joseph leaned back, turned toward AD, and fired his Colt Navy pistol past the faces at the bar, each one disappearing from the view in succession. Crashing stools and diving men accompanied the splash from flying drinks coming from all directions.

AD pitched his tall frame down to cower from the bartender's side at the end of the bar. The gilded mirror and glistening bottles lining the walnut shelf above him begged for further impulsive destruction. Before the second bullet could be triggered, both of John's hands grabbed for Joe's firing arm. Too late, amber-filled bottles exploded with the second and third shots. The giant mirror crackled, and portions dropped on the dripping bureau and AD.

In a blurred tenor, Joseph shouted, "The state of me family is none of your damned business, Mr. ABC. I'll show ye Irish courage!" With that, Joe charged from his end behind the bar, left hand on the barrel of his revolver, handle in ready position to strike blows. With a horrendous crack to his head, Joe, instead, landed cold on the floor. The bartender had struck Joe's skull with a table leg, hidden and ready for such an invitation. Lying still in a natal position, the blood trickled down the side and back of his head to the nape of his neck and onto the floor. It joined the puddle forming from his left cheek that had met a shard of thick glass.

Φ

After Michael left Quinn's store, Ellen slowly led the blind mare around the side of a building atop the hill and peered around the corner. She had heard the shots that caused men to stream from the saloon.

Standing in his cart, Uncle Mike seemed to be looking for Joseph's face in the commotion. AD and a friend were galloping away. Quinn told Michael that AD had been the source of the problem.

Having been alerted earlier by Quinn, the sheriff charged toward the saloon as men attempted to flee. The sheriff, not sure if there had been a death, directed chosen witnesses at gunpoint to return to the bar and sit at a table and wait for him to dismiss them after a little talk.

Neither Michael nor Ellen saw Joseph, but Ellen had seen Michael and Mr. Quinn walk out of the store and place her saddle in his little cart. Michael covered it with grain bags from Quinn's store and headed down the short hill.

Ellen decided not to ride down to get the saddle or worry about her da. She led the mare back to the store, stepped off Quinn's porch railing above the street to mount her, and turned her da's blind mare back to the farm.

Whatever happened to Da, Ellen knew Ma was sure to learn later. Has Da been shot? Is he dead? She didn't want to know. Her heart had already been broken.

Breaking the loy and attempting to sell their saddle had not been Da's worst offenses. She'd say nothing to Ma that didn't need to be said. She had no news for Ma. She would let Uncle Mike share any tragic or embarrassing details when he arrived back at the farm with Da and, hopefully, her saddle.

It was nearly dark, and she was hungry. Ellen decided to stop at Mrs. Collins's house to see if she had something for her and Mary to eat. She'd talk about something else, but Elizabeth would ask Ellen if she had eaten. Ellen didn't know what to say if Elizabeth asked her why she was out alone riding the blind mare in the growing dark. If she got something for herself and Mary, then Ma would only have to worry about herself and the boys. Elizabeth knew they had to eat and that meals at the Quigley home were growing harder to come by. Ellen decided to tell Elizabeth that Da just hadn't gotten home with their tea yet, and she stopped by to say hello, but she knew Elizabeth would feed her anyway.

Φ

Back in Pleasant Hill, sitting in a chair against the wall on the other side of the jail bars, Michael saw Joseph beginning to stir. "Well, then, Joseph. I see yer still alive. It seems nothin' will kill ye. I'm sorry. Should I welcome ye back?"

Confused and not fully alert, Joseph could not reply.

Michael said, "The sheriff's still assessin' the bill that will far out-do the profit from any saddle. And then there are the stitches the doc put in yer cheek and skull. There's a drink tab as well. Mr. Hayes paid back the five dollars for the saddle, but he cleared out of the saloon without settlin' for the drinks or damage. Ye can certainly understand why."

Joseph reached up to his thumping head and then became aware of the sharp throb of his cheek as well as the barbs to his pride from Michael's inquiries. He did not speak. He looked at Michael and felt resentment.

"Should I spare ye the details, Joe, or are ye aware of what happened?" Without waiting for a response, Michael continued, "The doc's comin' back. He says a single shot of opium will take care of ye tonight."

The doc entered and spoke with a deputy who was preparing to go home.

"I was against the opium, but he says one shot will help ye sleep yer first night of three in jail and said ye won't get 'soldier's disease' in one night. Besides, we both agreed it's too late. He hopes ye won't die, but it will also be helpful to the deputies to keep ye 'relaxed.' He doesn't want ye to eat—not that ye could. He's afraid ye might vomit, and nobody will be here to help ye. I don't have food with me anyway."

Doc White entered with his bag, and the deputy brought his key.

Michael continued, "The sheriff can tell ye what's goin' to happen with bail. I'll take Fiona home and have Mary come in the morning."

There was no conversation as the doctor administered Joe's shot, gave him a few instructions, and abruptly tipped his hat and left.

Michael said, "They're lockin' up now. I'll take something for Mary and the children to eat. I'll let ye and Mary figure the rest out. Don't expect John and Mary McManus to pay for broken mirrors, furniture, and bottles of liquor. I hope yer still breathin' tomorrow after yer dinner of whiskey and opium. Make yerself a sincere Act of Contrition, brother, and God help ye. Ye break our hearts—I hope ye know that."

Outside, Mr. Quinn stood there with a small bundle of salt pork and a little cornmeal.

Michael thanked Quinn and trotted off to Joe's family.

When Ellen got her saddle back from Uncle Mike, the girls decided to keep it safely hidden in their bedroom.

Mike rushed home after handing over Fiona and leaving the food from Mr. Quinn. Ellen had brought home bread slices and a sausage from Elizabeth, and they had food for several days. Along with their few eggs and milk, things were looking all right, except that Da was in jail and in no condition to get up and come home. Ma refused to pay bail—even if she could. The sheriff's plan to keep Joe for three days brought a little peace and healing.

The girls, as usual, were especially helpful. They stayed home on their next school day so Ma didn't have to be home alone with the baby and Little Joseph. When things went bad with Da, so did Little Joseph, who didn't want to be outdone.

After several days, Ma took Thomas to town with her in the cart to get Joe. Joe did not speak a word after Mary talked the sheriff out of the excessive bond. They would get "caught up" at the court with their next good harvest, something Mary agreed to but knew couldn't be done.

As she recalled the horrible events after the locusts and droughts of 1874, Little Mary decided that things could only look up after that last October when her da broke her loy and went mad again.

Φ

The locusts were on their way within hours. Thinking better of it and with encouragement from his worried wife, Joe Quigley decided, on this Saturday evening in April 1875, to stay home. For several days, he and Mary had frantically scurried about, hauling things into the house, dragging things here and there outside, and making sure doors to the rooms could still be closed.

While Little Joseph's mattress of batting was piled onto the other bed, his side of the room was stacked with as much hay and feed that would fit. The spring evening was lovely, but, by nightfall, the number of grasshopper hatchlings had doubled.

After the children settled in, Ma quietly played a few of her favorite hymns, sitting in the dark at her spinet. She had started playing again at the church, and she liked to practice right after their night meal—if they had one. It soothed the children who eventually fell asleep. The chirping in the night intensified, and Ma couldn't cover the sound, so she gave up and joined the rest of her family in their restless attempts to sleep and wait for the second plague to arrive.

When the Quigley family met dawn the next day, there was an astounding darkness on the northern horizon and the familiar thunderous sound of millions of wings beating the air. The cloud was moving at a terrifying pace. Joe went out to the livestock. Ma yelled at Ellen to grab the bucket and milk Patches. Ellen took a cloth to keep the locusts out of the milk. She yelled at Mary to gather the eggs. Ma and Little Michael grabbed the chickens and took them into the house. She went back, grabbed the last of the straw and scratch, and set it on the floor of her parlor. The chickens would stay out of the bedrooms where hay and feed were since she and Joe tied their legs to the parlor chairs with string. Joe kept Patches tied under the shed roof.

They had two hogs left, so they generously fed them and gave their animals their last fresh water before it could be contaminated by locusts. For a short time, the children stood over their stock animals and swatted at the grasshoppers so they could eat. The higher the sun got in the sky, the darker the sky became.

Since the telegraphed warning that arrived in Pleasant Hill from Nebraska only a few days earlier, Ma had filled the washtub daily with clean water. She and Da had rinsed out and filled two empty pork barrels in their bedroom and one in the kitchen with water, which had only finally cleaned itself from the taste of locust a few months earlier. The kitchen barrel allowed some seepage and was to be used first. The water tasted of smoked meat, but it would be welcomed over the nasty, bitter taste of locust waste.

After much noise and chaos, they surrendered to their fate. They had seen the same event last summer, but this was worse. Eventually, the sky was black from end to end, and it was like a large blanket had come to cover the earth. From the obliterated sky, locusts landed, first one by one and then by the handful. After the best breakfast they had eaten in months, Ma nursed Thomas and placed him in his basket next to the straw. The girls had helped Joseph place his batting on top of the hay. Both he and Michael had perched themselves nearly touching the ceiling to sleep the night before, while Ellen and Mary once again slept with their saddle and other tack.

By midway of the first day of the invasion, the children were in the bedroom where they played word games and cried from fear. Ma, Da, and Ellen reassured them they would live through it. Mary didn't cry like the boys, but she could not reassure anyone. They heard grasshoppers falling on their roof. Mary closed her eyes and held her hands over her ears. Da opened the kitchen door to investigate the source of a different kind of noise. He found mice scrambling against the door to get into the house. He and Ma stepped on the mice and swept feverishly to get them and the locusts out of the kitchen and off the steps.

Mary called her family together, and they all sat on the parents' bed to pray the rosary. The girls had almost mastered the difficult Lorica in Irish. They took this opportunity to practice their memorization to perfection. Mary took out her beautiful blue prayer book and turned to its pages, reciting it all in her native tongue. It calmed them, and every day of the attack, they repeated the ritual of saying their prayers in Irish.

On the second to last day, they released their chickens to the outdoors. They ran wild, eating locusts and scratching in the dirt. Ma and Da scooped up piles of locusts along their walkways and out from under Patches.

Joe rolled up the last of the sacks and soiled straw off the parlor floor, threw the mess on the pile, and lit it on fire. They had done this as often as they could, repelling the assault and cleaning the mess.

As the last of the insects were landing, Mary read Psalm 91: "O lord, how great are thy works!"

Joseph said, "Ye must be kiddin' Mary. It was biblical, but I didn't think the plague was that great." He turned to the children. "How about you, little paistí / children?"

Three of the children giggled, and Ellen smiled. Da was throwing more blame than glory God's way.

Nose in her Bible, Ma read on: "The senseless man shall not know." Then, looking directly at Joe and trying to hold back laughter, she continued: "Nor will the fool understand these things."

Joseph burst out laughing and said, "Now, ye got that one right, Mary Quigley!"

When Joseph was together with the family and not working or drinking, he could be funny. They loved having him back for the rare few moments.

They had survived for two weeks and were no longer feeling in the need of prayer as much as they were for celebration that the sky had quit raining insects. Mary skipped down to the lines about the flourishing palm tree, the cedar of Lebanus, and then directly to "the Lord our God is righteous." With that, they ran outdoors to shovel up one more pile of locusts to burn.

The house smelled terrible. Everyone had spent as much time smashing insects as the tied-down chickens had defecated. The outdoors was relief, but the land was once again stripped bare—and there were no crops or trees. The fence posts were destroyed, the livestock were dead, and there were many other discouragements.

CHAPTER 22

FARM OF MARY AND JOSEPH QUIGLEY,
PLEASANT HILL, MISSOURI,
JUNE 1875–AUGUST 1877

By June 1875, the worst plague in America had lifted. The Missouri and Kansas farmers planted their corn, but by all logic, it was too late. However, the ground conditions were perfect, they had the seed, and there was nothing to lose. It was amazing providence for the Pleasant Hill community that after disastrous weather and millions of locusts stripping the land bare only four months earlier, perfect and late summer days brought families a bumper crop of corn. The pollination was not too dry, the silking stage had gentle rain, and the crop diseases that could take hold did not show up. In the longer-than-usual heat of summer, the family gardens revived. From late September 1875 through 1876 food was miraculously adequate, and in some cases, like corn, it was abundant. Thanks to a package of seeds mailed from Mary's mother, Mary Grant McManus, the Quigleys had yellow squash, green beans, large orange pumpkins, and other edibles that had become scarce or nonexistent for two years. Nearly all the Quigley prayers had been answered, and they were rewarded by their investment of backbreaking work and unwavering hearts.

The banks in Cass County were able to retrieve losses, forgive late fees, and move on—except for the Quigley family and any others whose mortgages were significantly in arrears and credit inadequate for loans.

After their first harvest, in September 1875, it was with unusual lightness, Mary and Joe Quigley made a double mortgage payment to a clerk who took their money and said nothing about their account. The manager and his assistant appeared to both be absent. Mary was glad that they had avoided a conversation with either.

Neither she nor Joseph wanted an argument or bad news to ruin an otherwise exceptional day.

While leaving the bank, Joseph's quiet and vulnerable mood grew dark. Regardless of his signs of amiability, he was a sleeping dog and would not be fooled. He was silently brewing over Michael and the hogs. He wanted to move forward with his plans. Mary was moving forward with hers, but both she and Michael were standing in Joseph's way—or so he believed.

Within two days, the Quigleys bought their new Holstein cow and her not-yet-weaned calf from one of the Reid families south of the farm. Cousins of Mary Murphy were packing up and returning to family in Indiana, so the price for these animals was exceptional, if not a gift to the Quigleys.

The girls rode on their mare behind the cow, which was tethered to the wagon Da drove. In the back was the bellowing calf, some fresh alfalfa to tease the cow forward, and Michael. The calf would be weaned as soon as they felt it was safe, and before winter, the cow would be adding her warm milk to the direct benefit of the family, not the calf. The milk was worth more than the cost of feed for the calf. They would build back up their little herd and benefit from this investment.

Any day, Joseph expected Michael to arrive with an offer of at least one hog and possibly piglets from the sow Joseph had "given" him. Better yet would be a sow and a gilt already bred. One morning, he was standing in the yard and looking toward Michael's. Joseph guessed that a gilt from the last batch was at least seven months old by now, and anticipating the young hog, he had talked to Mr. Dunn about bringing his boar back to breed with his two sows and the new gilt he would be getting from Michael.

Hogs usually gestated over winter and had their piglets in spring. After weaning the piglets, the sows were rebred for their second litter in the year. Now would be perfect timing for getting a gilt from Michael. Joseph had thought incessantly about buying a boar, but it was too costly. Irritated and feeling insulted, he decided to make a trip up to Michael's.

His October trip to Michael's, made in a sober state, did not result in a hog. It resulted in bickering and insults that, fortunately, Joseph did not take to the saloon to repress. Michael told Joseph he was jumping the gun and that he needed to wait for the next batch. Michael had already given Joseph's family at least two piglets of food in the last two years, and he could not afford to be "gifting" anything until he recuperated from the hard times himself.

After Joe returned home empty-handed, Mary convinced him to plant twice as much corn in the spring and buy a new sow, another heifer, and a cow. She wanted to hire Melvin back full- time so they could expand all they could to make a few more good faith payments. Surely the bank would not foreclose if they made as many payments as possible until they eventually got caught up.

Through the end of 1875 and the spring and summer of 1876, Mary sold fresh butter, eggs, and sometimes cream in town based on regular preplaced orders. Mary planned to hide some of the money in a tin under the front porch. She would divide the money while in town, secreting some in her petticoat, and not even the children would know it was there. Though Joseph didn't disagree with Mary's dairy plans, he continued to believe they also needed a substantially larger herd of hogs to meet their obligations with the bank. They couldn't afford to eat the hogs and buy hogs and cows at the same time, and the bank would not be giving the Quigley family a loan. They had no credit and little collateral. Being able to wean the calves as soon as possible kept the milk flowing—as long as they also kept the cows healthy.

In July, Joseph invited Mary to take a walk in a beautiful, tall cornfield. It was a perfect day, and their first corn crop in a long time was thriving. She had grabbed a hoe out of habit, but Joseph didn't have hoeing in mind. Thus, it was that Mary conceived her sixth child. When Joseph helped Mary up to dust herself off, some of her secret change fell from her pocket.

Having earlier seen Mary deposit their egg and butter money in the canister on the buffet, Joseph thought it uncharacteristic of her to not get it all in the can. He said, "Oops, Mary, maybe this is some of that money yer not earnin' with the butter. Holdin' out on us, Ma? Helping yer lady friends are ye?"

"How dare ye, Joe Quigley. Don't be accusin' me of holdin' out on anyone. I'm doin' plenty of work and worryin' as much as the rest of us. This is not the time for anyone to be throwing money away. You know that. You also know that I'm not the only one responsible for producing more mouths to feed, so don't be blamin' me for makin' us less than wealthy. Even if I were savin' a penny or two, ye know it would go to us and this farm."

When Joseph picked up the money, she snatched it back and said, "I'll take care of that." Because they had already counted the money that day, Mary was careful to add it to the tally on the bureau.

In their summer and fall abundance, it seemed to Mary that her husband had finally made a small attempt to rededicate himself to the love of his family. On their October ride to the bank, with the boys riding in the back of the wagon, Joe told his pregnant wife, "Mary, darlin', this day could not have been without ye. In all of it, ye've held steadfast and strong. I'm sorry yer dealin' with all me own shortcomin's. I think I was wrong about the saddle."

Here they were, two years later, and it was the first time he had mentioned the saddle episode among his regrets.

Mary reminded him that he had not yet apologized to the girls for the saddle. Mary said, "This is our third October since that event!" She was not sure if he had seriously lost track of time. He was still a young man.

Joe replied, "Ye have to be mistaken. Why would ye tell me that, Mary? I already feel bad enough."

Joe Quigley would hold on to irritants the same way he was holding on to the idea of getting his hogs back after two years. However, this had to be his mind losing track of time. She had thought his mind was slipping, but this was the first indication of how significant it was.

She thought he might be confused about the hogs. On every occasion he brought up the subject of hogs, it resulted in a shouting match. He spoke as if he had just handed over the hogs that Michael would feed for him. Frequently, he thought he would be getting his sows back any day, even after the fight. Joseph continued building up steam against Michael, but Michael and Mary thought the situation had been somewhat resolved.

Fortunately, on that day, he was unusually contrite and felt ill. The hogs were not yet in the day's conversation. He had not eaten since yesterday, and he was bent over and looked terrible. Joseph never thought he was in the wrong. There was usually someone else to blame. However, being older and when he was very sick, he showed signs of vulnerability.

"It was me illness that made me give up, darlin', you know that. Ye know I love ye and the children. I'm so proud of ye, Mary. Yer me salvation, love." Tears flowed from the corners of his eyes. Joe turned and kissed Mary on the cheek. He sometimes cried when he was sobering up and had done something unforgiveable like strike Mary.

Mary refused to get weak. She had quit—long ago—letting him off the hook for drinking and trying to manipulate her into thinking he was actually sorry for what he had done. "I know yer hurtin', Joe, but ye know it is not the stomach or yer insides. You can't help that the war tore ye up, but we both know it's the drinkin' on top of it. Ye've been doin' it every year of our lives, and even with dry spells, ye don't stop. Ye just can't take our money to the saloon anymore."

In more whispered tones, she continued to unload, saying, "The children can't keep sufferin' meanness because of it. The boys will grow up to shoot ye in defense—not in love or to help ye. Ye just don't have that many more chances, Joe. Yer killin' us all. And ye have to be nicer to yer brother Michael. He couldn't pay ye full for the hogs, and he didn't have to. He did ye a favor by takin' them on in the first place, and then he fed us. Mary and Mike have given so much, and the children depend on him when they can't depend on you. You know that. Let it go."

Joseph had not brought up the hogs, but it wasn't unlike Mary to bring up the past. She had now made him less contrite and more combative. A part of her wanted him to admit wrongdoing and suffer regret, but her confrontations turned the tide again.

"What do ye mean depend on him? I'm their da. They won't have to go to *almighty* Mike. I'll make sure they won't do it again. I promised I'll do better to not fall off the wagon. But Mike owes me. He promised to give me hogs back when things fell back to normal and he got some piglets. Things are better now."

Mary was exasperated by the time they reached the bank and stopped the cart. Joe wiped his tired eyes. Mary looked at her husband and thought he looked old and beaten. He was thirty- eight, but he looked like a skeleton with one foot in the grave. The visible scar on his cheek had also contributed to his sickly and unappealing appearance.

It seemed to Mary all their youth had vanished in the war, rotten crops, plagues, and drinking. In his frequent inability to eat or lack of proper food, he had turned into a decrepit being. His days of lying in bed with his insides bleeding contributed to his irascibility and were so rapidly contributing to his demise that Mary thought she was going to become a widow within the year.

When they entered the bank, the teller alerted the manager, and he motioned them back from the counter to his desk. The clerk opened a gate at the end of the counter and led them to the manager's desk. All the other customers could look over and see them "getting in trouble" like errant schoolchildren.

The manager smiled insincerely and said, "First, congratulations on your corn harvest and your recent payments. I've noticed that like some of our other clients in your unfortunate circumstances, you've attempted to pay something on your mortgage when you could."

Joseph felt humiliated, but he bit his tongue.

Mary felt like a confessor at the front of the line who could hear a deaf sinner in the confessional asking forgiveness. She thought, *They yell their sins at the priest sitting in the dark behind a screen, but because they cannot hear, they continue to raise their voices to the chagrin of those who can hear their darkest secrets.*

Joseph said, "Is it necessary for you to announce our unfortunate circumstances to the town? Maybe you've not had unfortunate circumstances, but the rest of us have. We don't choose our unfortunate circumstances. I do not welcome floods, droughts, or plagues.

You have no right to blame or shame us for our impoverishment; that's what yer tryin' to do. I don't like the tone of yer voice."

Mary said, "Our farm is everything to us. You know it's what feeds our children. We're willing to do whatever we can. We need another chance; we can catch up two payments."

Joseph snapped, "Shut the grovelin', Mary! The town crier here doesn't give a pig's tail about the Quigley children."

In a piercing baritone, the manager responded, "Before the plague hit, I see you were already four full payments behind. Where do you suppose that money went, Mr. Quigley? Most other farmers in your region were meeting their obligations at that time—even with poor weather."

From somewhere on the other side of the counter came a "Shh" from a customer and a masculine "Quiet down" from another who didn't want to hear the pompous manager belittle a fellow farmer. Mary cringed and cast her eyes down. *He knows Joseph drinks. Everyone in town knows. Because we're Irish, he knows Joseph drank up the mortgage payment or maybe the sheriff told him it went to the jail.*

Mary wanted to be able to defend Joseph, but Joseph said, "I'd bet you a few intoxicated German or English neighbors didn't get all their payments made while their crops were rottin' in the rain." The manager said again that the bank, as though it were a person, *appreciated* their bad luck and their hard work, but there really wasn't *anything* "they" could do.

Joe said, "Well, maybe they can't, but what about you? Don't ye have any authority here?" he asked loudly enough for all to hear.

Joe and Mary would be given leniency if it were four or fewer payments they were behind, but that's where "they" drew the line. Six was too many. Unless Joe and Mary were completely caught up by next year, the bank planned to go ahead and repossess the farm.

"And, yes, it seems so unfair after six years, but today is going to be your final warning. This is our position: enough is enough."

The Quigleys had been given more opportunities than most. The bank was "losing money" if they didn't cut the Quigleys loose now or the family did not "pay in full" by next September 30.

330

The manager put his hand out for Joe to shake and declared, "I guess you all have to go home and figure it out."

Joe did not shake his hand.

The banker turned his back on Joseph and Mary and walked past the counter and through a door at the back, leaving them in a position of having to turn around and see all the customers' eyes looking their way as they departed.

Mary kept her eyes down and walked behind her husband as they left. Fortunately, their neighbors—whether they liked Joe Quigley or not—made it clear that their sentiments did not generally align with the bank. Some tipped their hats and said, "Good day, Mr. Quigley, Mrs. Quigley."

On her way out of the bank, Mary could feel the heat in her rosy cheeks from the embarrassment and weight of their indebtedness. She felt her heart thumping and heard her own blood pumping in her ears as they climbed back into their wagon. She wondered if this might kill her, but she couldn't imagine God would take her, leaving her children behind in Joe's hands. She would have to swallow her pride and write to her sisters Margaret, Agnes, and Bridget. Margaret had already sent her beautiful Jersey Polly. Polly was helping her sell the golden cream that brought a bonus.

To some degree, they had experienced the same weather and locusts in Kansas; surely, they would be sympathetic. There were many differences that would make it possible for them to help, but it was so much now.

Φ

In spite of their finances and the plague, 1876–1877 had been one of their best-fed winters. As spring of 1877 approached, a new heifer gave birth, the chicks all hatched, and Mary's improved chicken and cattle enterprise was paying off. By June 1876, she had made regular deposits to her tin. Before her October trip to the bank, she had remained hopeful, relieved that she had already saved for one full makeup payment.

It was, however, in September, before their October encounter with the manager, that Joseph, searching for his hammer the boys had carried off, stepped around the south corner of the house. He backed up, back around the corner when he noticed that Mary had come out onto the porch and was kneeling, her back to him, on the ground beside the front steps. Hiding from the corner, he saw her reach in her pocket beneath her petticoat. She then bent down and placed something beneath the steps. When Joe heard the unmistakable sound of money dropping into a tin, he realized she had been siphoning cash from the butter and egg money. He thought, *What's she thinkin? Savin' pennies is foolish when I could make good money off a boar and grow my herd at the same time. Selling one egg at a time will not help us.* Joe was livid and convinced himself he was justified in retaliating, which was a common sentiment for him.

After Mary's end-of-October installment to her tin and several days after their experience with the bank manager, Joseph stepped around the house to grab her stash. It was an exceptionally warm day. He wiped the sweat off his brow, placed the surprising amount of cash into a pouch, and slipped it under his coat. Unknown to him, however, there was a little surprise behind the door to the porch.

On another day in July, Little Mary had also seen her ma slip money into the can after she returned home from her market day. Ma usually made her trip out to the front porch after Ellen started her practice and Mary was sent to the back clothesline on the opposite side of the house. The boys would be napping, playing either here or there, eating, and Da and Melvin still hadn't returned from the field for their noon supper.

It was accidental that the door was slightly ajar when Little Mary noticed Da out in the front. She placed her foot behind the door so it would not blow open, leaving a small slit through which she could peer. When she saw Da get down on his knees and reach, she knew what he was up to. She now had a second new secret to share with her sister Ellen: Ma was hiding money, and Da was stealing it.

After Da took the money, he nonchalantly walked back around the kitchen steps to return to the house through the kitchen door. He walked past the girls who were now doing their school lessons, and into the bedroom to get his gun. Little Joseph, now three and in tears, and Michael, five, were fighting over their only toy in the bedroom.

Da stopped in their room and asked, "Michael, lad, which of you is the baby? I honestly can't tell, Michael, because yer soundin' like you might be the baby—not Joseph. Ye need to let Joseph play the drum now."

Da roughly picked up Michael, plopped him out on the steps, and said, "Michael, it is yer turn to play with the dog. He's new and needs friends. I don't like him much, but maybe he'll like ye."

Michael started counting the dog's toes.

Da said, "Did ye know that even if ye can count, they won't let ye go to school next year if ye act like a baby? Boys who fight with babies over toys are babies themselves. Babies don't go to school." This made Michael angry, but he said nothing to upset his da.

Joe came back inside and asked the girls, "Where's yer ma?" Mary answered, "She's out weedin'. Where ye goin', Da?"

He answered, "I'm goin' to town to talk to a man about a boar, and then I'm goin' out to get one of me hogs back from Uncle Mike."

Neither girl objected or commented, but once they heard their parents' voices become agitated and loud, they started eaves-dropping. Joe and Mary argued unabashedly while Melvin helped Da hook his two-wheeled tip cart to the blind mare. Melvin took no side in the fight.

Ma asked, "Where are you gettin' the money for yer boar?" Da said, "What do you mean where am I gettin' the money? I'm usin' the only cash we have."

Knowing the only cash was on the bureau, Mary said, "Joseph Quigley, don't ye dare touch that money. That's money I've earned with the eggs and butter so we can keep the farm. That's not money to spend on a boar or whiskey. It belongs to me and yer children. I have to save this farm! Don't you lose it for us. Me own parents helped us get this farm, and I'll do whatever I can to keep it."

The girls listened as Ma continued shouting her case with Da. She had been saying many of the same things over and over since the girls could remember. Hogs was a subject variation on a theme of disharmony: "Don't forget, Joseph, yer brother has been down here to check on us, bringing food every time yer off. He's fed those hogs through two summers and a winter of hell. He owes ye nothin'. Forget the hogs; let it go. Besides, ye got nothin' in writin'."

"In writin'?" Joseph picked up a small bucket and threw it to the ground at her feet, popping the rusty handle from its sides. "Michael's a stonemason—not a scholar or a farmer. Since when does a starvin' Irish family put things in writin'? Writin's what yer soft-fingered friends at the bank do. Dammit all to hell, Mary! Michael doesn't know animals like I do. What do ye think I did in Kansas City since I was a kid?"

"Ye drank, ye gambled, ye fought, and ye slept with the mules." It was a terrible thing to say, so trying to calm him, Mary immediately suggested, "Go lie down and rest, Joe. Ye don't look well."

"Yer a peasant with small thinkin', Mary McManus. I'll be lyin' down for a very long time when I'm dead. Yer no warrior or land baron a McManus brags about bein'. Yer always complainin' about losin' the farm—that's all I hear—but hogs are how I can make money for the farm. So stop fightin' me, ye official know-it- all! Yer done winnin', Mary McManus. It's me turn to take things in hand now!"

Ma finally gave up and walked away.

Da would go off to Michael's and probably to town to carry on in a drunken rage. As he clumsily mounted the mare with Melvin's help, Mary shouted, "Jesus beside ye, Joe. May he keep His palm on yer arse! May he save yer family as well—somebody needs to!"

Da said nothing in return. Melvin remained silent, and then he walked away as soon as the cart was on the main road.

Ma anticipated disaster from this occasion. After Joe trotted out to the road with the clumsy tipcart behind his giant blind mare, Ma went into the house to check the money on the bureau. It was all gone—months of it. The blood drained from her face, and she turned a ghostly white.

That he had the gun was troubling. Last Easter, she and Michael expressed the fear that Joe was bound to use it on either of them at some point. Mary didn't think Joseph would kill Mary Murphy or Michael's children, but his anger raged out of control with Michael, which scared them both. Before Ma walked outside to fret over Da's gun and the lost money, the girls had begun discussing if it was time to tell Ma the money from the tin was gone as well.

Ellen said, "Maybe she doesn't need to know."

Mary didn't know where Ellen got that idea, but it usually stopped them from doing whatever they were contemplating. She said, "Maybe he'll go get drunk first. Maybe he'll be so drunk he'll forget about the hogs, and Ma can go to town and get her money back before it's all gone."

Da had been good for a long time, but it wasn't until that last trip to the bank that the constant bickering and a new sense of panic had put this event and others into motion.

Ma hadn't checked her tin because she didn't want the kids to see her, but the girls were watching her every move as she went out to sit on the front porch to cry. When they were in crisis, they stood by their ma for their security as well as to help her if she needed them.

Ellen went out to the field and rounded up Thomas and Joseph. In a crisis, the girls always brought the siblings together. Little Michael, hearing the fight, was already hanging around Mary and Ma. Mary had Thomas by the hand.

Ellen offered to ride up to Michael and Mary's house and bring Da home. Ma absolutely refused to let Ellen place herself again in the middle of a situation with her da. If anyone went anywhere, it would be Ma. She got down on her knees and reached her hand under the porch to find an empty tin. It was enough to drive her into a fit of anger. She directed the children into the kitchen to wait.

Ma ran out to the field with Thomas to tell Melvin to take him over to the Collins house. Mary quickly explained to Melvin about the money. He was to tell Elizabeth that she would be going to Michael's to stop Joseph if she could. She returned to the house to give her children instructions in the event she didn't come right back. She told them how to act if their da got home before she did. If he was drunk, they were to run to Elizabeth's and stay there. If Da went to Elizabeth's, they were to run toward home and hide along the creek.

As Mary stood in the kitchen, she suddenly felt dizzy and nauseated. Mary placed her hand on her ma's rock-hard stomach and asked her if she was going to have another baby. Ma answered, "Yes, I think I am," and then she ran out the door to vomit in the weeds.

Ellen ran out with water for Ma, and the girls begged their mother not to go to Mike's. While they were holding onto Ma's skirt, crying and trying to keep her home, Mary struggled up. Once on her feet, she passed out cold on the ground. Frightened, the children stayed by her until Melvin could help her to her bed. Marvin kindled the stove, and Ellen made Ma some tea.

Φ

When Joseph arrived at the T in the road, he decided to go to town and check at the store for a bulletin posted about anyone wanting to sell a boar. Quinn had a board where people placed ads for selling or buying livestock or farm equipment or to make announcements for one reason or another. There was nothing there regarding a boar, but when Joseph asked, Quinn suggested riding up to a farm near Lone Jack. A farmer was selling out, and he had a ton of hogs. He hadn't heard if he still had a boar, but based on the number of hogs he had, it seemed that he likely had owned several. Though Joe knew who he was, it was getting dark early—and it was too far out to go for nothing. Joseph decided to inquire closer to town.

He headed north up the road on the way to Lone Jack, but he stopped at a farm just past the fairgrounds. Joe had bought a sow from the farmer shortly after they had moved out to their farm on Big Creek.

Mr. Simpson had good stock, was a good farmer, and might know the hog farmer in Lone Jack.

Joseph stopped at the head of his lane and said, "Good day, sir."

Mr. Simpson asked, "May I be of some service? Are you looking for someone? Are you Joe Quigley?"

Joseph replied, "Yes, sir. I am. I'm lookin' to rebuild me livestock. I'm startin' over. Do ye know where I can find a good but reasonably priced boar?"

Simpson replied, "If you're starting over, I believe you have to start with a sow."

They both laughed.

Joseph said, "I have two and am going to pick up a third or gilt this afternoon from my brother. About five years ago, I purchased a sow from you, but I am told by Quinn at the store that there is a Frank Schnetzer in Lone Jack who has a sizable herd he's sellin'. Do you know him?"

"I sure do know him. I bought his top boar at auction last month. You're too late; he's completely sold out, including his farm. Now that things are settling down, people are coming back, and others are selling out. It's happening overnight. Two abandoned farms north just sold last week. Frank's going back up to Ohio to take over a large family toolmaking enterprise. He's out of farming altogether."

Joseph said, "I hear the banks are fixin' to jack up the land prices on abandoned property or foreclose on anyone they can. I was told I could sell me own farm in a week—if I owned it."

"Do you have a barn?" Simpson asked.

"Not yet, but we had hoped to build after we get caught up. Now we have several sheds."

"I'm sorry I can't help, but I have to be going. Do you know about the Grange? I'm off right now to attend an organizational meeting over at the fairgrounds. I'll be glad when it starts up and hope to be directly involved as an officer. The Illinois and Minnesota farmers have been successful in controlling rates for shipping corn and hogs. Those railroad men gouge us at every opportunity and hurt a lot of farmers. When the farmers get together and hold the line on costs, they can have a better profit. The Grange gets them organized so they can be better farmers as well. You should come along; I might need a few votes."

"Maybe I'll meet someone with a boar. Sure thing. I'll see ye there."

"Good. That's quite a cart, Mr. Quigley," Simpson said as he trotted off.

Joseph turned his cart around at the top of Simpson's lane and thought of how anxious he was to show the bank manager it would not be so easy to be rid of the Quigleys. Joseph imagined himself getting rich with a new boar and his two sows back. It was early afternoon, and the sun wouldn't set for about four hours. Michael wasn't that many miles down the road, and Joseph's giant mare didn't have that far to go.

Joseph knew that he wasn't really set up for a boar. He was so anxious to get that money and put it to work that he jumped the gun a little. It was not like him to not have prepared better, but it was too late now. He would get the boar home and then tie him up good away from the sows. He and Melvin would go back to town tomorrow, get the lumber, wire, and feed, and they would be set up in no time.

While hitching the aged tip cart, Melvin had asked Joseph how he planned to feed the boar as he was lounging around the farm for half a year, waiting for his next sow service. The boar would be idle for months unless Joseph let him out to other farms. Even then, they all took their piglets and sows to market about the same time, so breeding happened in a fairly short time only twice a year. Joe knew all that.

Melvin had also asked about the possibility that the boar would bring diseases back that would kill all the hogs. It was a well-known risk if he planned to share his boar for profit. Joe said he'd worry about that when the time came.

Melvin was from a large Amish family with solid livestock experience and success. Though he was only eighteen, he was trying to be helpful because Joseph was acting impulsively and irrationally. Melvin said he didn't think the tipcart could accommodate a large hog because it was built for hay. He told Joseph that it needed some additional work.

Joseph said, "Why is it that everyone wants me to save the farm, but when I decide to take action, everyone tells me why it can't be done? You know, Melvin, that there isn't a wealthy farmer around who doesn't own his own boar—or take a risk to have more. Wealth and success require investment. Every wealthy man in Kansas City spent a lot of money gettin' that way. I'll have to start somewhere, and we have to build now—or else there will be no farm come next October."

Joseph just didn't listen to the good advice he was being given.

Φ

While Ma was lying in bed, pale and sweating, the children were calling on Melvin to go to Michael's to get Da home. Maybe Da would come back if he knew how sick Ma was—and the money would still be in his pocket.

"Please, Melvin," Little Mary said. "I watched Ma knockin' on doors, takin' orders, and carefully packin' fresh eggs, cream, and butter back and forth while takin' care of us, cleanin' the house, milkin' the cow, and weedin' the garden. She needs Da to come home with that money. He needs to help us so she won't die."

The children started to cry.

Michael asked, "Is Ma goin' to die?"

Mary answered, "No, Michael. She's havin' a baby. She was sick before Joseph was born. Can ye blame her for that?"

Joseph hit Mary and ran off chanting, "Ma's havin' a baby; Ma's havin' a baby."

"If you weren't here to help, Melvin, she'd be worse," Ellen said. Melvin finally complied with the request to go to Michael's, but when he got there, they hadn't seen Joseph. When Melvin went to the saloon, he sent someone in to look. Nobody had seen him there either. Quinn told Melvin that he thought Joseph was in Lone Jack. Lone Jack was too far—he might miss Joseph—and he returned to the farm.

He had told Michael, Quinn, and the bartender that Mary was ill. Michael told Melvin he would not go down to Joseph's farm—even if Mary was ill. That's when Melvin told Michael that Mary was expecting. Michael assured Melvin that, under those circumstances, Mary was probably fine. He said that Joseph had been so vile that he didn't want to go to the farm for fear of being shot.

He thanked Melvin for warning him about the sows. Michael and his boys would deal with it if Joseph showed up, but there was no such agreement that the sows would be returned. They had been payback for the horse and cow feed and food Michael had given Joseph's family. He said, "Melvin, you know, Joseph can't hear what yer sayin' when he has his mind made up on what he wants to believe. I think he's finally lost his mind. I can't talk to him at all anymore. I've fought with him his whole life, and all we've done for two years is argue over pigs. I'm not turnin' over my sows to a madman. If he wants a boar and a new breeding line, all he has to do is keep a male piglet and get a new sow.

"Tell Mary I'm sorry that the bank wants the farm back. Joseph has known what was expected since they bought the farm. Anyone who's behind or abandoned their farm is going to be foreclosed on because the price for land is goin' up rapidly—and the bank wants new buyers. People want to come here. That's been the story since after the war. I can't help unless I planned to buy them out. They know I can't. Tell Mary that Mary Murphy and I and the children will pray for her as we always have. That's all we can do. I wish the best. Mary McManus is a wonderful woman, but she married the wrong man. He's not well, but things may be easier when he's gone. I'm sorry to say that."

Φ

When Elizabeth arrived at the Quigley farm, she rapped at the kitchen door and walked in with a chunk of pot roast, honey, and a quarter pan of corn bread. "Mary, darlin', yer guardian angel is here." She kissed baby Thomas on the cheek and patted Joseph on the head. "How are ye doin' sweet boy?"

Elizabeth always said that if you repeat how great a child is enough times, they begin to act as though it is true. The children loved her because she was kind and very generous. As long as Elizabeth was around, they would not starve.

Ellen took the pot roast wrapped in meat paper and placed it in their little cooler, which was ineffectively fed by underground air through a stove pipe.

Elizabeth went into the bedroom to see Mary. "I've brought roast, a little honey, and a fresh piece of corn bread. Do ye think ye can eat?"

"Maybe I can now."

Elizabeth asked, "Are ye expectin' Mary?"

"I expect so." With that, Mary chuckled, got out of bed, and went into the parlor to sit in one of her good parlor chairs—next to the one reserved for company. Elizabeth would have been horrified to see chickens tied leg-to-leg onto the ornate tapestried chairs only seven months before. Mary was proud that nobody could still smell the residue from that crisis.

"I'll go make more tea and will bring yer food. I think ye need some beef, Mary." Elizabeth had sliced little pieces of the pot roast and placed them on the corn bread and drizzled it with honey. She gave everyone a fair-sized bite. As Mary had her snack, she told Elizabeth what was happening. Elizabeth listened, but she sensed no resolution for Mary. There was nothing she could suggest to help her. She didn't know how Mary could stand it, but she knew Mary's faith kept her bound to Joseph more than her love for him did.

After Melvin returned from town and gave his report, Elizabeth left. She didn't want to be there when Joseph came back. In spite of all her help, Joseph called Elizabeth "the meddler."

Meddling was not her personality. It was a way Joseph could blame her when things were his fault—and she was taking up the slack for his failures. Elizabeth and her husband, Lawrence, thought Joseph's charm had steadily diminished with each act of selfishness or violence.

CHAPTER 23

FARM OF MARY AND JOSEPH QUIGLEY, PLEASANT HILL, MISSOURI, AUGUST 1877–SEPTEMBER 13, 1877

Joseph was impressed by the Grange meeting and decided he might join. Two of the men he knew from the saloon were headed to town and invited him to come along with them for a couple of shots of whiskey and a discussion about the Grange. Off Joseph went—with his pockets full of money and a long-denied thirst to be quenched!

After numerous drinks by all, his friends agreed that he needed to go get his hogs back from the errant Michael, though all who knew him did not think of him in that regard. After hearing Joseph's side of the story numerous times, however, they had no sober question that he was deserving and long overdue. Before he got help to climb on his big mare, he purchased a new bottle of whiskey to take home.

By the time Joseph arrived at Michael's farm, he realized he was not able to stand upright on the ground, so he stayed on his mare and shot off his gun to call Michael out. Through a partly opened door, Michael shouted at him to throw the gun down on the ground or he would not come out of the house. Joseph did not comply. Instead, he yelled out orders to his brother and his sons, John and Thomas, who were out in the barn. They were finishing their chores, and it was beginning to get dark.

Joseph demanded that the boys tip the cart down and bring him his sow and a gilt. John, eighteen, who had come out of the barn was terrified by Joseph. Joseph continued to point the gun at John and in the direction of the barn door. John yelled at Thomas, seventeen, and told him to stay where he was.

Michael shouted at Joseph that nobody would give him anything while his gun was in his hand. Michael said he'd shoot Joseph with his rifle if he didn't either let his boys go or throw the gun down.

Joseph said, "No, you won't. Yer too good for that. Our da wouldn't stand for it. Give me back a sow, and I'll go. John, tip me wagon down, and you and Thomas bring me one of my sows."

John answered, "Your sow hasn't had her piglets. She will in a month."

Michael shouted, "We'll bring you a male and a female piglet after they're weaned, and then we're done with ye, Joseph. Besides, yer wagon is not suitable. I'm surprised ye'd want to put even a piglet in it."

Joseph answered, "I want the sow tonight. I'll bring you a piglet after it's weaned. Come out here Michael and give me my sow—or I'll shoot John."

Michael came out of the house and tipped down Joe's rickety wagon, and the boys disappeared into the hog shed. John returned with the sow, and Thomas stood by the barn with a rifle pointed at Joseph's back.

John shouted, "Drop that pistol to the ground, Uncle Joe, or Thomas will shoot the sow."

Joseph heard a large crack in the air. The shocking noise and the start in his mare caused him to drop his pistol. It was an accident of his intoxication.

Michael took the rifle from Thomas and kept it trained on Joseph. John and Thomas forced the sow into the broken-down cart. The back would not adequately close up, so the boys grabbed some jute and tried to tie it securely. The sow was squealing and beside herself. The sides of the cart didn't come up to her blades, and Michael wondered how she would ever get to Joseph's. However, he was not going to load it into his own wagon and subject his boys to the danger of delivering it.

Michael said, "Face yer cart out to the road, Joseph, and I'll follow behind with the rifle until ye get to the main road. Joseph, we'll throw the pistol in the cart and keep the rifle aimed at ye until ye clear the first hill. If ye take off runnin' before, ye'll never get that pistol back."

As Joseph headed for the road, he said, "Michael Quigley, don't ever come to me farm again. If ye do, I will kill ye. Did ye hear me, Michael? Tell yer family that they are not welcome in me home—nor will me wife or children come ever again to yer home."

As Joseph moved the cart forward onto the road, John and Thomas walked behind their father until they reached the main road to Joseph's farm. Before Joseph's cart wobbled on its wheels over the small hill in the road, Michael directed John to shoot off all the bullets in Joseph's gun and throw it into the cart. They could barely see in the darkness as they returned to the house.

Anxious to get home and get the sow off the cart before he passed out, Joseph gave his mare a kick into a faster gait. They were going up a slight incline where wheels had dug ruts with hard-as-concrete clay ridges left high and dry. The pressure from the rough road on the right wheel was too great. Just where the road leveled out, the wheel wobbled dramatically. Joe's mare reared up and backed down toward the ditch, the direction in which she was being pulled by the crumbling wheel. As it wobbled off, the gilt fell down on her front knee, rolled onto her back, and crashed over the side of the cart. She landed headfirst on her side into the deep, narrow ditch of standing water.

The cart's second wheel was sinking into the ditch as the mare went back and sideways. The shafts of the cart were pressing hard against the mare's sides. As his horse danced and twisted sideways to get away from her predicament, Joseph tipped over and held tight to the right shaft. There, Joseph hung, in his sickly, drunken state, with a dying pig and a mare suffering under the twisting pull of two shafts digging into her sides and holding down the hog.

Joseph fumbled, swore, and tugged at the straps buckled behind his seat. They held both the saddle and shafts tight to his panicked mare. Finally, he unloosened the buckle, which released the saddle that twisted and slid out from under Joe.

Tipped over, nearly headfirst, feet on the mare, and holding the right shaft in midair, Joseph tried to think of what to do next. The mare instinctively lifted her massive shoulders, dug in her hooves, and heaved herself forward and out from under the traces holding the cart.

Joseph and all the fittings immediately slid off the horse, and the second wheel and the rotten cart toppled on top of the wounded gilt in the ditch. The steadfast mare stepped on Joseph's arm as she turned toward home.

The beautiful, pregnant sow that had become Joseph's obsession and had caused him to abuse and reject his last-known sibling, lay silent with a broken body. She was unable to wriggle and squirm out from under the wreckage that had crashed on top of her. There, she lay, drowned under the tip cart, and Joseph lying spent halfway in the ditch water and passed out in a drunken state.

Joseph's tired, beloved mare immediately trotted down the road and smelled her way into her yard, pawing the ground as she arrived. Melvin was coming out of his quarters beside the hog shed to check on Mary and the kids in the house when he saw and heard Joseph's mare without the tip cart or Joseph. Using his lantern, he saw the mare was in a lather and needed water and attention. Melvin took her to the pasture and asked Ellen and Mary to take care of her.

Melvin hitched the small cart to Mary's mare and headed up the road to find Joseph. He had affixed two extra lanterns to the cart to see better. Not a mile down the road was the accident. Joseph was lucky. He had neither been hit in the head nor drowned. His bruises were not all noticeable.

Melvin dragged Joe's head and shoulders up and out of the ditch. He retrieved his pistol from the side of the road. Joseph was in such a state that he didn't notice when Melvin took the money pouch out of his inside breast pocket. Melvin threw the whiskey bottle farther down the ditch, away from the wreck, reached down, and slit the gilt's throat. If she bled out, she could be slaughtered soon. He saw that this was not a prime sow; it was only a small gilt.

Joseph came to, climbed into the cart, and immediately slumped into a heap.

On a blanket, Mary, Melvin, and the girls dragged the featherlight Joseph from the yard where he had crawled from Ma's cart. With Ma's help, they pulled him into the house, laid him out on the parlor floor, and left him to dry out and sober up for the remainder of the evening.

He did not protest because he was in no condition to do so.

On their way to school the next day, Mary, Ellen, and their brother Michael saw the tip cart and Uncle Mike's dead pig in the ditch. Ellen and Michael rode on to school together, but Mary refused to go. She rode their pony to Uncle Mike's, knocked on the door, and asked if he had given her da a pig.

Michael said, "Darlin' Mary, why do ye ask?"

Mary replied, "Because Da's tip cart and a dead pig are lyin' in the ditch along the road to the farm. Da's still drunk—so he's not talkin'—and we're not sure whose pig it is. If ye want to butcher it, it's still lyin' in the ditch with a slit throat." Swallowing tears, Mary asked, "Did she have babies?"

"No, Mary, she didn't have babies. Don't worry. She didn't lose any babies in the accident."

Mary said, "I hate me da. I don't think it was his pig, and I'm sorry, Uncle Mike, that he may have killed yer pig. It was a terrible thing to do, and Ellen and I are mad about it, but I don't think Da meant to kill yer pig. Da loves his animals. It's not like Da to be mean to animals. He's mean to Ma and us—but not to his animals. I have to go to school, but please don't tell Ma or Da I came here. Da doesn't like tattlin'."

Uncle Mike kissed Mary's cheek and whispered to her that everything she said was a secret between them and nobody else. "I have a secret that you can't tell yer da, but ye need to tell yer ma for sure. Yer da does not want yer ma, you, Ellen, or the boys to come up here to this farm anymore to get help, or for any other reason—no Christmas parties, birthdays, Thanksgivin', or Easter dinners. 'Tis not safe because yer da has forbidden it. I promise I'll love ye'all forever, but ye have to stay away as long as yer da is still livin' and yer still his children."

Though his life had been filled with much sadness, Michael could not recall ever feeling more hurt than he felt in that moment. To protect his own family, he was abandoning Joseph's. They didn't deserve it; they were good, and he sincerely loved and would miss them. It rekindled the grief he and his young half siblings felt as they were ferried away from Staten Island, leaving the deceased half of their family to lie in the unmarked graves of paupers.

It was the same for Mike as when he, Joseph, and the youngest of them left sister Margaret to become an orphan in New York— and when they said goodbye to Ellen and precious Charley in Pennsylvania.

The evening before was the last breaking apart of the immigrant Quigley family. Joseph had broken the last bonds holding together what Michael cherished as a family. He said, "Little Mary, I guess me own da would be disappointed that I didn't stop yer da from all the drinkin' and meanness."

Little Mary gave him the answer and saved the moment for him. The kind and loving child threw her arms around Uncle Mike's sturdy frame and said, "It isn't yer fault. Ma says Da makes the choice to do bad things even when he knows better. Ye been tellin' him, Ma tells him, the priest tells, and he knows better. I love ye and Aunt Mary and me cousins forever. Ye know where we live. If we have to go away, I'll find a way to tell ye first." Mary ran off Michael's porch, jumped on the painted pony, and galloped away, hurting under the dark shadow of her father's failings.

Φ

After milking, Melvin and Mary returned to the ditch to retrieve the wreckage. The broken cart was there, but the pig and most of the bloody water was gone. It was as though it had never been there. They were both relieved the gilt was gone, and they thought Michael might have ridden down the road to learn whether or not his gilt got home. With its throat slit, he might have thought that Melvin or Mary were inviting him to reclaim what he could.

Φ

Later that day, while Joseph slept off his intoxication, Ma and Thomas took the money Melvin had retrieved to the bank. She covered the amount needed to complete a single payment, but she could not put the remainder into savings without her husband's signature.

She planned not to give this to the bank unless she could guarantee that they had enough to live on until another full payment could be made. What was left, she took home, placed in a different tin, and—like a dog with a bone—hid it in a new place that was away from the house.

She reasoned that Joseph might think that the person who came upon the pig might have taken it. More disturbing was the thought that Joseph might blame Michael for taking back the pig and stealing his money as well, though she doubted that he would think that of Michael. If Mike never came to their farm again, Joseph might think that he was ashamed of taking the money— even though he told Michael to stay away. She would have to wait to see how it all washed out, but she knew Joseph would find a way to be angry with anyone but himself for what had happened to the hog.

Mary knew that the pig was not pregnant. She was probably an infertile gilt, and Michael and his mature sons had put one over on Joe because he was acting a drunken fool. Nobody told Da that it wasn't a pregnant sow. He might grow even more disturbed.

That evening, when Ma put her children to bed, Mary whispered into her ear that they could no longer go to Uncle Mike's or Da might kill him. Mary had also warned Ellen and her brothers. Mary told her ma the big lie that they had seen Michael on their way to school and that's what he told them. She didn't want her ma to know that she told Uncle Mike about his dead pig so he could go get it back. However, Ma knew Mary and Ellen sometimes could not restrain themselves from working up the courage to demonstrate their good character. She felt it was a McManus quality, and she saw it in abundance with the girls and, somewhat, in young Michael. She would have to wait on her judgment of Joseph and baby Thomas, though he was a wonderful baby.

Ma reminded Mary that it's always best to be honest. Without telling Ma that she had lied, she knew that her ma had figured that Mike wouldn't be riding about so early in the morning for no apparent reason. Ma said, "Mary, where would Michael have been going instead of doin' his chores? He wasn't taking his grown boys to school, was he?"

Mary answered, "I think you're right, Ma." That was the end of it. When Ma walked out of the room, she said, "Don't forget this when you go to Confession next week."

Φ

Within a week, Joseph took his sorrel mare to town for kerosene. He saw his whiskey bottle on the far side of the ditch. He couldn't resist it, and even though there was very little in it, he drank the rest and threw the bottle back into the ditch.

Da had taken the money from Mary's hidden porch tin and placed it under their mattress in a soft pouch wrapped in a towel and flattened out. When he wanted to drink or buy extra things, he didn't ask Mary for money out of the crock, but he would borrow from the pouch and the crock. He no longer cared that they might not be able to make extra payments to keep up. He still thought that their egg and butter money had been stolen off the road by the person who took the pig.

Unfortunately, Joseph was amused that Mary was sleeping on her money from the tin and didn't know it. He knew it would crush her if she found out. He had some ambivalence, but he generally liked his "dirty Irish tricks." In a way, he thought she deserved it for being sneaky and not respecting him as the real head of the household. Like a real McManus, she often took charge, and it embarrassed him. He thought she was probably crushed about losing her egg and butter money. She hid her feelings and started putting money away in the same crock on the bureau. He had seen the empty tin still under the porch, and he assumed she had given up keeping her secret cache.

When he came home from town with kerosene, Joe had also bought some tobacco and several other small items Mary had neither asked for nor given him money to buy. It was obvious that he had been drinking. He fell asleep before eating and didn't help Melvin with the chores.

Mary didn't ask where he got the money, but when she went out the next day to check on her newly hidden tin, there was no money missing!

It was the day they went to do their banking that answered a question for Joe about who stole the pouch from his coat. Wanting to avoid his learning that she had completed a late payment without his knowledge, she tried to convince Joseph to stay in the cart. He had been drinking and was in terrible shape, but mostly, she didn't want him to realize that the money had been returned to her by Melvin.

Because of his intent to assert himself over Mary and the bank officers, Joe refused to stay in the cart. It was a humiliation for her to ask, and Mary realized she was in trouble.

When it was their turn at the counter, the teller said, "Congratulations on your makeup payment."

Mary stood there stone-faced and blushed.

Joe asked the clerk if he could "refresh" Joe regarding the date it had been made and the amount. Joe realized that it was the day he lay sleeping on the parlor floor nursing his body and pride after the cart incident, and it was much less than the amount of money in the pouch that had disappeared from the coat. It was not until they finished making their current payment and left the bank that the fight began.

"And so, Mary McManus, ye came up with the money to complete the deficit on a missed payment? And how did ye do that? Did you steal money from yer husband's pockets and hide the rest? I can't have a legitimate means of getting us out of our situation at the bank, but ye can hand our hard-earned money over to them at yer leisure?"

Nervously, Mary said, "I did it for us Joe, for the farm. Stop it right now!"

The couple walked down the frosty wooden walkway arm in arm, Joseph untied the reins, and they stepped into their cart.

Joe said, "Why make any extra payments when we can't possibly pay it all off? Yer handin' it over to the devil. We'll get nothin' back for it. Let someone else make payments for the farm if they're goin' to own it in the end! Should we not save what we can so we can start over? Don't ye want to start over, Mary? What's yer other choice, me love? How would we feed the children? Yer always worryin' about feedin' the children. Instead of giving money to the crooks at the bank, use the money to feed the children."

Mary said, "So, ye want to stop payin' altogether then, Joseph? What kind of reasoning is that? That's not startin' over; that's givin' up. Don't ask me to give up. You roll over drunk an' dead if ye like, but don't ask me to roll over with ye. Never!"

"Ye tell me, Mary. How in God's name can we start over if we have no money? The bank won't give it back to ye. They'll have our money and the farm too."

They were beginning to yell, frozen breaths roiling in the air and parked in the cart on the street, with four-year-old Joseph and two-year old Thomas Edward freezing in the little boot Melvin had made. "Joseph, here we are like two classless and orphaned guttersnipes fightin' over our last crust of bread. Christ beside us!"

"Think, Mary, when the bank takes our money and our farm, we'll only own mouths to be fed." He pulled up on the reins and called, "Step up." The cart moved forward.

Mary and Joseph rode in silence. She handed a small woven blanket under the front seat back to the boys, tucked them in, and said, "Joseph, if we don't make any payments for the rest of the year, they will evict us from our farm early and possibly throw us in jail. I don't want us to end up in an almshouse. Neither do ye. Do ye want these little babies to live among the impoverished orphans in a poorhouse? Jaisus, Mary, and Joseph, that's what drove our families from Ireland. How can we let that happen here? This is a land of great wealth. Who will our families think we were?"

"Of course not, Mary. I'd rather we all die first. Me da gave his last penny to keep us away from the poorhouse, but he had the penny to give. And don't tell me what it's like to leave children in the poorhouse. For Christ's sake, Mary, Mike and I had to leave me sister Margaret in a nunnery when she was thirteen years old. I had to give up me little brother Charley and sister Ellen as orphans when they were barely older than Michael. That's after we left half our dead family behind and went out into the world all as children. We can flee in the night if we think they're comin' for us. They'll tell us first. America's a big place; we'll find a better spot to be."

"I don't want to flee in the night. I want us to live a normal farmin' life like me own family in Kansas. How can we flee in the night if yer drunk and can't sit up in the wagon while I'm breastfeeding another baby? So how will our girls go to school or find proper husbands livin' in a poorhouse? Mary can become a nun if she wishes, but I'll be damned into hell before I'll be droppin' her off at their doorstep! If they go to a poorhouse, they'll never get out. What kind of men will Michael, Joseph, or Thomas be with neither a proper education nor a farm to make a livin'?"

Joseph said, "I certainly don't want them to grow up to be like me. Do ye? I wasn't in a poorhouse. Maybe I'd been better for it if me brother had placed me at a seminary in Cincinnati and left me."

Mary said, "Certainly I would have been the better for it as well! For God' s sake, Joseph, ye started yer own hauling business as a child. We did well and were happy in Paola. Ye bought us a farm in Wea. Ye built yer way up, but the more you've drunk, the less capable husband and father ye've become. Yer mean, and I cannot trust ye—and now ye don't trust me. Do ye hear the things ye are sayin' to me? Do ye hear how I'm talkin' to ye? I'm yer wife, and we're hidin' money from each other—and it's a pittance we're fightin' over. It isn't supposed to be like this. It has to stop. Stop drinkin' and wastin' money—and let me take charge. The cattle are doin' fine. Now, I'd do better without yer interference!"

Joseph said, "Ye think yer already in charge, don't ye? Maybe that's what's wrong, Mary. Do ye want to take over and have me abandon ye so ye can carry on by yerself? Maybe an assistant bank manager can take over yer payments and me family as well. That would be real interference!"

"Do ye really expect me to discuss our problems when ye talk to yer pregnant wife like that, Joseph? Let's stop talkin'. The children will be home from school soon, and we have to milk soon enough. I'll make dumplin's if ye can kill that old hen. She quit layin', and we all could use a good meal to lift our spirits. I still have a wild onion in the cellar. We need to be puttin' new ice under the ground in our cooler. It's gettin' freezin', and the summer ice is all melted. When I take out the milk, it's too warm. I can feel it's past time for new ice."

When they were finished with their meal and evening chores, the girls helped Ma wash the dishes and clean up. They helped her get the boys to bed, and they all prayed with their ma as she sat on the piano stool between the beds.

When they prayed for those worse off than they, Michael asked his ma who that was.

Lifting her dark curls off her tired brow, she declared, "Things can always be worse, Michael. There's always somebody worse off than you. You have a family and God, and yer ma loves you deeply, Michael. Ye have milk and eggs. People in Ireland didn't have anything but grass to eat when they came to America. Can you imagine not havin' anything but grass to eat?"

Ellen looked at Mary, smiled, and sarcastically said, "Yes."

Mary looked at Ellen and said, "Or, can ye imagine, Ellen, not havin' anything but grasshoppers?"

Ellen looked back at her and said, "Yes!"

They both laughed, but Ma did not laugh. She realized that those events were what her children were living. Even though she had come from Ireland, she had not faced such challenges until after she married Joseph Quigley. They had enjoyed some good days, but most of her married life had been wretched.

Φ

Joseph and Mary had entered a stage in their lives when they did not talk after they went to bed. Mary was usually so exhausted that she quickly fell asleep or thought and fretted through the stressful events or problems, especially how to save the farm and stop Joe's drinking.

As Mary lay in bed on that exhausting and cold day, the mystery at the back of her head was what had happened to the money in her tin under the porch. The money had not been accounted for in the total sum retrieved by Melvin from Joe's pouch. She couldn't understand where it had gone. Joseph did not buy a boar, and he hadn't paid for Michael's gilt. Even with the bottle of whiskey and the drinking, the money Melvin brought her from Joseph's accident was not enough to add up. Unless Joe lost it or gave it away, he must have hidden her money from the tin under the porch, and as he took money from the crock, he enriched it with the tin money. How else could he have purchased those extra things and had drinks at the saloon?

She could never trust him again. He would lie to her. She had already lied to him and prayed that he would not find the tin in her new hiding place. He was flaunting his power to control the direction of their destruction, and she believed it would get worse.

She was entering her fifth month of pregnancy and facing the cold, dark winter. She couldn't clean the barn or carry calves without dependable help. Joseph was no longer the physical strength of the family. After the pig incident, his arm had not fully recovered. Other than Melvin, her number one helper was an eleven-year-old girl.

Joseph lay in bed fretting as well. He was getting more and more angry with Mary. The only way to get her to give up the money she had hidden was to place increasing pressure on her until she broke. It became obvious to him that she had hidden the remaining money from his pouch that the bank had not gotten.

Thinking over their fight coming home from the bank, Joseph began to think that the children might be better if they were without him. Maybe they'd be better off without their ma. However, he couldn't imagine that. He was proud of their intelligence and talent. Mary was attractive and respected and a remarkable mother, but Joseph knew he was not a proper example of how a father should be. He just couldn't help it. Michael was a good father. His own da was wonderful, but a child needed a mother to be truly happy. He had lost most of his joy when he lost his ma.

He decided he was going to die from his stomach, his intestines, and his drinking, but he was going to get control of the money so the bank would not be the only beneficiaries.

On Saturday morning, Joseph said, "Tell me what ye did with that money from the pouch. I love ye, Mary Quigley, but I cannot let ye hand over money to the bank. It's ours. We need it. I know it's hidden, and I will beat the truth out of ye. Ye owe it to me."

That went on all morning long as they went about their chores and took care of the children.

Finally, Joseph exploded, "I'm goin' to town to get ice and hay. When I come back from town, ye better have the money found— or ye'll find out who's boss!" His days of sober sweetness were gone. He reached into the crock, took out money, and left.

Mary checked to see how much he had taken. As usual, it seemed more than necessary, so she guessed what his state would be when he returned.

Melvin knew what to expect when Joseph returned to the farm during the milking. He had used enough money to drink all afternoon. He had also hidden some of the crock money in his pouch under the mattress.

Though Joseph planned to take care of the hogs, Melvin had already done so earlier. When they knew Joe might not come home on time, they started chores a little early. Mary was exhausted and visibly pregnant, but she, Melvin, and the girls carried on with their-night chores as Joseph stumbled around until Melvin suggested he should go lie down.

Michael was now six and did fairly well helping with grain and hay-feeding the cows as they came into the milking shed. Melvin and Ma got the cows into their stanchions, and the girls brought out the clean pails.

After Melvin and Ma cleaned off their bags with water, the milking began. Melvin, Ma, and one of the girls milked. When the first pail was full, one of the girls poured it over the cooler and caught it in the second pail that would be covered to keep flies and dirt out. After supper, and all the cleanup chores were done, Ellen and Ma used their new separator. It was a bucket with a see- through glass window in the bottom half.

After the milk cooled and the cream settled on the top, Ma set the separator bucket beside the sink with the plug at the bottom hanging over. Ellen held a bucket in the sink that caught the milk after Ma pulled the plug. Ma let the milk run through until it reached the level of the cream. Over the sink, they had fastened a lantern holder so they could better see through the little window. Ma would place the plug back in to keep the cream in the container. She poured the cream into a separate pail where it all ended up and left it in the cooler before she made her butter. The sweet cream, if left cool, could sit for several days.

Ellen handed the separated milk to Mary, and she took out the bucket to pour in their two big pails with lids that fit tightly over the top. When full, each pail was capped. In hot months, the milk was placed in their cooler or in a large tub of water to continue cooling down until morning. When it was cold weather, it was left in the little room off the milking shed; otherwise, it might freeze.

They would wash out their containers at the well pump and set them upside down in a crib with the lids on to drain for the process that was repeated in the morning. After the children went to school, either Melvin or Da took the milk to town.

This cold December Saturday was one of those unpleasant nights when Joseph was drunk or sick, and everyone was forced to quietly do his work. The same was true on mornings when he was hungover or sick with his insides. Ma and the little kids were out in the dark early or late with the horses, cows, hogs, and chickens, trying to do as much of a man's work that they could. It was often emotionally as well as physically overwhelming for Ma and the children as they grew to understand the mistreatment that was being handed to them.

The girls were learning that among the town gossips or at church in Holden, their names were often preceded by "poor," as in: "Poor Ellen Quigley. We saw that child out in the corn, hoeing nearly all day, as her da sat in the tavern drinking."

Or "Poor Little Mary Quigley. She was out feeding the hogs as her ma did the milking and her da lay sick in bed. Then she managed to get to school on time! How do those poor children do it?"

Or, "Did you see Poor Mrs. Quigley at Mass? She looked so tired, and she's pregnant again. The poor thing. She appeared to have a black eye. Did you notice how she seemed to turn her head to the side?"

The girls were somewhat unique in others' perceptions of them. They learned who the other drunken fathers were from school and church. They began to assess their value, based on families headed by drunks.

For example, some drunken fathers had several older sons who, if the fathers were farmers, could more easily than the little Quigley girls do heavy chores with animals that didn't always cooperate or were too big, mean, and heavy.

The Quigley girls discussed the idea that if they had been blessed with older brothers, their ma's life would have been better. They sometimes wished they were boys and had been older at this stage. Having older brothers would have been easier for them. They would have been proud of an older brother who could take charge, much like Melvin who never complained.

They didn't feel useless, but they sometimes lamented that their little brothers depended on them. They clearly wanted it to be the other way around, but they did not resent their little brothers, who were no more to blame than they for their birth order.

On the first very cold Saturday evening of December 1876, Joseph came home late—and the chores seemed especially difficult. Instead of going straight to bed as usual, Da sat at the table growling about money. He was staring at them, and they felt intimidated.

As they were finishing up evening chores, Ma looked over and said, "Joseph, if ye'll go to bed, I'll come in and talk to ye about money, but I have little to say. Why are you asking me about money? I didn't steal the money out of the crock—yourself did." It was dishonest, but she didn't care.

She had been so tired and busy she hadn't noticed the bottle of whiskey on the table. A third of it had been drunk. "Joseph Quigley!" she shouted as she lunged for the bottle.

Joe forcefully grabbed her arms and squeezed tight.

"You know I don't want to see any drinking in this house," she continued.

"Then leave!" Joseph threw her arms down forcefully to her sides. "Go on—leave."

"Leave where? What about the children? It's freezin' out, and I'm pregnant and exhausted. Take the bottle and a coverlet out to the pig shed if you want to be alone to drink."

He said, "I wasn't plannin' on drinkin' alone, but I think it's a good idea. I want you to leave and take them with ye." Joseph nodded toward Joseph and Thomas. "I don't care where ye go, but this is me house—and I'll drink in me house if I want to. Ye need to go while you can, Mary. I'm done with this all. I'll sit here and wait till the bank comes."

"Ye'll have a long wait, Joseph. They're not comin' for ten more months. Have ye lost track of yer days?"

The girls had stepped into the house and heard their da tell their ma to leave and take the boys. They were in stunned silence. Ma quickly took them out the kitchen door and instructed them that when she went back into the house to talk to Da, they were to come quietly back through the front porch door, get all their warm coats and coverlets, go out to the big wagon, and wait. They were to ask Melvin to help put new alfalfa down in the wagon so they could lie on it. Ma would join them if or when she could, but they were to let Melvin take them away if he decided he should. "Just go with him and be good. Tell Joseph to behave himself. I'll find ye."

As she had done several times in the past, Mary prepared to die at Joseph's hands and walked back into the house.

Joseph had drunk more from his bottle. "I asked ye to get yer things and leave—and that includes the children."

The children quietly and quickly ran into their room, grabbed what they could to stay warm, and headed out to the wagon.

Mary wasn't sure he was fully aware that the children had left the house, but they were gone when he grabbed Mary around the neck and dragged her into the bedroom. He threw her cape at her, but he would not let her take the bedding off their bed. He let her grab her heavy coat off a hook and put it on, pull a pair of heavy stockings from the drawer, and place her blue prayer book in her pocket. He then grabbed her hair, accidentally loosening it out of the pins that held it up and shoved her out the kitchen door. She tripped and fell off the bottom step.

The children screamed when they saw their pregnant mother fall, and the tears began to flow.

She looked up to see the lanterns out in the shed, the large wagon, the shadows of the children, and Melvin getting them settled. "I'm fine, children. I'm fine," she called out.

Melvin ran forward and helped her up. She had to get on her hands and knees and reach out to Melvin to get up.

Joseph stood on the kitchen steps and yelled, "Get out of me sight. Don't come back unless ye give me money for me boar—and quit givin' money to the bank. Don't take that wagon anywhere. That's me wagon, and I need it for the farm. Ye don't have a farm now—so leave me wagon here. Take yer cart, Mary."

Melvin walked up to the steps and said, "How are they to leave without the wagon? They can't walk out of here into the frozen darkness without any place to go and any way to get there. The cart will not hold them all, and there's no place for them to rest in the cart. Be fair, Joseph."

Joseph yelled, "Don't ye dare go to Michael's. He's not yer da! He's a good da, but he's not yer da. I'm yer da—and don't you ever forget it!"

Ellen whispered, "How will we ever forget it?"

Mary answered, "How will we ever forgive him?"

Ellen answered, "I don't think we have to. We'll ask Father."

Standing at the bottom of the steps, Melvin said, "Joe, let me take the wagon over to the Collins's farm. Then, I'll bring it back and go home on my horse to ask my father what to do."

"Melvin, what I need ye to do is bring back a locksmith in the mornin'. We're goin' to lock them out. We don't even have a lock on the kitchen door, and Ma might break in."

Melvin said, "No, Joe. I won't do that to your family. Without your family, you really have nothing. This is their home. You don't know what' you're saying. You're drunk. I'm taking the wagon over to the Collins's farm. Maybe your family can stay out of the cold better and nobody will die."

Joseph said, "I'm going to sit behind that door with me pistol and finish me whiskey. Make them go and get the locksmith here in the morning."

"How would you feel, Joe, with new locked doors and a suffering family that can't come in out of the cold? Would you kill your little children with illness because you want to be passed out drunk in your house? I like you, and we've never fought, but you should sit and sober up and think about things until I get back. Can I take your whiskey with me, Joe? Can I take your pistol and your rifle so nobody will get hurt?"

Joe didn't answer. He just went back into the house.

Melvin turned to Mary and said, "Do not go near that door to-night, tomorrow, or the next day without the sheriff's approval. I think he has lost his mind, and he will kill you. I'm not bringing back a locksmith, but that doesn't matter. You and the children stay away from that house—no matter what."

Mary said, "What would I ever do without ye, Melvin? Ye are provin' yerself to be many times the man my husband might have been without the whiskey. It is good that yer people do not drink alcohol. Neither do mine, thank God."

As Mary and her children huddled in the heavy wagon and Melvin drove it to the Collins house, Joseph started a bonfire in the yard. He first brought out two kitchen chairs. As the fire grew, he threw Mary's precious rocker on top and went back into the house, too drunk and exhausted to finish the job. Mary's beautiful rocking chair was nearly destroyed. The varnish and tapestry had fed the fire to do its work quickly until there was nothing of value left to retrieve. When Joseph was drunk, he could be the meanest person on earth.

Φ

Joseph had several very sick and one tearful day before he saw his wife and children again. When he saw them, he laughed, and in his delirium, he asked if they had enjoyed their "vacation" from the farm chores.

Mary had ridden over from the Collins's farm to do chores with Mr. Collins's farmhands and Melvin for several days until Joseph had drunk his third bottle of whiskey and received a visit from the sheriff and the priest.

Mary had quietly burned the few remnants of wood left of her chair and had wept in the arms of Elizabeth as Joseph lay drunk in the house. Nobody understood why Joseph had decided to punish Mary by burning her chair.

The children were horrified. Where could the new baby be comforted and fed by Ma as they had been? They had all been alone with Ma in that rocker, and it broke their hearts.

The priest, the sheriff, Mr. Collins, and Melvin were at the Quigley farm when Joe's family was invited to return. Joseph promised the men and his wife that he would not drink again; otherwise, he was going to stay in the jail. The priest made him say he was sorry to Mary. He forgave Joseph's sins and gave him communion in his sick bed so he could save his soul and start over. The children dragged themselves and their bedding inside, and Joe promised them that he would not drink again. Among themselves, they didn't believe him. The priest told Joe that his wife needed to handle the money so he would not drink. Joe readily agreed. He told the priest that he no longer had an argument with the bank; Mary could make the payments if they had any harvest at the end of the growing season.

Joseph never revealed that Mary's tin money and part of her crock money were still under the mattress. He tried to convince himself that it was safe, but he knew why he hadn't revealed it. In the event he needed it, there it would be.

Before Annie was born, Mary sold her favorite cow, Patches, and her newest cow. She was forced to give up her butter and egg business to rest for the birth of Annie, but she kept Polly. It was the cow that Daniel and Agnes had sent after the locusts, and they loved her. The girls would decorate the hair between her ears and her tail with dandelions and daisies. She was treated like a doll.

Annie, a very tiny, red-haired baby, was born on March 12, 1877, the third of Mary's babies to be born in that month. Ladies brought over a rocker they loaned from an older grandmother who hadn't quite decided to let it go. They also came by fairly often in the beginning to check on a very frail Mary and help her daughter stay warm and fed and to get her small and struggling body through the spring.

Joseph was trying to be good in front of the unexpected guests who would stop by the house to see the tiny girl and keep Mary from working too hard. He knew the word was out, and because he was sober, he felt a degree of embarrassment, though he didn't like them or feel grateful that they were helping his wife.

Without Mary's constant support, Joseph struggled through chores until long after Annie was born. He often lay in bed coughing or bleeding from his sore colon as weeds grew in the corn. The children and Melvin could hardly keep up with the wood that was needed for the fires, but they did their best.

By May, Ma was getting stronger, and so was her infant. It seemed that the children loved their infant sister into better health.

By June, she began to be more normal. She was smiling and cooing, and Ma was drinking Polly's rich cream and regaining her color.

Most of the Quigley family had sable brown or black hair, but with her reddish-brown hair, Annie looked more like some of the McManus ancestors. All the Quigley siblings loved her novel appearance. Every waking hour, they pressed their faces up against her rosy cheeks and thick red curls to kiss and comfort her. Since Ma was in the barn less, they saw Annie as a baby like other people's babies: a tiny pink bundle who spent time in the house when it was too cold or too hot. The other children had spent many hours outside as infants, tucked in the hay or bundled against a chill so their ma could get her chores done in between the feedings and changes.

When Joe fell off the wagon as summer approached, the siblings circled around like prairie buffaloes to protect Annie. When chaos broke out between their parents, Annie was central to their plans. Even Little Joseph felt a responsibility to put forth effort on Annie's behalf.

The children were growing older fast, and Ma felt that when the bank came, she would be able to survive with her children by her side. Ma had not given up her secret that part of the money she earned from the sale of the cattle was securely hidden with the other money in her tin, but she wasn't saving it for the bank. She was saving it because if Joe ever did something again like he had done in December—or if she became a widow who needed to start over with her children—there would be savings nobody knew about, including the bank. She had resigned herself to the repossession that was coming. She had the minute rehearsed in her mind. She was preparing to become a widow with orphans who could flee in the night—from the bank or her husband. She would take the beloved Hiram's wagon with her.

As their crops were harvested at the end of summer, they were about breaking even. They had spuds, but they were not looking forward to new piglets. Why bother? Mary and Joseph decided not to pay their September mortgage payment when it was due. They would pay Melvin and just wait until the thirtieth and see what transpired.

The days wore on stressfully, and school finally started. There were now four Quigley children in school.

Mary was home with Thomas and baby Annie, and she tried to engage Joseph in a discussion about their departure plans. Joseph would not talk about it. He would only say, "We'll worry about it when we have to."

Then he started to drink. He sat in the saloon and threw down the last mortgage payment. The bartenders and saloon owners did nothing to help. The sheriff was too busy, and Michael could not help without being shot.

From the middle of August on, the children went to school— and Joe Quigley went to the saloon.

Φ

On the morning of Tuesday, September 11, Joseph took a can of milk into town and did not come back. He had eaten a few spuds and bacon, and he seemed to be better than any other days in the last few weeks of drinking, bleeding, and ranting. He returned before the children came home from school and had brought a bottle with him.

Before she went to the barn, Mary asked him if he would please give her the bottle. "Joseph, what if the bank comes and we have to load our things and leave? Ye can't be drunk because I can't pack everything by meself. The girls can't lift the piano into the wagon.

I want to take Polly with us. Please stop. And where's yer money? When are ye goin' to run out—or are ye just runnin' up a tab?"

Mary thought she had all their money put away.

On Wednesday, September 12, Joseph stumbled into town to get kerosene, cornmeal, salt, and soap—and to drink. Again, he did not come back. Mary was pulling the bedding off the bed to hang it in the sun when she saw a dollar and a few coins lying on the floor under the bed on Joe's side. His pistol was also on the floor. As she pulled up the cover on the mattress, she discovered a white towel under which was the white linen pouch she had not seen for a very long time. There it was: the stolen money. It was too late for everything, but she bundled up Annie and Thomas, tucked them into the cart, and headed for town. She pulled over on the road to nurse Annie and to let Thomas run around a bit, and then they continued into town.

At Mr. Cuttler's saloon, Joe's sorrel mare, Fiona, was standing dutifully at the rail over the horse trough with a feed bag on. Mary took off the bag, let her drink, and then tied the mare to the back of her cart and went inside. She stomped in and laid their last precious handful of crock money down on the bar.

"Mr. Cuttler, tell me how much Joe owes ye on his present tab. He's been in here daily for nearly three weeks. Please tell me how much money you would take to not serve this man one more drop. Would you like to buy me farm? I'm sure we've spent enough in here to be squared away so we could keep it ourselves. Thanks to the likes of ye and Joe Quigley, it's available October 1, and we have no place to go."

Mr. Cuttler seemed embarrassed and insulted. "It's okay, Mrs. Quigley. You don't need to pay me more than he owes."

Mary snarled and said, "Ye miserable excuse for a human being, ye owe me and me children—and ye know it. 'More than he owes' ye say I don't need to pay ye? Jaisus, Mary, and Joseph, so help me God, this is an evil place!"

Joseph fell over the bar and yelled, "Mary Quigley, get out of here now! Ye have no business in here embarrassin' me in front of me friends."

Joseph's "friends" all cleared out.

"And ye have had no right to embarrass me and lose our farm, Joseph. Yer comin' with me now. So shut it about ye and yer friends!"

Joe answered, "Mr. Cuttler, I'll have another, please."

"Mr. Cuttler, you give him another, and I'll tell the sheriff yer fixin' to kill me husband and the father of our six children. If I had his gun, I'd shoot ye meself—so what are ye doin' on our family's behalf if ye hand him another drink?"

Joe reached for his gun, but he had been stumbling around and unaware that morning, and he had no idea where he had placed it. Mary said, "Yer pistol was under the mattress where ye laid it, still drunk, when ye were stealing our money. It's safely at home in its holster. I'm afraid if it were here, I'd use it now on either of ye! God help me now. We'll be leaving then, Mr. Cuttler. Here's the money I'm givin' to buy me drunken husband back. He needs to sober up to help me pack up our children and belongings when the bank comes to take our farm. I'd hate to see him fall off the wagon and get lost on the trail or smashed under the wheels.

Wouldn't ye?"

Mr. Cuttler picked up Joe's glass, but Joe had already put a bottle in his saddlebag.

Joe struggled to get up on his horse until a man walked along and helped him slip his boot into the stirrup. Mary returned to the cart to check on Annie and Thomas, and they started out.

Since it was early in the afternoon, there weren't too many people in the street to see Joe with his horse tied to his wife's cart as he was hanging on in his stupor, being towed home like a bad boy by his righteous wife.

When they got home, Melvin and Mary got him into bed and started the chores as the children were coming home from school.

The next morning, Thursday, September 13, Joseph was sick in bed. By afternoon, standing before death, Little Mary recalled that not much earlier she and her siblings had been transfixed on the last confrontation between her parents. It had continued from the day before. From his sick bed, her da had been shouting at her ma in his pathetic state of withdrawal. "Mary McManus, how could ye do that to me? Ye know I'm sick, and ye ... humiliatin' me in front of Mr. Ball, Mr. Hinshaw, and ... everyone? Why not go to the bell tower and shout it to the world: 'Come and line up, folks! Let me give ye Joseph Quigley's last pitiful cent he stole from me. Let me buy me sick, rotten, drunken husband from ye! He's a disgrace to me lovely, fine family, and a no-good farmer who cannot provide for his own flesh and blood. See here, bartender! I'll give ye money for the poor bastard. You save yer golden pint for the next broken soul, Mr. Cuttler. Me miserable betrothed's not worth yer trouble. I, the high-and-mighty Mary McManus, will lower me aristocratic self and buy the skinny drunk back from ye. I'll take the weakened, sick devil off yer hands and sober him up till the banker comes for the farm. Our ilk is too mighty to let the banker or creditors see the worthless, sick drunk.'"

The young Quigley boys had heard the many drunken rants and were already in the yard waiting for the final act. It was what Mary and Ellen had heard next in the front room that became the worst turning point of their lives. There was a sound of movement behind the mostly closed door. "Hand it to me, Mary, and I'll take care of us both." With those words, Mary and Ellen glanced knowingly at one another.

Little Mary thought, *Has Ma stepped to Da's saddlebag hanging from the hook in the corner of the room and handed the gun to Da, thinkin' he might kill himself? Has Da crawled out of bed to get his weapon himself—and Ma has grabbed it?*

Mary and Ellen had spoken yesterday to each other about their fears. Da had held the six-shooter in his hands nearly the entire day before, and he had asked Melvin to get his brother Michael down to the farm "right now!" Mary was glad Melvin had not sent Uncle Michael to the farm.

Mary knew why her da wanted Michael there. He was going to kill him. To Mary, it was an inevitable idea that Da would kill some-one—if not everyone. It had worn on them for days, and they talked to each other about how much they wanted to be in school. They wanted to sing, read the books, and meet their teachers, not listen to fighting, hold Annie, and cry in fear for their ma.

Mary heard her mother's raspy, exhausted voice saying, "Ye do that, ye drunken coward. Ye go ahead and just do that to yer family. Yer crazy with the sickness, Joseph. It won't matter 'cause yer goin' to die soon—whether ye pull the trigger or not. Hand me the pistol, Joseph. I'll help ye do it. God, hand me the gun!"

It was then that Ellen called out to Melvin. Mary rushed to her mother's side to take the baby, and Melvin soon followed Little Mary into the tiny bedroom. Outside by the kitchen, with Michael and Joseph, Ellen clutched the hand of Thomas, and he buried his head in her petticoats.

Da said, "This time I'm going to do it, Miss Mary … only, I'm takin' ye with me! I'm takin' ye to hell with me, Mary, for all the insults and the belittlin' and the work, the pain, the love we can't have back, and the poverty. I'm sick of it all, and the bank's not gettin' our farm while I'm still alive! Nobody's gettin' me farm, and no man's gettin' me wife. Ye'll be leavin' with me, me beloved darlin' Mary." Shaking, he stood up on the bed and leaned against the bedroom wall.

Ma yelled, "I'll be stayin' here with our blessed Quigley children, Joseph! Hand me that pistol, and I'll do it for ye."

Their da's raging and weeping and their mother's desperate pleas to hold on to her life and the lives of her children were the last utterances the children heard from their parents. When they heard Melvin yell, "Give me the gun, Joe," the first gunshot rang out. Then the second—and then the third.

Readers of this novel need to know that every attempt to be accurate with historical information was made. The characters in the novel lived within the historical realities and events of the time period. For example, Mary Quigley was my paternal grandmother, and her da was my great-grandfather. The biographical truth comes from certificates of marriage, birth, death, and baptism; the states of Kansas and Missouri and US Federal Census Records; Civil War records; newspaper articles; court proceedings; and ship manifests. There are no other documents such as diaries or written anecdotes that accurately portray the day-to-day lives of the characters. For only noted political leaders of the time is information historically correct.

It is a fact that Lieutenant General John McAllister Schofield, who would have actually trained Joseph Quigley's company, is my maternal first cousin three times removed. I have a copy of his autobiography, *Forty-Six Years in the Army,* from which I gleaned his opinions and cavalry-related experiences during the Civil War. I also used many other references for Civil War and place-name facts. The first of hundreds of references used was Tom Rafiner's *Caught Between Three Fires* that provides an abundance of local information on the border conflicts.

Mary Quigley's mother was Mary "Kate" Grant McManus, my paternal great-grandmother, who claimed she was a first cousin of Ulysses Grant. We have a DNA link, and his grandmother, a Simpson, is buried only feet away from a paternal great-grandfather, Captain Matthew Scott (*surgeon to General George Washington*), in the Warwick, Bucks, Presbyterian Scots-Irish cemetery. Also another of the Scott descendants married an Ohio Grant outside Cincinnati. These are tantalizing links I hope to yet connect.

Mary Grant's father, John Grant, was a secretive and wealthy man whose wife was a Grogan and daughter to the Johnstown Castle, Wexford, Ireland, Grogan family of uprising fame. John made many trips to Ireland. The father of Ulysses, like John Grant, was highly secretive and had claimed to know very little about his family. The Grant, McManus, and other families of County Down, Ireland, were an intelligent, ambitious, and faithful lot.

There are more DNA links and genealogical ties: Lincoln's assistant secretary of war and railroad executive Tom Scott is one. These and other relationships dictate the imperative for me to be a credible and historically factual author, though I am not a historian. None would appreciate a granddaughter or even a distant cousin who would corrupt the truth in regard to the remarkable contributions they all made during this time period in America's history, just to tell a Romeo and Juliet–style story.

Obviously, the same cannot be said regarding the imaginary characters and circumstances I cobbled together to represent as closely as possible the enigma that was Mary Quigley's da. He was a talented and broken person whose better attributes I see in his descendants. It is my hope that this story has helped the family and nonfamily readers' historical understanding of the context in which he and others lived. He was one of thousands of Irish immigrants who arrived into a very dangerous and tumultuous time, many by themselves as young adults, and some, like Michael, with younger siblings and no parents to support them.

I cannot defend Joseph's "bad angels," but my goal was to put his life within a historically accurate context.

APPENDIX A

English Words Spoken in an Irish Accent

Irish accent - In order to preserve readability, only a few words were used to reflect the English language as filtered through Irish immigrant pronounciation. They are used within dialogue. The schwa "ə" is a very vowel-neutral sound similar to an "uh". There are three distinct Irish dialects. The following pronounciations do not represent any one of them.

a'been: *Have been*

bu'ercup: *Buttercup*

canna: *Cannot*

'cause (cuz): *Because*

da (daw): *Dad*

do na'(du nə): *Do not*

'em (uhm): *Them*

gonna: (gunnah) *Going to*

haird: *Heard*

i'tall (ih–tall): *It all*

i'tis (ih-tiz): *It is*

i'twas (ih-twaz): *It was*

-ing words: Verbs, primarily in dialogue, are abbreviated to an -in ending, as in doin', goin' , feelin', and so on

ma (maw): *Mom*

me (me or mə): *My*

pairfect: *Perfect*

'tis or 'twas: *It is or it was*

woulda: *Would have*

wouldna: *would not*

ye (yə): *You*

yer (yair): *Your or you're*

yerself (yair-self): *Yourself*

Irish Words and Phrases Not Defined in Text

beansidhe: *Banshee,* a woman of the fairy mound who announces death by shrieking

Cairan: Irish name, *gift of God*

cara: *Friend*

Cúramach: Irish name, *careful*

Lorica (Latin): Common name, *Prayer of Saint Patrick*

Lúireach Phádraig (Irish): Formal name, *Prayer of Saint Patrick*

Irish Slang

actin' the maggot: *Acting silly or defiant*

air biscuit: *Fart*

arse: *Ass*

cakehole: *Mouth of "mouthy" person*

eejit: *Idiot*

gigglemug: *One who frivolously giggles*

gobshite: *Person who never stops unwanted chatter*

guttersnipe: *Impoverished and neglected orphan of a ghetto*

Jaisus (Jay-sus): *Jesus*

"Jaisus, Mary and Joseph": *an exclamatory phrase that can be slang or a prayer!*

starvin' Irish: *Victims of the potato famine from about 1845-1850*

Uncommon Vocabulary

chinker: *A small stone with a flat surface that fills chinks (small spaces) in stone structures.*

lorgnette: *The most popular form of opera glasses that were held with a handle and a chain sometimes pinned to a vest pocket.*

loy: *Flat wooden spade used to lift sod.*

mea culpa, mea culpa, mea maxima culpa: *Through my fault, through my fault, through my most grievous fault. (Latin—from Catholic Mass in confession of sins.)*

scraplings: *Pieces of stone remaining after a stonemason chisels out a block. These are used for filling spaces in structures.*

secesh: *Civil War and pre-Civil War slang term for secessionist. seceshes: The plural form of secesh.*

snecked stones: *Stones that are a mix of square and rectangle shape and are of different sizes used together in buildings. It is a common style of Irish and especially Scottish masonry.*

English Words Spoken with German Accent

dat: That

dis: This

dos: Those

goot: Good

Gott: God

der: Their/there

mein: My

mit: With

tink: Think

trumbled: Trampled

vatch: Watch

var: War

vait: Wait

vat: What

vell: Well

vhere: Where

vill: Will

vent: Went

vorried: Worried

willkommen: Welcome

wunderbar: Wonderful

ya: Yes

Battles and Skirmishes—Before and during the Civil War

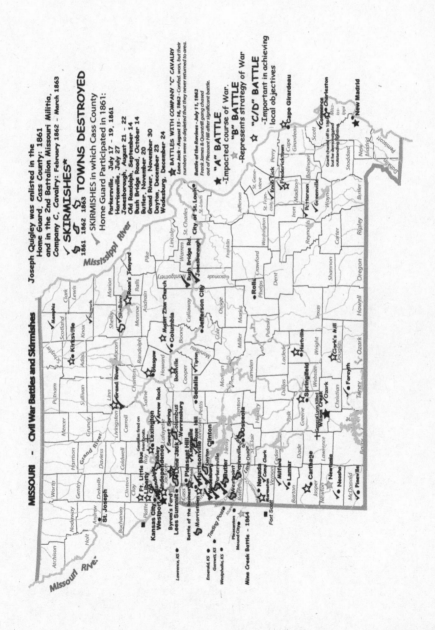

Printed in the USA
CPSIA information can be obtained
at www.ICGtesting.com
BVHW030407150823
668484BV00005B/17